BOOKS BY TIM MCBAIN & L.T. VARGUS

Casting Shadows Everywhere

The Awake in the Dark series

The Scattered and the Dead series

The Clowns

The Violet Darger series

DEAD END GIRL

DEAD END GIRL

a Violet Darger novel

LT VARGUS & TIM MCBAIN

DEAD
END
GIRL

PROLOGUE

Corduroy pants swished between Teresa's thighs as she crossed the parking lot. She had a headache. That drive-thru headset gave her a headache every damn time. The band squeezed her skull like an old man trying to find a ripe cantaloupe in the produce department. Pressing and pressing until her temples throbbed. When the headaches were really bad, she got the aura. And it was gonna be a bad one tonight. She could already tell. By the time she got home, she'd be nauseous from the skull throb along with the stink of fryer grease clinging to her clothes and hair and skin. Sometimes she swore she could feel it permeating her pores.

She placed a hand under the lid of the dumpster and lifted. The overhead lights in the parking lot glinted on the surface below. It looked like water, but it wasn't. It was oil. Every night they emptied the fryers, dumping the used oil into this dumpster. It was a disgusting task. Worse than taking out the trash on a 90-degree summer day, when the flies got real thick, and the meat went rancid almost as soon as they put it in the bin.

It was dead out. No traffic. No noise at all but her fiddling with the dumpster and the bucket.

Her skin crawled a little whenever she was out here this late. In the dark. In the quiet. A feeling settled into the flesh on her back and shoulders, a cold feeling, a feeling like after watching one of those scary movies when she was a teenager. It might have been a thrill while she was watching, but later on that night she'd always get spooked. She'd tremble in bed, too terrified to walk down the hall to pee. The house never seemed so ominously still as it did on those nights. Anyhow, she couldn't stand to watch horror movies anymore. Her weak stomach couldn't handle the gore.

Bending over the metal cart she'd wheeled along with her, Teresa scooped one of the buckets of used fryer oil and balanced

1

it on the edge of the dumpster. She tipped the bucket and watched as the gallons of brown grease oozed into the dumpster, disrupting the smoothness. Settled at the bottom of the bucket, there were clumps and chunks. Burned bits of fries and chicken tender crumbs. They splatted and splashed into the pool of liquid that looked black in the night.

That's when Teresa saw it. Something rising out of the oil, disturbing the otherwise unblemished surface.

Great. Some dumbshit threw two bags of trash in the grease dumpster.

Not cool.

Probably that Simmons kid. She knew he went out to his car on his breaks to smoke pot. Everyone knew. He always came back reeking of mouthwash and skunk weed. He even had a bumper sticker with those rainbow Grateful Dead bears. He wasn't fooling anybody.

She'd wanted to institute random drug testing, but the store manager wouldn't allow it. Something about the Constitution. Whatever.

She set the empty bucket down and let out the breath she'd been holding. The reek of old oil was heavy in the air.

Standing on her tiptoes and holding her breath again, she leaned over the edge, her arm swinging into the dark space but coming up empty.

Damn.

She hoisted herself up onto the side. With the edge of the dumpster jabbing her in the gut, she kicked one leg up onto the rim. One of her hands slid in a greasy residue, and she lurched forward, her upper body dipping into the darkness inside. For a split second, she was certain she was going in, all the way in, neck-deep into the foul muck. Her leg flailed behind her like a monkey's tail, struggling to regain her balance, and Teresa was able to catch herself at the last moment.

Cheese and crackers, that was close. Too close. She imagined herself teetering over the lip, plunging into the dark pool. That would have been awful.

She wiped her hand on her pants and peered into the inky interior. She wouldn't be able to reach the bags unless she got back up there, but she wasn't willing to risk taking a swim in a vat of grease. No way, no how.

Cursing the Simmons kid under her breath, she strode back inside the restaurant. A few moments later, the back door swung open again, and she reappeared with a step stool from the walk-in freezer and a pair of tongs.

The stool clattered onto the concrete. She shoved it as close to the dumpster as it would go with her foot, and it clanged against the metal. The sound reminded her of waves thumping against the side of a boat's hull.

Climbing atop the step, she gripped the tongs in her fist. Hovering over the gaping mouth of the dumpster, she swung her arm out, reaching for the first garbage bag. It rustled under her touch, and she clamped the tongs onto the flimsy black plastic. Tugging it a few inches closer, she felt the grip lose purchase. The bag was no doubt coated with a film of oil. Slippery as hell.

Damn it all. She should have brought a pair of gloves.

She clicked the tongs together in frustration, then redoubled her efforts. This time the tongs got a nice big bite of the plastic, as well as whatever was inside the bag. Clenching her fingers around the handle, she hauled the bag closer.

It was heavy. Probably the garbage inside was all sodden with oil by now. What a damn mess. She was going to end up driving home lubed up with the filth from head to toe.

The plastic crinkled as she lifted the bag. It was really gosh damn heavy. Something inside the bag bonged against the metal as she dragged it up along the corner.

She had it up on the lip of the dumpster now, and then she felt some resistance and a sort of stretching feeling and then the pop as the plastic ripped, and then the garbage was tumbling out, half on the ground and half back into the grease with a *sploosh*, and there was an odd thud of something hitting the ground — it sounded kind of like dropping a head of lettuce or something — and then she looked down, and it wasn't a head of lettuce, but there was a head, alright. A mannequin head, still connected to the torso, though there was a big crack along the neck. The arms and legs were gone, and just as she started to wonder why in the world someone would toss a broken mannequin into their grease dumpster, she realized it wasn't a mannequin at all.

It was a body. A limbless woman. Her eyes closed. Her skin as pale as bone. Red flaps of meat exposed where each arm and leg should be.

Teresa's breath hissed in her throat. She clambered down from the stool and scrabbled back in a crabwalk, the corduroy seat of her pants dragging over the asphalt in jerks.

She retreated without thought. A blind panic that bashed her shoulder-blades-first into the steel door twice before she realized what she was doing and got a hold of herself.

Her eyes stayed fixed on the grisly scene, and one word reverberated in her mind:

Gore.

CHAPTER 1

The smell of solvent hung like a cloud over the workbench. She sprayed a cotton rag with Hoppes solution, attached it to the cleaning rod, and forced it into the barrel of her Glock 22. When the white rag had turned dark gray with carbon powder, she traded it for a new scrap of cotton, sprayed, and started again.

She'd done well on the range today, practicing with a QIT-99 target. She managed to score 96% despite the fact that she hadn't shot in over a month. Well over the 80% required to pass her annual qualification test. She glanced over at the paper target riddled with bullet holes. Fat lot of good it did when she was stuck behind a desk most days.

Lately, she'd begun to question her decision to leave her position as a victim specialist. Violet Darger had spent her first four years at the FBI in the Office for Victim Assistance before giving up her position to become an agent trainee. She knew her colleagues thought she was nuts for making the move. Victim specialist jobs were highly competitive. To give that up... to start over at the bottom of the special agent chain was something almost everyone had counseled against. Not that she'd asked for their advice. "Impulsive" was the word her former supervisor had used. That was almost two years ago now, and she'd brushed them off at the time. They didn't understand. She didn't expect them to.

She moved on to the wire brush. She pushed the copper bristles through the barrel once, removed the brush tip, and then repeated the motion. A guy at a nearby table was using his wire brush as well, and he inserted it into the barrel and shimmied it back and forth. The sound of the wire fibers scraping against the inside of the barrel sent goose bumps scuttling over the flesh of her arms. Worse than nails on a chalkboard. Not because the sound was even so bad, but because she imagined the abrasive brush scratching the steel

5

surface of the barrel, throwing off its accuracy micron by micron.

She mentioned this fear once, to the firearms instructor at Quantico. He'd laughed.

"You need a chemistry refresher, Darger. Brush is made of copper. Barrel's made of steel. It won't scratch."

Darger didn't care what he said, and she didn't bother trying to correct anyone else either, but the sound of it still set her teeth on edge. Her brush went into the barrel only one direction: the same direction the bullet traveled. Out and only out.

After another pass with a fresh cotton cloth, she ran her bore snake through the barrel.

Her attraction to the FBI was something she'd never really tried to explain to anyone. Not in any kind of honest way. But deep down, she knew what pulled her in. She wanted to be part of the best. She wanted to spend her life fighting for something.

On the simplest level, a battle of good and evil still existed in the world. People did unspeakable things to each other. Rape. Murder. Human trafficking. Mankind devoured itself the same way it always had. The same way it always would. The big ones ate the little ones. The monsters defiled the meek.

And yet others existed who dedicated their lives to stopping the violence. To fighting the monsters.

Violet Darger wanted with all her heart to be part of that. She wanted to stare into the abyss, to do her part to keep the darkness at bay.

Twenty-some weeks at the training academy plus nearly two years in the Crisis Negotiation Unit, and she found herself looking around her beige cubicle and wondering, "Is this what I signed up for?" It was just another desk job most days, more bureaucratic than anything visceral. Hardly the change she'd been expecting when she transferred from OVA. She yearned to work the cases up close, but so far that hadn't happened yet.

The FBI spent half of the training time telling them it's not like what they saw on TV and in the movies. In other words, the prospective agents shouldn't expect their days to be filled with car chases and explosions and shouting into walkie-talkies.

More often, it was paperwork and court dates and an endless string of meetings with your superiors. And then in the next breath, the instructor would be telling them all about the crazy shit they've done — kidnappings, bank robberies, active shooters.

Darger worked over the frame with a toothbrush, then wiped up the excess solvent with a dried out baby wipe.

Just as she twisted open the top of the bottle of gun oil, her phone rang.

She removed one purple nitrile glove and tossed it on the workbench. She retrieved the phone from her pocket, saw that the caller was Cal, and swiped her thumb across the screen.

"Hot Pocket Ryskamp I presume," she said.

She put the phone in speaker mode, set it in her lap, and slid her hand back into the glove.

Cal's chuckle crackled out of the tinny speaker.

"Funny. But I don't know if that's the best way to answer when the new Deputy Assistant Director of CIRG calls."

"Holy shit."

"Yeah."

"You're serious?"

"Yep."

She stopped oiling the barrel and picked up the phone.

"Congratulations, Cal. Or should I say, *sir*. You're a sir now, huh?"

"I guess so."

"So for future reference, how should I answer the phone when you call from now on?" Darger asked.

"DAD Ryskamp would be fine."

"Mister Critical Incident Response Group. Hot damn."

"I know. So, hey, I didn't just call to gloat."

"Yeah, right." She dabbed oil into the creases and the slide, then used another rag to oil the recoil spring.

"OK, it was mostly to gloat."

"I knew it."

"Seriously, though. I have something for you."

She set the phone down again and returned to her task, working oil into the nooks and crannies of the gun frame.

7

"Is this like the time you set me up with that guy that thought that dinosaur fossils were a hoax?"

"You're not ever gonna let me forget that one, are you?"

"It's kind of unforgettable."

"Yeah. Well, we're consulting with the Athens County Sheriff's Department out in Ohio on a case of theirs—"

Darger snorted. Of course. He was going to try to send her out to some BFE resident agency to play Sheriff's pet.

Cal was still talking, ignoring her derisive sigh.

"—multiple cases, actually. The most recent victim was found in garbage bags in a Burger King dumpster. Dismembered. I don't know if you've seen any of it in the news, but they think they have a serial murderer out there. They're calling the killings the Trash Bag Murders or the Doll Parts Murders. But if you're not interested, I can try to find someone else."

The smirk on Darger's face vanished.

"Are you jerking me around?"

"Nope. I'm dead serious."

"You know, people always complain about cronyism," she said, "but I don't really see what's so bad about it."

"Ha. So listen. We already have an agent out there, and therein lies part of the problem. Guy's a real piece of work."

"How so?"

"Oh, he's one of these BAU hotshots who thinks he's Christ returned. Still thinks it's 1982, and he's hunting Ted Bundy or something."

"Ted Bundy was arrested in 1978."

"Whatever. You know what I mean. He's the type that refuses to work with other agents, constantly submits reports late, if at all, and generally drives guys like my new boss totally apeshit," Cal said. He had a habit of cracking his knuckles when he was stressed out, and while she couldn't hear it over the line, she still imagined him doing it while they talked.

"Victor Loshak, I'm sure you've heard of him," he added.

A row of creases appeared on her forehead.

"Yeah. I've heard of him." *Who hadn't*, was what she didn't say. She cleared her throat.

"So am I to take it that you want me to head out there and… what? Report on his findings?"

"Exactly. He hasn't touched base with the liaison in the Resident Agency out there in three days, so we're in the dark."

That was disappointing. This was starting to sound a little more like a babysitting mission and lot less like her profiling dream job.

"And look, I hope you don't think I'm only sending you out to the boonies to play nanny to some pain-in-the-ass old timer."

"I didn't think that." She hoped he couldn't hear the smile in her voice. He knew her too well.

"The truth is, I'm just as interested in hearing your take, and I suspect the local law enforcement would feel the same. You and I both know that you're the best profiler in CNU. You were spot-on with that active shooter in Phoenix. You saved lives."

She frowned and said, "He turned the gun on himself. I didn't do anything."

"What are you talking about? That was in your profile, that he'd take himself out. So we sat. Who knows what would have happened if we'd sent HRT in right away? He might have killed one of our guys. Might have killed another hostage," Cal said. "Don't get humble on me, Darger. It doesn't suit you."

There was a brief pause.

"Or are you trying to tell me you don't want this assignment?"

"No. I want it," she said.

"Good. Then have your butt on a plane to Columbus tomorrow morning. I'll get a copy of the files ready for you before you head out."

Darger was scribbling instructions for herself on a scrap of paper while Cal continued to talk.

"The way I see it, we're killing two birds with one stone. We're kept in the loop, and you get your foot in the door with BAU. I know the weirdo stuff is kind of your thing."

"The weirdo stuff. Nice."

Cal chuckled. "You know what I mean. What I'm trying to say is, I've gotten the impression that there are people that would love for him to be out of the Behavioral Analysis Unit.

All the talent in the world is worthless if you won't be part of the team."

"And he doesn't get reprimanded for… I don't know, not playing well with others?"

"Yes and no. He has friends higher up the chain, and like you said, cronyism is alive and well in the FBI. He's totally protected. For now."

Personally Darger wasn't interested in FBI politics. Actually, it was more than that. She detested it. But she kept her mouth shut and let Cal go on.

"Anyway, it was held back from the press, but there's a witness. A failed abduction. The girl — Peters is her name, I think — gave a full account. With your experience counseling victims and witnesses, I figure who better to talk to her? I'd start there and see what you come up with."

The conversation ended, and Darger dabbed her finger at the touchscreen to hang up. She went back to cleaning her weapon, her lips curling at the corners but not quite smiling. The new assignment was good news, she thought, but she wasn't going to get excited about a one-off case like this.

Of course, the rapid beating of her heart said otherwise.

CHAPTER 2

By the time she arrived in Athens, she'd gone over the files. Cal had them waiting for her at the front desk of his new office, along with a ticket to Columbus departing the next morning and a voucher for her rental car. She'd spent that evening acquainting herself with the crimes over a large cheese pizza and garlic bread from Giovanni's.

Three girls, all from the Athens and Hocking county areas, kidnapped, murdered, dismembered, and dumped in public places.

The first victim, Cristal Munroe, was found in an empty lot next to a roller rink, her body wrapped in black plastic garbage bags. Cristal was from the poor side of town. She shared a trailer with two other girls. The three of them had all worked at the same strip club, a seedy joint that was well known to have girls who would do more than just take off their clothes. Despite the fact that Cristal had recently left her job at the club to enroll in classes at the local community college, police still initially suspected her murder was the by-product of a trick gone wrong.

It wasn't until a second girl went missing that the media started speculating about a serial killer. Local law enforcement had no interest in the sensationalist murmurs from the press and denied any connection between the two girls. But when Katie Seidel's body was discovered a few days later, mutilated in a strikingly similar fashion to Cristal Munroe, they were forced to reconsider the serial killer angle.

Less than a month later, a third girl named Sierra Peters was abducted. She was able to fight off her attacker and escape. Police suspected the man that tried to abduct her was the same man that had killed Cristal and Katie.

Then, nearly a week ago, the body of Fiona Worthington was found — also in trash bags — this time in the dumpster of a Burger King.

Fiona was a 27-year-old graduate student at Ohio University

in Athens. Her parents lived nearby, her father being an English professor at the university. She was everything the first three girls were not — upper middle class, photogenic, and well-educated. The kind of victim the media always had a hard-on for.

Indeed, the third body started a media shitstorm, and that was when the local authorities called in the FBI.

The tires bumped over a railroad crossing, and Deputy Donaldson aimed a finger at a rectangular brick building. The structure looked dark, half the windows were broken, and the sign out front read "B I AM HOE ACE CO."

"That there is the former Brigham Shoelace factory. It was a major blow to the local economy when that place closed down. Now, I know what you're thinkin'. Who'd imagine you'd need a whole factory just to make shoelaces? Well, you'd be surprised. That place was the backbone of this town."

Darger grunted agreement. They passed another crumbling brick carcass, and the Deputy nodded toward it.

"Used to manufacture washing machines over there. They ship these jobs off to China or wherever, and then send us back this crap that lasts two years before it falls apart, so we constantly have to go buy new crap to replace it."

"Right."

"My parents gave me a toaster oven as a graduation gift when I went off to college. Lasted me 26 years before I decided it was lookin' a little hairy. Figured I'd get something that looked of this century. So I go out to Wal-Mart and get me a slick-looking Black and Decker, same exact brand I had before, mind you. Piece of crap burns out in eight months. And the real kicker? I would have gone back to the old one, but I already donated it to the Sally Am. I even went around lookin' for it. No dice."

Darger clenched her jaw, felt the muscles ripple. She wanted more than anything to be alone with the file and the crime scenes and her thoughts. She didn't need someone else's rambling observations gunking up the works. But Donaldson was a talker. She knew that the second he waddled out of his office to shake her hand and went off on a tirade about the "ongoing embarrassment that is the Bengals secondary."

What she was most worried about was that they'd get to the crime scene, and he'd really go off. Spewing out his own pet theories. That was the last thing she wanted.

In her opinion, there was more than one way to contaminate the crime scene, and one of them was with talk.

She'd seen it plenty of times. Cops are on the scene. Someone says, "looks like the husband did it." And based on the numbers, maybe it's not a bad guess for a shot-in-the-dark. But that kind of guesswork often led to tunnel vision, no matter anyone's best intentions. Suddenly people were looking specifically for evidence that backs up the narrative they've already accepted, excluding anything that didn't fit.

As a rule, agents working on profiles made an effort to maintain the purity of their own assessments. Darger wanted to get a feel for things without outside opinions. She had explicitly skipped over anything in the file that leaned toward analysis. She wanted only the facts. It was also one of the reasons she wanted to visit the crime scenes before meeting with Agent Loshak.

She wondered, again, if she was overstepping. No one had specifically told her to work up a profile, and based on all she'd heard, she didn't figure Loshak would be too keen on the idea.

A pothole in the road rattled Darger out of her thoughts. She realized the Deputy had stopped the running commentary somewhere a few miles back. She had a sense that her silence was becoming awkward. She forced herself to say something.

"How long have you been with the Sheriff's Department?"

"Coming up on a quarter-century next year. And I don't mind telling you I've never seen anything like this. We usually have a few cases of arson every year, and then there are the sexual assaults, the drug-related crimes, the domestic disturbances, but we've only had ten murders in-county in the last decade or so. Until now, of course."

"Wow," Darger said. "I guess that's why you called us in."

"Absolutely. If it were up to me, I'd hand the whole thing off to the FBI. This is… well, it's not what I imagined when I signed up for the force."

Donaldson took his eyes off the road to glance at her.

"I'm assuming you've read the book?" he said.

"The book?"

"The one Agent Loshak wrote? *Killer Instincts*?"

"Oh, right. Of course."

He shook his head.

"I got it out from the library after I heard it was him who was comin' down to help out. Figured it wouldn't hurt to do my homework, so to speak. But I couldn't do it. Couldn't get through it."

He suddenly looked more serious.

"No offense."

One of Darger's eyebrows quirked upward.

"None taken."

"It wasn't the writing, mind you, but the content. Crap gives me nightmares. I can't imagine gettin' in the heads of these sickos. I mean… I don't want to know."

Darger didn't know what to say to that.

"What'd you think of it?" Donaldson said.

"Of Loshak's book?"

The deputy bobbed his head once.

"He kind of wrote the textbooks for the field, so… I've learned a lot from him even though we've never met."

"Never met? How is that possible?"

"We're in different units," she said, "and Agent Loshak mostly works alone from what I hear."

"Oh, I must have been way off. I thought you two were related."

"What gave you that idea?"

"When I dropped off the files and photos at his motel room, I saw that he had a picture up on the night stand. It was a girl who looked quite a bit like you. I thought so, anyhow. Younger, of course, but I just thought…"

Darger thought about it a second before she remembered hearing the news about Loshak's family.

"He had a daughter who passed last year. Cancer."

"I'm sorry to hear that. I mentioned the photograph, even, and he didn't say anything. I didn't think much of it at the time.

Me puttin' my foot in my mouth is nothing new, I guess."

The turn signal ticked as they waited to make a left turn. Looking down the hill, Darger could see the circular Burger King sign rising above the roofs of the businesses below. The marquee sported a message offering Buy One Get One Original Chickens.

It wasn't until they wheeled into the parking lot that she realized Donaldson hadn't actually talked about the case at all.

CHAPTER 3

Deputy Donaldson slid the gearshift into Park but left the car idling. Darger moved to exit the vehicle, but she stopped when she noticed that Donaldson wasn't stirring.

"You coming?"

"I'll, uh, sit this one out, if you don't mind."

"Alright," she said, not minding at all.

"To be completely honest with you, I have a tough time with all of the… the blood and all."

He gave a sort of sheepish twitch of his shoulders.

"I'm not proud."

She didn't know what to say, so she gave him a curt nod and climbed out of the cruiser.

Rays of sunlight slanted down through the trees above. She took a breath, the charred smell of flame-broiled burgers filling her nostrils. Pretty gross. Something about the idea of meat and murder in close proximity to one another made her a little queasy.

Approaching the dumpsters, she noted the yellow crime scene tape fluttering in the breeze. Something about the tape's flapping seemed serpentine to her.

She paused just shy of the dumpster itself. This was it. This was where a Burger King employee lived out a nightmare. Spilling a garbage bag of human remains onto the asphalt, blood and grease oozing in all directions. Darger closed her eyes and saw the crime scene photos in her head. Deep gouges pocked the torso, ranging from small slits showing red to gaping pits trailing off into the black of shadows. Fourteen stab wounds, if she remembered the autopsy findings correctly.

The angry slash across the neck went a step beyond the worst of the stab wounds, so deep it had nearly taken the head clean off. Had decapitation been his intent? She paged through the files until she reached the medical examiner's report. They found marks indicative of sawing in addition to the slash across the neck that served as the fatal wound. Maybe.

Darger skirted around the perimeter of the dump site, taking in the crime scene from different angles. Traffic whooshed by, an almost constant source of background noise. But it wasn't static. It undulated, like waves on a beach. Certainly not an isolated location. He picked it for a reason.

The faux shutter sound blipped out of her phone as she snapped photos from various vantage points. It was somewhat unusual for profilers to actually visit the crime scenes in person. Usually, they studied the case file, spit out a profile and move on. But she knew Loshak did it this way, and she wanted to do the same. There were things you could miss in police photographs. The atmosphere of a place.

That was the reason Darger also took her own set of pictures. She wanted visual reminders to bring back the feeling of actually being there. Personal documents. She wanted to be able to remember how busy the street was, what other businesses were in view, where the killer might have stopped or parked his car during the dump.

The dumpster of a fast food joint. The grease dumpster, she reminded herself. Might have been intentional. He might have thought the oil would further complicate things forensically. Or it could have been an accident. If he were in a rush, he may have mistaken it for a regular trash dumpster. He would have heard the splash of the first bag. But by that time, he'd already committed.

She moved closer to the dumpster now, imagining the course he would have taken driving into the lot. Parking. Getting out of the car. Opening the trunk.

There were dark oil spots on the concrete, and when she flipped open the file to the photos taken when the scene was fresh, she confirmed that these were indeed the places where the bags had rested upon being removed from the dumpster.

Emanating from the dark splotches were streams and smears. They were dry now, of course, but still unmistakably blood.

In the photos, the stains were wet. Glistening against the pavement. Pools of it, drying sticky and gelatinous. Gummy.

As quickly as the shutter on a camera snapping open and shut, a different image of blood on concrete flashed in her mind. And then the metallic scent of it, almost more a feeling in her nose than a true smell. Her breath caught in her throat.

The world blurred for a moment, pulse throbbing in her ears. She tasted stomach acid at the back of her tongue.

She crouched in front of the smears on the pavement and closed her eyes. From where the deputy sat in his car, it would appear she was getting a closer look. But the truth was, she was a bit concerned she might faint.

Darger wouldn't let it happen. She took a long, deep breath, and her mind flicked into an exercise to center herself.

My name is Violet Darger.

I was born on April 13th.

I am standing in the parking lot of a Burger King.

Today is Friday.

It is sunny out, barely a cloud in the sky.

By the end, her breathing had slowed. Her pulse still thrummed in her chest, and her hands felt clammy, but she no longer felt like she was going to throw up or pass out, at least.

The exercise worked. It always did. For now, anyway.

Violet took out her phone again and snapped a few photos of the stains. Looking at them through the lens of the camera helped calm her a little more. She felt once-removed from the scene.

She flicked backward in the file. The first two dump sites were entirely out in the open. No attempt at concealment. Did the move to a dumpster suggest he was ashamed of this one? Maybe something went wrong, and he was trying to cover it up?

Darger scribbled these questions on her notepad, then paused to chew on a fingernail.

Based on the lack of rigor mortis and the state of decomposition, the medical examiner estimated the time of death to be around 48-72 hours before she was discovered. She'd been missing around 72 hours.

How long had she been in the oil? Violet squinted, trying to remember the interview notes with Teresa Riley, the Burger King manager. The one who had found the body. She flipped through the file and confirmed that Ms. Riley stated that oil is deposited into the dumpster once a day after the store closes. That would suggest that the body was dumped the night before it was discovered, sometime after 11 PM. Although there was the suggestion by Ms. Riley that the oil may not have been changed then. Violet ran her finger under the letters of the interview transcript as she read.

DET. LUCK: So the dumpster would have been opened by one of your staff last night around the same time?
REILY: Well now, I didn't close last night. And sometimes the grease don't get changed, you see? Not when I'm here, of course. I make sure those fryers are cleaned out every night. But no one really likes to do it, so I know sometimes they aren't doing it. I know it. Because I come in the next day, and there's a smell, you know? The oil gets a bad smell if you don't-
DET. LUCK: OK, but generally, the oil gets dumped every night. Is that right?
REILY: They're supposed to. Yeah.

The misspelling of Ms. Riley's name by the transcription program irked Violet. It was a computer mistake, she knew, but one that could have been quickly and easily fixed by whoever finalized the transcript. She didn't allow for such errors in her own paperwork, and she didn't like it from others. If they couldn't be bothered to correct a simple spelling mistake, what else were they missing?

She clicked and unclicked her pen and refocused on the task at hand. It wasn't the time to get sidetracked by minutiae.

So in theory, the body was in the dumpster for less than 24 hours. That would mean the girl would have been dead for something like 48 hours before the dump. That was consistent with the findings for the other victims. The evidence suggested he was spending a lot more time with them after they were dead than he did while they were alive.

Of course, there were other possibilities. If the oil didn't get dumped the night before, for example. She remembered another one of Ms. Riley's lines from her transcript.

REILY: Sometimes I feel like I'm the only one holding this place together, you know? I'm the only one that cares. These kids, they don't care. They don't actually give a crap about doing a good job. And you know... you know, some of them are marijuana smokers. I know because I smell it on 'em.

Violet tapped her pen against the file and walked around the dumpster. So it was possible the body had been in the dumpster for more than one day. But three? She thought not.

She looked at the photo of the garbage bags again. The crumpled black plastic with a sheen of oily residue. One torn, one intact. Bags for trash. And wasn't that what these girls were to him? Human garbage? Disposable pieces of flesh and bone? Just here for him to consume and then throw out when he's finished.

She doubted he was trying to say that explicitly. He likely chose the bags for the sake of convenience. The word echoed in her head. Convenience. She glanced at the Burger King sign towering above and thought about the significance of the body being dumped at what one might consider a Mecca of convenience. Your way, right away.

In the next series of photos in the file, the body was more clearly visible. At first glance, it really did look like an assortment of doll parts. Close-up shots taken after a destructive toddler has had his way with a Barbie doll. But upon closer inspection, the gruesome details became more clear: the stark white of protruding bone against a backdrop of torn red flesh. The pallor of the skin a mottled mixture of purple and gray. Strangely opaque.

Darger frowned at a picture focusing on the neck wound. There it was again. That awful, jagged slash. Was he really going for a decapitation? A new part of his ritual? Or had he cut further into the neck by accident this time and figured he might as well go all the way, only to find he lacked the proper tools? Or the time. Or perhaps the stomach.

Her eyes ran over the carnage again. No, she thought. He certainly didn't lack the stomach for it.

On the ride to the next dump site, Deputy Donaldson heaved a long sigh and broke his silence.

"I'll be glad when this is all over. Haven't had a good night of sleep since it started."

Darger couldn't remember having many restful nights in the past three years. But she said nothing.

"Wish I could stop thinking about it, that's all."

"Soon, hopefully," Violet finally said.

It was bullshit, of course. These grisly details, the images of these dismembered girls wrapped in plastic, would stick with him forever. Same for all the cops who worked their piece of the investigation. Same, too, for most all of the people who lived in this little swath of the Midwest and had become familiar with the crimes. Hardly a day would go by without these nightmares opening in all of their heads.

She didn't have the heart to tell him. A case like this would never be over.

CHAPTER 4

Darger repeated her ritual at each scene. Taking photos, jotting notes, comparing what she'd read in the files with what she saw with her own eyes. When she was finished, she glanced at her watch, surprised to see that it was already early evening. She hadn't meant to take so long.

By the time she climbed back into the deputy's car for the last time, the sun had begun to set. Deputy Donaldson maintained a thoughtful silence as Violet consulted the file and scribbled in her notebook.

"Before we head back to the station, can you take me to the spot where the Peters girl was abducted?"

Donaldson wore a smirk beneath his sandy mustache.

"Sure, if you can tell me which one."

"I don't follow."

"I suppose you don't have the updated file. The Hocking County guys had her in two days ago for another interview, and she kind of canceled her prior testimony out."

Darger flipped through the file until she found the witness statement for Sierra Peters. She scanned it again, refreshing her memory.

"She recanted?"

"Not exactly. But a lot of the details — which were fuzzy at best to begin with, mind you — changed."

"Maybe she started to remember things more clearly. I mean, what about her story changed?"

"The beginning, middle, and end, mostly. I expect it's hard to keep the details straight when it never happened. Listen, when I drop you off, I'll radio inside and have Marcie make you a copy of the most recent statement. You can go in and grab it before you leave."

"But you think she made it up?"

"The girl has a history. On and off drugs. Meth and painkillers, depending on her mood. She calls our department.

A lot. Filing noise complaints. Reporting suspicious activity in the neighborhood. Calling in ex-boyfriends for things and refusing to press charges two hours later. Crap like that. You take enough of these calls, and you start to take what she says with more than a few grains of salt. Add to that the fact that her supposed abduction happened the day after the press started up with all the serial killer hullabaloo?"

He shook his head as he finished his thought.

"A little too coincidental for my tastes."

Damn it all. If she'd made up the story, that wouldn't just scratch up her profile. It would mar the entire investigation. What doors had been closed because of her statements? What assumptions had already been made and hardened into fact in the minds of the investigators?

Donaldson was still rambling about the girl's history as a troublemaker.

"She went away to a real rehab out in Arizona a while back. Forty days of peace and quiet around town without her calling something in every few days. It was heavenly. Rehab didn't take, though. Two days after she gets back, she gets in a heated altercation at a convenience store and gets busted for possession."

There was a pause, and she could hear the suctioning sound of him sucking his teeth before he continued.

"She's a dead end girl, that one."

Darger had been almost convinced to drop it until that last remark. Her history didn't preclude her from being a victim. Besides, she'd met witnesses who had second thoughts before. It was scary to get mixed up in a murder investigation. Scary for a reason. Sometimes the risk involved was very real.

This thought triggered memories. Bad ones. Darger ground her teeth and blocked the worst of the lot before it had a chance to fill her head with images best forgotten. There would not be a replay of the spell she'd suffered in the Burger King parking lot. She wouldn't allow it.

"That's the thing about the boy who cried wolf, Deputy," Darger said, returning her focus to Sierra Peters. "That last time he really *had* seen a wolf. I'd like to talk to the girl. See what I think."

Deputy Donaldson scoffed.

"Be my guest. If you're in the mood for a goose chase, that's no skin off my nose. I don't pretend to be an expert in homicide investigations. Barely seen one up close myself before all of this. I know people, though. About 80% percent of 'em are good. Maybe not quite that many, but close to that. The other 20% can't connect to anyone else. Some of 'em lie and cheat and steal. Some of 'em kill. I suppose some do all of the above. Our girl isn't the worst of the bunch, but… I think you're wasting your time if you go talk to her. Like I say, though. Maybe I'm out of my element. This is a rural county. A different way of life than what you'll find a lot of places. But I've been patrolling these streets for 25 years. I've observed the human ape in his natural habitat."

He fell quiet for a beat. The car thudded over black stripes of tar where the road had been patched.

"I guess they say people can change. I'll let you know about that if I ever see it for myself."

At the station, Donaldson stopped the cruiser near the front walk. Darger thanked him for accompanying her before she closed the car door behind her. Over the sound of her feet slapping against the sidewalk came the electric whir of a car window.

Donaldson called out through the open window.

"Oh, and Agent?"

"Yes?"

"If you do go talk to the Peters girl, I'd suggest you keep a running inventory of anything that isn't nailed down."

Darger had stopped walking. She stood there on the pavement, squinting back at him.

"How's that?"

"Our star witness is a bit of a klepto. Liable to steal whatever she can get her hands on. Pawn it for drug money and whatnot."

He chuckled like it was a joke of some kind.

Before she could say anything in response, the cruiser propelled forward, coasting to the edge of the lot. Darger watched it wait there, turn signal blinking on and off like a lightning bug until it merged into traffic and traveled out of sight.

CHAPTER 5

The manila envelope was ready for Darger at the front desk, just as Donaldson said it'd be. She thought about waiting until she got back to the motel to go over the newest witness statement, but her curiosity got the better of her. As soon as she was in her rental car, she pinched the metal tab securing the top flap and poured the papers and burned DVD into her lap.

She drummed her fingers impatiently on the center console while her laptop booted. The desktop background appeared, and she jammed the DVD into the drive, clicking a file named 11932_SPeters_Int_1.avi.

The first interview took place the night of the alleged abduction, and the girl's appearance certainly backed up her story. In the video, Sierra's hair was wet and disheveled. Smudges of black makeup ringed her eyes. She wore blue hospital scrubs, her own clothes certainly taken as evidence. Darger knew that the trace evidence found on her clothes had given them nothing useful.

DET. JANSSEN: OK, Sierra. Why don't you start from the beginning? Where were you when he picked you up?
SIERRA: I was… on Vine Street. Savarino's.
DET. JANSSEN: Savarino's. The Italian place?
Sierra nodded.
DET. JANSSEN: Can you answer Yes or No?
SIERRA: Yes.
DET. JANSSEN: So you're on Vine Street, near Savarino's. And what were you doing there?
SIERRA: Walking.
DET. JANSSEN: Walking. Right. Where to? Where from?
SIERRA: Huh?
DET. JANSSEN: Well, you weren't just out walkin' for your health at 2 AM, were you?
SIERRA: No, I was at Jimmy's.

DET. JANSSEN: Jimmy. Does Jimmy have a last name?
Sierra sobbed.
SIERRA: Oh God. He was gonna kill me.
DET. JANSSEN: Jimmy was gonna kill you?
SIERRA: No! The guy that took me! He was gonna kill me.
DET. JANSSEN: OK, so what happened at Jimmy's?
Sierra abruptly stopped crying then.
SIERRA: Nothing. I went there to see if he was home, but he wasn't so I left.
DET. JANSSEN: And what had you walkin' over to this Jimmy guy's house at 2 AM? He your boyfriend?
SIERRA: What? No. I don't... Forget Jimmy, OK? He wasn't there. He wasn't a part of it.

Darger throttled the pen in her hand. What the hell was this? She'd had the same feeling reading the interview the first time. The video was even worse. This Detective Janssen seemed like he was interrogating her more than taking a witness statement. She let her gaze fall back down to the screen.

DET. JANSSEN: OK, so you go over to this Jimmy's house, for God knows what reason, and he's not home, so then what?
SIERRA: So I started to walk back home. And that's when this guy pulls up.
DET. JANSSEN: Can you describe him? What about his car?
SIERRA: He had dark hair. It was wet. Like he just took a shower or maybe had some mousse or somethin' in it. And glasses. Big glasses.
DET. JANSSEN: And what about the vehicle? Car, truck, van?
SIERRA: Car.
DET. JANSSEN: Do you remember what color?
Sierra folded her arms over her chest and hugged herself like she might be cold.
SIERRA: It was dark.
DET. JANSSEN: The car was dark, or it was too dark to see the color?
Sierra shook her head, seeming confused.
SIERRA: Both? I mean, it was dark outside, but the car was

dark, too.

DET. JANSSEN: OK. Big or small?

SIERRA: Um. Big? I don't know about cars, really. It didn't seem super old.

Janssen's mustache quivered while he ponders this revelation.

DET. JANSSEN: So you think it was a newer car?

SIERRA: Not brand new, but… newish.

DET. JANSSEN: Darkish, biggish, and newish. Got it. And how did he get you in the car? He call you over, then grab you? Hit you or something?

SIERRA: Uh-huh.

DET. JANSSEN: "Uh-huh?" Does that mean, Yes, he grabbed you? Yes, he hit you?

SIERRA: Uh-huh. Yes. He hit me. I got in the car, and he punched the side of my head and put something that smelled like rotten fruit up to my face.

Sierra gestured to nose and mouth.

DET. JANSSEN: Did he say anything to you before that?

She brought a knuckle to her cheek and rubbed at it.

SIERRA: He asked me if I wanted a ride?

DET. JANSSEN: Is that a question? Or a statement?

SIERRA: What?

DET. JANSSEN: You didn't sound sure.

SIERRA: He asked me if I wanted a ride.

DET. JANSSEN: OK. And do you normally accept rides from strangers?

SIERRA: I don't… I didn't… I didn't accept a ride from him.

DET. JANSSEN: You didn't? Because you said he asked if you wanted a ride, you got in the car, and then he hit you.

SIERRA: No. No. That's not what happened.

Sierra's chest started to jerk a little, like a child that's just stopped crying but is thinking about starting up again.

SIERRA: I didn't get in the car. He made me get in the car.

DET. JANSSEN: OK, OK. So you're in the car. Does he say anything when you're in the car?

SIERRA: Well, I wouldn't know, would I? I was passed out.

DET. JANSSEN: And when did you wake up?

SIERRA: On the floor.

DET. JANSSEN: Not where. When?
Sierra spoke slowly and deliberately.
SIERRA: When he put me on the floor. How am I 'sposed to know when? He took my phone. Wasn't like there was a clock in there.
DET. JANSSEN: In where?
SIERRA: In the room.
DET. JANSSEN: What was it? Like a house? An apartment?
SIERRA: No. The floor was hard. And cold. Cement.
DET. JANSSEN: Like a basement? Or a garage?
SIERRA: Garage. I think. I think it had one of them doors that go up.
Sierra pantomimed a garage door opening.
DET. JANSSEN: And he didn't have you tied up or anything?
SIERRA: My hands were tied, yeah.
DET. JANSSEN: Not your legs, though?
Sierra started to cry again, rocking back and forth.
SIERRA: I don't know. Maybe. Oh my God. I should be dead. He was gonna kill me just like those other girls.
DET. JANSSEN: But he didn't. Right, Sierra? Sierra.
Sierra wiped her nose and looked up at the detective.
DET. JANSSEN: He didn't get you. Stay with me for a few more minutes, and then we can take a break.
SIERRA: OK.
DET. JANSSEN: What could you see outside the door?
SIERRA: I don't know. I don't remember.
DET. JANSSEN: Think about it for a minute. Were there houses? Other buildings? A parking lot?
Sierra shook her head.
SIERRA: The lights were too bright to see anything.
DET. JANSSEN: What lights?
SIERRA: The headlights. On the car.
DET. JANSSEN: So you were on the floor, tied up, and then what?
SIERRA: I could hear rain on the roof. Sounded like metal. I thought I was in my apartment, but the rain didn't sound right. And I opened my eyes, and I was on the floor, and when I tried to touch where my head hurt, my hands were tied. And then I

could feel that my feet were tied-
DET. JANSSEN: So your feet were tied?

Darger wished for a time machine so she could travel back just to jump in at this point in the interview and tell Detective Janssen to shut the fuck up and let the girl talk. Sierra had been on a roll there — the most lucid she'd seemed in the entire interview — and he had to go and interrupt.

SIERRA: Yeah.
DET. JANSSEN: It's just that before, you didn't seem to remember.
SIERRA: Well now I do. They were tied.
DET. JANSSEN: Go on.
SIERRA: I woke up, and I didn't see the man. So I ran.
DET. JANSSEN: I thought your feet were tied.
SIERRA: They were. I got 'em loose. Obviously.
DET. JANSSEN: What were you tied with? Rope? Duct tape?
SIERRA: Rope. Or more like... twine, I guess.
DET. JANSSEN: What did you see when you got outside?
SIERRA: Nothing, really. It was dark. And the headlights made it so I couldn't see nothin'.
DET. JANSSEN: So you couldn't tell where you were at all once you got outside?
SIERRA: No. Just that it was rainin'. And then I ran through some woods. And I was sure he was right behind me. I was so scared. I was so scared he was gonna get me.
DET. JANSSEN: Did he see you get away? Did you hear him or see him?
SIERRA: I don't think so. But I just knew he was gonna kill me. I wasn't 'sposed to get away.
DET. JANSSEN: How long did you run through the woods for? Do you know?
SIERRA: Five or ten minutes? Maybe. I don't know. It was dark. And I thought he was comin' after me. I don't know.
DET. JANSSEN: And did you find the payphone right away, or did you have to walk for a while?
SIERRA: I don't remember. I just remember seein' lights ahead,

through the trees, and I thought, "A little farther, just a little farther." And the whole time, I was sure he was right behind me. And he was gonna grab me at the last second and kill me just like he meant to in the first place.

Detective Janssen tilted his head to glance at the clock on the wall.

DET. JANSSEN: OK, Sierra. I think we'll take a little break now. You want something to drink?

SIERRA: Diet Coke?

DET. JANSSEN: I'll be back.

The tape cut out and began again some time later. An open can of Diet Coke rested on the table in front of Sierra, and she spun it around idly, tapping her finger against the aluminum.

DET. JANSSEN: Let's talk a little off the record for a minute. And be honest, Sierra. You were partyin' tonight, weren't you?

SIERRA: No, I was not.

DET. JANSSEN: Come on, Sierra. Not even a few drinks? Maybe smokin' a little somethin'?

SIERRA: No, sir. I been clean. I been clean two weeks!

DET. JANSSEN: OK. Alright. It's just that your speech is a little slurred, you know?

SIERRA: I told you! He hit me in the head, and then he gave me that chloroform!

DET. JANSSEN: Chloroform? How'd you know it was chloroform?

SIERRA: Well, whatever! Isn't that what they usually use? On a rag?

DET. JANSSEN: Isn't that what *who* usually uses?

SIERRA: In the movies!

DET. JANSSEN: And what about this woman you saw?

SIERRA: Woman? What woman? There was no woman.

DET. JANSSEN: Says here you said you saw a woman jogging by. A witness, I guess.

SIERRA: No. There wasn't a woman. It was just the one guy.

Darger cringed at that last bit about the chloroform. It sounded... fanciful. A detail thrown in for maximum drama. Darger could see how that — coupled with her history — might make someone look at Sierra's testimony from the beginning and start to doubt it.

She double-clicked the next file.

As the second video played, Darger followed along with the written transcript. Sierra's demeanor and appearance were much changed in the two weeks since her first interview. Her hair was dry, her makeup unsmudged. Her eyes were no longer wide and blinking with fear. If anything, she looked a little bored as she took a seat in one of the plastic chairs across from Detective Janssen.

DET. JANSSEN: We wanted to go over a few things if that's alright.
SIERRA: Fine.
DET. JANSSEN: Let's start with where you were when he first got you in the car.
Sierra was combing her fingers through her hair as the detective spoke, and she stopped abruptly, hands floating back into her lap.
SIERRA: I was by McHappy's.
There was a long pause as Janssen stared at the file in front of him.
DET. JANSSEN: McHappy's? The bakery?
Sierra studied her fingernails and nodded.
DET. JANSSEN: Now hold on a minute. Last time you said you were on Vine St. Near Savarino's. Visiting someone named Jimmy.
Sierra's head shook from side to side. She didn't look confused or baffled by Janssen's statements. She seemed utterly calm.
SIERRA: No. That was wrong. I said it wrong. I was at Jimmy's, but earlier. Way earlier. When the guy got me, I was by McHappy's.
Janssen crossed his arms over his gut with one fist over his mouth. He stared at Sierra for several seconds before moving on.
DET. JANSSEN: OK. Let's talk about how he got you in the car, shall we?

32

Sierra shrugged.

DET. JANSSEN: There was some confusion last time we talked, about whether or not he offered you a ride. Did he offer you a ride?

SIERRA: Yes.

DET. JANSSEN: And you got in the car with him, and that's when he hit you?

SIERRA: No. I kept walking. I'm not an idiot. I didn't get in the car with no stranger.

DET. JANSSEN: So he pulls the car up to you as you're walking, asks if you want a ride, and you keep walking?

SIERRA: Uh huh.

DET. JANSSEN: And then what? He stopped and got out, or what?

Sierra crossed and uncrossed her legs.

SIERRA: Yes.

DET. JANSSEN: And you didn't run then?

SIERRA: Huh?

DET. JANSSEN: I'm just saying, some stranger asks you if you want a ride… probably creeped you out a little, right?

SIERRA: I guess.

DET. JANSSEN: And then when you say no, he doesn't drive off. He keeps right along with you. Stops the car. Gets out. Seems like you'd know then that something was off.

SIERRA: Well, I…

DET. JANSSEN: I mean, it would make more sense, for example, if he had kept on driving, and maybe, I don't know, pulled into an alley or something down the street, waited for you to pass, and then grabbed you.

SIERRA: Yeah. Well. That's… that's what happened.

DET. JANSSEN: It is?

Sierra nodded.

SIERRA: Yeah. He went into a parking lot up ahead of where I was walkin'. Only I didn't see him. And that's when he got me. He came up behind me and grabbed my hair and put the rag over my mouth and then I passed out.

DET. JANSSEN: Last time you said he hit you on the side of the head.

SIERRA: Yeah. He hit me, too
Janssen licked his lips and glanced at the camera.

Darger tapped her pen against the screen through the next
section as if that might speed things up. Janssen and Sierra were
stuck rehashing the vague details about the man and the car.
Caucasian male. Hair, dark and wet. Big glasses. Car, dark
sedan.

DET. JANSSEN: And you woke up where?
SIERRA: In the room. It echoed funny.
DET. JANSSEN: Echoed?
SIERRA: Yeah. Like the way his feet scraped against the ground.
DET. JANSSEN: The ground? Like dirt?
SIERRA: Umm… I guess.
DET. JANSSEN: Before you said the floor was cement.
A line of wrinkles arranged themselves across Sierra's forehead.
Her eyes squinted and closed and then she shook her head.
SIERRA: I don't remember for sure.
DET. JANSSEN: What about the door. Before you said you
remembered a door like on a garage.
Sierra blinked four times, eyes fastened on the tabletop in front
of her. Finally, she spoke again.
SIERRA: Yeah. I think so.
DET. JANSSEN: So maybe a shed instead of a garage?
SIERRA: Maybe. It's hard to remember.
DET. JANSSEN: And is there anything else you can think of?
Sierra scratched her eyebrow.
SIERRA: No.
Janssen flipped the folder on the table closed and stood, moving
to the door and opening it.
SIERRA: I can go?
DET. JANSSEN: Yeah. You're done. Talking with you has been
ever so helpful.
Janssen made no attempt to disguise his indifference. Sierra rose
from the molded plastic chair and left the room.

Darger was about to close the video player when she heard

something. She rewound the video and increased the volume on the computer. It was Sierra's voice again. Softer now that she was away from the microphone in the interview room. She had to put the speakers at full volume to hear it.

SIERRA: Wait. I think…
Detective Janssen was still standing in the doorway. He rested his fists on his hips.
SIERRA: I think there was a pool nearby.
DET. JANSSEN: A pool? Why is that?
SIERRA: I don't know. A feeling I guess.
DET. JANSSEN: And you just remembered this now?
SIERRA: I just… got a flash of it. In my head.
DET. JANSSEN: A pool, then. Got it. Thank you for coming in.
The screen went to black.

Darger frowned over the paper transcript. That last section wasn't even on it. She rewound the last bit of the interview and replayed it. Then she leaned over and grabbed the file from where it rested in the passenger seat. She flipped open to one of the autopsy reports, skimming. She jabbed a finger at the page. Her eyes glittered like a cat stalking a bird.

"Gotcha."

CHAPTER 6

Her motel room featured lush carpeting the color and texture of moss, and she thought the quilted floral bedspreads draped over the mattresses clashed with the moss quite well. All red and green and ancient like Freddy Kruger himself did the interior decorating circa 1984. The room had that stale smell Darger associated with all motel rooms: must and industrial cleaners and a hint of old cigarette smoke from years gone by.

The bed springs squeaked as she dropped her suitcase on the nearer bed. She poked her head in the bathroom just long enough to see her reflection in the harsh fluorescent light, and that pretty much completed the tour.

Her palms went clammy again. She was nervous about meeting Agent Loshak.

Better to get it over with then, she thought.

She marched out the door and down the concrete catwalk that gave access to the second floor rooms. She paused in front of the neighboring room, fist poised to knock. She hesitated. The door suddenly seemed intimidating. Agent Loshak wouldn't be happy to have another agent sent out here to check on him. Less than another agent, maybe. A glorified babysitter. She steeled herself for combat.

Her knuckles rapped against the door. One, two, three.

A grunt answered from inside the room, then the squeak of a creaky subfloor, and then silence. Darger figured Loshak was watching her through the peephole, and she made an effort to look official, standing straight and tall with her chin lifted slightly.

Finally, she heard the clatter of the door being unlocked. The knob turned and a pair of red-rimmed eyes surrounded by pale flesh peered back at her through the crack. Despite the sickly pallor, there was something striking in his gaze. A wry look. Clever.

"Special Agent Loshak?" Darger said. He kept staring, so she continued. "I'm Special Agent Darger."

She held out her hand, but Loshak made no move to take it or to open the door further.

"Your ID."

"Pardon?"

"Let me see your badge."

He made a gesture with his hand that indicated she should get on with it.

"Alright," Darger said. She pulled it from her pocket and stepped forward to hand it to him. Something about this exchange made her feel as if she were a dog in a pack, being challenged by the alpha. She wondered if it was on purpose. On second thought, it was *definitely* on purpose.

Loshak took the badge, rubbing a paw over several days' worth of stubble on his chin as he studied it. When he handed it back, they locked eyes. This time, Darger wasn't going to let him dominate. She held his gaze, unblinking, and it was Loshak who looked away first. He opened the door a little wider, but he didn't quite move to let her in.

"You know, you coulda called ahead."

Darger noted that he was changing the subject. Defensive. Another sign of weakness. Odd. This wasn't what she'd been expecting.

"I did. Both your cell and the room number. You didn't answer." She glanced over his shoulder and took in the room quickly. "Your phone is off the hook."

"Well, yeah... I find it rings less that way."

Loshak's face pulled into a grimace, and he held up a finger. "Excuse me for a moment."

He turned, walking quickly to the bathroom at the back of the room. The bathroom door banged shut behind him. He left the front door open with Darger standing in it.

She heard a gagging sound and then the slap of liquid on liquid. He was vomiting. Delightful.

She looked both ways down the second story balcony, feeling awkward standing outside of the open door. Screw it. She took a step inside and pulled the door closed.

After about a minute, the toilet rumbled and flushed. Water

ran in the sink, and then Loshak reappeared.

She blinked a few times, debating whether to address the puking elephant in the room or try to ignore it.

"Are you OK?"

Loshak waved her concern away as if it were a fly circling the potato salad at a Fourth of July picnic.

"Just a little under the weather. Want some advice? Stay away from Savarino's in town. Bad scallops, I think."

"Duly noted," she said.

Loshak sat on the bed, tilting his head to look at her with a clever look about his eyes.

"I assume you've seen the file?" he said.

"Yep. And I visited the crime scenes in person."

"Thorough."

Loshak fell back into the bed with a groan.

"Well?" he asked.

She raised an eyebrow at him, not sure what he wanted.

"Your thoughts?"

"Oh," she said.

She hadn't expected him to want to hear her take. After all the talk about him being difficult, he seemed neither surprised nor particularly bothered by her presence. Maybe a little curious. She'd come prepared for a fight. In the absence of conflict, she felt a little shy.

She moistened her lips with the tip of her tongue and began.

"Based on the race and age of the victims: white male, between the ages of 25 and 35."

"Uh-huh. What else you got?"

"Alright," she said, swallowing. "The fact that there are extensive stab wounds present lends itself to an anger-retaliatory profile. These crimes are first and foremost expressions of rage, a fetishization of power that finds its voice in excessive displays of force. In this case, stabbing a corpse fourteen times and just about cutting off the head."

"So he's not a sadist?"

Darger felt her shoulders jerk, some involuntarily twitch of the muscles there.

"No."

She realized how visceral her reaction had been and made an effort to loosen up. Did he think the killer was a sadist? Or was he testing her? She started to worry she'd missed something.

"Why not?" he asked.

"Because aside from the fatal wound, the medical reports suggest almost everything else is post-mortem. If he were a sadist, he'd keep them alive for that. Looking at the probable timelines we have, he probably kills or incapacitates them quickly after the abduction. He displays no particular interest in making them suffer."

"Agreed. Go on."

So he *was* testing her. Darger bit her lip a little and continued.

"I found it interesting that the most recent victim had her head almost sawed off. Makes me wonder if he was interrupted."

"Or gave up," he commented. "Why do you think that's significant?"

"He's taking the dismemberment further. Wants it to last longer, wants to be more elaborate... with the time he spends defiling the corpses."

For a moment, it was a little too real, this monster they were hunting. She tried to imagine the type of person who would find enjoyment in butchering a human body. She almost missed what Loshak said next.

"And so far, nothing's missing, if you know what I mean. But I doubt that'll last."

Darger flashed back to the motel room.

"You think he'll keep a body part as a souvenir?"

"Yep."

It would make sense, she realized. Like so many other serial killers — Bundy, Dahmer, Kemper, Gein, Kearney — much of the obsession was focused on the dead body itself. The product the killing rendered rather than the process of the killing itself. Many of these types wound up keeping body parts. Maybe even most of them.

"What else?" Loshak asked.

"He's not stupid. The precautionary measures — choosing dump sites that ensure evidence contamination, the bleach to degrade DNA — those suggest at least average intelligence."

Suddenly Loshak held up a hand, and Darger worried she'd made an error.

"Wait."

Again he got up and made for the bathroom. When he returned, he fell back onto the bed with a sigh.

"OK, continue."

"Are you sure?" she asked. "We can do this later."

He ignored her.

"You don't think the public dump sites might suggest that he's a dum-dum? I mean, there are an infinite number of places out in the woods he could dump 'em. Places where they might never be found."

"It's risky, yes," Darger said. "But it's clearly calculated. It's a territorial display. These are his trophies, and he wants everyone to see them. He's brazen enough to do it. Confident enough that he thinks it won't get him caught. He likes taunting us."

"Us?"

"Society at large. He's a loner. He feels persecuted. Like society is shutting him out. Keeping him down. Dumping the bodies in public places is a way to direct the rage at everyone."

Loshak nodded.

"That's pretty good, actually. You know, the lower intelligence, disorganized types are less apt to move the bodies. If they make any attempt to conceal their crimes, it's usually near the scene and a poor attempt — a shallow grave, shoved under a porch, or in their basement. They do the bare minimum. Like a kid who spills grape juice on mommy's white couch and covers it with a pillow. They know they have to hide it. They just don't put a lot of time and effort into planning it. I guess they can't."

A sound like sandpaper on wood came from Loshak's face as he rubbed at his unshaven cheeks.

"But this guy... he cleans up. Bags them. Puts them in his car. Drives around. And then, instead of going where no one would find them, he dumps them right out in the open. Where everyone will see. He covets the attention."

Loshak rolled onto his side, propping his chin up with a fist, and fixed his gaze on Darger, those lines smiling around his eyes again.

"But this is supposed to be your profile. Go ahead."

And now the meat of it, she thought.

"I would expect him to have had a traumatic home life with a domineering maternal figure who likely abused him — physically and mentally — mother, stepmother, or grandmother. Possibly foster care. That trauma created and reinforced a narrative of him being worthless. He's conflicted in his feelings about women. He's attracted to them, but he hates that the attraction gives them power over him. He's intensely afraid of rejection. He's convinced, in fact, that almost any woman would reject him, and that idea is what fuels his rage. He has a totally warped sense of self. He thinks of himself as an outsider. Someone somehow apart from the rest of the human race. Unlovable."

Darger was staring at a painting of a lighthouse hung next to the bed, not really seeing it, but looking through it.

"As I said before, he is not a sadist. He kills them quickly because a dead girl can't laugh or cry or recoil in horror. A dead girl is his completely to do with as he pleases. They can't reject him. They can't talk back or spit in his face. He has total control. That is his fantasy."

He made a face, squinting at her.

"What's your background? Academically, I mean."

Violet looked up from her notes.

"I have a Masters in Forensic Psychology."

Had she made a mistake? She frowned down at her notes. No. Her profile was sound. It was based upon the facts of the case. No profile was ever 100% accurate, but she was certain hers wasn't straying far from the standard.

"And at the Bureau?"

"I started in Victim Assistance. Sex crimes and human trafficking, mostly."

"You left OVA to become an agent?"

She shrugged, affecting an air of coolness. Inside, she was

anything but. She hated that this always came up, anytime someone asked what she'd done before becoming an agent.

"I liked the job, but I got tired of sitting behind a desk. I wanted something... more proactive," she said. Not totally a lie. "Less talk, more... hunt down the bad guys. Maybe I was jealous of you agents getting all the limelight."

He studied her for a moment and then gave a nod.

"You can go on."

"I'd expect him to be socially awkward, even with men. Not necessarily a recluse, but no close friends. Maybe a few acquaintances he socializes with on occasion. Drinking buddies. Hunting trips or a bowling league. But all of his relationships are superficial. No one really *knows* him. Though anyone that has spent any amount of time with him probably would have witnessed at least a few incidents of impulsiveness. Outbursts of anger. Violent behavior. These events would be perceived by his peers as out of character. Especially because his so-called normal demeanor is usually extremely controlled."

Paper rustled as Darger brushed a page out of the way.

"Military experience is possible. The power and respect would appeal to him. If so, it likely ended in dishonorable discharge as he fails to get along with authority figures. He probably works a menial job that he considers beneath him and—"

Loshak interrupted a third time to go vomit. When he came back this time, Violet couldn't ignore it any longer.

"Have you seen a doctor?"

"For food poisoning? It'll resolve itself."

Loshak laid an arm over his eyes, possibly an attempt to block out the light from the bedside lamp.

"And how long has this so-called food poisoning been going on? Quantico has been trying to get in touch with you for days. Food-borne illnesses generally run their course in 24 hours."

He peeked at her from under his arm.

"You didn't mention you were an MD."

"I'm not."

"Then don't worry about it."

There it was. A touch of the prickly disposition she'd

anticipated. Still, she'd expected him to push back more, to challenge her. Maybe it was the sickness keeping him docile.

"Now what's your take on his method of collection?"

"Collection?" she repeated, not sure what he meant.

"How he chooses the girls. How he takes them."

"Oh," she said. "I guess that depends on what we think of the interviews with Sierra Peters."

"Pretend we don't have a supposed witness. What would you guess, based on the rest of the profile?"

Violet scratched at the back of her head. She was winging it now. Most of her profile had been put together as she walked the crime scenes, and at that point, she'd been taking the legitimacy of Sierra's story for granted. The ground beneath her feet suddenly felt less solid.

"This is based on gut instinct more than fact—"

"Every profile is, don't you think?" he asked.

"I guess."

Violet chewed a fingernail.

"There are two options, really," Loshak said. "Is it random? He sees a girl walking down the street and just grabs her? Or does he watch them a while? Figure out their patterns. Wait 'til they're alone."

"I don't think it's random."

"Me neither," he agreed.

Loshak crossed one ankle over the other.

"And what about getting them in the car? Ambush? Or finesse?"

Darger thought for a second.

"If he talks them into the car, that suggests some sophistication — he's confident in his ability to get what he wants with words."

She thought of Ted Bundy and Charles Sobhraj, charming and conning women to get close. Ed Kemper made himself seem unimposing and dorky to disarm women, despite the fact that he was 6'9" and 300 lbs.

"But if he threatens them with a weapon, or maybe drugs them before they know what's happening, that's different. Forcing someone into a car — even if he incapacitates them or points a gun at them — is still risky on his part. Some of them are bound to scream or try to put up a fight. It could be that he gets off on the use of force. Or he might lack the confidence to try subtler means."

"If. You said 'if' before both scenarios. Which is it?"

She sighed.

"My gut says he does something to catch them off-guard. A con of some kind. Maybe he's able to talk some of them into the car. I could buy that with Cristal and Sierra. Maybe Katie. But not Fiona."

Loshak pinched the bridge of his nose and fell silent for a moment. Darger wondered if he was going to throw up again. When a minute passed by with no further expulsions or conversation, Darger cleared her throat.

"Speaking of Sierra Peters. What do you think of her statements?"

Loshak grunted.

"Hard to say. She contradicts herself so many times. Makes it almost impossible to decide what might be true. I'm disposed to ignore all of it for the time being. It's a shame, too. Having a failed abduction attempt could have been a real boon. That's what got Bundy caught. The first time, anyway."

"Even with what she said about the pool?" Darger asked.

"The what?"

"Have you seen the video of the second interview? Or only the transcript?"

Loshak lifted his head, frowning at her.

"The transcript. You got video?"

Darger held up a finger.

"I'll be right back."

She hurried next door, grabbing her laptop bag from the bed. In the mirror over her motel room's dresser, she noticed the manic, gleeful look on her face. Violet reminded herself that three girls were dead. She'd do well to curb her enthusiasm.

Back in Loshak's room, she skipped to the end of the video and cranked the volume.

SIERRA: I think there was a pool nearby.

DET. JANSSEN: A pool? Why is that?
SIERRA: I don't know. A feeling I guess.
DET. JANSSEN: And you just remembered this now?
SIERRA: I just… got a flash of it. In my head.

"Well I'll be goddamned," Loshak said.

"I'm assuming the fact that they found traces of bleach on the bodies was held back from the media?"

Loshak bobbed his head once.

"Then she's telling the truth," Darger said, her voice coming out a bit more excited than she'd intended. So much for curbing her enthusiasm. "What are the odds she'd randomly guess that? She didn't smell a pool. She smelled the bleach he dumps on them."

Loshak was still staring at the screen, the blue tinted light from the TV reflected in the wetness of his eyes.

"Maybe."

"What do you mean, maybe?"

"I'm not disagreeing with you," he said. "I'm just saying, she didn't specifically say she smelled it."

Darger chewed her lip again.

"What?" Loshak said.

"What if that's why he took Fiona Worthington? Sierra was who he really wanted, but she got away. He was angry. Impulsive. Lashing out. And he happens to see Fiona jogging by. That could be why she doesn't fit the victim profile as well."

Loshak pondered the ceiling for a while.

"It's possible. But your theory relies heavily on a girl known for telling stories."

"That's why I want to talk to her," Darger said. "I think I might know why she changed her story."

This finally snapped Loshak out of his trance. He ruffled a hand through his hair again and snorted, half-amused.

"Just what every junkie wants, right? A house call from a federal agent."

CHAPTER 7

Their task tonight may be to watch for a serial killer, but all McAdoo wanted, for the moment, was to open his damn snack cake.

The wrapper on the Honey Bun crinkled as Officer Dan McAdoo's pudgy fingers worked at it. He grit his teeth, pulled with all his might. The oblong food item quivered in the open space between his hands, but the plastic sleeve wouldn't budge.

"Piece of shit thing," he muttered under his breath.

He swiped the back of his hand at his brow. Despite the night's chill pressing at the windows, it was warm in the car. Stuffy. He took a breath and went back to it.

The bun shifted in his hands, hammy palms mashing the icing to the plastic as he tried again. With the amount of force he was applying, he couldn't help but picture the wrapper shredding apart all at once, the Honey Bun somersaulting out and belly-smacking the floor mat. Instead, the stupid thing just shook like mad and rasped out that cellophane sound.

His partner, Officer Chuck Novotny, was his opposite physically — tall and bony with a long face that was almost 50% nose. He watched the portly cop from the driver's seat, jabbing his gums with a toothpick, something between a grimace and a smile pulling on the corners of his mouth. His face couldn't seem to decide if it was amused or disgusted by what he was seeing — a grown man fighting like hell with a snack cake and somehow losing.

"Give it," Novotny said finally.

"Huh?"

The crinkle of the plastic ceased.

McAdoo turned to look at his partner as the man spoke, breaking eye contact after a moment to watch as the toothpick bobbed with every syllable.

"Give me the damn thing."

Novotny put his hand out, and McAdoo's eyes drifted from

the toothpick to the outstretched palm, hesitated there a beat, and flicked to the Honey Bun pinched in his fingers. He stared at the oval of cake for a long time before he handed it over.

"Something's wrong with this piece of shit thing."

Novotny had snatched it and popped the top of the package open before McAdoo had even finished his sentence. He shook the opened Honey Bun, the rich aroma of artificial flavors filling the vehicle, and McAdoo plucked it from his hand, lips twittering as though mumbling something to himself without sound.

"You're welcome," Novotny said.

They fell quiet again as McAdoo peeled away the plastic and bit the snack cake. The pudgy cop tried to think of something — anything — to say as he chewed. He hated the quiet. It made the time go slower, he thought. He came up empty, though. Maybe they'd talked themselves out over the past several nights.

Novotny spoke up then, mercifully shattering the silence.

"Tonight's stakeout was brought to you by the Federal Bureau of Investigation," he said.

McAdoo chuckled. They both knew that they were out here because of Loshak. The agent had impressed upon the Chief how certain he was that the perpetrator would return to one of the dump sites. Apparently these sickos did that on a regular basis. So here they were. Bored. Constantly either too hot or too cold. Shoving junk food into their mouth holes all night.

They'd set up shop in the parking lot of an apartment complex across the street from the Burger King where the most recent body had been found. They were tucked back in the shadows pretty good, their car nestled among the sedans and mini-vans of the people who lived in the building, but they had a clear view.

Both officers sported plainclothes, of course, and they sat in Novotny's Mustang rather than their standard cruiser. McAdoo decided to wear his holster since that wouldn't blow their cover so long as he stayed in the car, but he found himself unable to get comfortable with the gun in these bucket seats. Everything was so much smaller and more narrow than what he was used to in the cruiser. It didn't make much sense to him, but no matter which way he shifted, the gun kept digging into his hip.

Novotny switched out his toothpick, replacing it with a wad of Skoal from the hockey puck sized can he'd removed from his breast pocket. With the tobacco secured in his bulging lip, he lifted the binoculars to his face, and McAdoo followed his gaze. They looked at the Burger King across the street. The image of that bloody bag of body parts flashed in the portly cop's head, but the lot was empty. Dark.

"See anything?" McAdoo said, his mouth full of snack cake.

"Nope."

"Think he'll come back?"

McAdoo tried to sound nonchalant as he asked, but he was pretty sure his chalant was showing nevertheless.

"FBI people sure seem to think he will," Novotny said with a shrug.

McAdoo stopped himself short of asking, "What if they're wrong?" It would have been a silly thing to say, he knew. Between the two of them, Novotny and McAdoo had worked 11 years at the Athens Police Department. Neither of them had witnessed a homicide scene in real life before all of this, let alone worked a serial murder case. Special Agent Loshak knew more about violent crime than he would in 10 or 20 lifetimes working this jurisdiction.

"So they really do that?" McAdoo said after a lull. "Go back to the scene, I mean. That's, like, a thing?"

"Oh yeah," Novotny said, bringing the binoculars down to his lap. "Ted Bundy used to go back up into the mountains to his dump sites and sleep with the dismembered bodies."

McAdoo paused mid-chew, suddenly less interested in the second half of his Honey Bun.

"For real?"

"Yep. Used to jerk off into their mouths and stuff. He had problems."

"Yeah, I guess so. Where was that at? Somewhere way out west, right?"

"Washington state. Utah. Colorado. A couple in Florida, too. Maybe three."

"Yeah. So pretty far from here."

Novotny's head swiveled to face his partner, and he locked eyes with him.

"You think it doesn't happen around here? Ohio had one of the first famous serial murder cases. The Cleveland torso murders."

McAdoo's mouth suddenly seemed very dry.

"Torso?"

Novotny tilted his head and squinted, narrowed eyes still focused on his partner.

"Yeah. Torso. Please tell me you're not asking what a torso is."

"No. I just... I mean, I didn't know if that's what you said, or..."

"I said torso murders. Cleveland, Ohio. Twelve vagrant victims. Dude beheaded them while they were still alive, then cut off the arms and legs and dumped 'em. They never found about half of the heads as a matter of fact. I think he emasculated some of the male victims, too. Cut their junk right off. Snip-snip."

Novotny scissored his index and middle fingers a few times as he finished his thought, chuckling a little at his sound effect.

A sigh escaped McAdoo's nostrils like he'd sprung an air leak.

"Jesus, man. Who would do something like that?"

"Don't know. They never caught the guy. Investigation dragged on for years."

The Honey Bun sank as McAdoo let his forearms fall to rest on his legs. What the hell were they talking about? What the hell were they doing out here at all?

"This is so morbid. Remember when our job was handing out fix-it tickets for people with busted out taillights?" the fat one said. "Now we're staking out a goddamn serial murder scene. A goddamn Burger King where they found a goddamn dismembered girl in a garbage bag."

Novotny lifted a styrofoam coffee cup to his face and spit tobacco juice into it, nodding as he did it.

"Yep. I remember it well. But someone has to do the job, my friend. Some psycho wants to hack up a bunch of girls and

49

shove the pieces into garbage bags? Well, someone has to stop 'em. That's the police, right? And that's us. We'll get the piece of shit."

They were quiet for a while. McAdoo watched the shadows over the empty Burger King lot. The lights inside the building were on for anti-theft purposes, of course, but the big orange and red sign held dark. He could picture the killer swathed in half-light, struggling to get the bloody bag over the lip of the dumpster. His shoulders quivered a little when he thought of it.

"But those Feds," Novotny said, interrupting the vision. "They ain't real police. Always remember that."

McAdoo thought about this notion, couldn't make much sense of it.

"What do you mean?" he said.

"I mean we're the ones pounding the pavement, knocking on doors, sitting out at damn Burger King at 2:00 am for Christ's sake. We're the soldiers, you know? We're the ones doing the real job. Those FBI people? They're eggheads. Cracking psychology books. Writing term papers and shit. They mean well — maybe they even help part of the time — but they ain't the real thing. Bureaucrats won't stop this monster. All the paperwork in the world won't stop him. The police will."

Again he dipped his head and spurted brown juice into the styrofoam spittoon, licked his lips.

A rebuttal tingled on the tip of McAdoo's tongue. He didn't agree with his partner. At all. The police around here were in way over their heads with the Doll Parts case, and anyone who wasn't thankful for the FBI's help was a fool. He almost said so, but he hesitated a beat too long. The quiet encroached, filled the emptiness. The moment seemed to have passed, and he said nothing.

He finished the Honey Bun and crammed the plastic wrapper into the ashtray.

"I can't wait until I'm away from all of this," he said, finally. "Once I get my boat, I'll just be drinking and fishing. Drinking and fishing. Drinking and fishing. Not worrying about speeding tickets or serial killers or any of this shit."

Novotny sighed.

"Yep. You and your damn boat."

They sat in the quiet as the night dragged on and on, staring into the gloom of the parking lot across the way. The killer didn't show.

CHAPTER 8

The building at 2926 Susannah Lane was an ugly, squat little duplex. Like most of the homes and apartments in this neighborhood, it was painted an industrial blue. Darger figured it must have been the cheapest paint money could buy at some point, and the slumlords went wild.

A fat man stood on the lawn, overseeing two boys in their late teens or early twenties hauling boxes out of the house and piling them at the curb. His hands rested on his hips, his swollen belly showing his t-shirt absolutely no mercy. It almost looked like he was trying to smuggle a watermelon in there.

A girl with her hair pulled back in a messy bun fluttered next to the pile, hopping toward the man like an angry sparrow.

"You be waiting to hear from my attorney," she said through clenched teeth. "Expect a lawsuit come Monday morning."

The girl plucked something from one of the boxes and added it to a separate pile accumulating next to the mailbox.

"Oh, I'm sure that will happen," the man said, folding his arms over his chest and smirking.

Violet parked the car on the street and got out.

"Miss Peters?"

The girl kept screaming.

"This is how you treat people? Toss their stuff in the street like garbage? I have rights!"

The large man had moved up onto the porch, and he hung over the iron railing to taunt the girl.

"You want to talk to me about rights? Try payin' your rent once in a while. You were notified of the eviction proceedings by verified letter, each and every step of the way. Hell, you've had a whole week to collect your belongings."

"Sierra Peters?" Violet said, her voice getting lost in the din.

The girl's finger stabbed the air.

"I have friends, you know. I have friends I can call."

Violet got within a few steps of her and said more firmly,

"Excuse me. Are you Sierra Peters?"

The girl whirled around, and for a beat, Violet thought of a cobra rearing back, poised to strike. She almost stepped away, almost flinched, but stood her ground.

Sierra lifted her chin, clinging to her defiance, but the slightest waver in her voice betrayed her.

"Who're you?"

Violet held out her badge to the girl and handed her a card with her name and phone number on it.

"My name is Violet Darger. Could we talk for a moment?"

From the stoop, the landlord called out.

"You're the cops? Good. I was just about to call you. My tenant here — *former* tenant — is harassing me."

"I ain't harassing—"

"Issuing physical threats against my person and my property."

Sierra spun around to face him again, voice reaching a new shrill pitch.

"Threats! I did not threaten—"

She turned back to Darger, voice flipping back to a more reasonable tone.

"He's lyin', officer. He's making shit up. I did not—"

Violet put her hands out.

"Miss Peters? Sierra? If you can calm down a minute, I'm sure we can get this sorted out."

Now that she was closer, she noted that Sierra's chest huffed in and out like she'd just run the Yellow Brick Road training course at Quantico. Beads of water collected in the corners of eyes ringed with black liner. Violet wondered if she had asthma.

"She got a record, you know. Drugs and thievin' mostly," the landlord said.

Sierra whirled back around to face the man and hissed, "You shut up."

"Sir?" Darger said, leaning around Sierra to try to catch his eye.

"In fact, I'd wager you'd find an awful lot of stolen items in them boxes."

He had one hand rested on the fullness of his belly, rubbing in circles and drumming his fingertips. It reminded Darger of a mannerism a pregnant woman might adopt.

"You're a liar!"

Sierra's breath almost whistled in her throat. Tears were streaming down her face.

"Sir! Please go inside."

Darger advanced, hand raised.

"I didn't realize it was against the law to stand on my own front lawn."

Darger felt her fingernails digging into the palm of her hand as she struggled to compose herself. What was this guy's problem?

"If this situation continues to escalate, you might find both you *and* the girl arrested. Now please go inside. I'll be in to talk to you in a moment."

It was a bluff, but Darger saw a flash of fear in the man's eyes, which he covered quickly. Pursing his lips, he nodded to himself.

"Within my rights. A hundred percent," he muttered.

Finally, he went in, the screen door banging closed behind him.

When Darger turned back to Sierra, the girl was busy trying to pick through the belongings piled at the curb. Mascara-tinted tears ran down her cheeks, and her breath was still a rasp. She coughed out a sob as she tipped a box full of coffee mugs into the grass. With the box empty, she began packing up a few things she'd pulled from the jumble — a photo album, a large cosmetics bag, and a stuffed animal in the shape of a giraffe.

"Sierra," Violet put a hand on her arm, and the girl wrenched away.

"No! I didn't do nothin'! It's not fair that he just throws all my shit out, but I'm the one that gets in trouble."

Her voice trembled again, and fresh tears fell from her eyes. She swiped a hand at her cheek, leaving a black smudge of makeup behind.

"Sierra, I'm not arresting you, OK? I'm not even a police officer. I'm from the FBI. You're not in trouble."

Eyelashes thick with clumped mascara blinked together

rapid-fire. Her shoulders convulsed with each breath.

"I'm not?"

"No, honey. I only want to talk to you."

Violet was patting her back now and talking in a soothing tone.

"Sierra, it seems like you're having trouble breathing. Do you have asthma?"

Sierra's head bobbed furiously.

"Do you have an inhaler?"

Again the nodding. Her hand flailed in the air, gesturing at the house.

"You think it's still inside? Can you tell me where?"

"Medicine... cabinet..." Sierra wheezed.

Violet could see beads of sweat forming on her upper lip and at her temples. The wisps of hair at the base of her neck were sodden.

"OK, Sierra. I'm going to go inside see if I can find it. In the meantime, why don't you sit in my car? I'll turn the AC on for you, and I want you to focus on calming down, OK?"

Violet guided her to the passenger side and opened the door, then went around to the driver's side to turn the key and crank the air on.

"Do you know any centering exercises?"

By the look on her face, Violet might as well have asked her to recite the Pythagorean Theorem from memory.

"That's OK. It's easy. I want you to choose five things. Five facts about yourself."

Sierra looked dubious.

"For example, I would say, 'My name is Violet Darger. My favorite color is blue.'"

Violet pointed at Sierra, indicating it was her turn.

The girl swallowed, still appearing unsure.

"My name is Sierra Peters," she croaked. "My favorite color is orange."

Violet gestured at her, urging her to continue, but Sierra shook her head, still too rattled to come up with her own.

"My birthday is April 13th and my star sign is Aries," Violet said.

"My birthday is January 4th, and I'm a Capricorn."

"Got the hang of it?" Violet asked, and Sierra bobbed her head, yes.

"You keep going, and I'm gonna go see if I can find your inhaler."

Darger paused after opening her door, her foot hovering over the ground. She remembered Deputy Donaldson's warning about Sierra having sticky fingers. For a brief moment, she considered the wisdom of leaving Sierra in a rental car with the keys in the ignition, but she pushed the thought away. The girl was in the midst of an asthma attack. She wasn't going to steal the car.

Violet knocked on the door, then stepped to the side as the boys hauled a dresser through. She held the door for them, and then the man welcomed her inside.

"Alright, sir. I'm going to take her in before things go any further," Darger said, making no attempt to clarify what that meant.

"Good. She been nothin' but a pain in my sack for two years. Noise violations, domestic incidences, not to mention the drugs—"

"Shouldn't be a problem for you any longer," Darger interrupted. "Before I go, could you show me the bathroom?"

She flipped open the mirrored door on the medicine cabinet and began rifling through the makeup and toothpaste and pill bottles.

"Hey, what are you—"

She found the inhaler tucked into one corner and wrapped her fingers around it.

When she turned to leave, the landlord was blocking the door, hands on his hips. He puffed out his chest.

"Technically that belongs to me now," he said, pressing his lips together. "Everything here does."

Darger glared at him, the dead look in her eyes speaking loud and clear.

The man's posture loosened, shoulders twitching and drooping a little.

"But you can take it. Just make sure that girl don't come

back here."

Back in the car, Violet handed the inhaler to Sierra. Her breathing sounded a little less labored now.

The inhaler let out a hiss as Sierra depressed the button and took the medication into her lungs.

Violet looked at the clock. 9:21 AM. She was going to go out on a limb and guess that with all the excitement going on for Sierra this morning, she probably hadn't eaten.

"Hungry?" Darger asked.

Sierra nodded without hesitation, her bottom lip still quivering like a powerless child's.

CHAPTER 9

Darger put the windows in the Camry down, and the wind whipped their hair around as they made the drive across town to the State Street Diner. The cool air — coupled with the asthma medication doled out by the inhaler — calmed Sierra enough that her breathing had returned to normal by the time Darger slid into a parking space. A good thing, too. It was always easier to talk to a witness when they were breathing.

Inside, Darger chose a corner booth toward the back, hoping for at least the illusion of privacy. The decor had an art deco feel. Red leather seats. Black and white tile floors.

"This is about the killer, huh?" Sierra said.

Darger nodded. She was glad Sierra had broached the subject first. It hopefully meant she'd be willing to talk about it.

"I know everyone thinks I'm a liar."

A wispy lock of hair had come loose over her ear, and Sierra reached up to tuck it back in place. As she lifted her arm, her sleeve fell down, revealing a crosshatch pattern of white lines from wrist to elbow. Scars. A lot of them.

Violet winced and looked away.

"Who's everyone?"

"That detective. Janssen. All the cops, really. I seen how they looked at each other. Little secret looks like they think I'm too stupid to figure out they think I'm trash."

"Well, I don't think that."

Sierra shrugged, looking unconvinced.

"I don't," Darger repeated.

Damn that Detective Janssen. She was going to have to tread lightly with this one.

"We don't have to rehash all of it again. I'm sure you're sick of talking about it. I know I would be."

The waitress arrived with menus and a carafe of coffee.

"Coffee for you ladies? I got decaf, too."

"Regular is fine," Darger said, righting the upside-down cup

58

on the table so the waitress could fill it with the steaming black brew.

Sierra followed suit. Darger drank hers black, but she watched Sierra add four of the small creamer cups and approximately eight teaspoons of sugar to hers.

Darger smiled to herself.

"I like your porcupine," the girl said.

Darger's confusion must have registered, because Sierra lifted a finger and aimed it at Darger's lapel.

"Your pin."

Violet tucked her chin to glance at the little gold brooch.

"Oh! It's a hedgehog, actually. And thanks."

The teaspoon in Sierra's hand tinkled against the ceramic of her mug as she stirred her coffee.

"Is it old? Like a family heirloom or whatever?"

Darger fingered the tiny gold spikes on the hedgehog's back.

"It's supposed to be vintage. 1950's I think. But I haven't had it long. It belonged to—"

Her voice trembled ever so slightly, and she cleared her throat to cover it.

"—a friend."

Sierra tapped her spoon against the cup, then laid it to rest on a napkin. Coffee bled over the papery surface.

"I've got this ring," Sierra said, extending her hand. "It was my grandma's. My dad's ma. 'Sposed to be a moonstone, I think."

The stone was an oval of milky white set in a claw of sterling silver. A simple leaf pattern adorned the band.

"It's very pretty," Violet said.

Sierra wiggled her fingers, admiring the stone.

"Supposedly moonstones enhance your psychic abilities. If you believe in that kind of thing."

"Do you?" Violet asked.

The girl pursed her lips.

"Sometimes."

"Well then maybe you've already guessed…"

Sierra looked up at her.

"There is one thing I wanted to ask you."

Well, she hadn't run off yet. Darger took that as a sign to continue.

"I was wondering," Darger said, then looked down into her coffee. "It's silly, but I thought we might try it anyway."

"What?" Sierra's head tilted to the side. Her expression reminded Darger of a cat whose curiosity has been piqued.

"Well, you have to close your eyes."

The girl's chin jutted out.

"I told you it was silly. It's just, sometimes if you close your eyes and picture being somewhere, you can remember things you thought you'd forgotten."

She waved her hand, indicating they should forget it.

"But we don't have to."

"I'll do it," Sierra said.

"You will?"

The coffee was hot enough that it scalded her mouth a little as she took another slug. Just how she liked it.

The girl indicated she would with a nod.

Darger leaned forward slightly, so she could speak softly and still be heard.

"OK. Close your eyes."

The girl's eyelids fluttered closed. Darger could still see her eyes moving back and forth behind the thin layer of skin.

"Breathe in slowly, counting up to three, and clear your mind."

Sierra inhaled, nostrils flaring slightly as she did so.

"Now hold that breath, and then let it out of your mouth all at once. Feel the tension leaving your shoulders and your chest and your neck."

Darger watched as Sierra's torso deflated.

"Your mind is a blank canvas. Endless black."

Sierra's head bobbed almost imperceptibly.

"You mentioned something about a pool. Near where you escaped."

Again the girl nodded.

"Did you see it? Maybe the lights people sometimes have in them at night?"

Sierra shook her head.

"What then? How do you know about the pool?"

There was a pause, and Darger thought she might not answer.

"I smelled it. I smelled the chlorine!"

A tingle of excitement spread through Darger's chest. Now they were getting somewhere.

"Good. OK. Let's go back. Back to when he first took you. It's late. 2 AM. It's dark except for the streetlights. There aren't many people out. You're walking down Vine Street. Are you heading toward the university or away from it?"

Darger held her breath.

"Away," Sierra said.

Darger bit her lip, forcing herself to continue.

"When do you notice the car? Do you see the lights first?"

"No," Sierra said, shaking her head. "I hear the engine."

"Is it loud? A broken muffler?"

There was a clatter of dishes and silverware as their waitress cleared away the dishes from a nearby table. Darger watched her slip the cash tip into her apron pocket and move on. Luckily, the distraction hadn't seemed to rattle Sierra, who still sat with her eyes closed.

"No, normal sounding. But I hear him coming. And he pulls a little ahead of me before he stops."

"You can see the back of the car?"

"Yes."

"What about the license plate?"

There's a pause. Sierra's forehead wrinkled.

"No. It's too dark."

"Is there anything else? Anything about the car you can think of?"

Sierra's shoulders rose and fell with her breath.

"I don't think so."

Violet tapped the top of Sierra's hand.

"That's OK. Thank you for trying. You did good."

"That's it?" Sierra said, her tone sounding disappointed.

Darger leaned forward.

"Hey, you remembered that you smelled chlorine, right? That's something."

Sierra rubbed the palms of her hands over the tops of her thighs.

"Doesn't seem like much, though."

"It's more than you realize. You never know what small detail might turn out to mean something big," Darger said, and she couldn't stop the corner of her lip from turning up.

Sierra had already told her quite a bit. More than she probably even realized.

She hadn't corrected Darger when she started the narrative on Vine Street, walking away from campus. That was from Sierra's original statement. In her second interview, she'd insisted she was several miles away, near McHappy's bakery.

But secondly, confirming that she had indeed smelled chlorine — smelled bleach — proved for Darger that Sierra had been taken by the same man who had killed the other girls.

When they'd finished eating, Darger paid the bill at the front register, then returned to the table to leave a tip.

"I'm gonna hit the bathroom before we go," she told Sierra.

The girl started to scoot out from the booth.

"I need a smoke. I'll be outside."

The diner's ladies room reeked of cinnamon scented Glade, and the water pressure was such that everything in a three-foot radius of the faucet got sprayed when Darger turned the sink on.

She made a fruitless attempt at blocking the spray with an outstretched hand before turning the water off. She dabbed at the front of her shirt with a wad of paper towels and scowled at her reflection in the mirror. Should she keep playing it slow with Sierra or push her a little? Time was ticking. It was very possible another girl could go missing in the next few days. Then again, she might scare the girl off and lose the best lead they had.

As she passed by their table on the way to the door, Darger noticed that while the $5 bill she'd left was gone, the dishes hadn't been cleared away.

Bit of a klepto, Deputy Donaldson had said. Darger sighed, removed another bill from her wallet, and tucked it under the pepper shaker. She'd made her decision. Or maybe Sierra had made it for her.

Tendrils of smoke spilled from Sierra's nostrils. She leaned casually on the hood of Darger's rental, not looking the least bit guilty for stealing the tip.

Darger wondered if she should give her the benefit of the doubt. After all, the waitress may have grabbed the money and intended to return for the dishes. But Darger thought not.

They got in, buckled their seat belts, and Darger steered them onto the street.

Sierra sat up a little straighter when they turned onto Vine Street.

"I haven't been this way since…" she said and trailed off.

This was good, Darger thought. Very good. She slowed the car down a bit.

"You said you heard him first. Can you show me where you were when you heard the engine?"

Sierra's eyes were wide now.

"Sierra?"

"Stop the car."

"What?"

Sierra undid her seatbelt and then she was wrestling with the door, trying to open it. But the lock was engaged.

"Sierra, wait. I just want to know what really happened."

But she wasn't stopping. She'd found the unlock button and pressed it, and now she was yanking the handle, opening the door. Darger brought the car to a halt, her seatbelt going taut across her chest at the sudden stop.

Sierra scrambled out of the front seat, then went to the back to get her things.

"You tricked me!"

"I didn't mean to trick you." Violet put the car in park and started to get out. "Just hold on a second, please."

"No way. You all think I'm a liar, but you all are the liars!"

She slammed the door and started to run down the sidewalk.

"Sierra, wait."

Darger scrambled back into the car to follow.

"Leave me alone!" Sierra screamed back at her, then jogged

up a side street marked "One Way."

"Shit," Darger muttered and sped around the block. By the time she'd found a way onto the street, there was no sign of Sierra. Darger did a few more loops, hoping to catch a glimpse of her, but it was no use. The girl was gone.

Having nowhere else to go, Darger returned to her hotel room. She took off her boots and paced over the green shag carpet, periodically moving to the window to gaze through the glass before pacing some more. She'd knocked on Loshak's door, but he hadn't answered. She didn't know if he wasn't in or if he was still recuperating from his illness. In either case, it was probably better that he wasn't answering. She'd wanted to impress him, and somehow she thought that scaring off their best witness wasn't going to do that.

Fuck. If she'd just been patient. But no. No, she had to push. And she'd pushed because she'd been annoyed about Sierra stealing the tip if she was being honest with herself. Stupid.

She didn't want to sit around moping in her room, but she had nothing else to do and nowhere in particular to go in this unfamiliar town, so she decided to take a walk. Clear her thoughts.

It was a nice enough day that it almost didn't matter that the motel wasn't located in the most picturesque spot. Across the street was a gravel-paved lot shared by two different used car lots. She knew the Hocking River was somewhere off to her left, but she couldn't see it through the trees.

Violet had progressed nearly a mile down the road and was passing the Squeeky Kleen Carwash when her phone rang.

"Hello?"

"Special Agent Darger?"

Darger stopped walking and held very still.

"Sierra?"

"I didn't know who else to call," Sierra said, then started to cry.

"It's OK. What's wrong?"

"Can you come pick me up?"

Darger scribbled the address on her hand with a ballpoint

pen from her pocket.

"Stay right where you are, OK? I'll be there in ten minutes."

When she pulled up to the house, Sierra was sitting on the curb smoking a cigarette. Her makeup was smeared again and her possessions were set in a neat pile next to where she sat. Darger unlocked the doors, and Sierra climbed in after stowing her box of rescued things in the back seat.

"Did something happen?"

"Sometimes you think people are your friends, but…" Sierra said, wiping at her cheek. "No one cares."

"That's not true, Sierra. I care."

It wasn't just a platitude, either. Violet had spent the early part of her career counseling girls a lot like Sierra. Girls with addiction and untreated mental illness. Girls with a history of trauma and abuse. Girls that felt lost and unloved.

She tried to avoid making spur-of-the-moment diagnoses, but she suspected Sierra may have borderline personality disorder. It would fit with her wildly shifting moods, her chaotic relationships, her impulsiveness. And the scars Darger had noticed at the restaurant… It would explain those, too. People suffering from BPD were often cutters.

But Sierra wasn't listening, and when Violet got a look at her pupils, she could tell she was high.

"Sierra?"

"I need to use your phone."

Darger handed over the phone. Sierra sniffled as she dialed.

"Mom?" she said after a moment. "Listen, I need to ask you somethin'. Yeah. Yeah, but—"

The next thing Darger knew, Sierra was shouting into the phone.

"No. No. No, that's not true!"

She backed down a little, her tone coming out more of a whine.

"You're not listening to me. Why do you always take his word for it?"

There was a pause, followed by more screaming.

"Fine! Take his side, I don't care! I hate you!"

Her fingers gripped the phone so hard that her knuckles were white, and Darger worried for a moment that she was going to smash it against the dash.

"Sierra."

The girl blinked at her, and Darger thought she might be so angry and so high that she'd actually forgotten where she was and who she was with.

The tears returned.

"This isn't fair. I was doing good. I tried really hard. And then all this stuff happened. I give up."

Violet reached out and squeezed her shoulder.

"Look, my room has an extra bed. Why don't you stay with me for the night? Everything else can wait until tomorrow."

CHAPTER 10

Sierra told her where the good pizza was in town, and they stopped at Angelo's on the way back to the hotel. While she waited for the order, Darger went to the liquor store next door and grabbed two six packs.

They arrived back at the room and dove into the beer and pizza — half with mushrooms for Violet and half with pepperoni and extra banana peppers for Sierra.

Darger turned the TV on for background noise, and time moved in fast speed as three-quarters of the pizza disappeared along with several beers. It felt good to not talk, to not think, to just funnel food and drink into her face. The girl was right about Angelo's, too. Tasty.

Carbon dioxide hissed as Darger twisted the cap off her third beer. Sierra was on her fourth. Violet tipped the bottle back and took a slug, wondering at the ethics of getting drunk with a witness.

"Oh well."

Sierra looked over at her.

"Huh?"

"Nothing. Just talking to myself."

Sierra stared at her for a moment, then grinned.

"You're wasted."

"I am not."

A snorting sort of laugh came out of Sierra's nose.

"Yeah, you are. Lightweight."

"You're the one that sounds a little tipsy with that Miss Piggy laugh over there."

Sierra was in the midst of taking another drink from her beer, and a fine mist sprayed out of her mouth as she laughed again.

"Miss Piggy?!"

White foam oozed from the top of her beer bottle, and she quickly held it to her mouth so she could slurp it before it dribbled on the bedspread. After that, she sat still a moment.

"You're not like all them other cops."

"I'm not a cop, really."

"FBI, whatever. Once a cop, always a cop," Sierra said, smirking to herself.

"Pretty much."

"But you weren't?" Sierra asked. "A cop before, I mean?"

Violet shook her head, suddenly somber. Sierra had pushed her sleeves up, and she'd caught another glimpse of her scars. Coupled with this line of questioning, it had her mind going to all the places she'd been trying to avoid lately. Violet's gaze strayed to the window. Between the parted curtains, she could see the orange sodium glow of the streetlights shining on the cars in the parking lot. Blood on pavement looked black under those lights, she knew. Black blood and the tangy, acrid smell of spent gunpowder.

"Agent Darger?"

Darger's head snapped up.

"What did you do before this?"

Another swig of beer washed the bad taste from her mouth.

"I was a Victim Specialist. Still FBI, but… Sort of like a counselor. Or a therapist."

A moth fluttered at the window, wings beating against the glass before it moved on. Violet stared down the open mouth of her beer bottle. Tiny bubbles broke on the golden surface below.

"I was seventeen the first time I got drunk. I was at my best friend's graduation party. She had a big family, and there was plenty of booze to go around, of course. We waited until after the party, when almost everyone had gone home, and we snuck outside to the coolers and snagged some leftover Boone's Farm. Sangria. Tasted like grape juice and piss."

Sierra snickered.

"I used to love the Strawberry Daiquiri flavor."

"We each had our own bottle," Violet continued. "And at first we only took one sip. And then we waited. We kept saying, 'I don't feel anything!' And then we'd take another sip. And pretty soon, we'd each drank half a bottle."

"I bet you felt something then."

Violet's lips stretched into a smile.

"My friend stood up to pee and almost fell over. She hadn't even taken a step or anything. And that set me off giggling. I thought she was faking it until I tried to stand up, too. I stumbled sideways and took out a table lamp."

They both laughed.

"It wasn't long before it all caught up to us, and we were running for the door so we could go puke in the backyard so her parents wouldn't hear."

Darger tilted her head back and sucked down the last dregs.

"Haven't touched that stuff since. Even real Sangria makes me a little queasy."

"I don't remember the first time I got drunk for real," Sierra said, running a finger along the wallpaper and frowning. "But I do remember the first time I drank a beer. It was me and my neighbor, Kylie. We swiped a can of Bud Light from my mom's fridge. And one of her cigarettes, too. And then we crept out to the woods behind our houses, and we practiced holding the beer and cigarette in the same hand, the way our moms did."

She grabbed a pen from the bedside table and demonstrated.

"I don't think we even drank half of the beer. We thought it was disgusting. Same with the cigarette. We didn't inhale or nothin', just held the smoke in our mouths."

Sierra had that faraway smile people got when remembering fond times from their childhoods.

"How old were you?" Violet asked.

Sierra chewed her lip.

"Nine, I think. Maybe ten."

"Young," Darger said.

"I guess so. It was so innocent, though, you know? We didn't know what we were doing. It was only a game. Playing grown-up."

Darger tapped her fingernails against the beer bottle in her hand.

"When I was ten, I wanted to be a paleontologist."

"Which one is that?"

"Dinosaur bones. Or at least, that's what I was interested in."

"In other words, you were a huge nerd."

"Hey!" Darger protested, then laughed. "Well, yeah. Pretty nerdy."

"I'll try to hide my shock and surprise," Sierra said, and Darger threw a pillow at her.

She was feeling a little giddy from the beer.

"Didn't you have dreams when you were a kid? Something you wanted to be when you grew up?"

"Not really."

"None at all?"

She thought, tilting her face toward the ceiling as she did.

"A dancer."

Violet slid off the bed so she could sit on the floor with her back leaned against the mattress.

"No judgments, but are we talking ballet dancing or g-string dancing?"

Sierra tipped her head back and laughed.

"Not that kind! Like you said, ballet. And tap and jazz, too. I used to take classes."

"Why'd you stop?"

She shrugged noncommittally, and a cloud seemed to descend over her face.

"Come on, there had to be a reason."

"I grew out of it, I guess. I dunno. It's kid stuff, isn't it? You can't be a dancer for a living. Not that kind anyway," Sierra said, and a trace of a wicked smile returned.

"Well maybe not everyone can be a professional ballerina, but you could be an instructor. Teach kids."

Sierra was shaking her head.

"Nah. I don't think I'd have the patience for that."

They were quiet for a while, the only sound was canned laughter from the sitcom on TV that neither of them was watching. The laugh-track was the perfect counterpoint to the exaggerated beer sadness Violet felt. The girl gave up so young.

"I did these cosmetology courses in high school," Sierra said, and her eyes suddenly brightened. "I could see myself doing that."

"Yeah?" Darger said. "Then you should."

Sierra shrugged again, looking a little embarrassed. Like

70

admitting she wanted something in life made her feel sheepish.

"I don't know."

"What did you like about it?"

With one thumbnail, Sierra picked at the label on the beer bottle. The scratching noise was the only sound for a while.

"We used to go to this old folk's home," Sierra said. "We'd practice on the ladies there. Do their hair and makeup, give them manis and pedis. Those old ladies always looked so happy when we were done."

Violet pulled her knees to her chest and rested her chin on top, watching the girl.

"Sounds like it made you pretty happy, too."

"Yeah," Sierra said. "Yeah, it did."

They had settled into a strange comfort with one another by then. They flipped through the channels, pausing once on the shopping channel where some sort of strange boob cushion was being advertised. Sierra laughed so hard she rolled off the bed.

Darger was surprised to realize she was actually having a good time. It was not what she'd expected when she'd first invited Sierra to stay with her.

When she considered bringing up anything about the case, she felt a twinge of guilt. Not only because she didn't want Sierra to think that had been the reason she'd offered to help her. But maybe because it had been at the forefront of Violet's mind when she'd made the suggestion.

Violet didn't realize she was chewing on her nails until Sierra's hand latched around her wrist.

"Damn girl. You need a manicure."

"Oh. Yeah. Bad habit," Darger said, studying the jagged edges.

Sierra bounced off the bed and went over to the pile of possessions she'd scavenged from her eviction. When she came back to the bed, she had the little train case in her hands. The top unfolded, revealing two shelves with around a dozen compartments each. There were eyeshadows and lip pencils and brushes and sponges. Sierra reached for an emery board and a pair of nail scissors.

"You were serious?"

71

"Uh-huh."

Her open palm beckoned. She started with the scissors, evening out the broken edges and trimming a few hangnails. After that, a few sweeps of the file rounded what meager tips Darger hadn't already chewed off. Massaging a dollop of conditioning cream into each fingertip, Sierra clicked her tongue.

"You need that stuff they have for dogs."

A breathy laugh puffed out of Darger's nostrils.

"What?"

"It's like sour apple or something. 'Sposed to keep 'em from chewing."

Violet laughed.

"That might work. But I'd probably end up developing a taste for sour apple fingernails."

With a large wooden Q-tip, Sierra did battle with Darger's ragged cuticles, prodding and poking them into submission. A calmness came over the girl as she worked. A focus Violet hadn't seen before.

Another specialty goop came out and Sierra began massaging her hands and forearms.

Darger let her eyes fall closed.

"All I need now is a lounge chair on a tropical beach and a cute cabana boy to bring me a margarita."

"Tell him to bring me one, too," Sierra said, chuckling.

Darger lifted her free hand and gestured to the imaginary cabana boy.

"Make that two margaritas, Butch."

When it came time for the polish, Sierra selected a bottle of nail polish in a very loud shade of blue. A metal BB rattled against the glass as Sierra shook the lacquer, and Darger eyed it dubiously.

"Are we sure about this color?"

"Yes, *we* are sure about it."

"It's just so… blue," Darger said.

"The blue of a tropical ocean."

"Does it come with a cabana boy named Butch?"

"It's called Cerulean Sea, and it is very *in* right now."

Sierra fixed her with a stare.

"You're the one that said I should follow my dreams."

"And that involves painting my nails the color of cotton candy?"

"Cotton candy is pink."

"Pink! Hey, there's an idea. A nice traditional shade."

"Let me do them in Cerulean Sea, and if you hate it, we can take it off."

Darger surrendered her left hand, still clutching a beer in her right.

When she finished, Darger admired the glossy enamel. The girl had done a good job, and the color — while not necessarily something Darger would have chosen on her own — wasn't quite as garish as she'd expected.

"See?"

Darger wiggled her fingers.

"You do good work."

"Thanks," Sierra said, beaming. She bent over her own hand, applying the same blue shade to her fingertips.

Her face was placid. As tranquil as the tropical lagoon that the nail polish was named for.

Darger swallowed, worrying she might ruin what rapport she'd achieved so far. Maybe she should wait.

But again, the tick-tock of the clock counting down to the next victim demanded she do it now.

Finished with her first hand, Sierra screwed the top back on the bottle and waited for the polish to dry before she did the other. She blew on the nails and reached for the pizza box with her dry hand.

"So this Jimmy guy you were talking about earlier," Darger said, even though Sierra hadn't actually mentioned him. "Is he your boyfriend or what?"

"God, no," Sierra said, too quickly, and Violet realized there was almost certainly some kind of history there. She'd only intended to use the boyfriend angle as a segue.

"Friend with benefits, then?"

A slice of now-cold pizza hovered in front of Sierra's mouth, and she almost choked on the bite she'd just taken.

"Probably what he thinks," she said.

"And he's someone that can get certain things that people might want. Am I right?"

Sierra's eyes flicked up to meet hers for a moment, then focused back on her pizza. She pinched a piece of pepperoni between her fingers and pulled it free, depositing it in her mouth.

"I guess you could say that."

"Is that why you're protecting him?"

Sierra's jaw moved up and down.

"Sierra." Violet's tone was gentle but insistent.

"I don't know."

"Because no one's interested in whatever goes on at Jimmy's house. At least I'm not. All I care about is catching the guy who took you. If he's the same guy who killed those girls, Sierra, he's going to do it again. Soon. You know it, and I know it."

The chewing stopped. A faraway look entered the girl's eyes. Darger thought she could see tears forming, but she wasn't certain.

"I know."

The girl's voice was barely a whisper.

Violet didn't dare move. She held very still, and very quietly she spoke.

"So tell me what happened."

She had been at Jimmy's for most of the day. Getting high, watching TV, playing video games.

"Mostly him and his friends play, and I watch. I'm not really into that stuff."

At around 2 AM, she left Jimmy's to go home.

"You were going to walk home? It's kind of a hike, isn't it?"

Sierra shrugged.

"Jimmy wouldn't give me a ride, and he said I couldn't stay because he had to get up early the next morning, so what was I supposed to do?"

Violet tried to think if she'd ever met any drug dealer that had to "get up early in the morning." More likely, she was too naive — or in too much denial — to recognize when she was being blown off.

She'd only gone about a block when she heard the car. And that was where Sierra's story got interesting.

"He said..." Sierra said and then seemed to stop herself.

Violet waited. The last thing she wanted to do was interrupt.

After a long pause, Sierra started again.

"He stopped the car, and I..."

Again her words faltered, and Sierra covered her face with her hands.

"Sierra," Violet said softly, "I'm not going to judge you. I'm only interested in finding the man who tried to kill you. I need to make sure he never hurts anyone else, and I need your help to do that."

"I know, but... what if it was my fault a little bit? What if I got into the car with him?"

"That doesn't make it your fault. Is that what happened?"

An almost imperceptible nod of Sierra's head told her it was.

"What did he say to you?"

"He asked me... he asked if I wanted to party."

Darger could almost hear Janssen's accusatory tone in her head, *And do you make it a habit of getting into cars with strange men like that?*

A sniffle escaped the girl's hands, and Violet scooted closer so she could rub Sierra's back.

"I know this is hard. And I'm sorry you have to keep going over it again and again. But I promise you, it will help us find him. You're the key, Sierra."

The girl took her hands away at that, wiping at her cheek with the collar of her t-shirt. Violet leaned over and snatched a tissue from the box near the bed, and then handed it to Sierra.

"What do you mean?"

Darger licked her lips and tried to figure out how to explain it.

"In most homicides, the way we solve it is by tying the murderer to the victim. It was someone they knew. A family member, a co-worker, a spouse, a rival gang member. We can usually narrow things down by determining whether or not it was a crime of passion or something that seemed planned. If it was a crime of a passion — a husband catches his wife in an affair, or two people have an argument and one pulls a gun — then we knew where to start looking. Likewise, if it seems planned, then we start checking out people who would have benefited from the death, whether it's about money or drugs or a custody disagreement.

"But serial killers don't fit into the normal way of solving a homicide. And usually that means we have to get lucky. Or clever. Or both. In this case, I think it's both."

"*We* got lucky," Darger said pointing at herself, "because *you* were clever enough to escape."

Now she aimed her finger at Sierra.

"I still don't see how it helps that much."

"Sierra, believe me. This…" she waved her phone in the air, which had been recording their talk, "this whole conversation is everything. We are going to find him because of you. Because of the things you've told me here tonight. I know it."

Sierra had stopped crying now. She looked down at the wadded up tissue in her fist.

"Do you think you can tell me what happened after you got in the car?"

Sierra's head went up and down.

The story from there on out was similar to what she'd told Janssen. Almost as soon as she got in and closed the door, he hit her on the side of the head and clapped a rag over her mouth.

"It smelled kind of… sweet, but also like alcohol. Like really rotten bananas. But it made my nose so cold."

She woke some time later on a cold floor. She still wasn't certain about it being a garage or not. When she got to the part about running into the woods, Darger stopped her.

"How long do you think you ran through the woods?"

Sierra scratched under her chin.

"I don't know. It seemed like a long time. An hour? Maybe two?"

Darger knew from the timeline that it couldn't have been two hours. Sierra was picked up around 2 AM, and her 911 call was noted in the file as occurring at 3:16 AM. An hour was possible. Then again, it could have been more like fifteen minutes and felt like much longer in the dark, terrified, with her brain addled from chloroform.

Suddenly the girl's back straightened.

"I threw up."

"In the woods?"

"I don't know. Maybe. Or maybe in his car? I just know that when I was talking to the 911 operator, I could taste it in my mouth."

She made a face, the memory of the taste eliciting fresh disgust.

"Could you see the payphone you used when you first came out of the woods?"

Sierra shook her head.

"No, the first thing I saw was lights, way up high. Streetlights. And maybe the lights on a billboard. It's all kind of blurry. Once I saw the road, I kept walking along the edge of the woods until I saw a place with a phone. I was afraid that if I went to the road and tried to get someone to stop, that it would be him. Like in scary movies."

Violet exhaled when they were through, pleased with herself. Pleased with the girl. Turning off the recording app on her phone, she looked Sierra in the eye.

"Thank you, Sierra. Really."

Sierra nodded once.

Even if the girl didn't believe it, Darger could feel its presence — the little glimmer of light shining on this case, even if they didn't fully understand it yet.

Their beer buzzes had faded out to exhaustion, so they prepared for bed after that. Teeth were brushed. The taste of the beer washed away with Aquafresh and Scope. Darger rinsed her face, the cold of the water somehow dull against her cheeks which felt almost bloated with heat.

Sierra already looked unconscious by the time Violet closed the curtains and reached for the switch.

When the lights went out, the darkness once more surrounded them.

CHAPTER 11

McAdoo shambled into the Shell station restroom, his gut gurgling like a washing machine. He'd known the gas station microwave burritos would be a mistake, and Novotny had tried to caution him on top of that, but these warnings failed to stop him from slathering the damn things in the hottest salsa he could find and inhaling them, chewing sparingly, and washing them down with 20 fluid ounces of Dr. Pepper.

He stumbled into the stall, fingers scrabbling at his belt. Mentally, he focused on nothing, instinctively falling into some attempt at a state of zen that he hoped may prevent a pants-shitting nightmare right here on the cusp of relief. He thought about his boat, the one he'd buy some day, the one he'd been dreaming of owning since he was a kid. He didn't picture himself on it physically, but he imagined what it'd feel like to finally have it. It seemed to help a little. After much flubbing about with his hands, his pants came undone, the weight of the gun dragging them straight to the tile floor with a clank.

It wasn't where he expected to be at 2:32 AM, but here he was.

McAdoo's middle flexed and cramped and shuddered as he vacated the vile mixture of beans and peppers. Beads of sweat stood out on his forehead, visible in his reflection on the chrome toilet paper dispenser. If the salsa had been hot upon entry, it was liquid fire on the way out. A form of torture that was surely a major human rights violation. He gripped the bar meant for handicap assistance to help brace himself, wished like hell he had something to bite down on.

The door into the men's room swished open, and his squirming atop the toilet seat cut out all at once. He listened.

Footsteps. Coming closer. The door swished again, closing this time.

Silence. Someone was in here with him. Someone holding perfectly still on the other side of the stall door.

78

He tried to stop himself from considering it, but it was too late: Could it be the Trash Bag Killer? He was, supposedly, likely to revisit the Burger King a half a block down after all.

His eyes snapped to the holstered handgun resting on the bathroom floor. Jesus. Anyone could peak under the stall door and see straight away that he was essentially unarmed. It'd take him a beat to get hold of the weapon and unsnap the button on the leather strap to free it from its sheath, more than enough time for a damn psychopath to end him in some grotesque fashion.

Blood beat through his temples, seconds trickling past like hours. He thought about his options, coming up with three.

He could either go to scoop the gun now, he could try to say something, or he could opt for the church mouse method and sit here as quietly as possible. Each came with risks and rewards. He had no damn idea which to go for.

Think, McAdoo, think!

His gut convulsed endlessly, oblivious to the life and death situation transpiring around it. *Stupid gut!*

His lips parted, seemingly of their own accord. That settled it. He'd say something. That's what he'd do.

The urinal flushed. A hiss and spray that caught him off guard, killed the words in his throat.

"You all right in there?" a voice said. It took him a second to realize that it was Novotny.

Of course.

"Yeah," McAdoo said, his voice cracking a little. "Yeah, I'm fine."

"OK. Seems like it's taking a long time is all."

"Yeah. Well, it might be a while yet. My belly kinda rejected those burritos. Violently. Like how you said it would."

"'K."

"Hey listen. I want to apologize for the horrendous smell I'm creating in here. I know it's especially hard for you on account of that tremendous nose of yours."

In the ensuing scuff of shoes on tile, he couldn't tell whether Novotny had laughed or not. Then he heard water in the sink, and the door swished opened and closed once more. It almost seemed funny now, how scared he'd been just seconds ago. Almost. Having stared into a garbage bag full of human limbs recently, he guessed it didn't take much to frighten him. Too many damn serial killer stories from Novotny lately, too. Between the two of them, maybe being terrified was understandable.

Jesus. This was all so morbid.

McAdoo's gut lurched again. He looked at his watch. It was 2:36 AM. He did a little mental math. Figured he'd be lucky to be out of here by 3:00.

Shortly after he finally exited the gas station restroom, McAdoo fell asleep in the car, his chin slumped down onto his chest, little snuffling sounds coming out of his mouth and nose on occasion.

Novotny didn't wake him. There'd be no point in it, he thought.

He could watch the Burger King parking lot on his own, and he didn't mind being the one to actually do the job. McAdoo was good company — a good sidekick and a great guy. But Novotny simply felt most comfortable doing things himself and knowing they were done right, felt better with the responsibility in his grip alone. It wasn't out of selfishness, just a genuine sense that things were simpler and more efficient when he carried the load. He had always been that way, maybe.

He was an all-state football player as a freshman and sophomore in high school. In fact, he still held the Division V record for kickoff returns for touchdowns, both single-season and career. He wasn't big — only 5'8", 165 pounds at his brawniest — but he could run away from everyone. One of those little waterbug types nobody could hit cleanly.

All the big schools came calling after the regional quarterfinal game when he returned two kicks and a punt for TDs. Even the wide receivers coach from Ohio State came around a couple times that summer. Novotny's grades were in sad shape. Even with two years to work on it, he was unlikely to qualify for the NCAA minimum standards, but all the coaches told him that was no problem. A year in a prep school or a junior college would get everything straight academically, and he was gifted enough to be worth the wait they all said.

Every door in the world was wide open. For a little while.

He tore up his knee in the first game of his junior year, however. No one even touched him. He just pushed off wrong making a cut to get out and cover a back in the flat. He knew it was bad right away. The pop in his knee reminded him of a cork jettisoned from a bottle by a spray of champagne. He felt the bones shift, and the pain was incredible for a split second. Then the endorphins kicked in, and he felt almost nothing at all from his mid-thigh down.

ACL. MCL. Meniscus. He shredded all of it. The doctors in Columbus said the bone bruising was the worst they'd ever seen.

When he made it back onto the field his senior year, he'd lost a step. Maybe a step and a half. He still had a decent season — rushed for 1,457 yards and took 3 more kicks back for scores, but a lot of it was grit and effort now rather than sheer quickness and speed. He'd been reduced from greatness to merely very good by small school standards.

Not scholarship material. Not even close. One Division II school in Indiana wanted him to walk on. They sent him recruiting letters right up until they got a look at his transcripts, and then that door closed as well.

But he'd gotten his glimpse. He'd seen the open doors, and he knew what was possible. Football was over for him, but he knew some guys on the police force. He knew he could make detective in time. Only a few years, maybe, if everything went well. He'd juggled night classes at the Rio Grande Community College in Pomeroy for his first three years in law enforcement. Got a two-year degree in criminal justice, and now it was a matter of time before he worked his way up the chain. He'd make detective soon enough, maybe not in the APD, but somewhere local. Maybe even within the next year, he thought.

He lifted a styrofoam coffee cup to his lips and spit tobacco juice into it, looked across the street where the shadows encroached on the Home of the Whopper. Nothing over there moved.

CHAPTER 12

Thanks to the beer, Violet fell asleep easier than usual. She did not dream, or if she did, she retained no memories. It was just as well, really. More often than not, her dreams turned dark these days. If they weren't outright nightmares and flashbacks, then they were filled with sadness or a sense of dread. She longed for the anxiety dreams of her youth, when her angst could be boiled down to a perpetually forgotten locker combination. Or realizing she had a test in a class she'd never been to.

It was still fairly early when she woke. A few minutes past 7 AM according to the bedside clock. Sierra snored from the next bed, and a thin band of golden morning light spilled through the gap between the blackout curtains.

The bathroom door rattled as Violet pulled it closed behind her, and she squinted through pinched eyelids when the overhead lights flickered to life. She spread a glob of toothpaste on the end of her toothbrush and set about whisking away the stale taste of morningbreath. In the reflection of the mirror, Darger noted the towel hanging over the shower. Right. She'd need to go get some fresh towels from the front desk before she jumped in.

Back in the room, Darger slipped her blazer over the thin cotton t-shirt she'd slept in. Sierra had rolled over, no longer snoring. Gripping the keys in such a way to keep them from rattling together, Darger tiptoed across the room and out the door. There was a humid chill in the morning air, and it smelled of dew and cut grass. Darger inhaled deeply. It was going to be a good day. She'd talk to Loshak, tell him what she'd learned, and they'd put together a game plan. She wondered if they should alert the media, tell them that people should be wary of accepting rides from strangers in dark sedans.

But first, she needed that shower. The front desk attendant reminded Darger not to forget about the free Continental breakfast offerings as she handed over a fresh set of towels.

82

Darger grabbed two juice boxes and two blueberry muffins on her way back to her room. She tried to be as quiet as possible re-entering the room. She set the food on the table beside the door and lowered the key ring gently. A little smile played on her face when she thought of how she'd been worried to leave Sierra in the car with the keys the previous morning. And now that she'd spent some time with her, Violet didn't think Sierra had taken the tip from the diner table, either. She'd prejudged her, jumped to conclusions, just like everyone else.

Shampoo lathered into a white froth atop Darger's head. She rinsed the suds and then applied conditioner. And to think that Deputy Donaldson wanted to write Sierra off as a liar. What a mistake that would have been. This could be a big break for them. For the case. She wondered how many killers got away because of the shortsightedness and bias of the local law enforcement. A shame, really.

The tub handles squeaked as she turned the water off. Darger pushed the shower curtain aside and steam billowed out into the open air of the rest of the bathroom. She wrapped a towel around her head and got dressed.

After drying her hair and applying a bit of makeup, Darger flipped off the bathroom light and opened the door. The room felt a little cold after standing in the post-shower humidity for so long, but Darger barely noticed.

What she did notice was that both beds were now empty.

She took a step forward. Probably Sierra was off to one corner, looking for a bit of extra privacy while she got dressed. Darger leaned around the wall. No Sierra. No nothing.

"Sierra?" she said, stupidly.

She knew she was alone. She could feel it.

That was when her eyes noted that her purse was on the end of her bed. Violet didn't remember putting it there… knew she hadn't put it there, in fact. The bag was tipped on its side, a packet of travel-sized tissues and a tin of breath mints pulled out.

Maybe Sierra had needed a tissue?

Sure. But there was a box on the nightstand.

Well, she just hadn't seen it. Right?

Darger's eyes darted over to the table near the door. Her keys were gone. She lurched forward, then stopped.

Wait. Slow down. She could have run out to get a change of clothes or something else from the car. Sierra would have checked the purse for the keys before she spotted them on the table. It was fine. Everything was fine.

Violet forced herself to walk slowly to the window. One hand lifted the drapes out of the way so she could get an unobstructed view of the parking lot below. When she saw the empty parking space where her Camry had been, her head fell forward, clunking against the glass.

The smooth surface was cool on her shower-warmed skin.

"Shit."

CHAPTER 13

She waited, giving Sierra a chance to… what? Change her mind? To prove once and for all that Darger was just as prejudicial as the local cops when Sierra poked her head back into the room with fresh coffee? Right, she'd only popped out to grab something better than the swill offered with the continental breakfast in the lobby. Maybe she'd grab them both Egg McMuffins, too.

That would explain the missing cash. Sierra didn't have any money. They both knew that. She'd probably figured they'd both go out and grab something to eat after Violet got out of the shower anyway. Might as well save a trip and have breakfast waiting. A small gesture of thanks.

Except that she'd emptied *all* the cash from Violet's wallet, almost $200. That was a shitload of Egg McMuffins.

Violet knew she was kidding herself, of course. Sierra wasn't coming back.

Keys, car, and cash. Violet wondered what else was missing.

She had a spare key for the room at least. She supposed that was standard for a double room, even though she'd specified one occupant when she checked in. Probably they'd charge her some kind of "lost key" fee if she didn't turn both in at check out. Part of the whole scam. How many people lost a key during their stay, forgetting there had even been two in the first place?

In any case, at least it was one thing she didn't have to worry about.

A sudden panic overtook her, and her hands fluttered into her pockets and over her person. When she felt the prickle at her chest, she exhaled. For a moment, she'd worried Sierra had stolen the hedgehog brooch. Violet held her hand over the small pin for a while, taking comfort in its presence.

Eventually, she could put it off no longer. She walked down the catwalk and knocked on Loshak's door.

There was no answer.

She knocked again, louder this time.

"Loshak. It's Darger."

Leaning over the railing, she double-checked that Loshak's car was still in the lot. It was.

After a third fruitless attempt at knocking, she went down to the office.

The motel employee jammed the key into the slot, turned the lock, and opened the door. The privacy chain hadn't been engaged, so when she turned the knob, the door swung all the way open, a wedge of sunlight piercing the gloom.

"Loshak?"

Expecting further unresponsiveness, both women started a bit when he shook himself awake and sat upright in the bed.

"Whaddafuck?"

Darger let out a breath.

"So you *are* alive. That's good, at least."

She turned to the girl from the motel lobby.

"I'll take it from here. Thank you."

The girl headed back for the front office, leaving Darger alone on the threshold.

Loshak swiped a paw at his eyes. He looked even worse than he had two days ago. Face puffy, eyes bloodshot, with dark rings underneath.

"How'd you get in here?"

"I knocked. About a dozen times. You didn't answer, and all things considered, I thought I should make sure you weren't dead."

He grumbled something unintelligible.

"Did you even leave your room yesterday?"

Instead of answering, he squinted at the clock.

"What day is it?"

"Christ. When was the last time you ate something?"

Loshak ran a hand through his disheveled hair.

"I don't remember."

"Hold on a minute."

She ducked outside and left Loshak sitting in bed, rubbing at his face and likely still wondering what the hell was going on.

Darger returned a few moments later with one of the juice boxes and muffins she'd grabbed from the breakfast spread earlier.

"Here," she said, setting the food on the night table.

"You never answered my question. How the hell did you get in here?"

Violet paced back and forth in the narrow path between the beds and the dresser.

"The girl in the front office let me in."

"Oh. Lovely. So anyone can waltz in and get access to my room with a *Please* and *Thank you.* That's cute. Real nice privacy policy they got here."

She rolled her eyes.

"Don't worry. She said no at first, but I flashed my badge and told them it was official FBI business."

He picked up the muffin, started to unwrap it, then set it back down. Instead, he lifted the box of apple juice and stabbed the straw through the top.

"You pull that kind of crap often enough, and word'll get back to the higher-ups. Believe me, they love nothing more than writing people up for the little things."

"Jesus. It was for your benefit, not mine. I was worried you might have died in here," she said.

"Uh-huh. So why do you look like a house cat that just spotted a bird on the other side of the window?"

"What?"

He waved a hand at her.

"You're all keyed up. Pacing around like a caged beast."

She halted, falling back into a chair against the wall, started to pick at her nails, and stopped herself.

"Well, we do have a little problem."

"Oh?"

She made eye contact with Loshak briefly but broke it in favor of staring at her boots while she spoke.

"I went to talk to the Peters girl. And things actually went well. She told me everything."

Between sips of apple juice, Loshak glanced up at her.

"Yeah… and? How's this a problem? Sounds like good news

to me."

Darger had an urge to cover her face with her hands. Like maybe if she had something to hide behind, it would make it easier to say. She forced herself to sit up straight. She would walk tall and proud to the firing squad. But even with all of her noble intent, her voice pronounced the words barely above a murmur.

"She stole my car."

Loshak practically spat out the mouthful of juice.

"Pardon?"

"The Peters girl stole my car."

Loshak's lips pulled into a strange grimace, and it was a moment before she realized that he was trying his damnedest not to smile.

"And how did you manage that?"

"How is this my fault? Like I'm supposed to know she's dumb enough to steal from a federal agent. Everything was going fine. Great, actually. I think you'll be very interested in hearing what she told me, but…"

"But she stole your car."

Violet grunted.

"And all the cash I had in my wallet."

Loshak finally lost his composure and started to laugh. If she was honest with herself, there was a tiny part of her that wanted to laugh, too. If it had been someone else, she imagined she would have found it highly amusing. But it wasn't someone else. It was her.

That lump was back in her throat. After the time she'd spent with Sierra, Violet had actually come to feel an affection for her. It was something she thought was mutual. Violet didn't really care about the money, and the car wasn't even hers. What bothered her was the betrayal. That's what it felt like, anyway.

"Are you done?" she asked.

Loshak wiped tears from his cheeks and let out one last chuckle.

"Phew. You know I think I'm starting to feel a little better."

The smile faded, replaced by a more sober expression.

"You didn't leave your gun in the car, did you? That's a

letter of censure right there."

"No," she said. "I'm not a complete idiot."

"And I assume you've reported the theft?"

"Not yet."

"Better call it in," Loshak said. "Given her familiarity with the local authorities, I'd bet they have a pretty good idea of where she might be. They'll probably be kind enough to keep it off the books, you know, to avoid any embarrassment. On your part, of course. But they'll still give you hell for it."

"Oh goody," she muttered as she got out her phone.

The tires of Loshak's car bumped over the lines of tar marking several years' worth of road repairs.

Damn Loshak if he hadn't been right. When she got Deputy Donaldson on the phone (her luck that it couldn't have been any other deputy), he managed a bit more self-control than Loshak. He didn't have to set down the phone to compose himself after rolling on the floor in laughter, at least. But the smirk on his face still came over the line loud and clear. As did the implicit tone of "I told you so," though he never uttered the actual words.

"I'll have someone swing by her former residence, though she'd be awful stupid to go back there… then again, she's awful stupid to steal from a fed, so…"

"I was actually thinking I'd go check on my own if you don't mind," Darger said. "And if one of your guys happens to find her before I do, could you give me a call and maybe let me handle it? I'm not pressing charges. We need her on our side."

"You still think so? Even after this?"

"Yes," she said, though she'd started to doubt things a little.

"Well, I don't mind telling you that I think you're letting this girl take you for a ride. Literally."

This play on words finally got a legitimate chuckle out of him.

Violet was halfway to Sierra's last known address when it suddenly occurred to her that she was headed in the wrong direction. If she were an addict suddenly in possession of two hundred bucks, she wouldn't go home.

She'd go to her dealer.

CHAPTER 14

The rhythmic rumble of a bass line rattled the screen door on the front of the little bungalow. Darger felt the boom of it in her ribcage as she lifted her fist to knock on the door. Someone had the subwoofer on their stereo cranked to eleven, and she had a pretty good feeling that someone was named Jimmy.

The interior door opened, just wide enough for a man's face to peep out at her.

"Who're you?"

Gaunt lines ran down from high cheekbones. He wore a black beanie and a single tuft of facial hair jutting out from below his bottom lip.

Violet did her best to seem unimposing.

"Is Sierra here?"

Cold eyes the color of hammered steel looked her up and down.

"Nope," he said and started to close the door on her.

She pushed back on the door with the palm of her hand. "Wait!"

He paused with the door open a crack, peering through at her with flared nostrils.

"Please, I'm her sister," Violet said. "I'm really worried about her."

A slow smirk spread over his face. It did not touch his eyes. He cupped his hand to his mouth and whistled. It was so jarring that her hand flicked under her jacket, her palm resting on the butt of her Glock in its holster, ready to draw.

Nothing happened for a beat, and then, from a window about three feet from where Violet stood, she heard a toilet flush. She understood at once.

"Sierra don't have a sister."

"Stepsister," she said, barely bothering to sound convincing at this point. "What does it matter? Will you please have her come to the door?"

"I already told you. She ain't here."

Violet sighed. She pointed at the Camry parked on the street.

"You see that car?"

He gave a nod, careful to look bored as he did so.

"That's my car. Sierra st—" she stopped herself from saying *stole*. "Sierra took it. So I know she's here."

"Listen, lady cop. Your stepsister story is real cute, but I ain't buying. But all that is like, moot, or whatever, because like I said: Sierra. Ain't. Here."

With a roll of her eyes, Darger pulled her badge from her jacket. The toilet flushed again.

"I'm not a cop. FBI."

"Even better."

"Alright, look. Tell her she's not in trouble. *No one* here is in trouble. I just need to talk to her. She doesn't even have to come outside. I'll stay on this side, and she can stay on that side."

He frowned and appeared thoughtful, stroking his chin theatrically.

"Don't you gotta be smart to be in the FBI?"

"Sure. Why?"

"Because you're either deaf or dumb, bitch. I already told you three times that she ain't here."

Violet bit back her anger. The bass continued to pulse from within the house, and Darger felt her heartbeat thudding along with it.

Again the sound of the toilet flushing came from the window.

"Listen, you little shit. I don't care about whatever your friend is flushing in there."

She jabbed a finger at the nearby bathroom window.

"But if you don't get Sierra out here, I *will* care. I'll care a whole lot. I'll get a warrant and tear this shithole apart. I'll snake the goddamn drains if I have to. I've seen your rap sheet. We'd only need to turn up a single pill for you to be back in county lockup. Or you could just let me talk to Sierra."

It was a bluff, of course. Nothing he was doing fell under federal jurisdiction, and she wasn't sure the Sheriff would play along if she wanted to push it, especially as far as any drain snaking. Not that Jimmy knew any of that.

His grip tightened on the door, knuckles going white.

"How about this? How about you get the fuck off my property until you got a warrant, or I'll call the fucking cops myself and report you for harassment?"

Darger clenched her teeth, pissed at herself that she'd lost her temper. She should have known it wouldn't get her anywhere with a guy like Jimmy Congdon. Then again, maybe nothing would have.

As she turned and started to walk away, he called out.

"You think she didn't warn me you were comin'? She come up here snivelin' and cryin' 'bout how she didn't tell you nothin' — not that there's anything *to* tell, mind you. She's all *please, Jimmy, don't be mad at me.*"

He did the last bit in a mocking falsetto that she supposed was his attempt at impersonating Sierra.

Violet whirled back around and narrowed her eyes.

"So she is here."

"Was. Past tense and shit. And that's all I'm tellin' you. She was here, and she left. And now you can do the same. Later, lady cop."

He shot her a wink before the door thumped shut, and the metallic click of the deadbolt followed.

Darger stomped back down to where Loshak's car was parked. She got in and summoned all of her angst leftover from adolescence in order to slam the door as loudly as possible. The engine thrummed on, and she drove away from the house, taking a left onto Vine Street.

At the next cross street, she hung another left and did a loop back, coasting onto one of the side streets that gave her a view of Jimmy's house. She turned the key, killing the engine.

Twenty minutes. Maybe less. That was how long Darger guessed it would be before she watched Sierra Peters slink out of Jimmy's front door and down to the *borrowed* car parked out front.

Twenty minutes passed, and then forty, and then an hour. Darger settled in. Probably getting high with whatever they hadn't flushed. Or already high. Could be a while, in that case. If she snorted enough Oxy, Sierra could be in there for hours. Zoned out and staring at the wall.

Violet tried to remember exactly how much cash she'd had in her wallet. More than enough to get high and stay that way for a while.

She flipped around on the car radio now and then, a wide array of terrible music and worse talk shows at her fingertips. She couldn't stand any of it for more than ten minutes at a time.

As the afternoon waned into evening, doubt finally began to creep in.

What if Jimmy had been telling the truth? What if Sierra was there that morning, but had ducked out before Violet showed up?

But no. That didn't make sense. The car was still here.

Unless… unless the killer had come back for her.

Oh, Christ Jesus.

CHAPTER 15

Jeff Grady shook himself awake at the sound of the engine outside, the low growl idling at the end of the block. He blinked a few times in the dark, a sandy grit assaulting his eyes, and then he glanced at the alarm clock on the nightstand. Red numbers glowed there, revealing the time to be 5:36 AM. Christ. The sun wouldn't be up for another 90 minutes or so, and this was his day off. He wanted nothing more than to go back to sleep, but he had to know.

It could be the dumpers out there.

Over the past six months, someone had been dumping bags of trash in the woods at the end of the street. Being on a dead end made them a target for that kind of crap, he thought. He grit his teeth when he thought about it. Someone dumping leaky bags of diapers and orange juice cartons and those disgusting bloody styrofoam trays that had held chicken breasts or hamburger in them. Black plastic bags so full they're bulging like ticks stuck in a dog's neck, ready to pop. Then the coons and possums came along and tore the shit open, the used coffee filters and wads of soggy paper towel and plastic rinds from bologna winding up strewn about the woods. Looking like hell. And of course the city wouldn't do nothing about it, would they? Not unless someone caught the bastards in the act.

But then again, maybe it wasn't the dumpers. The car had been sitting there a long time already it seemed like. Did lingering like that make any sense for someone dumping trash? He thought not.

He lay back, but he kept his eyes open. There was a chance it was only a neighbor. Sometimes that Jenkins guy from the end of the block seemed to head out in the pre-dawn hours like this. What was his first name, again? Something like Dale or Daryl. He was always out tinkering in his garage at all hours and almost never wearing a shirt. Weird guy. Anyway, Grady would feel pretty stupid if he crawled out of bed this early over nothing.

The engine's rumble held steady for a long while, the droning note eventually relaxing him, coaxing his eyelids closed. He drifted a little, his consciousness fading down to just the sound of the car idling outside.

The metallic slam jolted him awake again — the trunk of a car banging shut — and somehow he knew it wasn't the Jenkins guy.

No, no. This was the work of dumpers as sure as he was alive.

Goddamn dumpers!

The droning engine note changed pitch as he went into motion.

He threw the blanket back, untangled his legs from the sheet and rose from the bed. The wood floor transmitted a chill into his feet, and his legs felt a little unsteady beneath him, his muscles still half asleep. His hands patted along the top of the dresser for his hooded sweatshirt, and he pulled it on.

And then he froze. Listening. The car outside was speeding away, engine shrieking out high notes after so long singing bass. He ran to the window and looked out, a deep breath exiting his nostrils and steaming a cloud onto the glass before him.

His eyes traced the asphalt to one end of the street and then the other. Shit. It was gone. He could hear the engine trailing away in the distance, but he was too late to get a glimpse.

Goddamn it. Why had he been messing with the sweatshirt? Like he could run out there and stop it from happening or something? Some kind of anti-dumper superhero or some goddamn thing. Why didn't he just look out and try to see who it was like a normal person? Maybe he wouldn't have been able to make out a license plate number in the dark, but he could at least get a make and model. Maybe even get a look at the driver for a police sketch or something.

Idiot.

He looked one more time, eyes swiveling to the outlet end of the street and finding nothing at all. No traffic. Not a single light on in any window on the block, at least from his vantage point. He pivoted to look at the dead end side. Nothing there, either.

But wait.

There was something there. He could see what looked like black plastic tangled in the brush, flapping a little in the breeze. A garbage bag, maybe. And there was a pale bulk near that, under the dead end sign. Whatever it was, it lay just beyond the perimeter of the last streetlight, swathed in the darkness. That combined with the tall grass made it hard to make out.

He looked at the alarm clock again — 5:41 AM. Only a few minutes had passed. His gaze fell upon the bed. The blanket was peeled back like an open door inviting him to return, and he could imagine that warmth surrounding his body again, pulling him down into a peaceful dream for as long as he wished to stay.

But no. Of course not. He had to know.

He pulled on a pair of jeans, the denim so cold against his legs that it almost felt damp. His skin bunched into goose pimples, all tight and weird, his scrotum shriveling something awful. And this was supposed to be his damn day off.

He dug around in the junk drawer in the kitchen until he found the little flashlight, and then he headed out, sliding the hood up over his head as he crossed the threshold.

The air felt heavy, and the grass glistened with frost. He made sure to stay on the sidewalk to avoid the wet, stepping into the street and walking the diagonal line toward his destination.

Now that the sound of the car had faded entirely, it was impossibly still out here. It felt a little wrong to be moving about in these dark morning hours, like he was violating some agreed upon morning sanctity.

The wind picked up for a moment, and he could hear that plastic flailing again, rattling the branches of a bush. It did look like a garbage bag, and it was wound up in the brush pretty good.

The mass below it was still shrouded, but whatever it was almost glowed a little. Something creamy white reflecting back a purple radiance in this muted light, he thought.

He licked his lips. That crawling skin tightened him up all over again, but it wasn't from the cold this time. Something wasn't right.

When he got close, he clicked on the light. The flashlight

was about the size of a cigar, but the LED bulb packed the illumination of something much bigger. A shaft of bright white light shot out of the tiny tube, and he swung the circle toward that bulk on the ground. The dead end sign reflected its glare back at him as he swung it past, beaming yellow and black. It stung like smoke getting in his eyes.

When he saw the foot, he stopped in his tracks. The light shook, the image flickering in a strobe effect for a beat. Jesus. A foot. A human foot. Attached to a leg that disappeared into the weeds about mid-calf.

It had to be a mannequin, right? The little scuff of dirt wrapping around the ankle gave it a realistic feel, almost like a patina, but it couldn't be real, could it?

And then the newspaper stories flashed in his head. Those cut up girls in garbage bags dumped around the county.

Oh, Jesus.

He stood there a moment, knowing his next move would in some sense define his life in a way that would always be known only to him. A private memory he would turn over and over in his brain, trying to decipher exactly what it meant about who he was for good or ill. He wanted to run back into the house and call the police. Let them deal with it. But he couldn't do that now.

He had to know.

He licked his lips again, and then he shuffled forward into the darkness, his breath coiling steam out of his mouth and nostrils.

He pointed the beam a little further, and the light danced over that pale bulk, the foot muted in the gray shadows in the foreground. The other foot came into view a few inches beyond the first. Milk-white. Not dirty like the other.

His heart pattered like a hummingbird flittering away in his chest. He could hear the blood pounding in his ears. Could feel his breath sticking in his throat. But he didn't stop walking this time. He had to see it before he could think about anything else.

The naked girl lay face down in the dirt, leafless twigs poking out of the ground all around her like miniature spikes. Her head seemed to be concealed in that black plastic tangled up in the bushes, but he could still tell her gender by the curve of her hips and waist, the somehow feminine way her legs tapered from thigh to knee to ankle.

The circle of light paused on the small of her back, and her pale skin shimmered under it, a bloodless tone of tissue that he found upsetting. Disturbing. Like the milky flesh of some segmented worm that squirmed so deep in the Earth that it would never be touched by the sun.

She sprawled with her arms down at her sides. Prone. Defenseless. The vulnerability accentuated by her pose. Those arms were in no position for her to catch herself when she was dumped here.

He shuddered, and he swung the light down to his side.

The body seemed to turn purple again now that the light was ambient instead of direct, but she glowed just the same. A glimmering dead thing all stretched out.

Yes. She was real, and she was dead. He was sure of both things now. And it turned out that knowing didn't help him at all. It brought him no satisfaction. No sense of peace. Failed to still the fluttering dread inside of him.

How could he live in a world where such a profane image could be real, where such a cruelty could be actual? She was dumped in the open with only this last hour and a half of dark to conceal her. By the time the sun came up, the whole neighborhood would be able to see the corpse plainly from their windows. And someone must have wanted it that way. They risked much to ensure it.

The wind picked up again, cold on his cheeks. It rattled through the foliage, swirling through the scene to move all of the pieces. The black plastic flapped up from the corpse, and he gasped.

There was no head.

The neck sheared off into nothing on a jagged slash, stringy red muscle tissue visible at the mouth of the wound.

His eyes recorded this image. Seared it into his skull for keeps.

A naked woman flopped flat on the ground with her head cut off. Dumped right out in the open.

CHAPTER 16

The wind rips against the windshield. It slaps at the car. Sounds solid.

He feels the cold radiating off of the glass. It chills his knuckles where they grip the steering wheel.

The land here is vacant. Barren. Empty. Snapped cornstalks bend to kiss the dirt. The fields of them are endless. The rows of broken plants sprawling toward the gray sky in the distance.

In the car he is alone. Always alone. His thoughts twist up. Mangle themselves. Spiral into nothing.

The engine throbs. Hums endlessly.

Lights jam the dashboard. Needles twitch along with the car's movements. He pays them no mind.

Stares down the road. Long and dark.

Never is the distance between him and the world more clear than in this car. The void. The gulf that grows between him and everything. Between him and everyone.

He tries to fight it. He searches inside and out for anything else. For any glimmer of hope. But he finds only the void. The abyss. The big nothing that exists just beneath the surface of all that we see.

Black. Empty. Cavernous.

His vision flicks to the duffel bag in the passenger seat. He watches it a second out of the corner of his eye. Licks his lips. Looks away.

He brings a hand to his pants. Smears his palm on the denim. Sweat slicks his skin despite the cold.

He tries to think of what to say to her, but he can't. Not yet. It's not right. Maybe it never will be.

He grits his teeth. Grinds his foot into the accelerator.

The car lurches. The needles on the dash shudder. He feels his lower back lift a little out of his seat for a moment before it resettles.

His eyelids flutter. His lips pop open. Breath explodes out of him in a hiss.

There is no other movement for miles.

Nothing.

No one.

It is always empty out here. Always gray.

And when he's alone his wound opens up. A kind of hurt he doesn't understand. Can barely comprehend. It's always there, he knows. But it only comes clear when he makes this drive. This high speed burn to and from the city.

The isolation lays bare the damage. The cold and lonesome drive sharpens his focus on this injury.

But not now. He can't now.

He concentrates to slow his breathing. Feels the blood glug along in his neck. The pulse decelerating. He can't let the rage all the way in. Not now.

He has to go to work. Soon.

His eyes stay fastened to the horizon, and he sees the city take shape there. The specks at the edge of the world grow. The buildings pointing their tips at the heavens. Part of him is disappointed to see this. Disappointed to know that the real world exists on the other end of this empty road.

And yet a calm comes back to him as he watches the buildings expand. The numb of daily life returns. The wound is tucked away and forgotten. Like the tools in the glove compartment.

Like what he has in the duffel bag.

CHAPTER 17

The first sensation Darger noticed was that she was freezing. The air seemed especially frigid as she inhaled. And a little moist. Had she left the air conditioner on? And that odor… why did it smell like fake lemons and sour milk?

She straightened her neck and aching pain shot from her shoulder up to her ear. Her eyes snapped open, and she blinked half a dozen times against the bright sunlight streaming in through the windshield before she remembered where she was and what she was doing. The clock on the dash read 6:08 AM. She must have fallen asleep sometime last night. The last thing she remembered, it had been around 2 AM. Drowsiness had started to take hold, and she'd told herself: just another half hour. Apparently, somewhere in that thirty minutes, she'd dozed off.

Rubbing her eyes and then waiting for the blurriness to clear, she noted that her rental car was still parked in front of Jimmy the drug dealer's house. Maybe Sierra was still inside, but Darger was starting to feel more and more certain that she wasn't. After a brief moment of panic the previous afternoon, she'd ruled out the possibility of Sierra being taken again. It was too risky — returning to the same location, grabbing her in broad daylight? No. He wasn't that impulsive.

And yet the longer the car sat in front of Jimmy's the more Darger began to admit that Sierra was long gone. It made more sense than her keeping the car, really. She wouldn't have any reason to think Darger *wouldn't* call the cops, and Sierra was a smart enough girl to know that being caught with the car would be much worse for her. Better to ditch it and move on.

Reluctantly, Darger started the engine of Loshak's car, slid the gearshift into Drive, and pulled away from the curb.

When she arrived back at the motel, she noticed that Loshak's curtains were wide open. She grabbed two cups of coffee from the free breakfast table before trudging up the steps.

102

She knocked lightly at Loshak's door, and he answered quickly, almost as if he'd been waiting.

"Sorry, I didn't mean to keep it overnight," she said, tossing him his keys. He caught them with one hand. The styrofoam cup she handed over more gingerly.

"Christ, you just got back? They find your car?"

"I found it."

"All by yourself. Good for you."

He peeked out the window.

"Where is it?"

"Still sitting outside the dealer's house."

"Why didn't you call one of Donaldson's guys and have them help you drive it back?"

"Because I still don't have the keys."

Loshak tried to mask his smirk by sipping at the coffee, but she wasn't so easily fooled.

"I'm glad that everyone is getting so much amusement from this."

"So you found the car. What else is bothering you?"

"Pardon?"

"You seem on edge."

"There's a serial killer on the loose and a witness stole my car." She frowned into the steaming brown liquid. "Also I think this is decaf."

Darger set the cup down and shoved her hands in her pockets.

"Why shouldn't I be on edge?"

"I'm just saying, seems like something else is eating at you."

Violet peered through the gap in the plaid curtains. She didn't want to say it out loud. Saying it out loud would make it more real somehow. Superstitious thinking, she knew, but also one that held a lot of power to the human mind. She knew that from her years of victim counseling. People often feel that if they never utter the words, they can make them go away. Bury them deep enough, and it's like they never existed. It wasn't true of course. But that didn't stop her from doing it anyway. She was only human, after all.

"I'm gonna go take a shower, maybe try to grab a quick

nap." She rolled her head around in a circle and flexed her shoulders. "I fell asleep in the car and really jacked up my neck."

She hadn't even finished undressing for her shower when she got the call. It was Donaldson. Assuming a patrol from his department found her car, she interrupted.

"I'm guessing your guys found the car, but it's too late. She's moved on."

"I don't… what?"

"Or did you find her?" She felt an odd mix of dread and hope. If they'd picked up Sierra, maybe she could go down to the station and get her to talk. On the other hand, if they were holding her, she'd have every reason *not* to talk.

There was an uncomfortable silence, and she was about to ask if Donaldson was still there when she heard the rustle of his breath in the receiver.

"I guess it depends on which 'her' you're referring to, ma'am."

"Sorry, I don't follow."

"We've got another body. Athens PD got the call twenty minutes ago, and I thought you ought to know."

By the time she reached the balcony, Loshak was already locking the door of his room. He still looked a little under the weather, and she resisted an impulse to ask if he was feeling up to a field trip. It would only piss him off, she figured. Instead, she kept her mouth shut and followed when he spoke.

"We can take my car."

CHAPTER 18

The parking lot at the airport bustles. Cars and trucks and vans shamble in and out. A line of them forming at the toll booth.

The Buick zigs and zags through the rows of vehicles. Eventually parking under a sign that reads "Employees Only" in red letters.

He hesitates a moment in the strange silence that the engine's rumble had occupied for so long. Squirms a little in his seat. Swallows, his throat clicking.

He places a hand on the duffel bag. He swears he feels a jolt of electricity. A pulse rippling into his palm as contact is made. But he leaves his hand there for a long moment and feels nothing more. He doesn't want to, but he plucks his fingers from the nylon canvas.

He turns from the bag. Shoulders squared to the driver's side window. Again, he pauses.

He lets his gaze fall through the glass to the steel door that stands between him and that other world.

The hinges squawk and the door slams shut behind him a beat later. The chilly morning air swirls around him. Touches the wet places.

His thumb depresses the button on the key fob. A series of clicks issue behind him. He wills himself to not look back at the duffel bag resting on the passenger seat.

His fingers touch the cold steel. Wrap themselves around the door handle. He steps through into—

— the office.

He strode inside and warmth enveloped him at once. As he walked the few paces over the perforated welcome mat to make his way behind the counter, a kind of reality he couldn't quite remember in the car snapped back into place. People. This was what it was like to be around people. The muscles in his chest and jaw went strangely slack, some tension he hadn't quite been aware of relieved all at once, and a tingle pricked along his scalp, his head going light, going faint.

The sudden shift away from isolation was disorienting to an alarming degree, filled him with some sense of teetering on the edge of things, on the edge of reality itself, poised to make that final plunge into madness. He thought it was a little like a bout of vertigo, the change in atmosphere negating his feel for direction and place. For the moment, he was nowhere. No solid ground beneath his feet. He straddled the crack between two worlds. One foot in each. It was impossible — overwhelming and strange — but it was happening.

And yet this crazed feeling came with a swell of pride. He thought it likely that it was a state most people couldn't handle, that something this jarring would break weaker minds, shatter them like broken mirrors, but not his. This was the one way his mind was strong. He was used to weird shit.

Movement to the right caught his eye. Lucas nodded a greeting from where he worked the drive-through window, making change for an elderly black man in a Lexus SUV. As far as coworkers went, Lucas was alright. A slender, quiet guy who mostly kept to himself. His teeth were all rotten from drinking Coca-Cola all night, every night to keep himself awake during third shift.

A gravelly voice spoke up from behind him.

"Hey-y, alright. It's the Ripper. On time and everything. For once."

Meaty hands squeezed at the trapezius muscles on each side of his neck. Laughter hissed, and Kurt could feel breath and flecks of spit spattering his neck. This was Chip. The boss. Portly. Balding. Obnoxious.

"M-morning, Chip," Kurt said. He turned to face the man, but his gaze fell to the ground to avoid eye contact.

"And top of the m-morning to you, good sir. You have a big weekend, Ripper? Get into any trouble?"

Ripper was the nickname Chip had come up with. Kurt Van Ryper was used to it.

His eyes darted over the floor as he searched for an answer, taking in the ankles of Chip's ridiculous distressed jeans. His boss always stood with his legs a little more than shoulder width apart like some kind of superhero, and he could just make out the hulking torso above them. A sheet of fat swaddled a broad chest and shoulders, bolting a gut onto what must have once been a heavily muscled physique.

"Not really," Kurt said, finally.

"That's too bad. Me? When I was your age? I was out there tearin' it up, man. That's what life is all about. Carpe diem and what not."

"Yeah."

Now Chip shifted his position, the width of his stance tightening a little, hips rotating that beefy torso so it was no longer facing Kurt straight on.

"So listen," the boss said. "I know you hate it, but we've got you over in the second booth today."

They both turned to look across the asphalt drive. The lonesome booth's windows stood dark for now. It was an aluminum and glass structure, three foot by four foot. Cramped. Tiny. The furnace wasn't fully functional, either. On a chilly day like today, it was warmer than being outside but not by much. Kurt always felt trapped in there, encased in glass on four sides like he was on display in the meat department. Everyone complained about having to work the booth, though. Working the window in the office building, like Lucas was now, wasn't so bad. It provided access to the bathroom, break room, fridge, etc. The second booth offered no such perks.

"Nobody wants to do it," Chip said. "Nobody. It blows. I get that. But I know I can always count on ol' Van Ripper to fly solo over there, amIright?"

Kurt spoke his reply to the denim swaddled ankles.

"Right."

"Good man."

Chip clapped him on the shoulder, and Kurt winced a little, which embarrassed him. His cheeks warmed right away.

"Oh, and check the traps on the way over, too, would you?" Chip said.

Kurt's head bobbed once.

Chip pulled a large key ring from his pocket and pawed at it with his plump sausage fingers. He unlocked a cupboard under the counter with a snap of the wrist, and Kurt ducked to pull out a tray for the cash register. Nickels and dimes tinkled in the cupped spots.

"OK, well…" Chip said, no longer looking Kurt in the face. "I'll, uh, get out of your hair."

Again Kurt's head moved up and down one time. Chip mirrored the gesture and retreated to his office.

Kurt backed his way out the steel door to head outside, returning to the cold, the gray, the tray for the register balanced in his hands in front of him, little metal arms pressing down stacks of dollar bills. His eyes flicked to the car, to the spot where the duffel bag must be, though the glare on the windows blotted it out. And in the light of day, in the presence of Chip and Lucas, this all felt quite bewildering. What transpired in the car, what sat in the car even now, seemed unthinkable. A lump shifted in his throat, threatened to gag him.

Jesus, what had he been thinking? He needed to ditch it. As soon as he got out of here, he'd dump it somewhere. Toss it over the bridge into the river, maybe — bag and all. He had to be rid of the whole lot of it.

He sidled between two cars in the drive-through line to draw near to the tiny booth, stooping a second to check the live mouse traps along the curb there. Rats occupied both, the hunch-backed creatures recoiling a little as he drew near, scrabbling with no place to go, those disgusting pink tails dragging along behind them like tiny, segmented hot dogs. Unlike the humans forced to work it, the rodents seemed to love the little booth. They nested in the insulation in the walls, chewed the wires that connected it to the office, shat little black pellets everywhere. Hence the traps they'd set on the concrete around it.

Anyway, he wasn't the only one trapped in a little box today.

He stood, moved to the door, struggling to unlock it without spilling the tray of coins everywhere, but he managed it. Again reality seemed to shift as he stepped into the new space. The air was dry in this tiny building, and it smelled vaguely of mildew and rat shit. He set up the register, the tray of money disappearing into its little shelf like it had never existed. After that, he sat, holding totally motionless for a beat.

He looked at the grid pattern formed in the wire that ran through the safety glass surrounding him. Chicken wire or something like it, he thought. A perfect cage, indeed. He flipped on the wall unit furnace and the green light overhead so drivers would know the booth was open.

He gazed across the lane to the other window. Lucas had been replaced, third shift now complete. A feminine figure lurked there now, slightly obscured by the glare and the touch of fog clouding the glass, but after a second, he could make her out.

It was Candice.

She wasn't like the others. All of the other girls who worked here were stuck-up types. They loved sucking up to Chip, flirting with him and prattling on about nothing. They never shut their stupid traps, but not Candice. She was quiet and kind. She said hello and smiled at him whenever she saw him. A genuine smile, each and every one of them. She didn't have to be kind to Kurt like that, he knew, but she was.

A feeling came over him like he was floating in those moments when she smiled at him, all of his weight lifting off of the ground as though pulled by a puppeteer's strings. And in those flashes, he thought maybe it could all work out. Maybe he could meet someone, date someone — Candice or someone else. Maybe it really was possible.

Even now, seeing her as a dark smudge in a glass case in the distance, the feeling came over him. Maybe he could be part of it all. Maybe all of the voices in his head running him down all the time were wrong. Maybe it was just fear, insecurity, doubt. A mirage that would disappear if he got over the hump of getting to know someone. Maybe.

And then he remembered the duffel bag in the passenger seat of the Buick, and the weightless feeling left him.

His gaze drifted away from the office building across the way, coasting downward. Falling. He lifted his hands, looking down at the soft flesh of the palms, at the lines and whorls etched there.

He knew it could never be. Not with Candice or any other girl. Not with his crooked eye. Not with his chinless pig face. Not with the awkwardness he seemed to spread to all those around him like an infectious disease. Not with the general repulsion he created in women with both his physical presence and personality.

Not with the things he'd done.

A Ford Focus pulled up to the window then. Dark gray. The booth's window swung open, and the wind snuffled at the opening, a whoosh of cold air blasting him in the eyes. An older woman grimaced at him from the driver's seat. He took her ticket, took her money, made change.

This was how it went for him. The people came and went. The ticket and the money exchange accounting for the depth of their connections. Fingers almost, but never quite, touching. He sat in his box, an endless line of people just outside. He seemed to be surrounded by them, and yet he remained alone.

He looked across the lane of traffic again at Candice — at what he could see of her, anyway. She was locked behind glass from him like all the rest. She was something precious. Something important to be protected and kept in a special display case. Not him. He was one of the rats in the traps out by the curb. A loathsome creature. A wretched thing squirming in his own filth. All he needed was the hot dog tail to complete the picture.

Another vehicle approached the window — a Mazda 3, he thought. Red. Four college-aged males gibbered away within, their conversation not pausing as the ticket and money exchange repeated itself. When it was done, the window swung closed, and all was quiet again.

It occurred to him, not for the first time, that sitting in the booth was a lot like sitting in the car. When he closed the door, he closed himself off from people once more. All of humanity was locked behind glass from his vantage point. His isolation was complete. The feel of it — the feel of the void — would come back to him little by little. It had already started.

CHAPTER 19

The dead end street looked more like a street fair than a crime scene. Two police cruisers were parked horizontally across the entrance of the block to bar any traffic from coming in. A traffic jam of law enforcement personnel, news vans, and civilian vehicles prevented them from parking anywhere near the actual street.

Loshak eased the car up to the curb in front of a peach-colored Victorian house with a mansard roof. Behind them, Darger noticed an SUV pull up and park. The side was marked with the logo of the Columbus CBS affiliate.

"It's only been a week since the last one," Darger said.

"Yeah," was all Loshak said in response.

She supposed he didn't need to say more. She knew they were both thinking it. If this was the work of their killer, the time between kills was getting shorter. Was it because the last one had been unsatisfying somehow? She sensed that Loshak wasn't in a chatty mood, though, and kept the rest of her thoughts to herself.

The closer they got to the crime scene, the thicker the groups of neighborhood folk and other gawkers. They congregated on the sidewalks and in yards, a nervous chatter passing between them.

"They think it's him, the Doll Parts Killer from the news."

"Bill said he heard it was a hit and run."

"Oh my goodness gracious! I let my kids ride their skateboards up and down that cul-de-sac!"

"I tell you what, I got my daddy's old 12-gauge out when the killings first started. I keep it loaded and tucked under my bed, just in case."

The tension was palpable. A creeping, itchy feeling Darger felt along her spine and scalp.

She glanced over at Loshak, wondering if he sensed the fear coming off the mob as well. His mouth pressed into a taut line and his penny-colored eyes seemed to bore straight ahead.

"Worse than a goddamn circus," he muttered to himself as they rounded the corner that led to the dead end.

The bustle thinned a bit as the line of yellow crime scene tape came into view. A group of uniformed officers were doing their best to keep anyone unauthorized as far as possible from the line. One of the boys in blue approached, ready to tell them to scram when a familiar voice called out.

"They're OK, Pat. Let 'em through."

Donaldson pinched the brim of his hat at them as they passed.

A white and yellow tent had been erected at the end of the street. It functioned as much to keep the media from sticking their cameras where they didn't belong as it did to cut down on foreign contamination. Swarming around the tent were more police and crime scene techs, all decked out in white protective suits — another layer to prevent evidence contamination.

The polyester fabric shuddered and then the flap opened. A tall man in one of the white suits stepped out. He removed the blue gloves on his hands and the respirator-style dust mask over his mouth, but he left his hairnet in place. Adjusting the belt at his waist that held a walkie-talkie and some other gear, he looked up and saw them coming. He raised one hand in a greeting.

"Agent Loshak. I don't mind saying that I'm glad you're here."

"Of course," Loshak said, then tilted his head in her direction. "This is my colleague, Special Agent Violet Darger. Darger, this is Detective Luck."

He pulled off the hairnet, revealing a head of thick brown hair parted to one side and styled with a generous amount of mousse or pomade. Some product that kept it looking wet anyway.

"Casey," he said, extending his hand.

She shook it briefly, looking into his brown eyes. Right. Luck. The one with the sloppy interview transcripts. Too bad he wasn't as fussy about his paperwork as he clearly was about his hair.

"Are your guys getting video of the gawkers?" she said. "There's a chance he's watching this right now."

"Roger that. I have three officers sweeping the crowd for witnesses, all outfitted with bodycams."

Darger nodded approval.

"We can go in as soon as the techs are done. I'm trying to limit the number of people in the tent at one time. Better to not trample it any more than we have to."

He pulled a phone from his belt and tapped the screen.

"While we wait, I can give you a quick rundown of how she was found. The call came in at 5:57 AM from one of the local residents — a Mr. Jeff Grady. Lives in the mint green number right over there."

Luck waved a hand toward a Cape Cod house with a well-manicured row of shrubs along the front walk.

"Apparently people dumping at the dead end is a recurring issue. Not bodies, of course. Usually trash. A few larger household items, too. An old fridge. A dryer. A couple sofas. Some people can't be bothered to wait for the city-wide bulk trash day is how he put it. So he hears the sound of a car engine followed by the slam of the trunk, he gets up, figuring he'll take a peek, maybe snag the plate numbers in case they are dumpers — that's his word. Guy seems like a real busybody, if you know what I mean."

"So did he?" Darger asked, impatient to know whether he'd gotten a number off the car.

"What's that?"

"The plates? Did he get the license plate number?"

"Oh," Luck said. "No ma'am, that's a negative. By the time he got to the window, the car had sped off. He decided he ought to take a closer look and then came up here and found her."

Voices murmured from inside the tent.

"Coroner already came and went. He put time of death sometime in the last 24 hours or so."

That got Darger's attention, and Loshak's too.

"And you're sure it's one of his?"

Loshak had been mostly silent until now, but Violet knew he was thinking what she was. Twenty-four hours wasn't long enough for their guy.

"Oh yeah," Luck said, and his face went a little gray. "I have no doubt about that."

The tent rustled again and a man and woman, both clad in protective suits and carrying bins filled with evidence bags, filed out.

"We're all set, Detective."

"Thanks, Gertie."

Now it was Darger and Loshak's turn to don the white outfits. Detective Luck handed each of them a bunny suit. Elastic snapped and zippers whirred. Darger made sure to keep her phone in her hand so she'd be able to get some photos of her own.

Loshak ducked under the door flap first, and Darger made to follow when Luck caught her by the forearm. Her first thought was that he wasn't going to let her take any pictures. He'd use the excuse that they don't want to risk anything being leaked to the media, but that was bullshit. It was territorial nonsense.

Her lips parted. She was going to fight him on this. But he pointed a finger at her feet before she got a word out.

"Forgot your booties, ma'am."

Violet looked down at her boots, noting that Luck's feet were wrapped in fluffy-looking blue baggies that looked very much like the hairnets they were both wearing.

"Shit. Right," she said, bending and grabbing two of the disposable shoe covers from a box next to the one filled with gloves. "Sorry."

"Not a problem, ma'am."

When she'd secured the booties, Luck held the flap out of the way for her.

"After you."

She scooted into the interior of the tent. With the lack of direct light, it was gloomy inside, and Darger squinted while her eyes adjusted to the dimness. Already the ripe smell of decay was making itself known, and she could hear the buzzing of flies.

The girl was slightly northeast of center in the tent, sprawled in such a way that was almost inherently unnatural. Limbs akimbo, joints resting at awkward angles, shoulders frozen in an uncomfortable stoop. The corpse looked like a marionette dropped in a heap by a careless child.

She was belly down and nude. The settling of blood after death had stained her back in a mottled pattern. That meant she'd spent a stretch of time on her back postmortem before she was dumped here.

There was always an initial shock when seeing a body. Any body, whether the person died by violent means or not. Darger thought it was something about the human form, normally so full of movement and life: walking, laughing, chest perpetually expanding and contracting. Something about seeing it so still, rendered into nothing but motionless flesh and bone. It was once this shock had a chance to fade that she noticed a problem.

This girl was dead, yes. And dumped naked quite openly where someone would find her. But her arms and legs were attached.

"It's not him," she said, and Loshak turned toward her from where he squatted next to a bush up by the girl's shoulders.

"What's that?"

"Well aside from the fact that she's only been dead 24 hours, and he always keeps them for several days… she's not cut up," she explained. "It's not right. I don't think he's capable of straying that far from his routine at this point. It doesn't make sense."

Loshak had a pencil in his hand, and he used it to prod at something that was covering the girl's head. Darger hadn't recognized it in the low light, she'd thought it was part of the bush. But it was a black garbage bag tangled in the branches of the undergrowth.

She was about to point out that a garbage bag wasn't exactly an unusual item when it came to dumping bodies when the plastic crinkled, rising under Loshak's pencil, revealing the horror of the raw stump at the end of the neck. The bag wasn't covering the head after all. There was no head.

"Oh," Darger said.

Her gaze lingered there, at the flesh torn and bloodied,

before drifting down to the other features. It was like, in seeing the mutilation for the first time, she was forced to reset. The body became as strange and terrible as it had been in those first moments. Violet followed the peaks and valleys of her vertebrae. The two shallow dimples above her buttocks. The slender arms in position to catch her final fall. Pale lines marred the skin there. Impressions from the grass?

And the hands, looking like something carved in marble by an old grand master. The delicate fingers, long and white, softly folded in toward the palm. The curvature reminded her of the way a violinist might clutch their instrument. Soft but firm.

Upon closer inspection, Darger noticed that the pinkie was crooked, probably broken. Also, several of the nails were broken roughly, despite having been recently manicured. This girl had put up a struggle.

There was a strange flutter in her belly. A growing unease. What was it?

Two creases formed between her eyebrows as she mulled it over. And then it hit her.

Recently manicured.

Her eyes snapped back to the ends of the fingers. To the nails painted —

No, it couldn't be.

Nails the color of —

Violet's hands flew to her face, a spinal reflex beyond her control. Air sucked into her lungs in a wheezing gasp, and she felt her knees buckle underneath her, but Detective Luck caught her before she went all the way down.

"Whoa," he said, gripping her under the armpits.

Darger tried to speak, to tell them she was OK, but all that came out was, "Oh God. Oh God. Oh God."

Loshak pivoted from his crouched position next to the body to see Detective Luck guiding her out of the tent.

The glare of the sun shone down on them as Luck lowered her to the curb. Violet tugged at the mask over her mouth, desperate for fresh air. A beat later, Loshak popped through the door after them.

"Ah shit, Darger," he said. "I'm sorry. I thought you'd seen one in person before."

"No."

And that was all she said for a moment while she sat there on the concrete with the morning light beaming into her eyes. It was too bright and too hot and God, she thought she might throw up. She rocked back and forth, squeezing her eyes closed against the brightness and the heat and the horror under the tent lying just a few feet away. She clawed at the gloves on her hands, peeling away the hot rubber and balling them into her fist.

My name is Violet Darger.

I was born on April 13th.

Detective Luck squatted next to her and put a hand on her elbow.

My fingernails are painted Cerulean Sea.

She stared at her hands. At the cotton candy blue adorning each fingernail.

Cerulean Sea.

"Take a deep breath, that's it," Luck said and patted her arm.

Cerulean.

She inhaled, chest expanding.

Sea.

She let it out, forcing her lungs to empty themselves completely, feeling her ribcage squeeze in on itself.

"It's nothing to be ashamed of, you know. I've seen my share of bodies, but these last few…"

He glanced at the tent flap and then away, down the street. He didn't try to finish the sentence.

"It's not that. It's not the body," she said, shaking her head. "It's the girl."

Violet inclined her head toward the white fabric that shivered in the breeze.

"That's Sierra Peters."

CHAPTER 20

All of the air went out of Darger and seemed to stay out. Her lungs stuck in that deflated state, in that seemingly permanent exhale like the shock of this revelation had knocked the wind out of her.

Shock. Yes. That's just what it was, she thought. A feeling so big it left her numb. Left her empty while her brain tried to catch up.

Sierra was dead. Her body defiled. Last night they'd painted their nails together, feasted on pizza and beer, and now she was a corpse on display for all the world to see.

A dead thing. A small thing. So small.

How could this be real? How could life be so awful as this? To chew up a person and leave them on the side of the road — a real live human being with dreams and fears and hopes and flaws. All of it wiped away in a flash. Gone forever.

Sierra Peters had flitted from place to place in her life, from problem to problem. The bulk of her possessions were probably still sitting on the curb on Savannah Lane. In the end, she didn't even have a home. Darger thought maybe she never did. Not really.

She closed her eyes against the images of the naked body flashing in her mind. Dirty. Scrawny. Bled white.

She'd wanted to be a dancer, and then she'd wanted to be a beautician. Instead, her whole life led to this. Belly down in the weeds. Head hacked off.

How could the world work that way? It didn't make sense.

Darger gagged a little, her lungs quaking and clammy. She coughed, hacking out throaty noises like a barfing cat. It was the violence of the cough that brought the tears to her eyes at last. The wet spread down her cheeks. It seemed to bring her around some.

The numb retreated a touch, and nausea took its place. Her skin went damp all over, lukewarm and dappled with beads of sweat, and an ache balled its fist in her gut. For a second, she thought she might throw up, but she took a breath instead, the wind cool in her throat. At least she could breathe again.

She remembered then that she wasn't alone.

Luck's face was scrunched up in a look of utter confusion. "Wait. What?" Luck said.

Loshak sniffled, the corners of his mouth turned down. He also looked doubtful.

"Yeah. How can you tell? She doesn't exactly… you know… have a head."

Violet held up a hand, showing off her own fresh manicure in Cerulean Sea.

Loshak was still standing at the entrance of the tent. He glanced back at the slit in the fabric that marked the doorway but didn't go back in. He didn't need to. Violet knew he'd probably already recorded every detail of the crime scene. Snapshots etched in his mind.

"Manicures," she said, by way of explanation. "She took a cosmetology course in high school."

"Holy hell," Detective Luck said.

"She has a record," Darger said. "We can run the prints against the ones in her file to make an official ID. But it's her. No doubt."

She explained her most recent interview with Sierra, followed by the stolen car debacle, and then she brushed grit from her palms and made to stand. Luck scrambled to his feet and put out a hand. She waved it away.

"I'm fine."

"You sure?"

Gritting her teeth together, she bobbed her head up and down. She was angry for letting herself get shaken like that. And embarrassed that the two men had witnessed it. They'd think she was weak now. A delicate flower that needed to be shielded and protected.

"I'm ready to go back," she said, tugging at her mask.

A series of wrinkles formed over Loshak's raised eyebrow. "To the motel?"

"No," she said and pushed past him on her way through the

tent entrance.

Violet was aware of them taking surreptitious glances her way when they thought she wasn't looking. She ignored them, getting out her phone and preparing to take some photographs. The bright white of the flash lit the tent in a strobe-like glare.

"Ligature marks look different this time," she said, noting the wider bands of irritated tissue at the wrists and ankles. The girls before had thinner, deeper wounds consistent with a thinner rope or twine. "Duct tape?"

"Looks like it," Loshak agreed.

Another burst of light from the camera punctured the dimness under the tent. Darger was about to mention the bands of lighter flesh over the buttocks and shoulder blades — when she caught another glimpse of the grisly remnants of her neck. The hand gripping her phone fell to her side as she suddenly remembered something Loshak had said about the killer not taking any souvenirs. *So far.*

"You knew he was going to keep the head."

She'd barely said it out loud, more muttering it to herself than anything. But Luck's head snapped up, oscillating between her and Loshak.

"I had a hunch," he admitted.

She was aware of her jaw muscles clenching.

"Why didn't you say so?"

A knuckle gloved in blue ran itself over Loshak's chin. He pursed his lips.

"Kinda thought you'd figure it out."

Darger pressed her fingernails into her palms, feeling the little crescent-shaped claws dig into her skin. Goddamn it.

She was angry at herself for not figuring it out. Especially when she ran through their conversation again and remembered that Loshak had prefaced his half-prediction with a comment about the partial decapitation. He'd practically spelled it out.

"Sorry," the detective piped up. "Are you saying he kept the head? He didn't just... dump it somewhere else?"

Darger and Loshak nodded in unison.

"Geez," Luck said, tugging at the neck of his white jumpsuit.

120

"Why?"

Loshak gave an almost imperceptible tick of his head to indicate that Darger should go ahead with the explanation. Testing her again, she figured. Damn him.

"You may have heard the terms *process* and *product* when it comes to serial killers. A process killer is interested in just that — the process. They are torturers. Stalkers. Hunters. They get pleasure from the ritual, the violent act itself, the inflicting of pain. But this guy," Darger said, raising her palms, "he has all the signs of a product killer. He kills them quickly and moves on to his actual interest. The product. The body. Like Bundy and many others, he's a necrophiliac. But the bodies don't keep, and they present logistical problems for concealment and transportation. It's tough to hide 140 pounds of rotting human flesh in your apartment. So they tend to dump them quickly, but a lot of times they keep… parts."

She tilted her head, squinting at a bare white wall of the tent.

"They progress to that point. They have to push things further and further to satisfy the control fantasy, to make it last longer. So…"

"So he takes her head," Luck said.

His gaze fell to the body lying in the weeds.

"And believe me, if he could keep the whole thing, he would," Loshak said.

A voice called out for Detective Luck from outside the tent, and one of the uniformed officers poked his head into the flap.

"Now don't come stamping in here without a suit on, Bobby," Luck said, shooing the officer back out the door.

When he returned, he held an evidence baggie in his hands. Inside was a brown leather wallet, printed with the Louis Vuitton pattern in gold. Darger suspected it was a knock-off.

"Found this with a bag and some clothes dumped on the shoulder a few blocks away," Luck explained. "Contains the driver's license of one Sierra Marie Peters."

As they drove away from the scene, a cameraman stepped into the street ahead of Darger's bumper. He held up a finger, indicating he just needed a moment to get his shot. Darger laid on the horn until he picked his tripod back up and scampered away with a scowl.

"Fucking hyenas," Loshak said, slumped in the passenger seat.

The silence that followed felt oppressive. Adrenaline had helped carry her through the time in the tent. But here in the quiet in the car, the extent of the emotional toll began to lay itself bare.

She could still hear Sierra's voice in her head. Laughing. Calling her a nerd. Talking about how happy the manicures made those old ladies. Saying how no one cared.

And maybe that was mostly true. Maybe no one cared. No one was there for her in the end. Were they? Just an ambitious FBI agent who wanted to use her for a night like all the rest.

But no. That wasn't true. It wasn't. She'd helped a girl who needed it.

"Guess we know she was tellin' you the truth now, eh?" Loshak's voice broke in, breaking the spell momentarily.

"Huh?" Darger said, her thoughts still hazy.

"I mean it's obvious to me that the guy waited around in the same place he grabbed her before. Woulda really pissed him off that she got away. Once he got over the initial fear of being caught, you know?"

"Jesus," Darger murmured. She hadn't thought about it before, hadn't quite fit all the pieces together. "That's risky as hell. For him to go back there, where someone might have recognized him? Or the car?"

"Damn right. Probably got real paranoid at first, certain we'd come busting down his door any second. I bet he made a thousand promises to himself that he'd never kill again. But when we don't come for him, all the old urges return. They always do. So he kills Fiona Worthington, thinking that'll quiet down the thoughts. But he can't stop thinking about the one that got away. Unfinished business, so to speak."

And then the horrible realization: what if it was her fault? No one could say for certain what Sierra might have done or where she might have gone had Darger not interfered, but she *had* interfered. It was her car that got her to Jimmy's. Her money that had bought the pills that had probably made Sierra more complacent. Less fearful of the monsters lurking in the shadows. If she had left it alone, if she had never come here... would Sierra still be alive? She would never know.

But she would be asking herself that question for the rest of her life. That she was sure of.

CHAPTER 21

The office of the County Coroner & Medical Examiner was in a squat brick building that shared a parking lot with a Lowes and a UPS distribution center.

Darger squirmed in one of the low-backed chairs in a small reception area, surrounded by the sound of shoes squeaking over tile floors and voices echoing down the stark cinder block hallways. Across from where she sat, a vending machine hummed a single note.

She hit the replay button on the video she'd been watching on her laptop. She couldn't stop watching and rewatching Sierra's taped interviews, searching obsessively for something they might have missed.

The hinges of a door somewhere off to her left squealed upon opening then clacked shut. Footsteps approached, but Violet barely noticed. She was immersed in the screen.

It wasn't until she sensed the rush of breath as someone plopped down into the chair next to her with a sigh and said, "Agent," that she snapped out of it, jumping a little and yanking her earbuds out.

"Startled you," he said. It was Detective Luck. "Sorry about that."

She closed her laptop and rubbed at her eyes.

"Nah, I'm on about three hours of sleep, so I'm a little jumpy."

"Came down to wait for the autopsy results, I take it?"

"Yep."

He stared at the blank wall in front of them.

"Just got done notifying the family," he said. "Worst part of the job, bar none."

Darger studied her thumbnail. The blue paint was already starting to chip. She must have been chewing while she went over the videos. She hadn't even noticed she was doing it.

"Did they want to come do a visual? Her parents?"

"It's only her mom," Luck answered. "Her dad took off when she was a kid, apparently. There's a stepdad, but he's at work. And no, thankfully she didn't insist on seeing the body. What a cluster-eff that would have been, right? 'Sorry, ma'am, we can't show you the head because there isn't one.'"

He pressed his palm to his forehead, letting his fingers slide down over his eyelids, like maybe that would make the images go away.

"The mother seemed pretty indifferent about the whole thing, honestly. Which is a bummer in its own right."

"Different people have their own way of responding to news like that," Darger said. "Sometimes what looks like insensitivity is a mask. A strong face someone puts on. Grief makes you feel vulnerable. And there are a lot of people that would rather appear apathetic than weak."

"I hear you. You never know how someone's gonna react to it. But I don't know. She was pretty darn frigid."

Luck's phone buzzed, and he excused himself to take the call. He moved off down the hallway, phone pressed to his ear as he stalked over the gleaming floor.

Darger yawned. The lack of sleep was starting to get to her. That and everything else that had happened in the last 48 hours. She crossed the small waiting area to where the vending machine clicked and buzzed. She fed it two crisp one dollar bills. In exchange, it spat out a cold 20-ounce bottle of Coca-Cola.

Back in her seat, she unscrewed the cap, releasing a burst of carbonation and with it, the recent memory of beers shared over a pizza. Half mushroom, half extra pepperoni and banana peppers. Darger tilted her head back and chugged a third of the soda in one gulp. Too bad it didn't have any alcohol in it.

Luck sank into the chair beside her. He leaned forward and rested his forearms on his knees.

"We got a vehicle description."

Darger sat up.

"One of the neighbors out for a run with her dog this morning says she saw a dark blue Buick Lacrosse. She thought 2012 or so."

"That's awfully specific."

"Well, I should say she *thinks* it was something like that. Said her ex-husband used to drive one like it, but she admitted she hadn't been looking for a make or model, so she might be off on one or both. It was coming out of that blind alley at about 5:42 AM. Has some kind of running tracker app on her phone, so it keeps track of exactly where she was in her route by the minute."

"It would match the car description Sierra gave in her original statement. A big, dark sedan."

"Got something else from her."

"Partial plate?"

"Not quite that lucky. But when we asked if there was anything distinct about the vehicle — you know, a dent, or a bumper sticker — she says she did notice something dangling from the rearview mirror."

"Tell me it wasn't a pair of fuzzy dice," Darger said.

Luck smiled.

"Nah. Something orange. Flat, like it was made of paper or cardboard or something."

"Parking pass?"

"Could be. Could be anything. A price sticker from a used car lot. An air freshener. We don't know."

As Darger readjusted in her seat, the metal surface of her brooch caught the light. She looked down at the tiny jeweled face.

"Hey — the personal effects that you found — was there a moonstone ring with the clothes or the bag?"

Luck started to shake his head, lifted a sheet of paper on his clipboard and ran his finger down a list of evidence found.

"I don't see a ring here. Why?"

"She was wearing a ring, said it was her grandmother's. Might be a good idea to check with area pawn shops to see if anyone comes in trying to hock something like that."

"A moonstone, you said?"

The pen in Luck's hand scribbled away as he bent over his clipboard.

"Yes. And the band was silver."

"That's good, thanks," he said and took out his phone. "I'm

gonna call it in right now."

She opened her computer on her lap, and for a while, her fingers tapping on the keyboard was the only sound. Detective Luck was alternating between a stack of paperwork secured to a clipboard and his phone. Minutes ticked by on the big industrial-looking clock secured over the door. After an hour, Darger couldn't take it any longer. The yawning had grown more frequent, and her eyes felt heavy and sore. All the Coke had managed to accomplish was making her need to pee three times. She stowed her laptop in her bag, curled up in the cramped little waiting room chair, and leaned her head against the wall.

She'd just rest her eyes for a few minutes.

"Agent Darger," a voice was saying. A hand rested on her shoulder, shaking her gently.

Her eyelids parted. Detective Luck hovered near her face, looking a bit amused if she wasn't mistaken.

"Sorry to interrupt your nap, but the Doc's ready for us."

Violet straightened, untucking her legs and stretching out her arms and shoulders. Her neck was still sore from the previous night, and this impromptu snooze against the brick wall hadn't helped.

Luck led her down the hall to a doorway marked by a name plaque that read: *Joyce Kennard, DO — County Medical Examiner*. The detective's knuckles rapped at the door and a woman's voice beckoned from within.

"It's open."

"Dr. Kennard," Luck said by way of introduction, "this is Special Agent Darger from the FBI."

The county medical examiner was small and slight, with silver hair cropped in a pixie cut. Something about her reminded Violet of a bird. Maybe the way she inclined her head to one side and then the other, blinking frequently. They shook hands. The doctor's fingers were cold and dry, but she had a firm grip.

"Always unfortunate to meet under such troubling circumstances, but I suppose it's the nature of the job. Good to

127

have you here, Agent Darger."

Dr. Kennard reached for a pair of glasses tucked in the pocket of her lab coat while Darger and Luck took their seats in front of her desk.

"Thanks again for doing the exam so quickly. I know it's not the norm, and you're busy as it is," Luck said.

"Happy to do my part, Detective."

She unfolded the glasses and slid them in place. There was a black leather folio in the center of the desk, and the doctor flipped it open, revealing a tablet. Pressing a button on the side, the device blinked on. With a swipe of the thumb, she brought up Sierra's file.

"I'll start out by telling you that I've found nothing to suggest this isn't the same perpetrator as the other girls. That being said, we'll have to wait for lab results to get a match on the bleach, for example."

Detective Luck rubbed at his chin.

"But you're fairly confident it's him, right?"

"All preliminary findings on my end would suggest that yes, it is the same individual," Dr. Kennard said, adjusting her glasses so they rested lower on her nose.

Luck glanced at Darger and gave a nod.

"Cause of death, in this case, is asphyxiation due to aspiration of the blood from the neck wound."

"Ah, hell," Luck said. A sigh hissed through his teeth.

Violet felt her own involuntary reaction, a tensing of every muscle in her body.

It was more common — as was the case with the other three girls — for victims of a slashing-style throat wound to die as a result of exsanguination. They simply bled out. And while it was likely of little comfort to those girls, to die choking on your own blood was surely a more painful, tortuous death.

Violet tried to tell herself it didn't matter.

She's dead, Darger thought, but she felt a pain in her chest as if someone were squeezing her heart in their fist. Her hand moved up to grip the brooch fastened there. It was a movement she made without thinking, perhaps subconsciously knowing what would come next. The memories she tried so hard to bury.

The ones that always came back.

The smell came first. Gunsmoke and the metallic stink of blood. And then the sounds. Wet, gurgling noises. Choking gasps. Crying and whispering and shushing, a voice Darger knew was her own but didn't recognize as such. And last, the images.

Gushing blood that looked black in the strange shadows cast by the streetlight overhead. Zara's lips pressing together and pulling apart, trying to speak as her strength left her. As her lifeblood matted her hair into clumps. Smeared on the pavement, leaving stains and congealed pools. Soaked into Violet's clothes and shoes as she held the girl's body and waited for the ambulance to arrive.

It wasn't sirens that Violet heard, though. It was the whistle of a train. But there had been no train that night.

Her eyelids fluttered with the realization, trying to clear the memories away. She was back. In the M.E.'s office.

"— like the others, the weapon indicated would appear to be smooth on one side and serrated on the other. Like a combat knife with a sawback."

Dr. Kennard was still giving her report. Thankfully neither she nor Detective Luck seemed to have noticed Darger's distress.

"The knife wounds to the neck caused complete severance of the larynx and trachea, as well as the carotid and jugular vessels. Complete severance, again, of the sternocleidomastoid, esophagus, and thyroid cartilage. Once he reached the cervical vertebrae, he switched to something heavier and blunter than the knife to complete the decapitation. The markings on the vertebrae would be consistent with an axe or maul."

Jesus Christ almighty. Violet was glad she was already sitting. The last thing she needed was a replay of earlier in the day. She was still squeezing the brooch on her jacket so hard that her fingers were starting to cramp. When she released her hold on it, she noticed a pattern of tiny dots imprinted on her skin where she'd gripped the hedgehog's spikes.

"Any fibers?" Luck asked.

"You know the other three had bits of sisal embedded in

129

their skin from the rope. This time we have what looks like residue left from duct tape adhesive." Dr. Kennard's finger flicked at the tablet. "We'll have to wait for the lab to confirm that. We also found bits of gravel in the superficial scrapes on the back of the heels, elbows, buttocks, and shoulder blades. As if she were dragged over a dirty, rough surface."

"Like a garage floor?" Violet chimed in, thinking of Sierra's statement from before.

Good God, what would she have thought when she woke up back in that place again?

Dr. Kennard peered at Darger over her glasses.

"Could certainly be."

"That reminds me," Luck said, taking a notepad from his pocket. He flipped through some of the pages. "I had a question for you, Doc."

"Yes?"

The doctor regarded him from over her spectacles.

"Those marks on her back," Luck said. "From the pooling of blood?"

"Livor mortis."

"Right. That's an indication that she was on her back when she died, right?"

"Not necessarily precisely when she died. It's a process. But it does mean the body was in a supine position for the majority of the six hours immediately after death."

Luck studied the notepad in his hands. He seemed nervous to Darger. Unsure of himself.

"It was just something I noticed is all, that well… The first and second victim both had the marks on their backs, too. But the third, Fiona Worthington, the marks on her suggested she was face down in the hours after death."

Dr. Kennard brought a knuckle to her lips.

"One issue is that Fiona Worthington was submerged in oil, for how long we don't know. I'd need to look into what, if any, changes might occur with decomposition when a body is in oil. There's a wealth of information on the subject of bodies found in water, but oil is another subject entirely. Is there some significance to that, you think? Her body possibly being left face down after death?"

"Well," Luck said, rubbing the back of his neck, which had turned a bit pink now, "and maybe Agent Darger can help me out with this, but I was thinking that maybe it was a sign that Fiona was different from the other victims somehow. Like maybe he didn't want to look her in the eye while he went about the dismemberment."

He chanced a sheepish look at Darger. She remembered being at the dumpster crime scene then, critiquing Detective Luck's interview transcript and finding them lacking because of a misspelling. But perhaps there was more to him than she'd originally thought.

Of course, his theory contradicted her own. In fact, her own interpretation would have been that the killer *wanted* the girls watching him during the process. Fiona was different not because he didn't want her to watch, but because he didn't care. In fact, maybe he'd placed her face down while he worked so he could pretend it was Sierra Peters.

"That's… possible," was all she said. "I'll be sure to mention it to Agent Loshak."

Luck shrugged, trying to dismiss the potential importance.

"Anyway, it was just a thought."

He cleared his throat and refocused his attention on the forensic pathologist.

"What about bodily fluids?"

"We took swabs of everything. But like the others, I suspect the bleach will have rendered any samples useless as far as DNA or blood-typing goes. Doesn't hurt to keep our fingers crossed, though."

Luck lifted his hands and created an X with each fore and middle finger.

"I'll keep 'em both crossed in that case."

CHAPTER 22

The steering wheel shivers in his hands. Pulsing. Throbbing. Vibrations coil from the engine into his flesh. The tremor travels through his palms and forearms and elbows. Dissipating somewhere in the upper arms. Absorbed by the meat.

The stoplight shines red like a Christmas light. Tints the street scarlet. He waits. He watches. Eyes blinking in slow motion.

The duffel bag shimmers in the corner of his eye. A blurred spot shuddering above it like heat distortion. He knows this isn't real. That the shine wafting off of the bag exists only in his head. That the electric poke he felt when he placed his hands upon it earlier was a similar delusion.

The light flicks to green and the movement resumes. The car stalks forward. Its momentum somehow confident. Hungry.

He licks his lips. Twice. Hesitates.

"I'm not always like this."

His voice sounds thick. Sleepy. He clears his throat.

"I mean, I didn't want it to be this way."

His head snaps to the right and snaps back. He can't look at it for long. Can't maintain eye contact.

"It was the only way. That's all. It was the only way I could have you."

He knows that this, too, isn't real. It's a make-believe conversation he's attempting to strike up. It's pretend. But he wants it. He wants to believe it a little.

He's not insane. A little weird maybe but not insane. He wishes he was. That would probably make it easier.

Again he glances that way. His head swiveling in slow motion. The muscles in his neck twitching and quaking. The cords there stand taut. It is somehow a strain to turn his head a quarter of the way.

But he does it. Holds it. Looks.

The zippered mouth of the bag hangs open. Flaps parted as

though in surprise.

He can see the face in profile there in the opening. Her face. Nose pointing at the ceiling. Eyelids open barely a slit. The cheek bone stands out. The skin still drawn tight there. Smooth. She looks pale. Bled white like a maggot. But otherwise, she looks good. He can't quite make out the jagged edge where the neck once connected to the torso. Maybe that's for the better.

Electricity thrums through his veins as he takes the sight in. It jolts in his head. Coursing and popping. Behind his crooked eye. Behind his blank and empty face. Current radiating deep within his skull.

His breathing changes. Grows ragged. His heart pummels at the walls of his chest.

Looking at her, he wants to go back. Feels the draw to return to the scene like a wolf hearing the howl. Something animal. Primal. He wants to go back. Needs to go back. To feel it again. To live it again.

But no. No.

Not tonight.

It's a risk. Too big of a risk with that FBI bitch lurking. He'd seen the two of them together. He pushes the urge down. Shoves it away. For now.

Still, he's too keyed up to sleep. Wired.

He's not sure how long it's been since he slept. Three days? Four?

It matters not for now. Slumber isn't an option. It won't be for a long time yet.

He drives. That's all. He lets his eyes drift back to the road.

And the void is right there. All around him. Black nothing that stretches out forever in all directions.

He needs to go somewhere. To let the electricity in his skull burn out a little.

And he knows just the place.

CHAPTER 23

Darger had expected just the lead investigators from each case to be present at the meeting. Instead, there were the three detectives, two sheriffs, a chief of police, one prosecutor and two assistant DAs at his side, along with a handful of uniformed men.

Donaldson greeted her at the door and guided her over to the Athens County Sheriff.

"Sheriff O'Day, this is Special Agent Darger."

"There are two of you now, eh?" he asked rhetorically, shaking her hand in that confident way all politicians had. "Where's Agent Loshak?"

"On his way, I'm sure," she said.

Darger didn't tell him that Loshak hadn't answered his phone or responded to the several texts she'd sent. She figured he'd forgotten about her, even though she'd reminded him about the meeting twice before she left for the Medical Examiner's office.

Maybe it was his passive-aggressive way of telling her he wasn't as amiable to her being there as she'd initially thought.

"You sure you don't want a lift?" Luck had asked when Loshak hadn't picked up after their meeting with Dr. Kennard had ended.

"No, go on ahead. I'm sure he'll be here any minute," she said.

When Loshak didn't show, Darger had to call another Uber.

But the meeting had been going for ten minutes now, and there was still no sign of him. She started to get nervous. The Sheriff had specifically mentioned the "friends from the FBI" and how they'd "offer their insight" later on in the meeting. What if Loshak didn't show up?

She'd coordinated with local law enforcement before. But never for something like this. Never for a serial murder case.

It was Sheriff O'Day who finally took to the podium at the

front of the room and called the meeting to order. She supposed everyone was comfortable deferring to him considering they were in his building.

"I'd like to start off by saying that all information at this meeting is considered restricted in terms of the press and the public — no one should be talking to the press without express permission anyway. But the same goes for when you're at home. Anyone not in this room is on a need-to-know basis."

His eyes flitted about the room, and several of the task force members nodded like dutiful school children.

"Earlier this week we got the lab results back on the bleach samples from the first two victims. They are the same chemical composition, and the lab traced the samples to the brand name Tandil. Obtainable only at Aldi stores, which I'm sure most of you know we do have locally here in Athens, but also all over Ohio."

He glanced down at a computer printout.

"Over 60 stores in the state, and about seven are within an hour driving distance from Athens proper. Obviously we'll have to wait a bit longer to confirm that the bleach on the most recent victim is a match. The contamination on the third body makes a verification there unlikely."

Darger frowned down at the sheet that was circulated around the room. She made note of her concerns in that regard for later.

"Why don't we have the lead investigator for the newest fill us all in. Detective Luck?"

At first, Luck had the look of a kid who had been doing his damnedest to go unnoticed and had gotten called on by the teacher anyway. He stood, buttoned the top button of his jacket, and seemed to grow a little taller. He didn't falter when he began to give the room a run-down of the newest murder. He started with the who, where, and when, moving over to a projector connected to a laptop to show a few photographs of the scene. Darger forced herself to look, though she'd seen quite enough of the images of Sierra's defiled body to last a lifetime.

After that, the detective moved on to the M.E.'s report, summarizing the cause of death, probable weapons used, and the trace evidence collected.

"We also know now where Sierra was the first time she was abducted, and have every reason to believe that she was in the same place this time."

Janssen raised his hand and chimed in.

"Sorry, but why the hell would we assume that?"

"The vehicle," Luck's eyes glanced almost imperceptibly in Darger's direction. "The car Sierra Peters was driving was found parked on the street near the first abduction location. It also happens to be on the same street as her dealer, Jimmy Congdon."

"Great. I assume you got that shitbird in a cell as we speak, awaiting questioning."

"A CSI team is en route to collect the car, as well as an arrest unit for Jimmy."

"Wait, what?" Darger said. "An arrest unit?"

Luck smoothed his tie.

"That's right."

Her head was moving back and forth, partially in disbelief. She was appreciative that he'd covered for her, not blurting out that it was *her* car Sierra had been driving. Her car, that she'd been stupid enough to allow to be stolen. But this was the wrong move, and she couldn't just sit by and let it happen.

"Why would you arrest him? He's probably the last person who saw Sierra Peters alive."

Luck stared at her, not following.

"I'm confused. You're saying that *because* he's the last person to see her, we *shouldn't* arrest him?"

"Who the hell are you?"

Janssen was looking her up and down with wariness.

The Sheriff piped up as if she were incapable of speaking for herself, "Sorry, this is Special Agent," he gestured with his hand like he was trying to conjure a rabbit from a hat, "Darwin, is it?"

"Darger," she said through gritted teeth.

"Where's Loshak?" Janssen said.

"I've been asked to fill in for Agent Loshak for the time being," Darger said, embellishing a little.

Well, technically it was true. Cal had sent her out here

essentially for that purpose. And it was a good thing, too, considering the fact that he wasn't here.

She turned her attention back to Luck at the front of the room.

"My point, Detective Luck, is that Jimmy Congdon is already likely going to be a combative witness. Arresting him and treating him like a criminal is only going to make things worse."

"He has a record," Luck reminded her.

Like she'd somehow forgotten. She wanted to point out that if it weren't for her, they wouldn't even know about Jimmy Congdon, but she refrained.

"That may be, but if we approach him like he's guilty of something, he's never going to talk to us."

"You're saying we should roll out the red carpet for a known drug dealer?" Janssen said.

"I'm not saying we have to go pick him up in a limo, for Christ's sake," she snapped, then tried to reel it in. "I'm only suggesting that a more gentle, amiable approach might be more likely to gain his cooperation."

"Gentle and amiable. Un-fucking-believable," Janssen muttered loud enough for everyone to hear. "How do we know this Jimmy guy isn't the killer?"

"Because he doesn't fit the profile. He's too young. Too well-connected socially. We're looking for a loner. And the timeline of the abductions and body dumps have been consistent with someone working a first shift, Monday to Friday job. Congdon is technically unemployed."

She turned her focus back on Luck.

"Call it off. Now. Before it's too late. We'll only get the one chance. If you turn him against us, he'll never talk."

He seemed to consider it momentarily, but Janssen butted in again.

"Maybe he doesn't want to miss an episode of his favorite TV show?" Janssen said, only half-joking.

Loshak, where the hell are you? she wondered, sending out a psychic bat signal.

Janssen continued.

"Who can say why he does anything? Could be coincidence, couldn't it?"

Darger said nothing, trying not to lose her temper.

Cops loved nothing more than to assign the term *coincidence* to anything that didn't fit their personal theory, while at the same time insisting that any circumstantial evidence that proved their position was anything but.

Targeting Luck again, she sat forward.

"You're being short-sighted. You're going to throw away our best chance at catching a serial killer — a man who's butchered at least four women that we know of — for a petty criminal like Jimmy Congdon?"

Maybe it was her tone, or maybe it was the phrasing, but she'd obviously taken a wrong turn. Luck fixed her with a hard stare.

"Do you know how many overdose deaths we have in this county every year? That's not counting everything else that goes along with the drug trade: the robberies, the assaults, the prostitution, the toddlers left home alone wondering if mommy's gonna come back or if she'll stay passed out in whatever craphole she went to get her fix."

His face was red and the emotion in his voice wasn't phony.

"That may be petty to the FBI, but it sure as hell isn't in the eyes of our department."

Luck straightened a little taller, standing his ground.

"Sorry, Agent, but this is my call. My investigation."

Yours to fuck up, you mean, she thought to herself.

"Well, after that lively debate," Sheriff O'Day said, "why don't we turn over the floor to the Special Agent so she can fill us in from the profiling angle?"

Special Agent, Violet thought. She was certain he'd already forgotten her name again as she rose from her chair.

Luck took his seat and Darger replaced him at the podium. She wasn't sure how much Loshak had gone over with them, so she started from the top. She decided to leave out her pet theory about Fiona Worthington merely being a stand-in for Sierra Peters. It was still Loshak's investigation more than hers, and she wanted to tread lightly when it came to contradicting him.

138

They were a dutiful audience until she got to the head.

"Cutting off the head," one of the uniformed officers said. "That's like, depersonalization, right?"

Darger shook her head.

"Just the opposite. When a killer wants to depersonalize a victim, they'll often either cover the face or mutilate it somehow. Cutting or beating until it's unrecognizable. Removing the identity in some way. Making it 'just a body.' It can indicate remorse or shame. But not always."

She used the computer to flash through several photos of the first three victims.

"This guy leaves the faces untouched throughout the task of dismembering them. He *wants* them to still be a person. So much so that this time, he kept her head. Of all the possible parts, the face is the one that marks her as an individual more than any other."

The glare from the projector blocked Darger from seeing who asked the next question.

"The last two were dumped within Athens city limits. Doesn't that mean he's probably a local?"

There were murmurs among the group. Some seemed to be in agreement — mostly those from outside of Athens PD who no doubt wanted to believe it couldn't be one of their own.

"We don't know how much significance that has. For one, Sierra Peters was a break in a lot of the previous patterns."

"Looks like the same sick fuck to me," Janssen offered.

"Oh, I don't have any doubt that it's him, but I think he was rushed on this one. No stab wounds, no mutilation other than the decapitation, of course, plus the fact that he dumped her within about 24 hours instead of the usual 48-72 hours. He was in a hurry to get it done. And I think he was in a hurry to dump her."

"Doesn't that strengthen my point? He's a local guy, so instead of driving all the way out to Bumfuck, Egypt, he dumps this one close to home."

"It's possible," Darger said, trying to keep her tone level.

Something about Janssen rubbed her the wrong way. Also she was starting to get a mean headache.

"But even in a rush, he's still careful. I doubt he'd tip off where he lived that easily."

"Guy's a fuckin' psycho who gets his kicks cuttin' girls into pieces. How careful can he be?"

Darger ignored him, wishing again that Loshak was there to back her up. Massaging her right temple with a fingertip, she continued.

"There's another issue about the dump sites that I think we should all consider."

She gestured at the map projected onto the wall.

"Two different counties. Three separate jurisdictions so far. I don't think that's an accident."

"What do you mean?"

"I mean that your average citizen doesn't have a lot of knowledge of that kind of thing. City PD, Sheriff's Department, State Troopers… cops are cops to most people."

"You're saying you think he's a cop," Detective Luck said and there was plenty of grumbling dissent that followed.

"Not necessarily." Darger raised her voice over the din. "In fact, I think not."

"You just said—" Jannsen started.

"I said I didn't think he was your average citizen, in terms of police knowledge. But I also don't think he's in law enforcement. He wouldn't have the discipline."

That seemed to quell them a bit.

"However, it's possible that he's someone in the periphery of law enforcement. EMT, volunteer fire, or maybe a cop groupie."

"Possible, possible. Everything's 'possible' with you guys. Sounds like a bunch of mumbo-jumbo to me," Janssen said with a dismissive wave of his hand. "Might as well consult my kid's Magic 8-Ball."

"And you're welcome to take it or leave it, Detective Janssen," Darger said. "It's your case. Your board to clear. Not mine."

The room was quiet then, and she let it sink in. As elected officials, she knew the pair of Sheriffs involved were more than a little anxious to clear these homicides, and the only way that happened was finding the guy.

"Alright," Janssen spoke up again, "let's say you're right. He's from out of town. Maybe even from somewhere like Columbus. Why not dump the girls there? Murders are a dime a dozen in the city."

"For two reasons. One is for exactly the reason you said. He doesn't want to be a dime a dozen. He wants the spotlight. Even if that's not the case at first, these guys almost always find that they like the attention. The second reason is that, this being a rural area, he might be aware that you lack investigators with a lot of homicide experience."

It all came out in a rush. She'd been in the zone and wasn't thinking about the phrasing or the effects the words might have. But she immediately realized her mistake. What sounded to her like an innocent fact would come off as a dig to the men in this room, and not just the ones looking to fight, like Janssen.

Another silence followed, this one seeming more strained than the first.

Well, shit.

Janssen crossed his arms over his chest.

"What're you trying to say?"

Luck had been quiet for a while, but he spoke now. His eyes remained focused on his hands folded on the tabletop in front of him.

"I reckon she's trying to say that us country folk are in over our heads."

He effected a slight twang to his voice, which should have been funny but only highlighted more that he was angry.

Before she could defend herself or her words, the sound of someone clearing their throat broke through the awkward tension in the room.

"Why don't we wrap things up there for now?" Sheriff O'Day said, consulting his watch.

It was past five o'clock. She was sure he was rarely in the office this late most days.

Chairs scraped and voices babbled to one another. Violet raised her hand in the air.

"Could I speak to the lead detectives for a moment?"

Luck, Janssen, and Donaldson gathered around. Deputy

Donaldson rested his hands on his utility belt and looked attentive. Janssen regarded her with open disdain. Detective Luck, on the other hand, wouldn't meet her eyes at all.

She considered trying to make amends for the poor wording earlier but decided against it. Donaldson would probably accept the apology in earnest. Janssen would see it as weakness. And Luck… she didn't know how to read him at the moment. It could go either way. If he took it as insincere, she'd only dig herself deeper. Better to bulldoze forward.

"I think it would be wise to ask around among the escort community in the area, see if any of the girls have had a John recently who was… *off*. They usually have a pretty good read on that kind of thing, but they're often too afraid to report it, for obvious reasons."

Janssen scoffed.

"Escort community? Should we check their monthly newsletter?"

That was it. Darger squared her shoulders toward him and let out a slow breath.

"Actually, Detective Janssen. I had a specific question for you."

He grinned, mouth full of coffee-stained teeth.

"Yeah? And what's that?"

Darger leaned across the table and pulled the new forensic report closer.

"Am I reading this right… that the bleach samples for your murder weren't submitted to the crime lab until after the second body was found?"

"That's right."

"Can I ask why?"

"I don't know, can you?"

Janssen sneered, looking amused with himself.

Darger met Janssen's cold stare. Her third-grade teacher had used that exact same line whenever a student asked *Can I go to the bathroom* instead of *May I go to the bathroom*. Darger had always thought Mrs. Horvath was just asking for one of them to piss their pants in the middle of her classroom. Darger waited, and eventually Janssen pursed his lips and answered the question.

"Look, the first girl… the stripper? We had no reason to suspect it was anything more than a working girl who crossed paths with the wrong guy. Or maybe a pissed off pimp or dealer."

"Can we refer to the victims by name, please?"

He didn't look at her. Instead, he glanced at Luck, and they exchanged a look. Like Darger couldn't see them? She knew what they were thinking, too. *This bitch.*

"Cristal Monroe," he said, voice thick with attitude, "was an addict and worked at a club we know sells sex on the side. What were we supposed to think?"

"I still don't see your point. Or do you always conduct a half-assed investigation if you assume the victim was a sex worker or an addict?"

He exploded, leaping forward to shout in her face.

"Fuck you, half-assed!"

Darger took a startled step back. Donaldson and Luck moved into the gap between them, acting as a buffer.

"As far as I'm concerned, you can take your assessment or profile or whatever the hell you call it and shove it up your tight, little FBI ass."

He wadded up the sheet of paper with the profile notes on it and tossed it on the ground as he stomped through the door.

Darger listened to the thud of his boots recede down the hallway. She'd known it would piss him off, but he had more of a hair-trigger temper than she'd expected.

"You really know how to rally the troops, Agent Darger," Luck said, slipping past her on his way out the door.

She thought about going after him to try to apologize, but her pride wouldn't let her.

Not willing to press the hospitality of anyone on the task force, Darger opted to walk back to her motel. It wasn't too far, maybe three miles at most. She could use the exercise and the time to gather her thoughts. She was three blocks from the Sheriff's office when she heard the distinct rumble of an engine slowing behind her.

Her first thought, irrational as it was, was Sierra's

recollection of the first abduction. That was what she'd noticed first, after all: the sound of the car coming up the street.

It was a split second thing, but something her training had taught her to do: orient herself to her surroundings and to the location of her weapon, should she need it. There was a brick half-wall to her right, an ornamental feature she could dive behind if she needed to. As for her weapon, it was in her holster. She could have it in-hand in seconds.

There was a whining sound that she recognized as an automatic window rolling down.

"Need a ride?"

Darger turned. It was Deputy Donaldson.

Well, if he was offering…

Turning on her boot heel, she crossed the sidewalk and climbed into the car.

"I wanted to apologize. If you took offense to anything I said during the meeting, that wasn't my intent."

Confusion clouded his face for a beat, then cleared.

"Oh, the country bumpkin stuff."

She opened her mouth to explain that Luck had been the one that said 'country folk,' not her. But perhaps it wasn't the time for nitpicking.

"For my part, ma'am," Donaldson said, "I harbor no such indignation. You ask me, it's a damn good thing to be in a jurisdiction with such a low murder rate. Who wouldn't want that? The big city detectives can keep their so-called experience. It's not worth the cost of doing business."

Violet stared through the windshield, watching a line of maples go by in a blur.

"You have a point."

"As for your presentation, I found it all quite helpful."

"Thanks," she mumbled.

Traffic was thick in downtown Athens. They joined a long line of cars waiting to turn left at an intersection, and for a while the only noise was the periodic crackle of the dispatcher over Donaldson's radio.

"If you're in the mood to socialize, there's a place not far from here," he said. "Place you can unwind a little, maybe get to know the locals."

"Maybe some other time," Darger said. "But thank you."

Her head was almost throbbing now, and the thought of being in a loud bar surrounded by a bunch of cops who would sooner or later have it whispered in their ears that she was some big city FBI lady who thought she shit gold appealed to her not at all. She just wanted to get back to her motel and knock this headache out with an Advil and some sleep. Maybe a hot bath first.

Once they made it out of the downtown area, traffic lightened, and it was a short drive the rest of the way to the motel.

She slid down to the tarmac and thanked Donaldson for the ride.

"No trouble at all," he said, and then he was gone.

Before she let herself into her room, she marched over to Loshak's door. It was a moment before he answered, looking haggard.

"You look like shit," she said.

"And what a delight it is to see you, too, Agent Darger."

He left the door open and went back into his room. She followed him inside.

"I didn't mean to sound like an asshole," she said, realizing that it was apparently becoming a habit for her to be unintentionally insulting. "Where were you?"

"Where do you think? I was here."

Darger pressed the back of her hand over her eye. The pressure relieved the pain in her head ever so slightly.

"The meeting, Loshak. You missed the meeting."

"Aw shit," he said. "Shit, I'm sorry. How'd it go?"

"Fine," Darger said, too quickly. She scrunched her eyes up. "For the most part. I wasn't exactly prepared, you know."

Loshak chuckled to himself.

"Yeah, I bet you hate that."

Her head throbbed. She was tired. And hungry. And pissed off at herself. And not in the mood for Loshak's needling.

"What's that supposed to mean?"

"Oh nothing," Loshak said, leaning back on the bed with his hands tucked behind his head.

"Are you analyzing me?"

"Lord, no. Absolutely not."

"Because two can play at that game. This whole denial thing with you about being sick? You're beyond Type A. You're like Type Triple A Plus."

"Yeah, and you know what Freud would have had to say about your fingernail chewing."

Darger had the urge to hide her hands behind her back. Sierra had also picked up on it, and she hated that people noticed that about her. She made sure to never do it in front of people, but the more observant always saw the signs.

"And what would he have said about your being a stubborn perfectionist?"

"Anal fixation? Really? And just because I prefer things to be done a certain way does not make me a perfectionist."

Darger snorted and headed for the door, which was still open.

"Where are you going?"

"To sleep."

CHAPTER 24

The Elbow Room was a cop bar on Court Street in downtown Athens. It was just around the corner from the Athens City Police Department. Less than a block. And though it hosted any number of civilian patrons from night to night, the bulk of the local law enforcement workers comprised the regulars. Everyone from high-ranking members of the administration down to the freshest rookies occupied the stools at the bar nightly, and a few judges and attorneys from the area made frequent appearances as well. Its reputation as a cop bar was so strong, in fact, that deputies and underlings from jurisdictions as far away as Zaleski made the trip to Court Street a weekend ritual.

Kurt knew all of this well. He'd hung out here often for the last several years, listening to the cops tell stories, befriending them, at least so far as several considered him a drinking buddy. He felt as comfortable walking among them as he did any other group of humans. It wasn't so hard to hide among the crowd, he knew. Any crowd.

Parking the Buick in the lot out back had come with a certain thrill, what with the severed head in the bag in the passenger seat. His whole body tingled, needle pricks rippling up and down him as the car juddered over the pot holes and found a vacant spot. When he killed the engine, the tickle intensified in the quiet, brimming over into a painful itch. He clenched his teeth, jaw muscles flexing. After a deep breath, the itch died back to a throb.

He'd zipped the duffel bag up en route and now considered trying to stow it on the floor, but it didn't feel right, so he left it. He ran a hand over the rough texture of its material, a fingertip dragging over the interlocking zipper teeth. No electrical pulses assailed him this time. Ah well.

Yellow streetlights buzzed overhead, shining down on the chewed up blacktop and faded vinyl siding of the bar. No one stirred in the lot. No movement at all.

His fingertips found the door handle, and again, he left the strange insulation of the car, stepping out into the cold. He felt naked in the open air, the frigidity reaching right through his thin jacket and t-shirt to chill the flesh of his torso. He took a deep breath reflexively at the shock of it, and the cold sucked right down into his lungs, biting all the way down, making him shudder. It smelled like snow outside. Seemed strange for October.

His breath coiled in the air before him as he walked the concrete walk to the big wooden door, a ball of steam twisting and disappearing into empty space. He stopped shy of the door and waited, the thumping rhythm of the music inside faintly audible. It had been weird to think of the writhing mass of cops inside those walls.

After a long hesitation, he slipped into the bar and was absolved once more of the detachment. The old reality snapped back, some lost feeling restored, like waking up refreshed after being tired for so long he'd forgotten what that felt like. Even here, surrounded by cops, he found an overwhelming relief to be back among people, away from the loneliness. On another level, it was tense, of course, but he'd been here so many times. He could keep the fear in a little compartment and go through the normal routine unperturbed.

Bare brick walls and button tufted leather booth seats gave the place a rustic feel, but the warmth and lighting dominated his sensory circuits. It was hot in here, the air almost heavy with body heat. Sweaty. And the light controlled the atmosphere. Made him feel calm even with all the people flitting around. The dimly lit space seemed forever dulled to a soft focus, even when he was completely sober.

He nodded a greeting to familiar faces, collecting smiles and waves in return. Funny how that worked, he thought. He'd barely spoken to most of these people, but they must be able to call to mind memories of seeing him whilst drunk, perhaps watching at the edge of the crowd, laughing along with the stories and jokes, and that was enough. Somehow that nothing level of interaction had become a positive association, deemed him worthy of a subtle greeting. If he were a handsome man, he thought perhaps one of the lady cops or police groupies would have hit on him, even, but it hadn't happened. For once, being ugly provided a perk. He wanted to remain mostly anonymous. Unnoticed.

He scanned the room as he advanced toward the bar, squinting to make out detail in the shadowy areas toward each far corner. A fat man with a sports jacket over his polo shirt lifted his bottle of beer at him to say hello. He was bald on top with messy hair hanging down on the back and sides. This was John Wayne Porto, the Athens detective who ran his mouth about the case on the regular, the one Kurt was hoping to see tonight. The one he would sit near. The one who, if all went well, would tell him where the investigation stood.

Kurt plucked a bill from his pocket as he neared the bar. His heart beat a little faster as he waited for the bartender's eyes to find his, and when they did, he had to concentrate to keep his voice from wavering as he ordered a Budweiser. It was strange that ordering a beer made him more uptight than being around so many police, but seeing the detective made his adrenaline kick in or something. He remembered seeing a video about that being a poker tell. When a player has a big hand, their fingers tremble from the adrenaline.

He licked his lips. As soon as he had the drink in hand, he could disappear into the crowd and be no one again. Soon. He cleared his throat while he waited, let his eyes go a little out of focus, staring at the wall of bottles behind the bar but not really seeing them. Finally, the barkeep scooted the brew his way, and he took the glass to a table near the detective.

He sat in the part of the room where those dim lights began to give way to the shadows. He sipped his drink, looking at nothing and watching everything out of the corners of his eyes. The people roiled around him, strange hairless apes smiling and yammering at each other and clapping each other on the back, totally unaware of the Other in their presence. The still, silent figure sitting amongst all of their swirling motion, his shoulders rigid, a glass of beer sweating on the table in front of him.

There was something fun about it. Fooling all of them.

Duping the very people tasked with weeding out his kind. He couldn't help but smirk.

The bar seemed a little quiet tonight. Hushed murmurs overtaking the room in place of boisterousness. Voices all tight and small. None of the raucous cheer he usually encountered among these off-duty guys. He couldn't decide if this was a reverent quiet or a sleepy one. Would word about the latest kill have gotten around already? He supposed so. It had been more than 12 hours since he had disposed of the bags, though it didn't really feel like it.

As if on cue, shushes rose up from the mob and the murmurs fell off into total quiet. He swiveled his head just as the bartender turned up the volume on the biggest screen mounted over the bar. It was the Channel 4 news, the NBC affiliate out of Columbus.

The anchor's head occupied the screen, her bleached white teeth standing out from the orange glow of her tan. And a graphic of a garbage bag appeared over her shoulder.

"In another brutal twist in the ongoing story out of Athens County, a dismembered body was discovered in a trash bag in a residential area on the south side of Athens in the early morning hours, the fourth such body in recent weeks."

All sound seemed to fade out around Kurt as she went on. He watched her lips move, but he heard nothing. That itchy vibration crawled over his skin again, a crackle flickering in his head like the blue beam in one of those bug zapping lamps. He sipped his beer, unable to pry his eyes from the TV screen where the camera panned across the scene. It was old footage, he realized, from Burger King. The garbage bag there, the pool of blood surrounding it on the concrete shining back more black than red. The puddle looked thick. Shiny and gummy. Like the ring of leftover ketchup drying on the plate.

He flinched, unable to contain himself. One hard jerk of the shoulders and abs that throttled his body so hard that the legs of his chair scraped audibly over the floor as it scooted a few inches back from his table.

He froze. Eyes locked on the scuffed tabletop. Back hunched like one of those rats in the live traps.

After a long, still moment, he looked around. All eyes remained glued to the TV screen. No one had noticed his flailing, or if they had, they didn't care.

And it was now almost an out-of-body experience for him. His consciousness seeming to pull away from his person. Floating. Hovering. All sight and sound reduced to something fizzy, his mind retracting into the static of the abstract.

He swallowed, and it felt distant. Remote. Like it wasn't real at all.

A rectangular blob in the static dissolved, and the TV news anchor appeared there, talking directly into the camera, a sober expression on her makeup-caked face. He could tell that she was stuck up just looking at her. One of those haughty, la-de-da types. His teeth ground together, and something about the sensation of his jaw muscles tightening brought him back to the moment, brought him back to his body, turned the sound back on as the camera cut to the male anchor with teeth so white they must glow in the dark. The graphic next to the anchor's head had changed. No more garbage bag. Now it was a pot leaf. He talked about a string of robberies at local medical marijuana dispensaries.

The piece about the body was over. Good.

He took a breath, and once again his whole body tingled from head to toe, but this time it was different. More pleasant. Some orgasmic jolt of pleasure that he didn't really understand. Was it the attention? It must be. He was the top story. The case had made the news before, but now he was number one. He was the headline. He'd made something of himself.

And yet he could see his reflection on the table's veneer, and his facial expression remained completely blank. Fixed. Unblinking. His eyes pierced the empty space before him.

He sipped his beer again. Nursing it. He wouldn't drink enough to get drunk, he knew. He'd only have one or two depending on how long he sat here. But he didn't want to be so slow about it that someone might notice.

The chatter picked up now that the bit about the dismembered body was over, and the bartender mashed the remote in his fist, turning the volume on the TV back down.

"Sick fuck," Detective Porto said over his shoulder. "He kept the head. Probably defiling it right now. You know what I mean?"

The detective locked eyes with Kurt, so he nodded to answer the question.

"I mean the sicko is probably face-fucking the thing as we speak," Porto said. "That's what these perverts do. Like Ted Bundy and those types."

For a long moment, the two men just stared at each other, Porto's face as expressionless and unreadable as he knew his own to be. Neither of them blinked. The corners of the detective's mouth curled then, and he burst out laughing.

"Sorry," he said. "Guess I'm a sick fuck, too. Not like this monster or nothin', but still…"

Kurt laughed as well, and Porto clapped him on the shoulder.

"Jesus," Porto said. "What the hell is wrong with us, eh? I guess you have to be able to laugh to keep from cryin', you know?"

He tipped his bottle of Sam Adams back and glugged the second half of it down, signaling the bartender for another with a wave of the hand.

"You gonna catch the guy?" Kurt said.

Porto's smile vanished all at once.

"Oh, we'll get 'im. It might not be anytime too soon, but we'll get the bastard. I promise you that."

Kurt bobbed his head once.

"I'm sure you will."

He sipped at his Budweiser and turned back to his own table, content to recede back to the edges of things. That was where he was most comfortable, he supposed. An observer. An outsider.

An Other.

He couldn't remember for sure when the distance first opened in his head, the black seas of infinity that held him apart from everything and everyone. People had hurt him when he was young. Blurry memories — just flashes of her face twisted into a mask of hatred, the gouges in his skin where her fingernails had torn him open. A cliché story, he supposed.

The wounds became the cracks in his reality where the void seeped into him, and through the years, the little boy's weakness became the man's strength. The numb blossomed in him, made him invulnerable. Every one of his acts cemented this transformation. Proved it. And now he could sit among the very police looking for him and go unnoticed, totally indistinguishable from anyone else.

That was life's great secret that only people like him could truly grasp. No one could see what was behind any of those faces in the crowd. No one.

He listened to the cops jabber on for a time, but he knew now that he had nothing to learn from these people. They were clueless. He shouldn't be surprised.

"Way the FBI agents put it, the guy is a puss," a flat-topped street cop said. "That's what I heard anyhow. Said he's a, ah, inadequate type. Too timid to get his pecker up with the girls, so he freaks out and goes on a killing spree."

The pudgy guy next to him snorted before he replied.

"Christ, almighty. Someone tell this guy about Viagra for fuck's sake. Might save some lives."

He pulled the little card from his jacket pocket and looked at it, the one he'd found among the girl's things. Violet Darger, huh? Yeah. Probably just as stuck up as she looked.

CHAPTER 25

Victor Loshak was suffering worse than he let on. Dizzy. Shaky. His thoughts distorted by the whims of the fever. In his loopiest fever dream moments, he even thought he might be dying.

He lay on his lumpy motel mattress, blanket pulled up to his neck, unable to stave off the occasional shiver. A grimace etched deep grooves into his face, puckered his lips. He wasn't sweating anymore. He didn't know if that was a good sign or a bad one going forward, but he was thankful to be rid of the sogginess that had plagued him off and on over the past few days.

The TV projected blue flickers onto the drop ceiling, which he watched rather than the screen itself, too weak and confused to lift his neck or sit upright. He tried to sleep, but his eyelids kept peeling open to watch the light show up there. The glow lurched and danced in never ending variations.

He'd pushed himself too hard in venturing to the latest dump site. He knew that now. He'd wanted to be there as much for Darger's sake as his. She seemed to know her stuff, and she was more than eager enough to do a damn good job, but he was still the one with 21 years of experience. He figured he could help her one way or another, even if it was just encouragement. Of course, being there when a body was discovered had a way of bringing the behavior into sharper focus sometimes, too. And the police officers working the case always seemed to trust him more if he'd been there at the awful moment when they worked a fresh scene. In any case, he was paying the price for that choice now.

The fever had come back worse than before, and his thoughts jumbled and circled around themselves, bordering on hallucinatory much of the time. Bits of memories and dreams bobbed up into his conscious mind, movies playing that interrupted his internal monologue over and over.

He squirmed a little on the mattress, moving his arms and legs for no reason that he could figure. He had no sense of what time it might be. Had a night passed since he'd ventured out? Could it have been longer? The shades were drawn tight, offering him no clues.

He closed his eyes and thought about the case, grisly crime scene photos blinking on and off in his head like Christmas bulbs. The jagged wounds. That limbless, bloody stump of a torso. The rage toward women evident here was appalling, but he'd seen its kind many times. What stuck out to him more was the incredible feeling of inadequacy it implied.

Some of the guys committing these types of lust murders were run-of-the-mill rapists who developed a taste for murder and necrophilia by way of escalation, pushing their sense of depravity and control to the limit. The murderer working in Athens County was not one of those. Loshak was certain of it. He was a member of a much smaller group: killers who think so little of themselves that they become convinced the only way they can satisfy their biological urge to reproduce is by doing so with a dead body. This twisted fantasy exists in them before they ever start killing.

All of the evidence pointed to that type. Killing a woman was, of course, an expression of rage rather than one of sexuality, but the act was still clearly entwined with this desperate desire to assert oneself. There was a damaged sense of masculinity driving these things, Loshak thought. A sense of worthlessness.

This guy in Athens had an exceptional sense of inadequacy, and what struck him as most noteworthy about that were those signs of sophistication poking through despite that. The perpetrator was confident enough in his verbal skills to talk victims into getting into his car, at least some of the time, and he was organized enough to perform the abductions, murders, and disposals of the bodies without leaving much physical evidence. So this was a capable, possibly even intelligent, person who also had such deep fears and insecurities about women that necrophilia was the only way he could even fantasize about being with one.

But that raised the money question: How could the police use that information to help solve the case? He didn't know. Not yet.

His mind drifted for a time, nonsensical fragments of dreams rising up mercifully to erase the violent images from his head. He was in and out like that for a while, neither truly awake nor asleep. Hovering between them.

Shelly was there in some of the dream flashes, and she was OK. Just little snippets of random moments. Plopping onto the couch and pulling her laptop open on her lap. Sitting at a picnic table, eating a strawberry sundae at Dairy Queen. He liked seeing her in dreams now. When his daughter had first died, he couldn't handle the misery of dreaming her back into existence only to wake up and lose her again, but now he was just happy to see her, knowing down deep that it wasn't quite real.

In his most lucid moments, he knew that he needed help, that he should go to the doctor, but he couldn't bring himself to do it. He'd always been reluctant to seek medical treatment. Some phobia of the doctor's touch. And he supposed it had only gotten worse since Shelly died.

His mind snapped back to the killer. The subject was acting out his fantasies. Waking dreams where he had total power. Total control. The human bodies were his props. Objects he could dominate to make the fantasy exist in the real world.

This guy would want to go back to the scenes, both the dump sites and the place or places where he committed the acts themselves. He was sure of it. This subject's obsessive nature would require him to relive those moments when the fantasy played out, those fleeting segments of time when his power was real. Probably often now that his crimes were escalating.

The police were watching the scenes at all hours by his request, of course. That was what they had to go on for now, and it was being attended to by professionals. The tension in his neck seemed to release as he walked his fever-addled brain through this notion again.

Yes. Yes, that was something, wasn't it? Something important. Arriving at this point seemed to calm him somehow, and a peace settled over him. The resting grimace on his face smoothed itself out.

He knew he wasn't dying now. He only needed some sleep,

Dead End Girl

so he closed his eyes and slipped away.

CHAPTER 26

The chill of the seat seeps through his jacket and t-shirt and saturates the flesh along his spine. It makes his shoulders jostle. Makes his arms convulse for a beat. He cranks up the heat. Puts his fingertips to the vent. Feels only cold air.

The duffel bag shimmers in the corner of his eye again. That heat-distortion-like haze returned to its rightful place over his passenger's head.

Her face sticks part of the way out. Nose protruding from that zippered gap. Her skin is much colder than his. Icy. Her complexion looks strange under the yellow streetlights. The color of a lemon Starburst.

He brings his hands to his mouth. Cups them together. Blows into them. The warmth flares in his fingers. A little cloud of heat hovering in the hollow of his palms for a second before it fades. His hands feel wet after, so he wipes them on his pant legs.

Now he shifts gears. And the car moves to leave the lot.

He waves at a couple of the cops smoking on the sidewalk. They nod back. Gesture with their cigarettes. Steam and smoke coiling around them. Wafting in all directions.

Right away he brings his hand to her skin. Fingers pressing into her eyelids. So soft and so cold. The electrical jolt he feels is stronger than before. Somehow more exciting with the police right there. Just a few feet away. Utterly clueless.

The Buick declines down the mottled ramp of the driveway in slow motion. Absorbing two big bumps like a boat on a rocky sea. And then the car coils into a left turn onto the street. The sailing suddenly smooth.

He fumbles at his sleeve. Checks his watch. Eyes blinking a few times to make sure he's reading it correctly.

Only 9:16 PM. Good. There's still time.

When he speaks his voice is barely above a whisper.

"Gotta grab something from mom's house."

I know.

Finally. Finally he can imagine her responses. He can pretend. He feels his face flush. Feels his scalp tingle. Realizes that he is verging on tears. Jesus. Even he knows this is pathetic. But it is the only way. The only way. When she was alive, there was only the cold between them. Nothing there. No connection. This imagined relationship is something, though. It is something.

Anything is better than nothing.

He controls his voice when he speaks. Maintains a deadpan so she won't detect the emotion.

"I'm sorry to say that you won't get to meet her. Not directly. My mom, I mean."

I know that, too.

"Yeah. Yeah, I guess you would."

What he hears isn't really her voice. Not the person she was. It is someone new. A girl he invents as he goes along. This voice is a little thinner. A knowing delivery. Deadpan. She could be anything. Could be everything. Every possible girl.

They drive on. His breathing going a little ragged as the emotions well in him again.

"I'm so glad, you know? Glad that you're mine, I mean."

Me too.

The voice in his head doesn't sound convincing. He tries it again. Changing the inflection.

Me too.

No. It's still not right. He knows she doesn't mean it. Of course she doesn't. Why would she?

He adjusts his grip on the steering wheel. Fingers squeaking against the polyurethane.

It's OK. I understand that you're glad.

"OK. Just… You don't have to lie to me. You don't have to do that. I know how things really are."

OK.

The conversation trails off. The sounds of the night and the road rising up to take its place.

Fast food logos flit by on the side of the road. Red and orange and yellow lights. The only things out this way that keep the dark away.

CHAPTER 27

Violet lurched awake. The scratchy hotel sheets clung to her bare arms and legs. She was sweaty and breathing hard from a nightmare.

The dream's final image flashed in her head again: Sierra Peters' severed head in Darger's suitcase. The girl's mouth was open, swollen tongue protruding between her teeth. Her eyes were milky white, the same cloudy shade of the moonstone ring.

She kicked the stifling heat of the covers away from her and rolled over to check the alarm clock.

The red digits read 9:28 PM. Through the window, she could see the stars burning white against the blackened sky.

Great. Now she'd be up all night for sure.

After a cool shower and a change of clothes, she felt a bit more refreshed. Sleeping during the day always left her feeling groggy, though. She made a pot of coffee. What the hell? She might as well.

While the coffee brewed, she paced around the room. It still felt too warm, and the air was stuffy, so she opened the door to let the night in.

The grief welled in her again, brought stinging tears to her eyes. But she had to push it away. She knew that. Oh, it would torture her more. There'd be more tears. More nightmares. More panic attacks that made her knees buckle. Probably enough to last a lifetime.

But not now. Now, she had to work. That was the best way to honor Sierra. To do what she came here to do. To do her job.

To find this monster and stop him.

He'd make a mistake. That's what she'd told the task force. What she hadn't said was that she thought he had already made a mistake. Two, really. And the name of both mistakes was the same: Sierra Peters.

The first mistake was taking her at all. She'd proven that when she got away. Whether it was sheer luck on her part or was bound to happen because he'd chosen a girl who wouldn't go down without a fight, it hardly mattered. She'd escaped. And while she'd given them one hell of a knot to untie when it came to her conflicting statements, Darger was certain the answer existed somewhere in there.

The second mistake the killer made was taking Sierra again. Darger may have come to believe the girl, but she wasn't sure she'd have been able to convince the rest of the investigators working the case. Now that he'd killed her, there was no doubting her story, so long as they could figure out which detail would ultimately lead to his undoing.

The answer was right there. She knew it was.

Two cups of coffee later, and she was practically jogging back and forth in the room. She wanted to take a walk, but it was dark. She used to take evening strolls all the time. She liked the feel of the air growing heavy with the coolness of night. The sounds of the crickets and cicadas. But she didn't walk at night anymore. The light from the streetlights and the sounds of footsteps echoing over the pavement in the dark brought back too many familiar feelings.

She wished they were in a nicer hotel, one with a gym and treadmill. She needed to move.

If she had a car, she'd take a drive. At least that would be something. She crept to the door and peeked over at the neighboring room. Loshak's light was on.

She begged his keys off him, and a few minutes later she was behind the wheel with the windows down and the wind tangling her loose hair.

She drove past Vine Street gazing at the spot where Sierra said she'd been grabbed the first time. The second time she must not have even made it back to where she'd parked Violet's car. How long had he waited? Had he been waiting since his first attempt failed, hoping to see her again, desperately needing to tie up the loose end? Had he killed Fiona Worthington as a stand-in for the one that got away, only to find that the darkness inside him wouldn't accept substitutions?

Darger parked the car and sat, watching traffic roll by,

though there wasn't much. The windows at Jimmy's were all dark. Not even so much as the blue flicker of someone watching TV or playing video games. She hadn't yet heard whether or not he was arrested, but perhaps the lack of illumination suggested that Luck had gone through with it after all.

After a long time staring into the dark, Darger started the car again. She had one last place to visit before she headed back to the motel.

She did not turn up the dead end street when she reached it. She just rolled by slowly, letting her eyes gaze into the balmy night. She could see very little in the dark, but it didn't matter. It was there in her mind and always would be, long after the white tent was taken down and the last shreds of yellow police tape tore loose from the branches where they were tied.

The final resting place of a dead end girl.

CHAPTER 28

He waited on the stoop at his mother's house, the echo of the doorbell still ringing in his head. The duffel bag dangled at his side. Its cargo was deceptively heavy, he thought. About the weight of a bowling ball. He adjusted his grip on the handle, trying to somehow make the bag look less like a round, heavy object pulled it into an awkward shape, but nothing he did helped.

It felt wrong to bring it here. Not just dangerous. Not just morally or ethically objectionable. Wrong on some deeper level. A violation of nature itself, perhaps. And yet it filled him with an almost sexual excitement. Made his heart flutter. Made his mouth water. The impulse pounded in his skull, too strong to be denied.

He had to do this. Had to.

He'd parked the car five blocks off and walked here. He hated to do it. Missed the Buick already. But he had to. He'd seen someone this morning. He was almost sure of it. A jogger near the dump site. Someone who could've seen the car at the scene. So the car had to go. The risk was too high.

He swallowed, the dry flaps of his throat seeming to rise and fall in unison. For a crazy second he thought about turning and leaving the stoop. Even if he'd already rang the bell.

A silhouette took shape in the light beyond the window, the curtains ruffling a moment. Then the deadbolt clacked, and the door swung open, making that strange suction sound it always made when the metal pulled away from the rubber weather strip running around the frame.

His mother stood there in the opening, holding still for a moment, the diagonal wedge of light shining onto the back of her head so her face stayed mostly in shadow. All he could really make out was her tightly cropped gray hair and her general stature.

She was such a small person, something he always forgot

until he was up close to her again. She seemed somehow more substantial in his memories. Taller. More physically imposing.

"So are you not shaving at all now?" she said.

"What?" he said, fingers shifting the weight of the handle again.

"This," she said, cupping her fingers around her jaw to pantomime his stubble. "The scraggly hobo beard you've got going on. That's your new look, eh? Well, I don't even have to ask if you've met a girl, do I? Looking like that."

It's good to see you, too, Mom, he thought, a smirk curling his lip for a microsecond. She greeted him this way often, with a criticism rather than a hello. He didn't really get mad about it. Not anymore.

"Oh, I just forgot to shave is all," he said after a moment's hesitation. "I'll get to it tomorrow morning, I figure. Anyway, I just wanted to see how you were doing and grab a few things from my room."

She hesitated in the doorway.

"Right. Well, OK."

She took a step back, opening the way for him to cross the threshold into the house. He slipped off his shoes on the landing and climbed six steps into the dining room.

The decor had changed little since he was a boy. Everything looked nice enough — clean and in good repair — and yet it was all strangely dated, a blend of elements from the 70's, 80's, and 90's. This hadn't fully occurred to him until he was much older, but now he thought about it every time he walked past the weird painting of an owl hanging over the stairway, socked feet sinking into brown shag carpet, strangely meticulous and ancient all at once, almost as though this place had been shut up for years.

"I don't suppose you're hungry," she said, some distant injury clear in her voice.

He didn't like eating here, so he rarely did. She realized it at some point, and it seemed to hurt her, though she'd never addressed it directly.

"No, I ate earlier," he said, sliding the bag under the table and taking a seat.

She stood at the counter, partially blocked out from his vantage point. She seemed to look at him, but her eyes didn't meet his.

Sometimes he wished she was dead. Not out of any malice, though he thought she might even deserve some. Out of some feeling that he could never really be himself with her hanging around. That there was no way for him to sever this damaged connection, no way for him to escape this relationship and move on. It wasn't like she had any real feelings of warmth or affection for him, and the ones he had for her were conflicted and made him feel like a weakling.

Despite all of that, he couldn't abandon her.

She didn't know any better. That was all. Somehow it wouldn't be right to hold it against her. And in a crazy way, she was the only person who knew what he was. Something that was true on multiple levels.

"Almost forgot. I, uh, need to borrow the car if it's all right," he said, raising his voice so she'd hear him in the next room. "I dropped mine at the shop and hoofed it over here. Transmission's going, I think. This would only be for a couple of days, I'd think. A week or so at the most."

"It's fine. Take the Prius."

His tongue flicked out of one corner of his mouth and glided the length of his top lip. It felt dry and segmented like an earthworm.

What could he say? He couldn't tell her that he preferred the bigger sedan to the little hybrid, especially since the former was 25 years old. He'd pictured using the Continental the whole way over. Could see himself behind the wheel, an unconscious passenger slumped next to him, nestled safely out of view of the windows on the leather seat that was more like a plush couch than anything you'd find in a modern car.

"Are you sure? I don't mind taking the old boat."

"It's not like I have places to go. The grocery store once a week. You'll take the Prius."

They were quiet for a while, and then he heard her digging in the drawer for the extra key fob. He tried to shift his fantasy from the lux interior of the old tank to that of the tiny Prius.

Tried to imagine how he'd handle one of his projects in the smaller car. Maybe it was roomier than it looked, but he didn't like it.

"Do you ever see the guys from school anymore?"

Her voice startled him. It was close. He looked up to see her standing in the doorway, that hard look etched into her face seeming to have softened. She dangled the little black rectangle with the Toyota logo on it, and he took it.

"What?" he said.

"You know. Nate, Matt, and Kurt and everybody."

"Not really. I talked to Matt on Facebook a while back. He has a kid now."

"Oh, wow. I still remember him showing up at the door that day he'd colored his hair Bozo-the-clown orange. I had to bite the insides of my lips to keep from laughing."

She was quiet a moment, a faraway look in her eye, and then she went on.

"Seems strange, doesn't it? The way everybody grows up so fast."

"Yeah. Yeah, it does."

"I guess I'll never get to have grandkids, though. Not that it's any surprise."

She drifted out of the dining area, floating up the three steps into the living room. He sat at the table a moment, letting his leg lean into the duffel bag. No electricity, but it felt exciting somehow to touch it in this place.

Another memory flashed in his head, a picture and a feeling seared into his brain, into his memory, no matter how much he may have wanted to forget.

In third grade, he'd found a sky blue Bic lighter on the sidewalk a couple of blocks from school. Naturally he pocketed it, showing it around during classes. Word got around, and by the time recess hit, he was the talk of the playground. A group gathered near the merry go round to witness it, watching his thumb descend onto the flint wheel and flick and flick until the little flame hovered above his fist. They oohed and ahhed like cave-children seeing fire for the first time. He burned a few leaves and a box elder bug, its legs squirming furiously until

167

they vanished.

As far as he could remember, it was the most positive attention he'd ever received at school. Maybe, he thought, that was what it was like to win the spelling bee or become a star athlete. It was something like love.

When he got home from school, he showed his mom his new toy. He stood in this very dining room, back to the table. She stood in the doorway to the kitchen.

He flicked it just once before she ripped it from his hand and clubbed him in the temple with the heel of her hand. Her face twisted into that Halloween mask again.

She said that little boys who play with fire wet the bed. And that she needed to teach him to never do it again. To teach him in a way he wouldn't forget.

He waited. Swallowed. A lump flexing in his throat. His hair in his eyes from when she'd knocked him.

She came back into the dining room with a wire coat hanger, had him take off his shirt.

Bright bolts of pain flashed through his tiny torso, the flesh of his back torn open in strips from the sheer force of the wire. Each impact poked like an electric shock down the length of his spine, went numb for a split second and then burned like he'd been peeled open and had salt flung into the wound. He grit his teeth. Clamped his eyes shut as tight as they'd go. All he could picture was blood weeping down from his shoulder blades, sluicing over that expanse of torso, the skin peeling away in sheets to reveal all of the muscle on the backside of his body.

He tried so hard to hold still, to not let her have the satisfaction of seeing him squirm, seeing him suffer by her hand, but he couldn't. He knew, somehow, that she enjoyed that power. Had seen it in her wet lips, in the way her eyelids smiled even though the rest of her face grimaced. His spine twisted, flailed, arched back, unable to wiggle away from the hurt.

And then the rain of blows cut out, and everything stopped. Went dead quiet. Both of their chests heaving for a time.

She stormed off after a beat, and he stood there for a long time. His t-shirt killed every inch of the way down when he slid it back on.

Later that evening, when he hoisted himself to sit on the vanity and look at the damage in the bathroom mirror, it looked bad, but not nearly as dramatic as he'd imagined during the act. It looked like a cat had scratched him a few times. Scabbed up lines with purpled and yellowed bruising faintly visible around them.

Years later, he thought of this scene, of his mother towering over him with a coat hanger, when he killed her cat in the backyard.

His childhood bedroom smelled like a blend of Altoids and Right Guard, an odor that brought back another wave of memories, of dreams, of a visceral sense of the time gone by — the faintest tingle in his chest and head. All of the people he used to be, from the frightened child to the awkward high school kid to the serial killer on the news, they were all here with him now, all jockeying for control in his head. A head full of spirits, full of ghosts.

He stood still for a moment, looking upon this time capsule of a space. The same tattered bedspread still sprawled on the bed, a limp thing sporting faded blue and white stripes. Pale lines gouged the dark wood of the dresser where it had scraped the banister upon being moved in. The vertical blinds looked like jail cell bars with a couple of pieces missing. Snagged threads puckered up from the pond scum green carpet. It looked like it was installed in 1976, and it probably was.

The room was pocked and scarred and flawed the same way his skin was. All these years later, all the old injuries still showed.

He dug in the drawers in the desk, pulling free a couple of passports tucked in back. He hoped he wouldn't need either of them anytime soon, but it was better to have them at the ready now. It might come to that.

He unzipped the duffel bag, peered between those zippered lips into the dark. He pulled the gap open wide enough to see her, a sliver of the forehead and hair becoming visible. He felt his pulse quicken as he looked upon that image, his hand descending into the bag in slow motion.

He ran his fingers through the girl's hair. She was cold, but a strange warmth flushed his face and torso as his hand made impact. The heat in him welled just to touch her in this place, to feel her against his skin and know that she was his.

CHAPTER 29

Loshak woke to loud knocks on the door. Confused, he sat up. His eyes danced over a foreign carpet to find a crappy TV playing an infomercial for super sharp knives. The sound was all the way down. He felt the muscles in his brow tighten. After a beat of total disorientation, he remembered where he was in the universe.

Athens, Ohio.

He looked at the door, noticed that he'd left it unlocked.

"Come in," he said, feeling very strange to raise his voice after so long in the stillness of sleep.

The knocking stopped, and after a long moment, the doorknob turned in slow motion. The rectangle of wood seemed to stick in the frame for a second, coming free with a scrape, and then the light poured in where the door had stood.

Deputy Donaldson stepped into the room, took off his hat and held it in front of his chest. His smile faded as he sized up Loshak's state.

"Oh, hey. I ain't disturbing you, am I?"

"Nah. I've just been a little sick. Rest and fluids and all that."

"Right. Of course. How you feeling?"

"I'm getting better. What do you need?"

"Well, I, uh, wanted to give you a heads up. It's about Special Agent Darger."

"Oh?"

"It's nothing serious. Just… I'm privy to a lot of talk. A lot of it. Around our department and around other local precincts and what have you. Now, I know Agent Darger means well. I've talked to her. She… Well, she has some gumption, that one. Lotta gumption. A real gung-ho lady. But this talk I'm hearing… It's just that some of the others don't see it the same way I do."

Loshak smoothed his hair down the side of his head before he responded.

"And how do they see it?"

"Well, she's stirring the, uh, the pot, you know? She goes cavorting around with the Peters girl who turns up dead the next morning. She got in a big fight in the meeting last night. It was a bad scene. Now I got a call this morning and hear that she plans to go poking around again, bothering the families of the victims. These are people still reeling from family tragedies. People the local authorities have already interviewed. She's stirring the pot for no good reason. Is how they see it, I mean."

"Stirring the pot. I do see what you mean."

The Deputy cleared his throat, his hat twitching in his hands in front of him.

"Well, it's not me that's saying this, you understand. I mean, the stirring's not how I see it. She's trying to solve homicides. She has a passion for it."

"No, I understand what you're saying. Thanks for coming to me, Deputy. I'll talk to her about it."

"OK. Great. I felt like something should be said is all."

Loshak nodded, expecting that was the end of it, but the deputy only stood there. The agent turned his head, looked at Donaldson out of the corner of his eye.

"Anything else on your mind, deputy?"

"I kind of was wondering your thoughts on the Steelers this week. Four point favorites at home? Seems low to me."

Loshak shrugged.

"Could be. I don't have a strong opinion on that one. Not sure I'm comfortable laying more than a field goal with that offensive line, but…"

"Uh-huh. I see. Anything you like on Sunday?"

"Ravens-Browns under 44 and a half. Supposedly that's the sharp play. Might want to lock it in now. The number's likely to move."

Donaldson pulled a small notepad out of his breast pocket and jotted the note.

"Thank you, sir," the deputy said, licking his lips. "Ravens under. Anything else?"

"Not sure. I'm always tempted to bet the over on Cincinnati with that secondary. Not ready to make it official just yet."

The deputy rolled his eyes.

"Good lord. The Bengals secondary? Don't even get me started."

CHAPTER 30

The day dawned overcast, with milky gray clouds that reminded Violet of Sierra's eyes in her dream. A haze hung in the air, obscuring the sunlight and blotting out the color in the day. Everything was monochrome. A photograph in black and white.

Darger had tried to sleep after her night drive, but she'd only managed a prolonged session of tossing and turning. Eventually she crawled from the bed, made a couple of phone calls, and got out her laptop. She checked her email, and the new rental voucher from Cal's office was there. On the rental company's website, she arranged for the earliest possible time to have a new car dropped off at the motel.

When Darger went over to drop off Loshak's keys, she'd already formulated a plan for the day. After she got her new wheels, of course. She checked her watch. Any minute now.

"Have you talked to any of the families? Of the victims, I mean?" she said.

"I met the Worthingtons very briefly. But it was still pretty fresh, and they were a mess."

She could tell by the look he was giving her that he wanted to say more. Like maybe he wasn't sold on her idea of talking to the families.

"You do say in your book, we're profiling the victims just as much as the killer."

"It's not that," he said, eyes searching the room like maybe he'd find the answer somewhere on the ceiling. "Just... tread lightly."

That raised an eyebrow. She didn't need anyone to remind her how to handle victims or the families of victims. She had plenty of experience in that department, thank you very much.

He must have read the irritation on her face, because he added, "It's not the families I'm worried about as much as the feeling some might have that you're stepping on toes."

"Oh," she said.

"I'm only saying, it might be wise to have the blessing of the locals, so to speak."

"You're saying I should call and get permission to talk to their witnesses."

Loshak shrugged. "Sometimes it's best to seem like one of the guys."

"Sometimes?"

"Yeah well, sometimes it's not, you know. I'm assuming you'll need these, then?"

He held up the keys.

"Nope," she said, and her phone buzzed as if on cue. "In fact, I think that's my new rental right now."

She half-expected the rental company to give her some guff about one of their cars being impounded by the police, but no mention was made of the ordeal. She supposed that the kid dropping the car off — she figured him for about 19 and probably a college student — either had no idea, or if he did, couldn't care less. All in all, it took less than a minute for her to sign the new rental agreement and take possession of the keys.

She'd already talked to Donaldson first thing in the morning, but now she had to make the other calls. As she expected, Donaldson had no problem with her speaking to "his" witnesses. She'd planned on calling them in the order of least problematic to most problematic, and now she couldn't decide who was likely to be a bigger pain in the ass between Janssen and Luck. She figured it was a given that Janssen would give her some kind of grief. He was just an asshole like that. Luck, she wasn't so sure about. She opted for the sure thing.

When she got Janssen on the phone and told him who was calling, his response was less than thrilled.

"I was hoping you wouldn't mind my talking to the girls that lived with Cristal Monroe."

"Mind? Why would I mind? Knock yourself out," he said as dismissively as possible. "Is that it?"

"Yes."

"Great. Bye," he said, and the phone clicked out.

"Fuck you, too, Janssen," she muttered as she flicked through her contacts, looking for Detective Luck's number.

He answered on the second ring.

"Detective Luck."

"It's Agent Darger."

There was a pause, and Darger worried for a moment that he might hang up.

Finally he said, "And what can I do for you, Agent?"

"I…" the apology hung there in her throat. She was still a little irritated that he'd turned so hard on her like that during the meeting. Surely he knew she'd meant no offense. She was merely stating a fact, after all.

Fuck it. Loshak wanted her to play like one of the guys? Fine. Guys didn't apologize or worry about hurting each other's feelings. They got over it and moved on.

"I was calling to let you know that I'll be interviewing some of the families today. Of the victims. Professional courtesy and all," she said.

"Oh. Alright," was all he said.

Huh. That wasn't so bad.

"Great, thanks."

She barely had the words out before he was speaking again.

"So should I pick you up, or…?"

"Sorry?"

"I'm asking if you're driving or if I'm driving. Doesn't seem much point to driving separately," he said, then he added, just to make his point clear, "to talk to my witnesses."

So he was going to play the territorial game after all.

"I'd planned on talking to as many of the families as possible, for all four victims."

Might as well remind him that they weren't *all* his witnesses. Janssen and Donaldson had already given her the go-ahead.

"That's a good idea. One of us local guys really should be taking the extra step to pull all the strands together. Can you be ready in half an hour?"

She wasn't sure if he was being purposely obtuse or not. What was she thinking? Of course it was on purpose.

"Um. Yes. I'm ready now, actually."

"Great. I'll be thar faster'n green grass through a goose," he said, the fake twang coming back.

He hung up before she could respond, and her thumb hit the END CALL button so hard she thought it might go through the screen.

CHAPTER 31

When Luck arrived at her door, they both did their best to act like professional law enforcement personnel who had more important things to do than focus on petty personal squabbles. But it didn't last for long.

They took the steps down to the parking lot. Luck paused in front of a dark red Chrysler minivan, and it wasn't until he popped the back hatch that Darger realized it was his vehicle.

"Wait," she said, finding it difficult to hold back a snide grin.

He shot her a look.

"You're gonna give me crap about the van, right? Like I haven't heard it a thousand times before."

He pitched his voice into a mocking tone.

"'Hey Luck, did you have to trade in your testicles when they gave you the keys?' And on and on."

She bit her lip, trying to keep from snickering.

"No, no. I figured you were going undercover as a soccer mom."

She snorted at her own joke, and Detective Luck just shook his head.

"You'll see," he said, climbing in. "The Luckmobile is the sweetest ride in the Athens PD."

They lapsed into silence on the drive. Despite the joking, Violet couldn't let what happened at the task force meeting go. It was an annoying fly buzzing around her head as they bumped through potholes and over tarred patches of asphalt.

After several minutes of semi-awkward quiet, Luck gestured at the dash.

"I mean, you got your separate climate control for the front and back passengers, heated leather interior — LL Bean edition, no less. What more could you want?"

"Oh yeah," Darger said, "very luxurious."

Luck was mute until they rolled up to a red light.

"It's no Beemer or Mercedes, of course. I'm sure that's what

178

you highfalutin FBI people drive, right?"

She gave him the side eye.

"I drive a Prius."

Now he was the one chuckling to himself.

"Of course you do."

"What's that supposed to mean?"

"Nothing at all, Special Agent Darger."

She was beginning to loathe the way he said her name. *Special. Agent. Darger.*

Violet folded her arms and glared out the window. That's how he wanted to play it, huh? That she was some kind of pretentious city girl? She fixed her eyes on the double yellow line that ran ahead of them as far as the eye could see. This was going to be a long day.

"So," Darger said, searching for neutral territory, "Detective *and* SWAT?"

She'd noticed the black tactical bag embroidered with the white SWAT logo when Luck had opened the trunk.

"Yeah, well," he said, glancing at her as he drove, "it's a part-time thing out here, so a lot of the guys are on-call SWAT."

"You're like the FBI cream dream."

"Really?"

"Oh yeah," Darger said, looking him up and down. "Recruiters would be all over you."

His cheeks flushed pink, and she was amused to see that he was a little embarrassed now. Ha. Score one for Special Agent Darger.

Another stretch of road went by with only the sound of the tires humming over the pavement. Finally she asked the question she'd been dying to know the answer to since she called Luck this morning.

"What happened with Jimmy Congdon?"

"Dick and squat," he said with a bitterness that surprised her.

Had he changed his mind on bringing him in, she wondered? Taken her advice? She kept her eyes focused on him until he elaborated.

"It appears our dear friend Jimmy skipped town. Probably

heard some buzz about us finding Sierra and put it together that we'd be wanting to ask him some very pointed questions."

"Hm," was all she said in response.

"I'm sure you're happy."

"Happy?"

She gaped at him.

"Why would I be happy? I wanted to hear what he had to say just as much as you did. Just had a different idea of how we should go about it."

"Well if you ask me, him running off makes him ten times more suspicious."

"He's not exactly a law-abiding citizen. Him acting suspicious is like a fox acting sly. It's his nature."

Luck didn't say any more after that. He didn't have to. She knew where he stood and vice versa.

"I reached out to the few working girls I could think of. Like you asked."

"Yeah?"

She was a little surprised given how they'd parted ways at the meeting.

"It's different here. Prostitution, I mean. It's mostly done through the internet. And the girls are all the type that could be living next door, and you'd never expect it."

"Believe me, Detective, that's the case more than you realize. The streetwalkers make up a tiny percentage of sex workers, whether it's the city or the country," Darger said. "They are sisters and daughters and mothers. Sometimes the families know, and sometimes they don't."

"Well the two I thought might be willing to talk to me weren't. I suspect they knew why I was asking, and they'd rather not think about that."

Cristal Monroe had lived in a trailer park outside of Logan, Ohio. The grounds were clean and the units all fairly new, each laid out in its own little swath of lawn. The house she'd shared with two other girls was situated in the back corner of the neighborhood. An older model Jetta was parked in the driveway. Luck pulled to the curb and put the van in Park.

"I'll let you handle this one," he said.

She barely gave him a second look as she climbed down to the sidewalk.

Passing a lawn gnome squatting in a patch of shriveled daylilies, Darger reached the front door. Her knuckles rapped three times against the aluminum-clad screen door. She waited.

After a moment, she knocked again. She glanced over her shoulder at the car in the driveway. She had a feeling someone was home, but they weren't answering for some reason. She considered the fact that these had been Detective Janssen's witnesses. Given his low opinion of the victim, it didn't take a lot of imagination to figure that his disposition might have extended to her roommates.

Taking a business card from her pocket, Violet jotted a quick message on the back: *Please call me.*

She had a feeling they never would, but it was worth a shot.

When Darger returned to the van, Luck had turned the radio on and was listening to an Oldies station.

"No one home?" he said, looking unsurprised.

"Not for us, anyway."

"That was one of the reasons I stayed in the van," he explained. "Figured they'd probably had their fill of cops knocking on their door, asking 'em a million questions. Especially after Janssen was finished with them. I thought you might have a chance, being a woman, but I guess not."

She mentally crossed Cristal's name off her list. Cristal was originally from Florida and had no kin here. The family left in her home state rarely heard from her. They'd reached a dead end when it came to talking to anyone that might have known her well.

"Where to next?" Darger asked.

"Lancaster's only about 20 minutes up the road. That's where Katie Seidel lived."

"Let's go," she said.

When he answered the door, Darger was mildly surprised to find that George Seidel was older than she'd expected. Katie had only been 20 years old, but her husband looked to be easily in his forties. He was short, about the same height as Darger, with tanned forearms covered in a haze of blonde hair. There were deep bags under his eyes, and several day's growth of beard on his chin.

The small white house stood under the shade of a giant hemlock tree, but Mr. Seidel squinted at the daylight beyond the door as if he hadn't been outside in days.

"Come in," he said, curtly.

A baby had started to cry, and he ducked back into the house as quickly as he'd appeared.

With a nod, Luck indicated that Darger should enter first.

"Excuse the mess," George said, clearing away a basket of laundry from the sofa in the living room. "I'm still trying to get the hang of all this."

He set the plastic basket down and stooped to lift the crying baby from a bouncy seat near the TV. Another child, a boy of about two years old, turned to regard them from where he knelt in front of the screen.

"I told you not to sit so close, Damian," George barked.

The toddler did a frog-like hop away from the television and went to cling to his father's leg. He peered around a denim-covered thigh to peek at them, simultaneously shy of and intrigued by the newcomers.

"Hello, Damian," Violet said. "My name is Violet. And this is Casey."

Detective Luck waved at the boy, and Damian jerked his head back so he was hidden again.

"Don't be hanging on me like that," George said, giving his leg a shake. "Go on. I have to feed your sister."

The boy slid down to the floor, still watching Darger and Luck. He crept closer.

"Didn't realize this all had been turned over to the FBI," George said from the kitchen.

He pulled a bottle of baby formula from the fridge and gave it a shake.

"It hasn't," Darger said. "We're here to assist with the investigation, but it's still in the hands of the local jurisdictions."

George held the baby to his chest, balancing her small head

against the crook of his elbow, and plugged the bottle into her mouth. The crying cut off, turning into a series of pleased cooing sounds.

"Too bad," he said, looking up from the baby.

"Why is that?"

George Seidel lowered himself into a glider at the end of the room while the baby in his arms continued to suckle at the bottle.

"Why do you think? Cops around here couldn't solve a crossword puzzle. String of murders? Forget it."

He seemed to remember then that Detective Luck was present. He glanced up and said, "No offense."

"None taken," Luck said, though Darger wasn't sure it was true.

"Someone scratched up my rig and slashed my tires a few months back. And by someone, I mean the delinquent piece of trash at the end of the road, Bobby Ringo."

Darger had seen the truck cab tucked into the carport next to the house when she knocked on the door.

"What happened?"

"Nothing. That's the problem. Cops said without evidence that he'd done it, there was nothing they could do. But I know it was him."

"How long ago was this?" Darger asked.

She didn't think it had anything to do with the murder of his wife, but she didn't want to rule anything out.

"Six, eight months," George said, rocking back and forth.

"And why do you think he was the one that messed up your truck?" Luck asked.

"Because. He had a loud party one night, and I called the cops. Him and all his little punk friends got MIPs."

Luck shot her a look, thinking the same thing she had been. If Bobby Ringo was under 21, there was very little chance he was their killer. It didn't fit.

While they talked, Damian had scooted over to the end of the couch, inch by inch. Now, he clambered over the arm until he was face to face with Violet.

"Hello again," she said.

The boy still didn't speak. Instead, he reached out a finger and touched the golden pin on her lapel. Darger held it out.

"You like that?" she asked. "Do you know what kind of animal that is?"

Damian shook his head, eyes transfixed by the pin.

"It's a hedgehog. It's got little spikes all over its back to scare predators away, but under all that armor, it's actually a very nice animal. Friendly. Some people keep them as pets."

Damian crawled closer so that he could hold the pin in his hand, effectively winding up in Violet's lap.

"The lady doesn't want you climbing on her, Damian," Mr. Seidel said to the boy.

"He's OK," Violet said.

The boy lifted his head to look at her a second and then went back to the hedgehog on her jacket. Darger wondered at how the boy was handling the death of his mother. He hadn't uttered a word since they'd arrived, and she thought his choice to wriggle into her lap wasn't just about the shiny bauble that caught his eye. He wanted human affection. Closeness.

Darger was watching the boy's tiny fingers prod at the spikes on the hedgehog's back when she asked, "You were away on work that night? Is that correct?"

George stopped the swinging motion of the chair for a moment, staring at the worn blue carpet under his feet. The baby gave a restless squeal, and he went back to rocking.

"That's right. I mostly do short hauls so I'm not away all the time. But sometimes I take hotshot loads. That's what I was doin' that weekend. Drivin' a half-trailer full of boat parts down to Louisiana."

"Did she often walk to work?"

"Of course not," George snapped. "You think I'd let my wife walk alone at night like that? Hell no."

His jaw worked back and forth, molars grinding together. He seemed to compose himself then.

"Her car was actin' up. Needed a new, I don't know what… fuel-line sensor or some such. Used to be able to fix things myself, but these days everything's got these little computerized parts, and if one of those fails, then there ain't nothing to be

184

done but take it in."

"Her car was in the shop then?"

"Yeah, down at the Rider Brothers on Morton Street. Waitin' on an estimate."

"Do you remember how many days she would have been walking to work?"

"One or two. She got a ride from one of her friends the other days, but I don't know for sure which."

"And in the weeks before… did she mention anything strange or off? Any odd customers coming into the gas station? Unfamiliar cars hanging around the neighborhood?"

He shook his head. "No. Nothing like that."

The baby had started to cry again, and Darger gave Luck a look. George Seidel had his hands full, and they were only adding to the burden.

They stood, Darger lifting Damian with her before setting him on the ground.

"Thank you for giving us a moment, Mr. Seidel," she said, and then to the boy, "It was nice to meet you, Damian."

George went to stand, but Luck waved him away.

"We can show ourselves out."

Damian was still waving at Violet from the couch when she closed the door behind her.

CHAPTER 32

The drive back to Athens was made mostly in silence.

Detective Luck broke it once to comment, "Breaks your heart to think about that little boy growing up without his mom."

Darger murmured agreement.

They were quiet the rest of the way. The empty sound of the wind spiraling off of the van's windshield was the only sound until Luck announced that they'd reached their destination.

"Worthington house is up here to the left."

Fiona Worthington's parents lived in a house large enough to fit the homes of Cristal Monroe and Katie Seidel under the roof with room to spare. It was a newer build designed in a modern Queen Anne style with bayed windows and a turret on one corner. A two-story porch wrapped from one end to the other, and the house perched on a hill overlooking the town, with a view of the Hocking River and a round domed building she'd heard one of the locals refer to as The Convo. She figured it was an arena of some kind.

Fiona's mother greeted them at the door, addressing Detective Luck by his first name, and shaking Darger's hand.

In the foyer, Lois Worthington took their coats. Darger's boots clopped over the parquet floor. Tucked into the corner below the wraparound staircase was a small round table laden with a large floral arrangement and a pitcher of lemonade.

"Can I get you anything? Water? Coffee?"

"I'd take a glass of lemonade," Darger said, and Lois Worthington gave her an odd look. Like she'd used her salad fork when she should have used her dinner fork. No, that wasn't fair, Darger thought, correcting herself. Don't start with the judgments.

From beside her, she thought she heard Luck suppress a chuckle.

Darger glanced at the pitcher on the little table, and Mrs.

186

Worthington followed her gaze.

"Oh! No," Lois said, her hand flying to her chest. She started to laugh. "That's not real, dear. It's decorative."

She picked up the pitcher and waggled it from side to side, and the lemonade stayed bizarrely in place. No sloshing about at all, because it was solid.

Violet felt her cheeks go red, and she forced herself to titter nervously along with Luck and Mrs. Worthington, who were now having quite a laugh over it.

Probably happens all the time, Violet told herself.

"That's cute," Mrs. Worthington said. "No one's ever done that."

She actually wiped tears from the corners of her perfectly made-up eyes.

"Phew! It's been a while since I had a good laugh. That felt good."

Violet's unease only increased the further they made their way into the house. It was traditionally furnished to go with the historical architecture style: oversized gilt-edged mirrors, bookshelves topped with cloisonné vases, and heavy brocade window treatments.

The room Mrs. Worthington brought them into had a baby grand piano at one end and a white marble fireplace at the other. The carved marble slab was topped with a delft mantel clock and two large floral arrangements featuring hydrangeas and delphinium.

It was the kind of place that always made Violet feel acutely self-conscious. She started to notice all of her outward flaws. The lint on her jacket sleeve — a jacket she'd bought secondhand. The scuffs on her boots, which were not real leather. Her teeth, which were neither perfectly straight nor pristinely white.

She made a fist with each hand, obscuring her ragged and chipping fingernails.

There were pictures of Fiona everywhere. With the family, with friends, and many of her alone, on the back of a horse. In the more recent photos, her blonde hair was cropped short, but in all of the childhood and adolescent snapshots, her hair was long, almost to her waist.

"When did she cut her hair?" Darger asked.

She wasn't sure why she asked, the words seemed to tumble out of her mouth.

"About a year ago, I guess," her mother said, eyes locked on a photograph of Fiona smiling next to a black horse. "She was always very fashion forward."

"I imagine she had a lot of boyfriends," Darger said and instantly regretted it. What the hell was wrong with her? Why would she phrase it that way? "I mean... I didn't—"

Mrs. Worthington waved away Violet's apology, in that ever-polite way older rich women often had.

"I know what you meant, dear. And no, actually. She didn't date much, not even in high school when all the other girls her age were boy-crazy. Fiona was always very focused. Very driven."

"And what was she studying at the university?"

"It was a surgical scholarship. She got her DVM two years ago. Veterinary medicine."

Darger nodded while Fiona's mother went on about her daughter's achievements and virtues.

Fiona Worthington reminded her of many of the girls she'd graduated high school with. Maybe that was why she felt so out of place in her home.

Violet's father left the family when she was six. It was just her and her mother after that, and it was a struggle for them. When she was 13, they were evicted quite suddenly when it was revealed that the landlord they'd been renting from hadn't been paying taxes on the property. For three weeks they lived in her mother's car until they found a new apartment. And even though it was only three weeks, and she knew plenty of people had it worse, *much* worse, it left a lasting impression on her. She remembered the shame she felt as her mother dropped her off at school an hour early so Violet would be able to take a shower in the girl's locker room.

Things turned around quite suddenly when she was fifteen. That was when her mother met Gary. He was the corporate counsel for the real estate company her mother worked for, and within a year, they were married. Violet was sent to the local private school, where most of the students were from very wealthy families. She supposed she was technically from a wealthy family as well by then, though it didn't feel like it. It never felt like it, not even fourteen years later.

Money or not, she wasn't one of them. She knew it, and they knew it. It wasn't that any of the girls were ever directly unkind, either. Girls that age have a way of letting it be known that you are Out as opposed to being In without saying it expressly.

On one occasion, she remembered a girl named Bianca DeVos ranting about where people did their shopping.

"I cannot believe people actually buy clothes at Target. I mean, I've seen some semi-cute things there, but it's always like so last year and *so* cheaply made. I would be so embarrassed to have to tell people I shopped there," she said.

Violet had looked down at her outfit. She was fairly certain the pants she was wearing were from Target. And her shoes were most likely from Walmart, a fact that may have driven Bianca DeVos to a nervous breakdown, convulsions, and mouth foam on the spot, had she admitted it.

She'd never known for sure whether Bianca was saying those things because she knew Violet bought her clothes there or whether it had been a random, organic thought not directed at anyone in particular. She didn't suppose it made a difference. They remained separate, either way.

"I can show you her room if you like?" Fiona's mother offered, and Violet snapped back to the present.

Luck raised an eyebrow at her, which left her wondering if she'd been staring off like a space cadet.

"Yes, thank you," she said, and the procession headed upstairs.

Fiona's room was in the turret, with plenty of natural light coming in through the wrap-around windows.

"You can see that she was very proud of her trophies and awards," her mother said, gesturing to the wall covered in plaques and ribbons for various equestrian events Fiona had participated in over the years.

Darger thought that Fiona had likely been proud of a great

many things, then scolded herself. She forced the images of
Fiona's dismembered limbs jumbled in a black garbage bag into
her mind. Whatever Fiona Worthington had been in life, she
was a victim now. The same as all the rest: Cristal and Katie and
Sierra.

The awards outnumbered the personal photographs, though
Darger guessed that may have been different when Fiona was in
high school.

In the closet, there was a collection of bags and shoes that
probably equaled Darger's yearly salary.

Damn it. Violet wasn't sure why, but she couldn't think
straight in this house. She felt strangely claustrophobic in this
place filled with shiny, pretty things. Was she jealous?
Resentful?

She knew she was being silly. It hadn't mattered back then,
and it certainly didn't matter now. Fiona liked fine things. So
what? The only difference between them was that Violet was too
practical to spend $500 on a purse. And that wasn't a surprise
when the last purse she'd bought had ended up soaked in blood
and used as Government Exhibit #1-263 in a murder trial.

There was a bouquet of pink peonies on the bedside table,
and Violet reached out to brush one of the petals with a
fingertip. She was surprised to find they were real. She'd
assumed they were made of silk. Phony like the lemonade
downstairs.

"Those were her favorite," Lois said, then added, "I had
them flown in for the service, and I thought it would be nice—"

Fiona's mother gasped and covered her mouth with her
hand.

"Excuse me. It's the strangest things that trigger it. You
know, at first it was any little thing. The phone would ring, and
I'd think maybe it was her calling, and then I'd remember that
she wouldn't ever be calling again."

Violet swallowed thickly, gazing around the room. She took
in the bed with the gauzy canopy and the white velvet tufted
headboard. The chandelier that hung in the center of the
rounded turret area. She'd felt before that Fiona Worthington
hadn't fit the pattern, and now she knew she'd been right. She

190

had a strong desire to leave this place. As quickly as possible.

"Thank you for letting us barge in like this," she said to Lois, who shook her head.

"It's no trouble, really. Any time."

They shook hands again in the entryway, and Mrs. Worthington thanked them for their diligence.

"It means a lot. That you're all working so hard to find who did this."

As they rolled down the driveway, Violet watched the giant house shrink in the side mirror, down to the size of something she could hold in her palm.

CHAPTER 33

He exhales on the window. Watches the fog bloom on the glass.
He scoots back and the clouded circle recedes. Fades.
Disappears.

The booth smells like mothballs today. Astringent. Worse
than usual. The wire mesh veining the glass feels more like a
cage than ever.

So yeah. Just another day at the office. He doesn't know
what he does this for. What anyone does it for. The endless
hours of meaningless labor. The never-ending cycle of
production and consumption. What is he supposed to want
from this life? From this world?

The drive-through lane is dead. Empty. Utterly still. There
are no upcoming flights on the schedule. Nothing for hours.

This is the lull. The nothingness he stares into for hours at a
time. His mind grapples at the goddamn void like sense can be
made of black nothing. He can't help it. He knows the winding
thoughts are useless. Circular. Draining. But he can never turn
them off.

His eyes flick to the Prius across the lane. Her current
resting place. He misses her. She sits in her duffel bag in the
passenger seat. Zipped up tight. Being in the cold will do her
good. At least there's that.

Her complexion had gone gray recently. Ashy and mottled.
And he got a whiff this morning. Fouled meat. The cold would
preserve her some, maybe. Refrigeration. Crazy to think that she
would be too far gone soon. That it would all be over soon.

An image flares in his head. The knife slashing a line in her
throat. The flaps of skin hesitating a moment before they pulled
apart. Sheets of flesh like a layer of paper shrouding the meat
which shrouds the bones.

She leaks out everywhere. Red. Blood spurting out with
every heartbeat. A wild spray like a garden hose with a thumb
held over the opening.

192

She swoons right away from the blood loss. Eyelids drooping. Muscles gone slack. So scared and small. Her skin icy cold to the touch within seconds. Chest fluttering shallow breaths in and out, little choking gasps.

It is fast. Less than a minute from the incision to unconsciousness. Death arrives four minutes after that. It settles over the body as her self vacates the shell. For now and for always.

She doesn't suffer long. Barely has time to grasp what is happening. Maybe 45 seconds. He is glad for that in some mild sense. The suffering isn't his object. Not with her. Not with any of them.

Possession is.

And she wasn't his until the bleeding stopped. Until the patter in her neck ceased. Until the light drained from her eyes.

When she was gone. Evicted. Ejected. Permanently. Only then was she his.

This was the only way.

His own heart beats faster as the image occurs to him. Swells and wanes in a fraction of a second. His tongue juts out to lick his segmented lips. Fingers twitch a little like the paws of a dreaming puppy.

He is sorry she is dead. Sorry it works that way. But he feels no guilt. No remorse. It is just something that happened now. Somewhere back in the mists. In the past. No one could touch it anymore.

A twinge of warmth brings him back to the present moment. It's cold as always out here in the booth. But a little heat plumes out of the wall unit furnace now that it's been on a while. He tilts himself that way. Shoulder lit up orange from the glow.

His eyes look beyond the cage and dance across the parking lot. Flitting from sedans to SUVs and mini-vans. In the distance he sees the planes. Gigantic airliners waiting to shuffle people around the country. Around the world. The busy bodies never rest. They produce and consume and produce and consume. New cars to be bought. New TVs. New gadgets.

There are so many objects all around us, he thinks, and yet

this world is utterly, utterly empty.

CHAPTER 34

The haze from earlier in the day had thickened into a heavy fog. They came to a four-way stop, and Darger watched as the mist seemed to open and close like a curtain for the car in front of them, enveloping it in the cloud as it rolled through the intersection ahead.

"You alright, Agent Darger?"

"I'm fine. Why?"

"Just asking. You seemed awful quiet in there is all."

"So?"

"I'm just saying, you had lots of questions for George Seidel," Casey Luck said.

"Well, they're different, aren't they? Different victims, different families. Different ways of dealing with them."

"OK, I didn't mean anything by it. Was only curious. Thought you might have had something."

"Like what?"

"I don't know. A theory or something."

Darger just shook her head. She had no interest in revealing any of those particular thoughts. But he was still watching her periodically, glancing at her during long straight-aways and at stop signs. She needed to change the subject. Get his mind off her and onto something else. She went with what was surely his favorite topic: himself.

"So what's the story with the van?"

Luck smiled to himself. Like he'd been waiting for her to ask.

"Almost all the guys, aside from Patrol, drive cars from the police auctions. Whatever the department can get for cheap, you know?"

Darger gave a quick nod of the head. It was routine for property to be seized during a drug bust, for example, and then auctioned off. TVs, bicycles, jewelry, sometimes even houses. And of course, cars.

"This sweet ride," he said, patting the dash lovingly, "used to belong to a psychic."

Violet blinked at him.

"A psychic."

"Yes, ma'am. Used to do readings in her living room. Miss Valentina."

He dropped his voice and whispered as if he was sharing some big secret: "Her real name was Carol Smith."

Darger snorted.

"Anyway, there was a Mister Valentina. Her husband. And apparently Mister Valentina was like *the* cook when it came to MDMA in southern Ohio."

"Uh-oh," Violet said.

"Yeah, so, everything's going along in apple pie order. She's making her scratch gazing into her crystal ball, he's making ecstasy in the basement. Until the night Miss Valentina comes home to find Mister Valentina in bed with her sister."

"She called the cops on him?"

"No, no. She went after him with the 12-gauge they kept in the garage."

"Oh, Jesus."

"Yep, luckily it was loaded with birdshot. She didn't get him square, either. Got one arm and part of his back. She says she wasn't even trying to hit him, only wanted to scare him. But the neighbors heard the gunshots, and when the Sheriff's Department showed up, there were little holes blown all over the place."

"And then they found the lab."

Luck nodded.

"The funny thing is, had she not shot up the place, they might not have found anything. But she chased him all over the house with the gun, and the CSI's had to document each discharge of the weapon. Once they found the lab, that was it. They seized the house, the cars, all of it."

"The crystal ball?"

Luck laughed.

"Maybe so. She was pretty furious during the whole ordeal, apparently, and legend has it," again he dropped his voice lower in both pitch and volume, "she cursed it all. Including the ol' Luckmobile here."

He stroked the steering wheel.

"Now you know cops. Not a superstitious lot," he said with mock innocence, and Darger scoffed. "None of the other guys would touch this ride. And being that I was the newbie detective and feeling that my last name gave me some sort of anti-voodoo or whatever, they gave it to me."

"And?" she asked, waiting for the rest.

"What?"

"Is it cursed?"

"No," he said, indignantly. "If anything, it's the opposite. First time I drove it, I parked, got out, and boom — there's a $20 bill just lying at my feet."

Violet smirked.

"So it's the Luckmobile in more ways than one?"

"Darn straight."

It occurred to Darger, and not for the first time, that he had a curiously clean mouth for law enforcement. Well, she thought, it wasn't so unusual for there to be a few Boy Scouts in the group.

"You'd think she would have seen it coming."

"What's that?"

"Him cheating. If she was psychic, she should have seen it coming."

Luck chuckled.

"Maybe she did. I don't know."

"No way. She wouldn't have gone after him with the shotgun like that if she'd known."

"Maybe she was unprepared for how it would affect her."

"No, I'm saying that if she knew, she would have loaded the gun with something more than birdshot."

Luck fixed her with a look of combined amusement and awe.

"Remind me never to cross you."

They were on one of the back roads that ran through the countryside. Twice they saw deer on the side on the road, grazing in between rows of drying field corn.

The van slowed, taking a right onto a long driveway shared by three trailers. The homes were well-kept if not dated, the lawns freshly cut. A green John Deere tractor was tucked under a carport added on to one of the trailers. Luck parked the van outside the back-most of the three buildings, and they climbed out.

Gravel skittered underfoot on their walk toward the front door. Her boots thudded up a wooden ramp, and before she had even knocked, Darger noticed movement at the curtain over the door. A moment later, it swung open. The pinched and lined face of a woman was thrust from inside.

"If I have to tell you reporters one more goddamn time not to trespass—"

She must have seen Luck over Darger's shoulder, because she stopped mid-sentence.

"Oh. You again."

"We're sorry to bother you, Mrs. Peters," Violet said. "I'm Special Agent Darger. From the FBI."

"FBI?"

Mrs. Peters' penciled eyebrows levitated skyward.

"Fancy."

If she were actually impressed she didn't sound it. She struck Darger as a woman who was amazed by very little.

"Could we come in for a few minutes?" Darger asked.

The woman clicked her tongue against the roof of her mouth. Without answering, she opened the door wide, and they entered.

Inside was about how Darger had imagined. It matched the outside in its 1980s charm. Brown shag carpet on the floors, dark wood paneling on the walls, and a garish green and yellow linoleum in the kitchen. But it was clean and cared for. They stood around a bar area between the kitchen and dining room. Mrs. Peters slid a glass ashtray from one side of the counter and picked up an already lit cigarette balanced on the edge of it.

"Did you say something about reporters?" Darger asked. "Have they been bothering you?"

"About once a day, one of 'em comes up the drive. I tell 'em where they can go. I got nothin' to say about nothin'."

"If they're bugging you—" Luck started, but she brushed him off by shaking her head and throwing up her hands. A charm bracelet tinkled at her wrist.

"Nothin' I can't take care of myself."

She held the cigarette between pursed lips for a moment, inhaling. Plucking it from her mouth, she let out a long stream of smoke.

"You need me to identify the body or whatever?"

"No, ma'am," Luck said. "We've got her fingerprints on file, so that's all been taken care of."

"Of course you do."

Patricia Peters ground the smoldering end of the Newport into the ashtray, black cinders smearing the glass.

Violet cleared her throat to speak.

"And when the county releases the body — probably today, but sometimes it takes a little extra time in the case of a homi— in certain cases. But when they do release it, any funeral home should be able to help you arrange everything."

The woman's thinly penciled-on eyebrows drifted higher up her forehead.

"Funeral home?"

"For the service."

"I don't got no money for a funeral."

"There are programs to help cover some of the costs," Violet offered.

The woman scoffed.

"Yeah, I know how that all works. Rope me in with promises of financial assistance, do a whole big to-do, and then you get the bill and it's twice what they said it'd be, and the help I get is peanuts. No thanks."

Violet laid a hand on the woman's pruned fingers, which earned her a withering look. She pulled back as if she'd been burned by the woman's touch.

"I really think you should consider it. It doesn't have to be anything fancy, but taking a moment to remember Sierra with family and friends is an important part of the grieving process."

The woman's nostrils flared.

"Lady, have you ever had a daughter murdered by a mad

man?"

"I haven't," Violet admitted.

"Then do me a favor and don't be telling me how to mind my business."

Violet resisted the urge to shoot Luck an exasperated look.

"We're trying to get an idea of what Sierra was like. Who her friends were, what she did for fun, if she'd mentioned—"

Patricia Peters cut her off.

"Look, that girl has been acting out since she was twelve years old. You think she told me anything? When I tried to discipline her, it was in one ear and out the other. She ran off every other weekend. By the time she was in high school, I'd had enough. I kicked her out of the house when she was fourteen, and that was that. She only ever came around when she wanted something from me, and usually what she wanted was to steal something to pawn so she could buy more drugs. So I don't know what I could possibly tell you that would help."

Darger had years of practice reserving judgment from her time as a counselor. But reserving the judgment didn't always mean it wasn't there. She felt an intense anger at Patricia Peters. At the kind of parent who would throw their own child out on their own at the age of fourteen. She wanted to grab the woman by the shoulders and shake her and scream in her face. Her only daughter was dead.

"OK," was all she said.

Violet took a breath and gathered herself.

"And when was the last time you talked to her?"

Patricia Peters rolled her eyes and picked up her lighter so she could light another cigarette.

"I already told this one," she said, gesturing at Luck. "How many times are we going to have this same conversation?"

"Just one more time, if you don't mind," Darger said, pasting a weak smile on her face.

The Bic clattered to the table, and Patricia took a long drag.

"The day before, I guess it was," she said, smoke billowing from her nose and mouth as she spoke.

"And what did you talk about?"

"She wanted—"

Patricia hesitated. Her forehead twitched into a matrix of lines, but only for a moment. She lifted the cigarette, and her mask of detachment returned.

"She wanted to come stay here, I think."

Something familiar tugged at Darger's memory.

"Did you have an argument?"

Patricia stared her down with a defiant look in her eyes like she thought Darger was accusing her of something.

"Yes."

"Do you mind telling me what it was about?"

Patricia sucked at the cigarette.

"She came by last week. When I wasn't home. And she ain't supposed to come in here when I'm not at home because things have a tendency to go missing. But she managed to get by Terry, that's my husband. He don't know how to handle her. Anyway, I get off my shift and come back here to find that she stole a ring. It was her daddy's mama's ring, but he gave it to me. That is *my* ring."

Darger could still hear Sierra screaming into the phone, telling her mother she hated her, blaming her for taking her stepfather's side of the story over hers.

"Was it a moonstone ring?"

Patricia's head snapped up at that.

"Yeah. Why? You find it?"

"No, but we're on the lookout for it, in case it shows up at any area pawn shops," Violet said.

"Well if you do find it, I want it back. It belongs to me."

"Would you happen to have a picture of it?" Violet asked.

Bony fingers stubbed the cigarette out in the ashtray.

"No. Why would I? Who takes pictures of their jewelry? Is that a rich person thing?"

"I meant that maybe you had a photograph of someone wearing the ring."

"Oh," Patricia said, pursing her lips like she had a bad taste in her mouth. "Not that I know of."

Darger glanced at Luck. He shrugged at her like, *Don't ask me. This is your show.*

"I guess that's about it," Darger said with a sigh.

She took out a card and placed it on the table, writing her hotel room and phone number on the back, just in case.

"I think we've taken enough of your time. If you think of anything—"

"Yeah, yeah. I know the drill. Give you a call."

On the porch, before Patricia closed the door on them, Violet turned back.

"Mrs. Peters, would you… mind if I set up a small service for her?"

Patricia leaned through the door frame, one hand on the handle, ready to pull it closed.

"Do whatever the hell you want. Don't matter to me. And it definitely don't matter to my girl. She's dead."

The door shut with a thud and a rattle. It had started raining while they were in the house, and for a moment Violet paused there, listening to the patter. Without giving it much thought, she put her palm out to feel the cool sprinkle of the droplets against her skin. Some kind of habit left over from childhood, she supposed.

"You coming?"

Luck's voice broke the spell, and she crunched over the gravel and into the van.

"Christ," Darger said as her door thumped shut.

He started back down the driveway.

"I told you."

"Yeah. You did."

A somber quiet fell over them for some time. The steady drumming on the roof seemed to lull Violet into a kind of trance. She stared through the rain-streaked glass of her window. As they sped through an intersection, the green light from a traffic signal lit up each droplet.

Life was always ten thousand times more complicated than it seemed. In pitying Sierra, it was easy to blame her mother, but Darger had gotten her own taste of the mood swings and the treachery. Sierra would have tested the patience of any parent. She had likely been abused, had problems with addiction, and even if she'd had the resources to treat that and the underlying mental illness Darger suspected was there, life still wouldn't have been easy for her. It would have been marked by chaotic relationships and emotional struggle.

Her brow wrinkled as she thought of Deputy Donaldson's term for Sierra: dead end girl.

Violet thought of all the other dead end girls she'd come across. She thought about the men who preyed on them, and how even if they managed to catch one, to catch *this* one, there would always be someone else to take his place. Another killer. Another abuser. Another rapist.

She had the same thought she came to often after a bad day as a victim specialist.

The world is fucked.

She didn't know how long they rode in silence, but Luck must have been feeling the bleakness as well. Or maybe her cynicism was contagious, because he asked, "Feel like a drink?"

"God, yes."

CHAPTER 35

Judging solely by looks, The Elbow Room was a standard college town dive bar. The classiest thing in the place was probably the tin ceiling, which Violet figured was probably original to the building anyway. Icicle-style Christmas lights hung over the bar, and the brick walls were adorned with local sports memorabilia and neon signs for Budweiser, Heineken, and Jack Daniels.

But looks didn't tell the whole story. The clientele did. This was the cop bar Donaldson had mentioned. Most of the guys were in civvies, but that didn't matter. Once you learned to sniff out a cop, you could smell them a mile away. Crew cuts, mustaches, t-shirts with logos for the local Police & Fire softball league, those telltale bulges of firearms holstered to belts.

All of the seats facing the door were taken. Cops, even when they're supposed to be unwinding, can't get rid of the paranoia they experience day-to-day in their jobs. The habit of watching entrances and exits sticks with them whether they are busting a meth lab in some apartment downtown or having a basket of cheese sticks at the local Applebee's.

Those who stood did so in the bladed position: instead of standing square, one foot was in front, always the non-shooting side, so for most that meant their left. It kept their gun hip away from a potential suspect and provided more room should they need to go for their weapon.

All things considered, a cop bar was the last place Darger really wanted to be. First, because Luck was likely to have plenty of chums who would want to come chat, and all Violet really wanted was to have a drink or two while blending into the upholstery. And second, all talk would likely be about the murders, and she'd had about as much of that as she could handle for the day. Her nerves were fried. She could practically hear the sizzle of the electricity as the overworked synapses fired in her brain.

She kept her mouth shut, though. The last thing she needed

was to offer Luck more ammo to use against her. *Too good for a cop bar?* she could almost hear him ask.

They found a table at the back, in a corner dim enough that Violet felt at least marginally invisible. A willowy older woman with a black bob came by and took their order. She returned quickly with a Blue Moon — in the bottle, no glass — for Luck and a whiskey-ginger for Darger. Beads of condensation glistened on the glass, and the cold felt good under Violet's fingers. She brought it to her lips, wanting nothing more than to guzzle the whole thing down in a single gulp, but she restrained herself, sipping demurely at the little straw instead.

Detective Luck frowned down at his bottle, spinning it back and forth in between drinks. Darger took the moment to study him. His hair was long enough that he wore it parted to one side, and he didn't have a mustache. He also lacked the stereotypical coffee-and-donuts physique, but part of that was that he still had youth on his side. What he did have was the rigid, upright posture and the wandering eyes, constantly searching for potential danger.

"Luck!"

The voice rang out from a few tables away, and then a paunchy, middle-aged man was approaching their booth. He dragged an empty chair to the edge of the table and squatted over it with seemingly little concern for having his back to the exit. But Darger still marked him as a cop by the high and tight haircut and the way he held out his elbows when he walked.

"Heard you caught the latest Code 99 for the Doll Parts scumbag. Detective Lucky-fucker, am I right?"

"Yeah. Right," Luck said sarcastically.

He glanced sideways at Darger, looking markedly uncomfortable by this intrusion.

"Tell the truth, now. You shit in your pants a little when you realized he took the head, right?"

"We're not really supposed to talk about the details of the case," Luck said, and the man clapped him on the shoulder.

"Oh Jesus, Dee-tective! Lighten up. I'm just messin' with ya."

The man's eyes swiveled over to Violet, whose presence had

thus far gone unnoticed. It was a circumstance she'd savored while it lasted.

"Who's yer lady friend, Lucky Boy?"

Luck scratched at his eyebrow.

"This is Special Agent Darger of the FBI."

"Well dip me in shit and roll me in breadcrumbs," the man said. "They make a lady version now?"

Violet set down her glass and stared into the man's bloodshot eyes.

"Only for about 40 years."

The man's jaw went slack for a moment, and then he threw back his head with a harsh cackle.

"Scrappy as all git out, aren't ya? Detective John Wayne Porto, pleased ta' meecha."

He didn't reach out to shake Darger's hand so much as grab it from off the table, pumping it up and down. His fingers were warm and fleshy, and she was glad when he let go.

The waitress returned and Porto insisted on buying them another round. Darger took it as an excuse to drain the rest of her highball. She needed the comfortable cushion of booze if she was going to put up with this one much longer. When the woman bent to place fresh napkins on the table for the second round of drinks (or perhaps twenty-second round, for Porto), she caught Darger's eye, giving her a quick wink. Darger wasn't sure what that was all about until she took a mouthful of her whiskey-ginger and realized it was about 90% whiskey and 10% ginger ale. The next time the waitress passed their table, Darger lifted her glass with a smile and a nod. Apparently she wasn't the only one that found Porto hard to stomach.

Detective Porto pulled another cop sitting nearby into the conversation, and Darger took his distraction as an opportunity to mostly tune out. The Jameson helped, for sure, but being in the Worthingtons' house and then dealing with Sierra's mother had brought on feelings she hadn't anticipated. Dark thoughts and ugly memories created a fog in her mind as thick as the mist that had clung to the city all day.

Some time must have passed, and then Porto's voice broke through.

"I mean, I been with plenty of women that did a little too mucha this," he pantomimed a duck-like talking motion with his hand. "Now I mighta considered a gag or maybe some duct tape, but I never considered taking off the whole head!"

With this he erupted in laughter, his face splotchy from the alcohol and elation.

Darger's glass slammed into the table so loudly it startled her a bit, and she stood to get in Porto's face.

Luck must have anticipated what was about to happen, because suddenly his hand was on her arm. Before she got a word out, he tipped his head close to hers and muttered.

"Let's get out of here."

He stood, and she followed suit, reaching into her pocket to add a few extra bills on the table for the waitress. If the woman was that observant with all her customers, Darger expected she often left her shift well-compensated in tips.

Back outside, they passed through a cloud of smoke from the crowd of nicotine addicts gathered beside the door. Detective Luck slid one jacket sleeve over his arm and then the other. The van beeped twice as it unlocked.

"Sorry about that. Probably would have picked somewhere else if I'd been thinking."

"I guess at least now when we read in the paper about Sierra Peters' body being found with no head, we won't have to wonder where the leak came from," she said, climbing into the passenger seat and pulling the seatbelt over her chest.

"Come on, Porto runs his mouth a lot, but he knows not to talk to the press."

"He doesn't have to. This isn't just local business anymore. And the tabloids are sneaky as hell. And clever. If I were one of their snake-tongued reporters, the first thing I'd do is sniff out this bar, and anywhere else I could find cops hanging out en masse, downing liquid truth by the pitcher full."

"Ah, I see. This goes right with your dumb country boy theory from earlier."

She'd walked right into it, she supposed, but what the hell? If he wanted this fight, he could have it.

"That is total bullshit, and you know it. Correct me if I'm

wrong, but you've had three murders in your jurisdiction in over a decade. I was merely stating a fact, and it's a fact the killer could easily know and think he's taking advantage of. It doesn't mean you're not a good detective. Maybe you're the greatest detective in the world, but it doesn't change the fact that you've never investigated a murder."

Detective Luck stared at her, his features tinted red from the glow of the stop light above them. When the signal changed to green, he looked away, and the car lurched forward.

Seconds ticked by. Through the windshield, Darger studied the wet smear of the various light reflections on the road. Red from the taillights of an idling car in the parking lot. Blue from the neon sign of a pizzeria. Green from another traffic signal.

Luck sighed and muttered something under his breath.

"What?" she asked.

"I said, 'You're right.' OK?"

"Oh," Darger answered. She readjusted in her seat, feeling a little awkward now. She hadn't expected that.

"Maybe I didn't like how you said it. Didn't like thinking that, I don't know, you and Agent Loshak look down on us or something."

"We don't," she said, but he waved her off.

"I know. I guess… I guess I was shooting the messenger. Just because I don't like it, doesn't make it not true."

The tires of the van sloshed through a puddle.

"I really don't. Look down on you, I mean," she said, then added. "I suppose I could have said it more… diplomatically. I was a little nervous, to be honest."

"Nervous? About what?"

She couldn't believe she was admitting this.

"I didn't think I'd be alone there. I assumed Loshak would show. And I've never done this before either."

"What do you mean?"

"I mean this is my first time profiling for a serial murder investigation. I was in Crisis Negotiation. Still am, technically."

"Oh," Luck said, and nothing more was spoken until they reached the motel.

He put the van in Park but left it running. Cop habit.

"You really mean what you said about having a service for her?"

"Yes. Why?"

He shook his head.

"Took me by surprise is all. Not the usual way of doing business for the FBI, is it?"

"Maybe it isn't about business. Maybe, after all is said and done, after the media and the lawyers and the fucking people like us are finished picking over her carcass like a bunch of crows, maybe I can look back and think that at the very least, she went out with a shred of dignity."

There was more emotion in her voice than she'd intended, a scratch at the back of her throat that threatened to turn into something more. She swallowed.

"You think that I'm too much of a stuck-up FBI bitch to give a rat's ass about some poor trailer trash?"

The words came out before she could stop them. Venom meant to counteract any vulnerability she may have shown. The Jameson must have hit her a little harder than she'd thought after all.

Luck's eyebrows pitched ever-so-slightly upward.

"I never called you a bitch."

"Ah, but then I *am* stuck-up?" she said, and the corner of her mouth turned into a smirk.

Maybe Luck wasn't so bad. It was smart, what he'd done. Turning to humor instead of taking the bait she'd left for another round of arguments. And she was doubly grateful that he'd ignored the fact that she'd been on the verge of tears. No, he wasn't so bad at all.

She undid her seatbelt, watching the grin still spreading over his face.

Before her brain was able to analyze what the rest of her was doing, Darger had leaned across the console, grabbed a fistful of Luck's jacket, and pulled him closer. He smelled like the fall, a pleasant blend of cedar and juniper and maybe a touch of wood smoke. His lips were soft, and his mouth was warm, and good God, almighty. What was in that drink?

When she broke away, Luck somehow managed to look less

confused than she did, despite the fact that she'd been the one to initiate it.

Her mouth was still ahead of her thinking, because then she said, "I'd invite you up, but Loshak's right next door, so things could get awkward."

"Why, Agent Darger… I never put out on a first date," he said in a lilting southern drawl.

A tingle of heat spread over her cheeks. She'd only meant that it might be uncomfortable to have to explain things if they should bump into Loshak, but she realized immediately that it sounded like she'd been suggesting that not only would they be having sex, but it would be the kind of sex one might hear through the walls.

She wasn't sure if his joke made her feel better or worse. At least it was dark enough that he couldn't see her blush.

"You think that was a date?"

"Wasn't it?"

She thought he was teasing but wasn't sure.

"OK. I'm going now. Otherwise I might try to see if I can fit both feet in my mouth at the same time," she said, climbing out of the van.

She didn't bother turning on the lights after unlocking her door. The deadbolt snicked into place, and she kicked off her shoes. It was two steps to the closest bed, and she threw herself across it, barely making an effort to pull the blankets up.

Thanks largely to the whiskey, she fell quickly into a dreamless sleep.

CHAPTER 36

Loshak left his car at the gas station and began the two-and-a-half block trek on foot. The night air was heavy after the rain, and the chill swirled into his chest with every breath. He found himself a little lightheaded by the time he crossed the first intersection. Not a good sign.

He knew he was pushing himself too hard again. Out in the cold walking like this when he should probably be in bed. He just couldn't see it that way. Couldn't live that way. When he was honest with himself, he knew he wasn't getting better in any case. Not anytime soon. He could feel it. So he may as well do his job and worry about his health later.

He needed to get out there, be among the police working this case. It was part of his process.

The wind picked up, frigid air battering at his face, blowing through his jacket. At least he had the two hot cups of coffee to keep his hands warm along the way.

The Burger King appeared up ahead. Off to the right. The building offered no evidence of life, and the sign was dark, but something about seeing it seemed to steady his head anyway. Seemed to steel his resolve.

It was another half a block before he could pick out the blue Mustang among the cars in the lot across the street. He couldn't quite make out the shapes of the people inside it, though he knew they were there.

His gut started to ache again. A sharp pain in the upper abdominal region that radiated into the muscles in his back when it really got going like it was now. Jesus, it hurt. His body flexed out of instinct, as though his torso could cup itself into a c-shape to escape the pain. He had to fight the urge. He didn't want the others to see how he was suffering.

He lifted a coffee cup in his hand as he approached the sports car, tipped it slightly in what he hoped looked like a greeting. His teeth grit, jaw muscles clenching tight in agony. He could make out the shadows within as he got close, but there was something eerie about the way he couldn't read the expressions on either face until he was right on top of the car.

The man in the passenger seat popped the door open, and Loshak swung it wide with his elbow. He leaned in, handed off the coffees, and climbed into the backseat of the Mustang. They introduced themselves, and he knew right away that he'd be able to keep the names straight as Novotny was the one with the huge nose. Nose-votny.

"Thanks for having me tonight, guys," he said, closing the door and settling into his seat.

"Thanks for the coffee, Offic— uh, Agent," McAdoo said.

He popped the triangular opening in the coffee lid and held it just shy of his mouth. Steam coiled out of the mouth hole.

"You can call me Loshak. Pretty much everyone does."

Both of the officers nodded.

They sat quiet, all eyes drifting to the fast food establishment across the street. Nothing moved out there.

"Not a creature was stirring," Novotny said. "Not even a Whopper, Jr."

McAdoo clucked out a laugh at that. Perhaps out of courtesy.

Loshak fidgeted in his seat, trying to get comfortable. He doubted he'd accomplish it, but he tried anyway.

"Can I ask you something?" Novotny said, eyes finding Loshak's in the rearview mirror. He retracted the toothpick from his mouth as he waited for an answer.

"Sure."

"Why come out here and watch the Burger King with us? What is there to gain from it?"

Loshak hesitated a moment before he answered.

"Right. Let me try to lay it out. My job — profiling subjects — is part science, but another part of it is art, I think. I guess that's the nature of anything psychological to some degree. We're not working out a math problem with a finite solution. We're trying to predict the behavior of a human being — an erratic proposition in normal circumstances, let alone when we're dealing with one exhibiting such abnormal characteristics.

It's never black and white. There's always room for interpretation. Years of experience allow for a kind of inductive reasoning that combines all the known variables and tells you the most probable explanation. From there, you might need to make an intuitive leap or two to get really specific. And I find intuition sometimes needs external stimulus to pull its trigger. So I like coming out for things like this. Observing. Talking with the officers doing the real job. You can learn a lot just by being present and paying attention. And you never know what might pull that trigger."

They were quiet.

"That make sense?"

"Yeah," Novotny said. "Yeah, it makes a lot of sense."

He jabbed the toothpick between his incisors.

"So you think he'll come back here," McAdoo said, his delivery somewhere between making a statement and asking a question. "To the scene, I mean. You, uh, think he'll come back."

"This guy has been fantasizing about committing these acts for a long time," Loshak said. "And coming back to the scene allows him to relive that fantasy. It dredges up all the same feelings. That's what he's doing it all for. To serve this violent fantasy life that has gotten out of control. Do I know for sure that he'll come back? No. But the odds are that he feels a compulsion to do so, even if he suspects we might be watching."

He winced a little, the pain in his gut flaring as he finished. He saw a flash of recognition on McAdoo's face, but he met the portly officer's gaze, and the man said nothing.

"Without much forensic evidence to work with, I think this is our best chance. You guys are our best chance."

"Where does this guy rank?" Novotny said. "You've worked a lot of these kinds of cases. How does this sicko compare to the rest?"

Loshak took a deep breath, a little surprised that his stomach didn't deliver a jolt of pain at the apex of his chest's expansion.

"He's smart. Smarter than most. He's someone who knows how to hide in the open, how to conceal the darkness when people are around. And dumping the bodies in the open like he does? That's very aggressive. Very territorial. It's not a normal combination. Usually the more brazen types lack a certain amount of sophistication. They solve problems with blunt force, you know? No finesse. Their thinking lacks nuance, lacks self-awareness. I don't think this guy suffers that problem. At all."

They fell quiet for a long while, once again staring at the shadows draping the Burger King in grayscale.

"So what you're saying," Novotny said, "is that he's going to be a pain in the ass to catch."

Loshak laughed a little at that.

"Yeah, pretty much. But you know, you just work the case hard. You work every angle over and over. And somehow, some way, something shakes loose. Either of you guys ever read about the Joel Rifkin case in New York?"

Novotny tilted his head to one side.

"A little," he said.

"Well, he got caught because he was driving without plates. There was a high-speed chase that ended with him crashing into a telephone pole. The officers who made the stop noticed a foul odor coming from the bed of his truck and found the corpse of his last victim stored there, a 22-year-old prostitute. And a serial murder case I worked in Colorado hinged on a cop having a feeling about an SUV rolling through a stop sign. He was on his lunch break and thought about letting it go, but something made him flip the lights on. A feeling he couldn't explain. He probably saved lives by doing that."

Everyone held quiet for a moment as a Dodge Ram drove by, seeming to slow for a split second as it passed by the Burger King. Probably some gawker hoping to see police tape strung up around bags of gore, Loshak thought.

"So you're saying you think this guy will make some dumb ass mistake like that?" McAdoo said.

Loshak grimaced again and remembered to conceal it, hoping no one noticed.

"I'm saying we'll get him. One way or another."

They were silent again, and Loshak felt the need to go on.

"Doing this job, you see the worst of humanity. People do unimaginable things to each other. Rape. Murder. And worse. I once worked a case where a guy slashed holes in women and raped the wounds while they bled out."

He sucked his teeth, though he wasn't sure if it was from the memories of the case or the pain in his abdomen.

"But you also see the best of humanity. The absolute best. Because there are people who dedicate their lives to stopping the violence. They suffer greatly for it, but they do it anyway. Someone has to."

After a second, McAdoo spoke up.

"So what do you think that means about people? When you look at the best and the worst together, I mean."

Loshak thought about it.

"I think we're all connected, you know? What we see as good and bad, it's all part of human behavior. And it's on us to untangle what it means. Not only about the criminals but about ourselves. Because the guys who do these things, as awful as their behavior is, they're still human beings. They behave like monsters, but they're not. Not all the way.

"I read once about this idea that all of the universe was born out of a collective consciousness. Like one great soul, right? Another plane that's just energy. Just consciousness. Here on the physical plane, we all have our little shard of the great soul in our skulls. That's the divine spark that makes us all who we are, you know? But the pieces can feel that they're apart from the whole, that they're sealed off from everyone by a layer of flesh and bone. We can feel that something in our lives is missing. That we are somehow incomplete. And that creates the tension in us that drives us to endless conflict. Drives some of us to the worst kinds of madness."

They were quiet for a moment.

"I don't know. Sometimes I could believe something like that."

CHAPTER 37

It wasn't until she awoke the next morning and replayed the events of the prior evening that she truly felt the depths of her disgrace.

Oh God. Had she really kissed him? And then half-heartedly invited him to bed?

Setting aside the fact that it was completely unprofessional, she barely knew Luck. She had no idea how she felt about him, or he about her, for that matter. They'd only met two days ago. And not only had she practically thrown herself at him, but he'd turned her down.

Well, maybe she did know how he felt, in that case.

That was fine. It was all fine. She'd just never look him in the eye again, not for the rest of the investigation. Or anyone else he might tell. Oh, and wouldn't that be the perfect revenge against the stuck-up FBI bitch?

Her electric toothbrush whirred, producing a thick foam she spat into the sink. Now, now, she thought to herself. That wasn't really fair. He'd apologized after all. Or come as close to apologizing as most cops probably ever came. He'd admitted a fault, at least. That was something.

Under the heat of the shower, Darger reminded herself that this was why she didn't drink whiskey. The hangover was worse than the drunkenness. It made her paranoid and petulant, and while she knew she'd made an ass of herself, she had no idea how much.

Worse than the kiss, perhaps, had been her admission to being a newbie. Why had she done that? The only possible outcome would be that he'd take her and her theories less seriously. No good would come of that.

Damn it all.

She felt a little better after a coffee and a cup of yogurt she snagged from the meager breakfast spread from downstairs.

Checking the clock to make sure it wasn't too early to call, she dialed one of her old colleagues in Victim Assistance.

"Violet, it's so good to hear from you," Beverly said. "How are things?"

"Good," Violet said, sure to smile and try to mean it when she said it.

All of her old coworkers were psychologists and social workers, experts at reading your mood from the tone of your voice, no matter what your words might say.

"I'm good," she repeated.

"I'm glad to hear it. We miss you, you know," Bev said. "Judging by the time, I'm guessing you're not calling to chat."

"No, I'm not. And I think I probably already know the answer, but… is there a way to get assistance money for funeral expenses without the signature of next-of-kin?"

"You got one of those, huh?"

"Yeah," Darger said.

It was always surprising to her how often people didn't want to bother setting up a funeral for a loved one, even if the cost would be covered. Then again, many of the family members they dealt with were the same people responsible for abusing the victim, or kicking them out of the house, which ultimately led to them turning to the sex trade to make a living. And then, like she'd told Luck, people have all manner of defense mechanisms they use to try to protect themselves from the ugliest parts of life.

Bev exhaled loudly, her breath creating a static noise through the phone.

"You really can't get authorization without the family's consent. It's all supposed to be on the behalf of the survivors, you know? It's basically the same as if we can't locate next-of-kin. If there's no next-of-kin and no estate, then it's the standard state-funded indigent burial or cremation."

"That sucks."

It was what Darger had expected, but she was disappointed at the answer.

"Yeah, I know. The dignity of the decedent isn't really taken into consideration."

Violet made polite small-talk with Bev for a few more

minutes before ending the call. She sat back against the padded headboard.

She thought of Sierra's body, laid out on a cold stainless steel tray, draped with a white sheet. A morgue attendant would open the door to her compartment, her private, little refrigerated cubbyhole. The tray would roll out, and she'd be transferred to the metal gurney with a thump and a clang. The wheels of the gurney would squeak and bump over the grout lines between the tile as she was transported down a long, stark hallway.

In the incineration room, her body would be placed on a large conveyor belt. With the twist of a knob, the conveyor would start forward, bearing the remains into the cremation box. The incinerator door would slam shut with a bang, a lever lowered to secure it in place. A button would be pressed and flames would shoot out from the combustion chamber, lighting the room with a flickering glow. Sierra's flesh would blister and then blacken, any remaining blood sizzling and hissing in the heat as it literally boiled. The fire would consume her, every last eyelash and fingernail. Her bones would be nothing but charred dust in the end, stuffed into a box labeled with a case number and a name.

"Fuck that," Darger said out loud.

Loshak answered the door, sipping at a cup of tea.

"Cup of tea?" he offered, but she declined.

"Have you given any more thought to my theory?" she said.

"What theory was that now?"

Violet didn't want to sit. She'd sucked down another coffee after her phone call and the caffeine was humming in her veins.

"The one about Fiona being a stand-in for Sierra Peters. You sort of said it yourself at the crime scene, I guess."

"Did I?"

"You said he would have sworn off killing again after she got away. But when the urges came back, he went out and grabbed the first girl he saw: Fiona Worthington. I think this proves he was after Sierra all along."

Loshak swallowed a mouthful of tea and set the cup down.

"That might be a leap too far."

"How so?"

"Well to start, how do we know he doesn't have more than one girl picked out at a time? Maybe he screwed up with Sierra and moved down the list."

"But he took Sierra's head. With Fiona, it was like he started to and then changed his mind."

"Or was interrupted."

Darger sat down finally. She could see he wasn't going to be easily convinced. Like everyone else, Loshak was far too enamored with Fiona Worthington. She fiddled with the pin at her lapel.

"So what's with the hedgehog?"

"What?"

"The pin. Come on, it's too obvious. You haven't worn a lick of other jewelry since we met — no earrings, despite the fact that your ears are pierced. No necklaces, no bracelets, no rings on your fingers. But that little golden pin is there on your jacket every day. Who's it from?"

This was why she hated being around other profilers. They couldn't turn it off. Once you trained yourself to start noticing every little thing, you couldn't stop.

"It's not from anyone," she said. "I bought it. It's mine. End of story."

Loshak pursed his lips, not looking convinced.

"Whatever."

Darger took the opportunity to change the subject.

"I've been thinking about it, and I'd like to have a service for Sierra Peters."

She practically blurted it out, worried he'd cut her off before she had a chance to say the words.

"Huh," he said, then suddenly looked more awake. "Alright."

She'd expected some kind of resistance. When it didn't come, she almost didn't know what to say. So she said nothing.

Loshak rubbed a hand over his cheek and chin, massaging the skin.

"You know, we could have some guys in street clothes getting video in case anyone of interest shows up. That means we'll need to have the press run something—"

Darger sprung out of her chair.

"What? No. No way. That's not what this is about."

"What are you talking about?"

"Can't this girl get one day, one fucking day without it turning into a media shitshow?"

"Well, it's too late for that, isn't it? We can't control that, Darger. What's more, it's not our job. Our job is to catch the guy."

She set her jaw, teeth gritting together.

"No press," she said.

He held his hands out.

"Alright, chill out. It was just an idea."

It was quiet for a moment while they studied one another. Loshak broke away first.

"Look, I know you had a personal connection to her, but don't let it get under your skin. It's not good for you."

"It's not under my skin."

"You sure about that?"

"Yes," she answered, biting the word off quickly.

"Alright," he said, though he didn't sound convinced. "But don't let it become a habit."

She didn't bother putting up a fight this time.

"It won't."

"Have you arranged something like this before?"

"Exactly like this?" she asked. "No."

"I just meant a funeral, you know. I don't suppose you're quite the weeping widow, but I guess what I wanted to say was, don't let them take you for a ride. Whole business is a racket."

Darger thought Loshak was being a bit unfair, but she let it slide. She thought morticians probably saw about as much of the horror of the world as law enforcement did, and no one threw them any parades or lauded them for their bravery.

Violet would have been happy to report to Loshak that there was very little pressure to add any bells and whistles from the funeral director. Darger selected a modest casket and a simple service. She also made sure to warn him about the condition of the body.

"The body is not… intact. In fact, there's no head. At all."

"I see," he said, barely reacting with more than a series of blinks.

She wondered if his composure was real or something that came with years of practice.

"Obviously that means closed-casket, but in addition to that, I'd like to stress that there is an on-going investigation and the… condition… of the body is something we'd like kept out of the press."

The man folded his hands, one on top of the other.

"I can assure you that we are accustomed to being as discrete as is possible."

"I appreciate that. Thank you."

When it came time for the flowers, Darger pointed to a photograph in the brochure. It was an all-white casket spray with roses, tulips, and snapdragons.

"That one," she said, then something occurred to her. "Do you have anything with peonies?"

"Peonies would be out of season, so we'd have to have them flown in. $20 a stem, so $240 for a dozen, plus shipping."

Violet thought of Fiona Worthington's mother, sparing no expense to have her daughter's favorite flower on hand for the funeral and now at home. And then she thought of what Sierra's mother had said in response to Darger asking about a service. *Do whatever the hell you want. She's dead.*

And then there was Loshak's opinion of the business being a racket. Maybe he was right. And maybe Patricia Peters was right, too. But Sierra deserved something nice just as much as Fiona had.

"That's fine. I'd like to replace the roses with a dozen white peonies."

CHAPTER 38

All the lights in the funeral home were off when Tyler jammed the key into the lock and twisted it. The deadbolt clacked out of the way, and the back door swung open, just like that. He pushed his glasses higher up on his nose, a rushed breath hiccupping into his throat. Frigid electricity entered his bloodstream then. Like it always did. Key or no key, nothing made his heart pump icy cold all through him like breaking and entering. Nothing.

He kind of loved it.

The steel rectangle tilted aside to reveal the shadowy interior of the place, and Tyler led the way in, Sam following close behind.

They inched forward into the darkness, the kitchen counter vaguely discernible to Tyler's left. A gaping blackness pocked the center of it, and he gathered that must be the sink. With that as a reference, he knew the basement steps were somewhere to the right, though he couldn't see them. He shuffled that way, trying his best to remain soundless. The sheer quiet of the moment stretched out into something stimulating, and he couldn't help but smile, more little bursts of electricity flashing through the muscles in his cheeks.

"Can we get some lights on up in here?" Sam said, his voice practically full volume.

"Shut the fuck up!" Tyler whisper yelled.

He got a hold of himself and went on in a more hushed manner.

"They're sleeping upstairs. Right above us. Dickhead."

"Right. Sorry," Sam said, now whispering, though even that seemed too loud as far as Tyler was concerned.

Jesus. Maybe he shouldn't have brought this idiot along after all. This was all Sam's idea, of course, but when Tyler took an honest look at his friend he saw him for what he truly was — a mouth-breathing idiot who ate Flamin' Hot Cheetos for approximately half of his meals. Subtlety and finesse were foreign concepts to Sam. Tyler thought they always would be. Quiet was a language this fool could neither speak nor understand.

Tyler extended his arms in front of him, hands bobbing into the darkness like strange tentacle feelers, reaching out for some piece of wall to orient himself. Anything solid. The quiet bloomed again, and the stimulation made the skin on his chest writhe, the flesh pulling strangely taut with every inhale and then going slack upon releasing.

Though he'd never brought a friend along, Tyler had snuck into the basement of his uncle's funeral home a few times before, stealing enough embalming fluid each time to properly soak a few bags of weed. The high was pretty dramatic, supposedly indistinguishable from that of PCP. One of his friends, Anton, tripped so hard on the stuff that he wound up disrobing on a city bus and telling the other passengers he was a Native American. (Not true.) Upon being arrested for indecent exposure, he told the cops he was Jesus. (Also not true.)

Tyler had been in high school back then, though. Now he was 20, and this trip into the basement would land him something much, much better than a weird drug trip. He licked his lips as he thought about it. Sam's cousin had all the phone numbers they'd need to arrange the sale as well. It was too perfect.

His fingertips found purchase then, brushing the ornately carved wood adorning the edges of the doorway. He stopped, adjusting the trajectory of his shoulders, and then he skidded his feet until they felt the lip at the top of the steps. Good.

It was all downhill from here.

Upon reaching the hall at the bottom of the steps, Tyler felt along the wall and turned on the lights. The long fluorescent bulbs flickered and hummed as they came to life. He had to squint and let his eyes adjust to the brightness. He looked over his shoulder to see Sam doing the same, though he did it while breathing through his mouth, of course.

Maybe they would've been OK to turn the lights on in the kitchen as well, but he didn't like it. Not with his Aunt Alice,

Uncle Bob, and three cousins asleep just up the flight of stairs, possibly within viewing distance of the increased illumination. Down here, it'd be OK, though. He felt pretty good about that.

It was colder in the basement. The kind of cold that made Tyler's skin shrivel, all of his body seeming to shrink away from the dank air. He felt the muscles in his arms tense, seeming to pull the sleeves of his t-shirt higher up on his shoulders. His nipples were like the tips of ice picks.

Tyler pivoted, looking at the myriad of doorways leading off of this hallway. It all seemed vaguely familiar, but it took a second for the particulars of the layout to come back to him.

"This way."

He gestured to the lone open door to their left, and the boys stepped once more into the darkness. Astringent odors wafted about them, hovering somewhere between a medicinal smell and that of toxic chemicals, somehow mildly healing and harming all at once. Tyler again flipped a switch and waited that beat for the fluorescent bulbs to light the way.

Two metal embalming tables dominated the room, evenly spaced like a pair of hospital beds. Stainless steel. Little grooves ran down the length of each that somehow made them look like something his mom would roast a chicken on. The heads of the tables cut off into industrial sinks, some apparatus mounted underneath them with what looked like tanks and hoses coming out. Those must be the new embalming fluid pumps.

The blood goes out. The pink goo goes in. And now the meat will keep again.

Tyler couldn't help but consider the notion that one day his naked body would lie on a table just like these. He pictured himself sprawled out, skin puckered in the cold so little dimples formed everywhere like the saggy skin on a raw Thanksgiving turkey.

But no. No. It wouldn't just be tables like these. *It would be these actual tables.* Wouldn't it? Everyone in his family would surely have their funeral here.

He shivered, his t-shirt riding ever higher on his shoulders, and a lump formed in his throat, swelling up like a tennis ball.

He looked at the pearl and black tiles on the floor, all of

them leading slightly downhill to the grate in the center of the room. A drain, he remembered. In case it got messy and they needed to hose the room down.

"Jesus," Sam said, his voice again coming out full volume. "This is where they cut 'em open and shit, huh?"

Tyler swallowed the tennis ball and glared at his friend. He growled barely above a whisper.

"Shut the fuck up. If you can't be quiet, go wait in the fucking car. I can do it myself."

Sam reverted to his version of whispering.

"Sorry. Just… Well, where the hell is it?"

Tyler took a breath, the flesh on his chest crawling again.

"I forgot. This is where I stole the embalming fluid, but it's not where they, uh, store them. Store the bodies, I mean."

They looked at each other, and weird clucking sounds emitted from Sam's gaping maw. After a second, Tyler realized his friend was laughing.

Nice.

Tyler turned, and they crossed the hall, opening the door there and entering another dark room. He felt around for the light switch once more.

This space felt colder right away. He could feel the chilly air press through his jeans and coil itself around his legs, his torso shimmying a little at this unwanted touch. Again, the silence seemed to swell in that moment before the lights came on.

There. Yes. This was it, thank Christ.

The pair of refrigeration units looked like stainless steel filing cabinets along the back wall, each big enough to hold two bodies.

"Fuck," Sam whispered in an awed tone. "It's like those… um… things from TV. Those rooms where police keep bodies and shit. Can't remember what they're called."

"The morgue."

"Fuckin' right. The morgue, bro. Like the rue morgue and shit."

Tyler nodded, and then the two of them hesitated a moment just inside the door, not quite ready to cross the room and get hands-on with the metal box where the dead bodies lay.

Tyler felt a little twitch in his leg, and that seemed to spur him into motion. He stepped forward, his footsteps echoing off the tiles on the floors and walls.

He slowed as he neared the unit, his eyes flicking from door to door, trying to settle on which meat drawer he would slide open first. Top left made sense to him. May as well work it left to right.

He didn't wait around for the weird feelings to kick in. As soon as he was within arm's length, he reached out.

The stainless steel was frigid against his palm and thumb. He almost pulled his hand away out of instinct, but he caught himself. Time to be done with it.

He thumbed the button and pulled the door open, holding his breath. It took a second for his eyes to focus on what was there.

Feet. A girl's feet.

He squeezed his hand into a fist a few times and then reached in for the identification form — essentially a paper card in a laminated plastic pouch that lay between her ankles. The cold reached up to his elbow, threatening to go further, but he pulled the card free.

"What was her name?" Sam whispered from across the room. "Sienna or something."

"Sierra Peters," Tyler read from the card. "It's her."

He took a breath, his eyelids fluttering. They'd done it. The rest would be easy.

"Get your phone ready," he said to Sam, and then he turned to slide the shelf of corpse out of the meat fridge.

He wanted to yank the thing out and be done with it, but she was heavy, and it was too weird.

The drawer wheels squeaked as the naked body slid out on its metal tray in slow motion. The flesh of her legs was very pale, with bruises around her knees so dark they almost looked more black than purple. His eyes snapped away from the patch of pubic hair right away, but he found no comfort in looking at her breasts, like a pair of sunny side up eggs stretched over her chest. None of these horrors prepared him for what came next.

His hand jerked away from the shelf right away when he saw

it, a gasp torn from his throat. By the time he gathered himself enough to realize what he was doing, he found that he was standing halfway up the basement steps. He had no memory of sprinting out of the room and through the hall to get there, but he knew he must have.

He stopped, legs parted with a foot on each step. He blinked a few times before he could convince himself to go back.

The image came back to him. The stumped neck. The empty length of tray where her head should be. Jesus fucking Christ.

When he got back to the storage room, Sam was shooting video with his phone.

"You OK?" his friend said, stopping a moment to observe Tyler. For once, he knew enough to not laugh. He even closed his mouth for a moment.

"Yeah. I'm fine."

Sam went back to his cinematography, and Tyler looked at the naked, headless girl. The buzz of the fluorescent bulbs seemed louder now. They seemed to vibrate in his chest.

"We should cover her," Tyler said.

"What do you mean?"

"The tabloids will give us more if she's covered. A headless girl is one thing. They can go with the whole serial killer thing and sensationalize it. A naked headless girl, though? That's too much."

A thoughtful look came over Sam's face.

"Yeah," he said. "Yeah, you're right."

Tyler put two pairs of gloves on before he'd touch her. He draped a sheet over the corpse, running it under her arms so it might even look like a dress from the right angle. Then he folded her hands on her belly, almost like a real funeral pose.

Sam smiled as he fingered his phone to get the money shot.

CHAPTER 39

It was a brief service with less than a dozen mourners. Violet had left a message with Sierra's mother letting her know the time and place. She'd hoped Patricia might change her mind and attend, but she never showed. Loshak and Luck were there, along with Donaldson, the Sheriff, and a few other law enforcement personnel who got word and wanted to pay their respects. Even Janssen made an appearance, to her complete surprise.

The funeral home had recommended a local minister named Tabitha Watson, whom Darger suspected had plenty of experience officiating the funerals of strangers and nonbelievers. The funeral director asked Violet to choose three songs for the service. Figuring Sierra's tastes would have leaned to the somewhat contemporary over anything classical, Violet selected Bridge Over Troubled Water by Simon and Garfunkel, Jeff Buckley's cover of Hallelujah, and Angeles by Elliott Smith. After the first song, Pastor Watson read from Psalm 69:

"Save me, O God; for the waters are come in unto my soul.

I sink in deep mire, where there is no standing: I am come into deep waters, where the floods overflow me.

I am weary of my crying: my throat is dried: mine eyes fail while I wait for my God.

Let not the waterflood overflow me, neither let the deep swallow me up, and let not the pit shut her mouth upon me.

Hear me, O Lord; for thy loving kindness is good: turn unto me according to the multitude of thy tender mercies."

As her eyes meandered over the small crowd, Violet wondered if she'd made a mistake. Should she have taken Loshak's advice and invited the press? Even if they'd gotten no new leads from it, didn't Sierra deserve more than this?

Her gaze fell on the peonies laid over the casket. How many

mourners had come for Fiona Worthington?

Stupid question, she told herself. It wasn't a competition.

And still, she couldn't stop comparing the two. The snapshots of Fiona on horseback. Her room kept perfectly intact, with her trophies and awards proudly displayed. The fresh cut flowers placed on her bedside table. And then Sierra's mother, who had seemed the most animated during their brief interview when she wondered if they'd recovered the moonstone ring.

It wasn't just the material things Sierra had lacked. It had been a sense of home. A sense of family.

A sense of love.

Violet was so deep in thought she barely noticed when Hallelujah played, and when Pastor Watson began reading again, she assumed at first it was another Psalm. It was only when she got to the lines: "What hurts you, blesses you. Darkness is your candle," that Violet's head snapped to attention. Goose bumps prickled over her arms.

It was a Rumi poem. She recognized it because she'd once read it during a eulogy herself.

A surreal feeling came over her then, and she very much wanted the service to be over. She needed air. Clean air. Her jacket felt hot and cumbersome, and she resisted the urge to fidget.

Pastor Watson finished with the poem, and Violet tried to calm herself. She went through her calming exercise. Name, birthday, favorite color, but when she glanced up and saw the coffin at the front of the room, she lost any ground she'd gained.

Violet closed her eyes, hoping for a reprieve. Instead she saw blood on the pavement, dark red pools coagulating into jelly. Breath rattled in her throat as she inhaled, and though her head was bowed now, eyes fixed on her hands and the death grip they had on the folded program for the service, she saw Loshak turn to face her.

He leaned in.

"You alright?"

Not trusting herself to speak, she nodded and murmured, "Mmhmm."

Finally, Watson introduced the last song and thanked them all for being there to honor Sierra Peters.

The guitar came in, the rapidly fingered notes resonating over the speakers. The song built to the bridge and peaked, holding the room breathless for a beat and rolling back from there.

And that was it. The small group dispersed. It was over. It was done.

Violet rose and went to the head of the chapel to thank Pastor Watson and the funeral director again for their assistance. She paused at a table set up with a coffee machine to fill a paper cup at the water dispenser. It was pleasantly cool in her mouth. Crumpling the emptied cup in her fist, she tossed it into a nearby trash bin and made for the door. It was propped open with a potted palm, and she could already feel the breeze coming in. She slid her sunglasses on and welcomed the sunlight beating down overhead.

Darger had her nose stuck in her bag as she rounded the corner of the building on her way to the parking lot. She was trying to dig her keys out and having a heck of a time of it. The key ring was new, the feel of it unfamiliar to her probing fingers, not to mention buried under all the flotsam and jetsam she kept in her bag.

She heard the scuff of shoes on pavement, and when she looked up, she found Detective Luck leaning against his van, watching her.

"Detective Luck," she said.

"Special Agent Darger."

She hadn't talked to him since the dubious kissing incident. She'd even chickened out when she gave him the funeral details, sending a text instead of calling. So far he hadn't mentioned it, and she sure as hell wasn't going to bring it up. And that was that.

"No sign of her mom, huh?"

Darger shook her head.

"She wasn't home when I called. I suppose there's a chance she never got my message, but…"

"It was nice that you did it, anyhow."

Violet shrugged.

"I have something for you, actually," Luck said, opening the door of his van.

Violet waited while he sifted around between the seats, coming back with an envelope, which he handed to her.

"From me and a couple of the guys at work," he said.

Inside the envelope was a stack of $20 bills. She didn't count it, she just let the flap fall closed and held it out to him.

"I can't take this."

"Why not? We wanted to pitch in."

"I don't know," she said.

She couldn't explain why, but it felt odd for there to be cash changing hands over funeral costs.

"It's a lovely thought, really, I just…"

"Well if you won't take it, then donate it somewhere in her name."

Darger looked up, trying to see Luck's eyes behind the lenses of his aviators.

"OK. I like that." She put the envelope in her purse. "Thank you."

"Got dinner plans?" he asked, and she tried to keep her face impassive, forbidding her cheeks to blush or her eyelashes to flutter.

"I don't."

He spun his keys on his finger with what she had to assume was practiced nonchalance.

"Would you care to join me?"

"Alright," she said. He gestured at the van to indicate he'd drive, and she went around to the passenger side.

As he navigated the Luckmobile out of the parking lot, Darger did her best not to wonder whether this was supposed to be a date or not. But trying not to wonder was half of wondering, and so she failed.

It was after a funeral, and that seemed to her an inopportune time for a date. Then again, he had specifically waited for her in order to ask her to dinner, it seemed. Wasn't that the very definition of a date?

Maybe he felt bad, didn't think she should be alone after the service. He was only being chivalrous, perhaps.

Jesus, why did she even care that much?

"Where are we going?" she asked, thinking maybe the venue might offer a clue.

"I know some places. I'm sure they'll seem quite humble compared to whatever hoity-toity establishments you're accustomed to."

She glared at him over the edge of her sunglasses, and he winked at her.

"Any special diet considerations I should know about? Food allergies?"

"Yes, actually. On Fridays, I only eat things that are green. Wheat grass smoothies, kale salad, steamed soy beans, etc."

Now he eyeballed her, trying to decide if she was being serious.

"Kidding. Nothing like that, and I'm not picky."

"You like shawarma?"

"Yes," she said and decided that the garlic and spice content made for unlikely date fare.

Not a date then. Fine. Now she could relax.

It was a small place near the university campus, and judging by the line of young people picking up carry-out orders at the front register, a popular place among the students.

Their waitress was a small girl with her hair pulled back into a French braid. Despite her slight physique, she issued commands like a drill sergeant.

"How many?" came out more like an order than a question.

"Two," Luck said, and she led them to a table next to a window. Darger was glad for that after the somberness of the funeral home.

The food arrived quickly after they ordered, and they avoided talking much in the interim. Violet supposed funerals left most people feeling a bit introspective.

They'd been eating steadily and quietly for a few moments when Luck broke the silence.

"So?"

"It's good. Really good."

Darger dipped her falafel sandwich into a little cup of Lebanese garlic sauce and took a massive bite.

Luck smiled at her, looking genuinely pleased.

Darger noted a table of two men in one of the back corners of the restaurant. They were casually dressed and engaged in friendly conversation, but every five seconds, almost on the dot, one or the other glanced up and let their eyes do a quick search of the room.

"I see you've chosen another place favored by your fellow boys in blue."

"What?"

"Like half the guys in here are cops."

Luck craned his neck around. At a different table, two men immediately recognized him and raised their hands. Luck waved back.

"OK, so there are a couple."

Darger sipped at her tea, trying to disguise her smirk.

"So what?" he asked.

"Nothing. Just an observation."

"And isn't that the pot calling the kettle black, Special Agent Darger?" he asked, gesturing at her with a French fry before popping it into his mouth.

"How is that?"

"How is it not? Your so-called 'just an observation' is meant to suggest that I can't turn the cop part of me off, right? That I don't know how to just... relax and be a normal human being."

"No. An observation can just be an observation."

"Now that," he said, wiping grease from his fingers onto a napkin, "is the biggest bunch of bull I've ever heard. At least when it comes to you. I see you over there, watching everything, making little mental notes, brain going a mile a minute. I bet you profile in your dreams."

Darger tilted her head to one side, blinking thoughtfully.

"You know for all your talk about not having much experience, you're a pretty good detective."

He looked surprised that she'd paid him a compliment, and she thought his cheeks maybe went a little pinker.

"Thanks," he managed to mumble, and then seemed to

suddenly find the stack of pita bread on his plate fascinating. It was a while before he recovered from his bout of bashfulness.

"So, at the risk of asking the most cliché question possible," he said, "what led to you becoming an FBI agent?"

Violet plastered a polite smile on her face, the one she kept always at the ready for when someone asked that question.

"Why did you become a detective?" she threw back, raising an eyebrow.

"The same reason half these guys do," he said. "Runs in the family."

"Well, I guess you could say the same for me," she said, lying through her teeth. "So who was it? Your dad?"

Luck nodded, frowning into his hummus as if it might hold some existential truth.

"Was he a detective?"

Raising his eyes to meet hers, he shook his head.

"Nah. Highway patrol."

"And let me guess. You used to sneak into his room where he kept his badge and uniform, and you'd put it on and go stand in the mirror, pretending it was yours. Flashing it at your reflection and practicing your tough guy policeman voice."

She sat up a little straighter and looked him in the eye, squinting one side a little like she was in an old Western.

"Detective Luck. Athens PD. Freeze and put your hands in the air," she said, throwing her voice a little in an attempt to sound male.

Luck laughed.

"Um, no. But I'm starting to get a better picture of you as a kid."

Violet smiled and sat back, rubbing at her cheek. She liked Luck. Liked his laugh and the hint of crow's feet at the corner of his eyes. Proof that he hadn't lost his ability to smile on the job. She didn't like lying to him. But it was better this way. For all parties involved.

"You up for a drink after this?" he asked.

"At La Chambre Coude?"

Darger bent her arms and wiggled her elbows up and down. Oh good Lord. She was getting punchy. But the prospect of getting drinks made it seem again like this maybe-possibly-could-be a date, and as much as she didn't want to admit it, that gave her a little thrill. A warm, fluttering lightness in her chest.

"Sorry. I thought The Elbow Room might sound fancier in French," she said, clasping her hands together so she couldn't pick at her nail polish.

Luck ignored her outburst of dorkiness, thank God. He only shrugged, one corner of his mouth curving upward.

"Unless you'd rather go somewhere else."

She flapped a dismissive hand in the air.

"Nah, it's fine with me."

"Alright, but don't go spouting any of that French stuff in there. We're simple folk around here, and that kind of outlandish extravagance will likely get you kicked out."

Ice cubes tinkled as Violet set her glass down and gave him a hard stare.

"You're never going to let me forget that one, huh?"

"No ma'am," he said with a wink.

CHAPTER 40

There is no way around it. Rot is beginning to take hold of her flesh. Fouling the meat.

The head rests on a wooden rocking chair in the living room area of his studio apartment. It stands upright but tilted to balance its weight on the stumped neck bone and the rounded back of the cranium.

The mouth hangs open all the way. Like she reclines in a dentist's chair. Every tooth visible and reflecting light. Her tongue white and strangely spongy looking. Her gums have receded to the point that it's a wonder her teeth haven't fallen out.

Maybe that will be the first thing to go. It's inevitable. Isn't it? She will crumble. She will fall apart.

He looks at her again. Really looks.

The skin around the eyes droops unnaturally. Little puckers in the complexion like a silk shirt that needs ironing.

The skin sags along her jaw. Pulls into jowls that make her look much older than she is. Or was.

He watches the motionless head from across the room. Rubs a hand at the back of his neck. Feels the little prickle of the hair follicles there.

He hates to think it. To admit what is happening. But it looks like her skin is about to detach from her cheek bones and slide clean off of her face. Like a sheet of skin will flap off and melt into a puddle on the floor. Leaving exposed muscle and bone. Everything wired together with stringy connective tissue.

It seems so inevitable. The way she will come apart.

But he has a plan.

He approaches her and rotates the swing arm lamp on the desk so it points straight down at the face. It makes her cheeks look like they're glowing pink.

He kneels next to her and opens the makeup kit. He's no expert with cosmetics. He knows enough to know that a liquid foundation will bring back a more normal human color to her. So that's where he'll begin.

He loads the makeup sponge with the stuff and spreads the first swipe over the flesh. Hesitates. The streak of healthy pink skin looks so wrong next to the pale gray that has become the rest of her that he almost vomits. His throat flexes. Acid climbs his esophagus. But he keeps it down.

He lets his eyes go out of focus as he continues. Can't quite bear to look at that seam where death and the makeup touch unless it's a little blurry. A little fuzzy.

The smell doesn't help, of course. She is ripe. Has been for a while now. He thinks he's gotten used to it some. As much as he can. But it still makes him nauseous at times. It might be unavoidable.

Her shade brightens. An unnatural hue somewhere between peach and pink. Inhuman and strange.

He is painting her. That's all. It seems less upsetting to think of it that way somehow. Less profane. Like putting a fresh coat on the shed. Covering the wrinkles and flaking places.

He speaks in a whisper as he works.

"They could never understand it. Could they?"

I think not.

"But you do?"

Yes.

He dry heaves again. Tongue spluttering out between his lips. Epiglottis clicking deep in his throat.

His hands freeze for a moment. The makeup sponge holding still on her cheek. Warmth creeps into his face. Embarrassment.

"Sorry about that."

It's OK.

"I do this because I love you, you know. Because you're mine."

I know. This is the only way.

"Yes."

The lipstick and eyeshadow go on easier. Faster. And somehow the foundation looks less fake right away once those are in place. Something about the contrast of the mouth. The shape the shadow brings out. She looks feminine and... He searches for the right word. Eyes ticking up toward the ceiling as he ponders it.

Juicy. She looks juicy for the first time since before all of this.

Again, he whispers:

"You look so beautiful tonight. Like a proper lady."

Thank you.

He tries his best with the mascara, knowing it will get a little messy. Forgiving himself preemptively. Reminding himself he can wash it off and do it over if he needs to.

His hand shakes a touch as he brings it to her face. Applies it.

Not too bad. The darkened lashes make her look dainty again. Bring out a tenderness in her expression. Even if it's a little sloppy.

He steps back. A great relief washing over him. This could have gone so wrong. Could have come off so ghastly.

But it didn't.

He closes her mouth and the lipstick adheres the lips together in a pout for a beat. And she looks good. Really good. Better than he ever could have hoped for.

Then gravity flicks its wrist. Her jaw swings free. Falls. Falls. Bounces faintly when it can fall no more. The tiniest bungee effect when the cords pull all the way taut.

Careful to avoid touching the freshly wet area, he cups her neck to lift her and places her onto a cookie sheet. She reclines. Nose pointed toward the ceiling. He uses two cans of chunky soup to keep her from flopping over and smearing her makeup. Clam and corn chowder with bacon.

Lifting the sheet, he walks to the kitchen. Every step measured. Slow and even. The tray wobbling a touch in his arms.

The freezer door swings open. Fog swirling and disappearing in the frosty chamber. It stands empty. Vacant. Ready for its new occupant.

In she goes.

CHAPTER 41

They passed another group of off-duty policemen on their way out to the van. Luck greeted them with a polite nod.

He unbuttoned his suit jacket before climbing into the vehicle.

"I need to stop off at my house on the way," he said, sliding on his sunglasses. "Gotta feed my dog. The way he eats, it should take about 60 seconds, tops. I hope that's OK."

"No problem at all."

Luck fastened his seatbelt and rolled up his sleeves before reversing out of the parking space.

"What kind of dog?" Darger asked.

Luck peeked at her over the reflective lenses, looking sly.

"I'll give you three guesses, Miss Profiler."

"Oh, you want to play it like that, huh?"

"I can't help but notice that you're stalling."

"Pft. Alright. But if I win, you're paying for all my drinks tonight."

"Fair enough."

Darger tapped a finger against her lip.

"Well, there's the totally obvious choice for a cop."

"You have to say it, or it doesn't count as a real guess."

"German Shepherd."

"Nope."

"Didn't think so," she said, her tone light and dismissive.

Luck snorted.

"Yeah, right. See what happens when you make your little assumptions?"

"Pit bull," she said, ignoring him.

"Wrong again."

Damn. The sun was barely brushing the top of the tree line in the distance, and Violet stared at the last golden rays extending over the greenery.

"Black lab?"

Luck made a buzzer noise in his throat.

"Well?"

Looking smug, he said, "You're just going to have to wait and see now."

Luck's place was a small one-story ranch tucked in the middle of a block of similar homes. She guessed the whole neighborhood had probably been built sometime in the 1950s. Each yard had an attached one-car garage and two maple trees out front, and she guessed the interiors featured three bedrooms for the perfect nuclear family.

Inside, everything was as she'd expected. It was very clean, and decorated in what she liked to call "Modern Masculine Minimalist." The classic bachelor pad of the anal-retentive. She'd bet Loshak's house or apartment was almost identical. The walls were a neutral gray, the floors a mix of dark stained wood and stone tile. Stainless steel appliances adorned the kitchen along with black concrete countertops. The lone break from the so-called MMM aesthetic was a collection of brightly colored balls, stuffed animals, and pillows strewn about the living room. It was like a child's toy chest had exploded in the otherwise stark, manly space.

Luck gave a whistle and called out, "Morty!" and then she remembered. Of course. The dog.

From down a hallway, she heard the clickety-clack of nails on the floor. It rounded the corner, seeming to gain speed as soon as its master came into view.

Luck squatted low to meet the animal, and the dog rushed at him.

"Hey, buddy," Luck chuckled as the dog snuffled and licked him, hopping around on his hind legs with his tail wagging so fast it was a blur.

It was a scrappy, scruffy little thing in a red bandanna. He was barely bigger than a puppy, but Darger couldn't tell if he was young or just a small breed. One ear stuck straight up, the other flopped over on itself.

"So what is he?" Darger asked, patting the little dog's head as he went in for a sniff at her ankles.

Luck scooped a measuring cup full of food into a metal dish.

The dog instantly lost interest in Violet in favor of the food.

"Dunno. A mutt of dubious parentage is what I usually say."

If she had to guess, she would have said part Pug, part Chihuahua.

"How old is he?"

"Don't know that either," Luck answered, watching the dog inhale the kibble. "I got him from the shelter. They found him wandering the streets — no tags, no microchip, no nothing. They think he's probably five or six. I've only actually had him a few weeks."

That also explained the abundance of toys, Darger thought. He would have gone nuts spoiling the new dog.

When the dog had finished with the food, Luck went to a sliding glass door at the back and opened it a crack. Morty scurried outside and trotted around the yard, dutifully marking various landmarks on the way. Luck grabbed a plastic bag from a roll on top of the refrigerator and went out to collect the doggie deposits. Darger smiled to herself, figuring even before he'd gone outside that he'd be the type to never let a dog poo run astray. In fact, she bet herself that instead of depositing the bag anywhere in the house, he'd immediately take it either into the garage or outside. Wherever he kept the curbside trash bin.

Morty led the procession back into the house, and sure enough, Luck went to a door off the kitchen and returned without the bag.

She crossed her arms, thinking of a different wager then.

"You cheated, by the way."

"Cheated?"

He stooped, and Morty leapt into his arms. Luck stood up, cradling the dog in the crook of one elbow.

"You let me think you had a purebred."

"No, no, Special Agent Darger. You jumped to that conclusion all on your own. I tried to warn you about making assumptions."

She reached out to scratch the dog behind the ear, and Morty planted his snout against her wrist for a sniff.

"You never said what you wanted if I lost."

"I didn't," Luck said, something in his voice catching her

attention.

When she looked up to meet his eyes, his focus was fixed on her in such a way that her ears started to get hot, and her heart beat a little harder.

He leaned down and kissed her, and the heat in her ears spread to her cheeks and chest.

Morty was still clutched in Luck's arms, and he squirmed between them. Violet felt a warm, wet tickle on her neck. She giggled and pulled away from Luck and the licking dog.

"I guess he likes you, too."

"Too?" Violet repeated. "So that means you like me."

With an outstretched finger, she poked him on the arm.

"I don't know if I'd go that far," he said, setting the dog down and pulling her closer by the hand, "but you've grown on me a little."

He lifted her fingers to his mouth and brushed his lips lightly over her knuckles. The sensation sent a shiver down her spine.

"You still wanna go get that drink?"

"Later," Violet said, leaned forward to kiss him again.

Before long, he took her hand and they went to his bedroom.

CHAPTER 42

His apartment feels like a tomb. An L-shaped cavern with books and magazines piled along the walls. Dark. Dank. All the lights off. The curtains drawn as tightly as possible. The muted glow that spills along the edges of the windows is the only illumination.

It reeks of death blended with his own body odor. The putrid stench intertwining with a distinctly masculine musk. Leathery. Faintly acrid.

All of the stuff he'd pulled out of the freezer melts in a garbage bag on the kitchen floor. Hot pockets. Waffles. Little breakfast sausage patties. TV dinners. It will start smelling soon as well. He knows this. And yet he can't bring himself to make that trip to the dumpster. Can't bring himself to leave her alone in the cold.

The tomb feels empty with her gone. Even if she's just tucked away in the freezer. Not truly absent. It's not the same. Lonelier. More meaningless.

He speaks to the fridge door.

"I miss you."

There is no reply.

He paces the floor. Socked feet moving from the linoleum to the carpet cratered with cigarette burns. Black blisters in the beige that were there when he moved in. He rounds the bend in that capital L. Passes the mattress on the floor and turns back.

Nausea ripples in his gut as he treks toward the kitchen once more. The loneliness always makes him sick when it comes back full force like this. When reality encroaches on the fantasy.

He talks to the freezer door again. Eyes locked on the veins and wrinkles on that textured surface. Voice tight and small.

"I love you, and I hate you, and I miss you so bad."

Night falls. He lays in his bed. Blinking in the dark. Staring up into the emptiness.

He rolls over onto his side. Tries to find comfort he knows isn't there for him.

This separation is only temporary. He'd bought more time by using the freezer. Possibly quite a while. But knowing these things doesn't make it any less painful. She is apart. Not there. He can feel it in his guts. In the thudding in his skull. In the sweat on his skin.

He knows it's all in his head. Knows she is a girl he created. That he scripts her every word.

But it's real when he can believe it. The realest thing he's ever felt. That he ever will feel.

And it's real when she's gone. Whenever they're apart, the emptiness is right there. All around him. As big as ever. As close as ever.

He sits up finally. Faces the fridge. Whispers into the blackness.

"Goodnight."

He waits for a long time before he reclines.

She doesn't answer.

CHAPTER 43

The atmosphere inside the Elbow Room was different than it had been the first time. There was a strangeness Violet couldn't put her finger on. She wanted to call it subdued, but then it seemed like there was still an awful lot of chatter going on. Maybe more, even. But the voices felt hushed and almost furtive.

Luck came back from the bar carrying their drinks. As he slid Violet's over the polished tabletop, he glanced back over his shoulder.

"Weird vibe in here tonight."

Her eyes went wide when they met his.

"I was thinking the same thing."

"What's up with that, you think?"

Violet lifted her drink and took an unladylike gulp.

"I don't know, but I'd say we're probably about to find out," she said with a subtle nod at the rapidly approaching figure.

"Detective Casey Luck, everyone!" Porto said, clapping his hands in applause. "About to be Ohio's most famous boy in blue."

Luck shot Darger a disconcerted look.

"How's that?"

Porto chortled.

"Ho, ho! You mean you haven't seen it?"

"Seen what?"

Luck's lips were pressed into a firm line. Darger could tell he was starting to get annoyed.

Porto smiled, but it looked evil.

"Porto, cut the shit and just tell me what the hell is going on," Luck said, actually uttering a four-letter word for once.

Definitely annoyed, she thought.

"The Daily Gawk," Porto said.

Darger got out her phone.

"The Daily Gawk?" Luck said. "What are you talking

about?"

"Oh, for fuck's sake," Darger said.

"What?"

She held out her phone so he could see the headline plastered on The Daily Gawk's home page: **Doll Parts Killer keeps her head!**

"Aw, hell," he said.

Darger swiped the screen with her finger, and then she felt the bottom of her stomach fall out.

"There's a video," she said, not realizing for a moment that the tiny voice speaking was her own.

She didn't hit play. The video started streaming automatically.

Grainy, shaky cell phone video showed fluorescent light reflecting off of tile floors. The camera panned slowly to build the suspense. Scanning up from a set of bare feet, over the wrinkles of a white sheet. Hands folded over the chest in the stereotypical funeral fashion. At the sight of the fingers with the blue nail polish, Darger felt a twisting motion in that emptiness occupying her gut. A spiral. She'd wanted them to start paying attention to someone other than Fiona Worthington but not like this.

The camera continued its journey, moving upward from the crossed arms to the pale flesh of the collarbone and then the shoulders. And finally the payoff: where the head should be, nothing but a raw stump. Red meat with a single white bone protruding from it like a finger pointing at the stainless steel tray.

The shock shot tendrils of numb all through her as she watched this fresh profanity, and she felt her balance wobble a little atop her chair, forearms leaning against the edge of the table for support.

But after that initial wave of disbelief, a rage clenched inside of her. Something lean and hard and hateful growing tighter and tighter in her chest. The world just kept finding new ways to defile Sierra Peters, and it made her want to fucking explode.

And then Darger was on her feet. Moving. Her shoulder colliding with Porto and glancing off of his saggy torso, knocking him backward in a drunk stumble.

"Violet," Luck called after her, but his voice sounded small. Weak.

She didn't slow down. Pushing through the crowd. Through the steel door.

Casey caught up with her in the parking lot.

"Where are you going?"

"To figure out who took that video," Darger said.

"Yeah? And how are you going to do that?"

She dug her nails into her palms, holding herself back from directing the rage at him, but just barely.

"It was either taken at the morgue or the funeral home, and the funeral home has a shitload less security than the medical examiner's office."

Luck unlocked the van, and they climbed in.

"I told that funeral director to be discrete. God damn."

She ripped at the seat belt, tugging it across her lap and securing the latch.

As they pulled into the parking lot of the funeral home, Darger's phone rang. She looked down at the letters on the screen spelling out: CAL RYSKAMP.

"Shit," she muttered. "It's my boss."

She pressed and held the green button, then lifted the phone to her ear.

"Darger."

"Are you seeing this shit?" he asked without preamble.

Darger's head fell forward.

"Yes."

"Well, what the hell is going on out there? How did they get it?"

"That's what I was just about to find out. Someone must have gotten into the funeral home—"

"Yeah, and about that. What's this I hear about you trying to pull strings with Victim Assistance to get funding for the funeral?"

This new outrage caused her voice to rise an octave.

"What? That's not what happened."

"Look, I don't know how things worked over there, but that's not how I'm running things here. I figured you knew me well enough to know that."

"Cal, I—"

"No, Violet. I don't want to hear it."

The disgust in his voice was like a slap in the face. She knew Cal was probably taking some heat for the tabloid story. The Bureau hated bad press. But every iteration of the story she could find made no mention of the FBI's involvement in the case at all. So she couldn't figure out why he was so outraged.

Cal's voice dropped to a grating whisper.

"You're supposed to be keeping me in the loop, Violet. I've been in meetings the last two days and had no idea we even had a fourth victim until my boss dropped into my office to ask about this Daily Gawk clusterfuck."

Ah, so that was it. Cal had come across ill-informed in front of his boss and felt like an idiot. Now it was her fault. Then again, she'd been so caught off-guard by Sierra's death that she had maybe been shirking her duties a bit.

"I'm sorry," she said. "You're right. I should have notified you."

His breath rattled into the phone.

"From now on, I want daily updates. If you can't get me on the phone, send a text or an email. And I'll expect a field report from you no later than 0800 hours tomorrow morning."

Tomorrow was Saturday. She didn't suppose Cal would be there to read her report at 8 AM, in fact, she didn't think he'd even so much as glance at it until Monday morning when he returned to the office. This was punishment for sure. And rest assured, it would be worse if he got the report with a time stamp reading anything later than 7:59 AM.

"Yes, sir."

"And as for getting to the bottom of who sold the footage, drop it. I think enough of a mess has been made already. I didn't send you out there to be playing Scooby Doo games."

"I'm not playing—" she started to say, but the line was dead. He'd hung up on her.

So Cal was pissed, and Bev had sold her out. Not even sold

her out. Outright lied. Violet had paid for the funeral herself, despite knowing full well there'd be no funds from Victim Assistance.

Apparently, Violet had fewer friends in the world than she thought. What a shock.

She was still staring down at the now-dark screen of her phone when Luck reached out a hand and squeezed her shoulder.

"You alright?"

"Yeah. I guess."

He tucked a strand of hair behind her ear.

"You could come stay at my place for the night."

"I better not," she said, and his hand fell away. "It's not that I don't want to, believe me. But I have to write up a report before morning."

"Guess I should let you get back, then."

They parted without so much as a peck on the cheek, and she crossed the darkened lot to where her rental was parked. Violet wasn't sure if it was her or him or both, or perhaps just the events of the evening that put a damper on things.

Maybe none of it meant anything, she thought as she climbed the stairs to her motel room. Maybe it was all just an outlet for the maelstrom of emotions that come with a funeral.

Her keys clattered on top of the dresser, and she fell onto the corner of the bed with a bounce and a creaking of springs. Oh, how she wanted to crawl under those cheap hotel sheets and sleep for a week. For once she was certain that she'd zonk as soon as her head touched the pillow. But Cal wanted that report by first light. An act of penance if she'd ever heard one.

She slithered over to where her laptop slept on the bedside table and woke it with a brush of her fingertip across the touchpad. She had work to do.

CHAPTER 44

It was a knock at the door that woke her. The sharp rap of knuckles against the blue-painted steel.

Violet stirred, wiping at a swath of hair that had fallen over her face. What time was it?

11:38 AM according to the clock. She'd submitted the requested paperwork to Cal via email a little after 7 AM and supposed she must have passed out sometime after then.

The knock came again, and she scrambled out of the bed.

"Just a minute," she said, hurrying over to the chair where she'd tossed her dress from the previous day.

It was wrinkled from lying there in a wad all night, but it was the quickest manner of getting dressed at the moment. Violet pulled it over her head, then glanced in the mirror. Her hair was a mess, and she had a smear of leftover mascara under one eye. The hair she pulled back into a ponytail, and the smudge she removed with the swipe of a spit-moistened thumb.

She didn't check the peephole, she just swung open the door. She supposed she'd been expecting either Loshak or Luck. It was neither.

The woman looked frailer to Violet standing on the catwalk outside the room. Maybe it was the harshness of the sunlight, illuminating every nook and cranny of her wrinkled skin.

"Mrs. Peters," Darger said. "Come in, please."

It wasn't until she was pulling the door shut that she remembered the night before. The Daily Gawk video. Oh, Christ on the crapper.

Violet removed her bag and the other crap she'd dumped on the chair so that Patricia could sit. The woman's eyes were wide and darting back and forth, and she clutched at the purse handle that hung over her shoulder as if it were the only thing tethering her to reality.

"I saw..." Patricia said, then wiped a hand over her mouth. "I heard about it this morning. I had to go to the website. Had to

250

see it for myself."

Violet sat down on the bed across from the chair.

"Mrs. Peters, I'm so sorry. I wish you didn't have to see that. Especially not that way."

"So it's real, then? I mean, that was really my girl in that video?"

Violet forced herself to look Sierra's mother in the eye when she spoke.

"Yes. I'm afraid so."

It was the smallest of consolations, but Darger was suddenly glad the body had been mostly covered with a sheet in the video. Perhaps they would have blurred any nudity had she not been, but it would have been obvious nonetheless.

Patricia Peters covered her face with her bony hands. A long moan escaped through her fingers.

"Oh, my little girl. What did he do to my little girl?"

Violet reached out and gave Patricia's arm a gentle squeeze.

"I'm so sorry."

When Mrs. Peters looked up at Violet her eyes were moist.

"I just... don't understand how," she said.

Violet was about to explain (and profusely apologize for) the indiscretion of the funeral home when the woman went on.

"How could someone do such a thing?"

Now she wept openly, and Darger reached across the bed to grab the box of tissues.

Of course she was more upset about what had happened to her daughter than about the who, what, where, when, and how the damn pictures had been leaked. Come on, Darger, she thought to herself. Pull your head out of your own ass for ten seconds.

"He's sick," Violet said, softly. "And I don't mean that in the way that suggests that he could get better with therapy or medication or anything like that. The sickness in him is bone deep."

Patricia dabbed at her cheeks with the wadded up Kleenex.

"And he's still out there."

"Yes. He is," Violet said, looking down at her own hands. "But we're going to catch him. I promise you that no matter what happens, I won't give up on this case until we get him."

The woman was already shaking her head, expressing disbelief.

"But how? He's out there right now," she said and tugged at the neck of her blouse like she was trying to stave off a chill. "Livin' and breathin' and probably thinkin' about who he can do this to next. And I keep wondering about... what if he comes for me? He took her twice, my girl. That means he was stalking her. And you mentioned her ring being gone, meaning I suppose he took it. What if he wants more? Why wouldn't he, if he was obsessing on her like that?"

Violet patted the woman's knee.

"It would be..." she struggled to find the right words, "highly unusual for something like that to happen."

"You know that for sure?"

"I don't know anything for sure, Mrs. Peters. But my job is trying to figure out what he will and won't do and how he might make a mistake. Because that's how we're going to find him. We have police knocking on doors from dawn until dusk, trying to find anyone that may have seen something. We're watching the places we found the girls in case he comes back. If you'd like, I can talk to the Sheriff's Department and have them send a patrol by your house a few times a day. To keep an eye on things."

That seemed to allay some of the worry on Patricia's face.

"I don't want to be any trouble-"

"It's no trouble. That's what the police are there for, Mrs. Peters."

The woman bobbed her head, and an expression passed over her face that Violet couldn't read. Shame, perhaps.

"I've been feeling so much guilt since it happened. Guilty that I thought she was lyin' just like everybody else. Guilty that I didn't let her come home like she wanted. Guilty that I didn't go to say goodbye to my baby."

A tear ran down her cheek.

"You tried to tell me, but I didn't listen. And now I'll never get to see her again."

Violet handed her another tissue. She could tell the woman that guilt was a normal part of the grieving process, but she knew it wouldn't make her feel any better.

Bony fingers scrabbled at the purse, disappearing inside and searching for something.

"I brought these," she said, handing over a few faded photographs. With the pictures came a whiff of stale cigarette smoke.

Violet shuffled through the snapshots: Sierra, age 4, dressed as Dorothy from the Wizard of Oz for Halloween. Sierra, age 7, holding a ballet pose in a black leotard and pink tights, her hair pulled into a bun. Sierra, age 11, standing in a pool in a pink bathing suit. She had a blue popsicle in one hand and was sticking out her tongue to show off the matching blue hue of her mouth.

Violet felt a sudden pressure in her chest and struggled to maintain her composure.

"I keep seein' them use the same photo on the news, but that other girl, the one before my Sierra, the pretty one, they got all sorts of pictures of her. Didn't seem right that Sierra's was just the one. And blurry, too."

"Thank you," Violet said, setting the photos out of sight. "I'll make sure they're returned to you after I add them to her file."

She didn't bother explaining that she and the police had nothing to do with the photo selection on the nightly news.

"I was wondering," Patricia said, gazing down at the hands she held clutched in her lap, "if I might see the photos. Of my Sierra."

Violet wasn't sure what she meant at first. The photos she'd just handed over? And then it hit her. She was asking to see the crime scene photos.

Darger's head was moving before the words came, shaking vehemently.

"Oh, I don't think that's a good idea, Mrs. Peters."

"It's my right, isn't it? As a family member?"

Violet begrudgingly agreed.

"It is. But in cases like these—"

"I know," Patricia said, and now she was the one reaching over to pat Violet's hand as if their roles had been reversed. She sounded calm and reasonable. Like she'd already accepted what she would see. "I know it won't be pretty. But I already missed my chance to say goodbye in the flesh, and I think…"

She trailed off, eyes lifting to the ceiling.

"Have you ever seen one of those gory movies, Agent Darger? Where they show all manner of blood and guts and violence?"

"I suppose so," she answered.

"But there are other scary movies. Ones that don't show all the carnage and slaughter. They're quiet. They leave things to your imagination. And somehow I think they're much scarier for it."

Patricia's gaze swung down, and her piercing eyes fixed on Darger.

"That's what seeing that video last night was like. It was all light and shadow. Implied horror. I need closure, Agent Darger. I need to see her one last time. As she was. If I don't, I'm afraid what's in my imagination will keep on hauntin' me forever."

Violet suddenly had a feeling she'd gotten with Sierra. That there was much more to this woman than she'd initially realized. Again Darger was faced with the fact that she'd done the same as everyone else, as much as she wanted to deny it. She'd pigeon-holed Patricia Peters as a shallow, uncultured old woman who lived in a trailer on the outskirts of a small town. She was poor and from the country and may not know all there was to know about a great many things, but she was not ignorant in the ways of the world.

"OK," Violet said quietly. She stood and got her laptop, setting it on top of the dresser and crouching next to it. "But if it gets to be too much, we should stop."

Patricia nodded gravely.

Violet began with some of the least disturbing photographs first: shots of Sierra's feet and hands. She watched Sierra's mother for any sign that she might pass out or run for the bathroom to vomit. The woman kept an unblinking stare on the screen.

"Go ahead," she said, and Violet moved on.

A photograph of Sierra's buttocks and back. One of the garbage bag trapped in the undergrowth. And then a shot from further away, showing the body from toe to neck.

Patricia gasped then, and Violet stopped. Shit. This was a bad idea.

"I'm sorry, I shouldn't have—"

"No," Patricia said, squeezing her eyelids shut. "It's not that. It's not the pictures."

After an anguished moment of silences, her eyelashes parted.

"If I had—" Patricia pressed a fist to her mouth to stifle a sob. "Oh my dear Lord, what if she's dead because of me?"

"No. No, Patricia. This is not your fault."

"But she wanted to come home, and I wouldn't let her!" the woman wailed, and Violet scooted closer to embrace her.

"I know," Violet said, her own feelings of responsibility for Sierra's death filling her with remorse.

After a few moments, Violet pulled back and took one of Patricia's hands in hers.

"The reality is that when someone dies, there are always regrets. Those of us who remain can't help but wonder what we could have done differently. And how things may have ended up if we had."

Patricia sighed and lifted the balled tissue still in her hand to her mouth. A rattling cough racked her chest.

"Excuse me," she said, hoarsely. She swallowed and coughed again. "Could I have a glass of water?"

"Of course," Violet said, rising to her feet and grabbing one of the individually wrapped disposable plastic cups on a tray next to the TV. The cellophane crinkled as she tore it free and went to fill it in the bathroom.

As she held the cup out, Patricia fanned the neck of her blouse.

"Do you have any ice? I'm feeling a little warm."

"Oh," Violet said, peeking at the rippling liquid in the cup. "Sure. I just have to run down to the ice machine."

"I'm sorry to be such a bother."

"Not at all," Violet answered, setting the cup down in exchange for the plastic ice bucket. "I'll be right back."

When she returned, Sierra's mother seemed to have set

herself back to rights. Her eyes were clear again, her purse hung squarely from her shoulder, and her hands were clasped in her lap. Violet plucked a few ice cubes from the bucket with a pair of tongs and handed the cup over.

The woman's larynx bobbed beneath the loose skin at her neck as she drank. She gave a satisfied sigh and rested the cup on the table next to her.

"Thank you for that."

"Not a problem."

Patricia stood then.

"I think I've probably taken enough of your time, ma'am. Thank you for talking with me."

"Anything I can do," Violet said, clasping Patricia's hand as they moved to the door. "I mean that. If you need someone to talk to. I'm here."

"I appreciate that," Patricia said, then walked out the door. Violet watched from the balcony as she made her way to her car. Darger was still standing with her back leaned against the door frame long after the car had turned onto the road and faded from view.

CHAPTER 45

McAdoo gazed across the street where the Burger King parking lot looked as empty as ever. No movement. No nothing. The shadows that seemed so ominous when they first got this assignment now seemed non-threatening. Routine. It was getting hard to imagine they'd ever see anything out this way.

He cracked open his can of Monster, and a strange candy smell filled the Mustang.

"Can't believe you drink that shit," Novotny said.

"What? We're sitting out here bored to death all night. I need the extra caffeine and taurine and stuff."

"You ever heard of coffee? It's what adults drink in scenarios such as the one you've just described."

"Sometimes I drink coffee. Sometimes I drink Red Bull. Sometimes, every once in a while, I even drink Monster. It so happens that Monster is a better deal than Red Bull. You get like twice as much for the same price."

Novotny put his window down a crack and tilted his head toward the opening.

"Christ. It smells like gummy worms or something. Tropical punch and shit."

McAdoo didn't know what to say, so he took a sip out of his can, slurping a little. He checked the time on his phone, the little screen lighting up bright. It was 1:04 AM.

"Think Loshak is coming by tonight?" McAdoo said, not wanting to give the silence enough time to settle in.

Novotny shrugged his shoulders before he responded.

"Don't know. Why? You been missin' him?"

"Nah. He just breaks up the monotony, I guess."

"I see how it is. I guess, after all these years, I'm not enough man for you anymore. You need something more."

"Yeah. No. Very funny, shitbird."

McAdoo took a big slug out of his can of Monster, almost defensively. The acidic tingle snaked over his tongue and took the plunge toward his belly.

"Don't worry, Mac. I will personally make sure that Victor Loshak is there to hold your hand while we make the arrest. Might even be able to get a binky you can use during any interrogations."

"A… A binky?"

"That's what my little girl calls her pacifier. Thing helps her calm down when something spooks her. Of course, she's not quite two years old, but I imagine it'd work for a bigger baby such as yourself."

McAdoo said nothing. He slurped his energy drink. It could be worse, he knew.

Even when Novotny was in an antagonistic mood like this, it was better than the quiet. He had a habit of going mute, speaking not a word for hours at a time, and the silence bothered McAdoo a lot more than the ball-busting. Novotny communicated solely through glares and heavy sighs during those stretches. His presence became aggressive, pushing past uncomfortable into unpleasant. A great weight squatting upon the atmosphere inside the car.

Maybe there'd been less of that behavior since his little girl was born last year. McAdoo hadn't considered that before, but the timeline seemed to match up with his memories well enough. It was also something else the two of them had in common. They both had gotten married and had daughters in the last four years. Calmed down. Their talk had often come back to terrestrial stuff of late. Family stuff. Hopes and dreams involving simple things like vacations, holiday plans, a future involving preschools and beyond. McAdoo spoke often of owning a boat. His partner talked about making detective someday. In most every way, life seemed much simpler.

Until the Doll Parts Killer showed up.

"Jesus fuck," Novotny said, his voice thick and deep, barely louder than a whisper.

McAdoo looked up from his can, glancing over at his partner who sat forward in his seat, the binoculars pressed to his eyes, his mouth open wide. He followed the angle of the 'nocs to the parking lot across the street. Just as he went to reassure himself that his partner was further messing with him, he saw it: the dark figure creeping across the asphalt, disappearing behind the Burger King's brick facade.

He almost dropped his drink.

"What the hell? Jesus. Is it him?" McAdoo said, immediately a little embarrassed that his voice conveyed more open terror than Novotny's had.

Novotny lowered the binoculars, though his eyes stayed locked at the place where the figure had vanished behind the building. He answered without making eye contact.

"It's someone. Caucasian male in jeans and a blue jacket. Let's roll."

McAdoo struggled to nestle his Monster into the cup holder, the bottom of the can rattling along with the shaking of his hands.

Novotny cracked the driver's side door, kicked one leg out and paused in that position to draw his weapon. The gun swished a little pulling free from the holster.

"Wait," McAdoo whispered, still fumbling with the drink.

If Novotny heard him, he gave no sign of it. His brow furrowed, a fierce look about him like some kind of predator. He moved out of the car without sound, closing the door with great care so that it only emitted the thinnest click.

He moved out, his gun pointed in front of him. One finger rested on the trigger guard, and the thumb on the opposite hand rubbed at the button on his flashlight, ready to light this creeper up once he got close enough.

A wave of panic rippled through McAdoo as he watched his partner move away from the safe space the Mustang had become. After a frozen moment, he jerked into action. He wobbled back and forth in the bucket seat, flopping like a beached narwhal, trying to angle himself in such a way that he could draw his gun.

The voice in his head sounded sure of itself, so he listened.

Get out first. Then draw your weapon.

He stumbled out onto the asphalt, splashing through a mud puddle. He half-jogged, concentrating on getting his gun free from its holster without dropping it, fingers scrabbling over the metal and leather like the spindly legs of a baby deer. There. He had it. He picked up speed. The grip nestling into his fist, setting back against that webbed spot between his thumb and index finger. It felt right. More than right.

He felt in control. Realizing this made him shudder, his shoulders jerking in a series of spasms, but he didn't slow down.

It looked like something out of a movie. A point-of-view shot. The camera racing across the street, across the parking lot, drawing closer and closer to that point behind the Burger King. But it wasn't a camera. It was him.

He heard a voice from around the corner, a deep-throated growl that reminded him of his high school gym teacher, Mr. Norris.

"Hands up! Hands up!"

It took him a second to realize it was Novotny doing the yelling, though this brought no real relief.

He rounded the corner, eyes racing to find his partner. There. The other officer stood with his feet shoulder width apart, gun and flashlight pointed at... nothing? McAdoo stopped in his tracks, trying to make sense of it.

"He's in the dumpster," Novotny said, his voice closer to normal volume but maintaining a bit of the hard edge from before.

Sweet Jesus. The dumpster? The dump site itself? It really was the killer.

McAdoo's gun trembled before him as he pointed it at the green trash bin. Pinpricks ripped up and down his limbs, and his head went light. This didn't feel real. At all.

"Hands up!" Novotny bellowed again. "Right now! Do it! I want to see hands sticking out of that goddamn dumpster at all times."

Two hands rose above the metal side, the flashlight's beam reflecting off of the pale of the palms.

A strange slur spoke up from inside the metal trash bin.

"Do you want I should stand up?"

Novotny and McAdoo looked at each other before Novotny said: "What?"

"I said, 'Do you want I should stand up?'"

Novotny's body language changed all at once. His shoulders slumped, and he rocked his head back to look skyward as though rolling his eyes wouldn't be enough.

"Christ," he said. "Yeah, go on and stand up. That you, Carl?"

"Yessir."

The man in the dumpster stood. He looked haggard, his graying hair scraggly and his face visibly dirty.

"I take it you know him?" McAdoo said.

Novotny nodded.

"Carl Metzger. He's not the guy. It's the wrong dumpster anyhow."

As soon as he said it, McAdoo remembered that he was right. The body had been found in the grease dumpster located behind the building, not this one which was closer to the back of the lot.

"You out picking through the trash again, Carl?" Novotny said. "Carl here was in county lockup most of the past 60 days. Trespassing and contempt of court. Just got out three or four days ago, I think. Is that right?"

The guy in the dumpster bobbed his head slowly up and down. Smiled a little.

"So what do we do?" McAdoo said.

"Might as well take him in. Let the detectives clear him officially. Shit, they may as well get some extra paperwork duty out of this, too. Lord knows we will."

CHAPTER 46

Her phone buzzed that evening, just as she finished polishing off a takeout box of Chicken Lo Mein.

"Detective," she said by way of answering after seeing the name on the screen. She thought she heard cartoons in the background.

"Good evening, Agent Darger," Luck said, all official-like, and for a moment she wasn't sure if he was teasing or not. Then his voice relaxed. "How'd it go?"

"With my report?" she asked. "Fine. I've always had a knack for bullshitting my way through paperwork for some reason. If he really wanted to punish me, he would have made me present my report to a crowd while wearing only my underwear."

"I wouldn't mind seeing that."

Violet snorted, tracing the lattice pattern on the bedspread with a fingertip. The interlocking lines reminded her of a birdcage.

"I had an interesting visit earlier," she said.

"Yeah?"

"Patricia Peters came by."

"Oh. Merry Christmas," he muttered. "I hadn't thought about that."

"Me either."

"Was she pissed off?"

"She was more upset than anything else. Blaming herself, really. For everything. I think the reality of it finally hit her."

"Geez," Luck said, exhaling with a whoosh and crackle of static. "I can't even imagine trying to come to terms with something like that."

"Yeah," Violet said, and her eyes automatically went to the brooch on her lapel.

"Well, I know you got ordered to stand down as far as the leak was concerned, but I went over to the funeral home this afternoon," he said. "Put the screws to the director."

"It's Saturday. Isn't it your day off?"

"Yeah, well. You know how it is. We're never really off-duty, are we?"

Violet felt strangely flattered that Luck had gone out of his way to do that. Though she supposed she was being presumptuous to assume he'd done it for her. *You and your assumptions, Agent Darger,* she could hear him say.

"What did that sniveling reptile have to say for himself?"

"Wasn't him," Luck said. "He has a nephew that does odd jobs around the place. Of course, the funeral director swears he's a good kid, and it must have been some of his friends that pressured him into it."

"Peer pressure to defile a corpse. That's a new one," she said, shaking her head in disbelief. "You talk to the kid?"

"Yeah," Luck said. "Pretty sure he crapped in his tighty-whities, especially when I embellished the truth a little and told him it was a felony to profit off the desecration a human corpse."

"Nice."

Violet was sitting cross-legged on the bed, and she let herself fall backward. The back of her skull bounced when it made contact with the mattress.

"And if it makes you feel any better, I think between my little white lie and the hell he's gonna catch from his uncle, he'll probably end up donating the money to charity."

Darger's eyes traced the irregular outline of a water stain on the ceiling. It was shaped a little bit like a cowboy hat.

"That'd be something."

Luck must have heard something in her voice, because he sighed.

"You know it isn't your fault, right? You were trying to do a good thing."

"Trying," she said with a wry smile.

"You know what I mean."

Darger threw her arm over her eyes, blocking out the light in the room.

"Yeah."

"I just wish I could do something to cheer you up, that's all," he said.

Violet bit her lip, thinking of their encounter after the funeral.

"I bet you do."

"Now, now, Agent. Look at you getting all manner of salacious thoughts in your head. My intentions were all but pure."

"Right. Pure."

He laughed.

"Well, hey. I have family obligations tomorrow, but if I get any updates on anything, I'll let you know. Otherwise, I'll talk to you on Monday."

"Until then," Darger said and hung up the phone.

She wasn't going to check again. She didn't want to know. It only made her angry all over again.

She got up, took a step away from the bed, and then leaned down and took the mouse in her hand, unable to resist the urge.

She loaded the browser and typed the first few letters into the address bar. It already knew what she wanted and finished the URL for her. Her thumb stabbed the Enter key.

When she'd first looked, the funeral home video had 88 comments. The next time she'd loaded the page, it was up to 212. Then 492. That didn't count Facebook, which had added another 770 comments and over 4500 Likes. She tried to imagine the type of person who would "Like" something like that.

The page loaded. At the top was a story about some Hollywood producer's mental breakdown. Violet wondered sardonically if that would be enough to staunch the flow of new attention to the Sierra video. She had to scroll down through several posts to reach it, as the site seemed to have some new juicy tidbit of gossip every hour, if not more often. There was almost a day's worth of "news" covering the Doll Parts story now.

But she only got two posts down before she saw a new headline that caught her eye.

FBI Agent: "Doll Parts Killer is sick." These crime scene

photos prove it!

"Oh shit," Darger said.

The article had been posted 37 minutes ago. She wondered who the hell in the FBI would be so stupid as to give The Daily Gawk a quote.

Loshak? Never.

And she hadn't talked to any reporters. So who?

Her mouse clicked on the bold text, and she started to wonder if someone was trying to set them up somehow. Someone within the investigation. Who else would be leaking this stuff?

When the article loaded, she scanned down the page. It wasn't until she reached the third photo that she realized it was even worse than she'd imagined.

There on the screen, in full color, were the crime scene photos from Sierra's file. Darger's personal file. Darger's personal photos.

She was dreaming. It was a nightmare. It had to be. This could not be happening. Had she been hacked?

She squinted closer at the photos, realizing that they weren't "originals" so to speak. The quality was bad. Oddly pixelated. And there was a glare on some of them as if there was a reflection of the camera flash. In one photo, you could clearly make out the edge of a laptop screen.

Her laptop screen.

And then she finally put it all together.

Someone had taken photographs of her computer screen. That was when her eyes roamed over to a pull quote from the article. In big black letters it read:

"The killer is sick. And the sickness is bone deep." — Violet Darger, Superstar FBI Profiler

For the love of God. Superstar? Who wrote this shit?

It was at that moment that her phone buzzed. She didn't have to look to know the screen said, "Cal Ryskamp." She flinched as she pressed the Answer Call button.

"Darg—" He cut her off before she could even properly answer.

"Tell me I'm in the motherfucking Twilight Zone."

"Cal."

"Please tell me that, Violet. Please tell me that I've wandered into some kind of temporary alternate reality in which everything is upside-fucking-down, because I swear to God we just had a conversation yesterday about these tabloid leaks."

"I know, Cal. But listen—"

"No, no, no, Agent Darger. You listen. My goddamn neck is in the noose right now, so whatever you have to say, it better be good."

"The quote is a lie, Cal. That was something said in confidence to the victim's mother. I didn't know she was going to turn around and sell me out!"

"No? You didn't think everyone in that fucking podunk town was going to be looking around for ways to make a quick buck off their most famous resident at the moment? Wise up, Darger! I mean, Jesus God Almighty."

She knew Cal well enough to know that, while potent at first, his temper never sustained itself for long. She could hear in his voice that it was already starting to fizzle.

"What about the photos?"

"She must have got into them when I left the room for a minute. I mean you can obviously tell they're shitty cell phone shots of my computer screen, not the real thing."

"Jesus H. Christ," Cal said, laughing bitterly. "It's just one disaster after another."

"I'm sorry."

"Don't be sorry, Violet. Be better. I mean, fuck! You know this isn't how to play the game. I was trying to do you a solid here. I rub your back — help you get your foot in the door with Behavioral. But instead of rubbing back, you keep fucking me in the ass."

"That's a delightful image, Cal. Thank you."

She cared even less for the inference that any of this was a game.

"Don't get cute. I'm serious. This is your big chance. And mine," he was sure to add. "Do not screw this up. Got it?"

"Oh, I got it."

When Cal finally let her off the phone, she peeked her head

around her door. Loshak's blinds were closed, no light could be seen around the edges. Maybe he was finally sleeping off his illness.

How long had he been suffering now? It had to be coming up on two weeks. No way it was food poisoning. An ulcer, maybe?

A small wave of relief washed over her as she pulled her head back into her room. She'd had about as much disapproval and condemnation as she could handle for one day, anyway.

Tomorrow would be a new day. And who dared to dream what new horrors it might hold?

CHAPTER 47

Violet was already up when the knock came at her door. She likely wouldn't have slept well as it was. Her sleep schedule was shot to hell. And that was on top of everything else.

Loshak's grim mug greeted her when she opened it. So he'd finally seen it for himself.

"I can explain," she said, but he held up a hand to cut her off.

"Save it. I'm sure you'll have plenty of time to do some of that when we get to the meeting."

"Meeting?"

"Yeah. Sheriff O'Day called an emergency meeting of the task force."

Loshak cocked his wrist toward his face.

"Starts in 20 minutes, so we better get going."

Darger was already reaching for her jacket.

"It's a Sunday."

"Well, I don't suppose our local boys were too thrilled when they saw that their case had made the tabloids twice in one weekend."

The dryness in his delivery only made the words sting more. She knew the worst was still to come.

When they reached the parking lot, Darger headed for her car instead of following Loshak to his.

"I'll follow you in my car," she said.

The last thing she wanted was to be trapped in a moving vehicle with Loshak's wrath.

But even as they filed into the conference room on the second floor of the Sheriff's office, he said little. She couldn't figure it out.

It was a smaller group this time. No lawyers and no uniformed officers. Just the three detectives and their bosses. From the icy stares aimed in her direction, she could have sworn the room was about ten degrees colder than the rest of the building.

"Well, well," Janssen said. "If it ain't our resident Superstar FBI Profiler!"

Violet cringed internally but kept her face calm. She risked a glance at Detective Luck, and he gave her what she thought was an encouraging blink.

Sheriff O'Day spoke up then, calling the meeting to order.

"I know that none of us are thrilled to be here on a Sunday. I'm sure we all had been looking forward to spending some much needed time with our families," he said.

His top lip and mustache quivered with irritation.

"But I think some things in terms of this investigation and this task force need to be addressed. Chief Haden, I know you had a few things you wanted to say."

Luck's boss moved to the front of the room, hitching his belt up over an ample belly. He cleared his throat before speaking.

"I've already discussed this with my detectives at length, but I figured it would be wise to reiterate to the rest of the group: from this point forward, there should be no extraneous photographs taken at crime scenes. Myself and the two Sheriffs have agreed to this effect. The crime scene techs and the coroner should be the only ones with cameras anywhere near a scene. Period. End of story."

He made no secret who that comment was aimed at, staring at Darger for the duration. She clenched her jaw, wishing she had the power to go invisible.

"Furthermore, I've canceled the stakeout detail for all crime scenes within Athens city limits, effective immediately," the Chief of Police said.

"I've pulled my men off their details as well," Sheriff O'Day added.

Loshak held up a hand.

"Hold on, now. Let's not be hasty about that."

"Hasty?" Sheriff O'Day said. "What's the point of staking out the dump sites if he knows we're watching now?"

Loshak gaped for a moment, and then his gaze roamed over to Darger. His eyes held a look of incredulity. Oh boy. That wasn't good.

She was starting to think Loshak hadn't actually read the article. Hadn't known about the stakeout being blown.

She'd only mentioned it to Patricia Peters to relieve the woman's paranoia. To let her know they were doing everything they could… Of course, Darger knew now she'd been conned. She didn't think Loshak would care for her excuses, whatever they may be.

"As far as I'm concerned, it's all down the tube now," Sheriff O'Day was saying. "All those extra man-hours. The overtime. This operation cost our department a lot of money."

"Ours, too," the Chief agreed.

She knew that her one job at this meeting was to keep her mouth shut. Avoid digging herself into a deeper hole. Head down, lips zipped. But she couldn't help it.

"Thank god you all have your priorities straight."

"Let's not overlook the most obvious fact," the Sheriff said, ignoring her, but struggling to keep his voice level. "This makes all of us look bad."

She thought of Sierra's broken body, defiled and on display now twice for anyone that wanted a peek.

"You think you look bad? You should see the girl," Darger said with a snort.

Sheriff O'Day's spine straightened, and he squared himself toward her.

"Thanks to you, Agent Darger, the entire country has seen her."

Out of the corner of her eye, Darger thought she saw Detective Luck wince on her behalf.

"Well, I guess it's a good thing the FBI is here so you can blame us for everything when re-election time comes around."

"Gentlemen," she could hear one voice saying over the din.

She thought it might have been Loshak, but she was too embroiled with the Sheriff to look.

"You have a lot of nerve to go lobbing suggestions like that—" the Sheriff started to say, and Darger got louder to match his voice.

"Balls, Sheriff. They're called balls, and it's a good thing at least one of us has a pair!"

She was vaguely aware of other voices around them, trying to interrupt, but a match had been struck and the flame had been kindled. She couldn't even hear her own words among the uproar, let alone the Sheriff's or anyone else's.

And then a high-pitched whistle sounded. They all turned. Luck removed his thumb and forefinger from his mouth.

"Everyone here has one objective, and that is to find this guy. Hopefully before he kills again. It's not going to happen if we keep doing this," he said, gesturing at the group. "Agent Darger made a mistake. I don't think there's any argument there. But what's done is done. We have to move forward with a new plan."

"The detective is right," Chief Haden said. "I think we better adjourn this meeting before things go too far. I say we take a day to gather our thoughts. Maybe two. We can regroup later in the week when cooler heads have prevailed."

The group disbanded, scattering like a flock of seagulls in a busy parking lot.

Loshak was halfway down the stairs when Darger caught up with him.

"Loshak," she started to say, but when he wheeled around and she caught the fierce look in his eye, the words died on her lips.

"Not here," he growled.

The knot that had been in her gut since the previous evening grew two sizes. She stood frozen in the stairwell until she heard the door open and close. It wasn't until Janssen of all people stopped next to her to scowl and gruffly ask if she was alright that she was able to move again.

Luck must have taken an alternate route outside, because he was waiting near the front door when she came out.

"Hey," he said.

Darger kept walking.

He kept pace with her, putting an arm out to try to slow her down.

"Violet."

She recoiled from his touch, finally stopping next to her rented car and fixing him with a contemptuous glare.

"Thanks for going to bat for me in there," she said, the sarcasm sharp in her voice.

"What the hell are you talking about?"

"They practically blamed me for the leak, when the reality is that Patricia Peters could have gotten photos from anywhere. She's a family member of the deceased! She could have submitted requests for the entire file, the autopsy, you name it."

She unlocked the car and climbed into the front seat. Luck had a hand on the car door, keeping it open while they argued.

"Yeah, but those pictures *did* come from you."

Her fingers wrapped around the steering wheel, squeezing until her knuckles felt like they might pop out of the sockets.

"I can't believe you think this is my fault!"

"Listen, Violet, you're not the only one that got chewed out over this, alright? I spent the first half of the day getting reamed by the chief. That was *my* crime scene. I'm the one who let you take the pictures. I'm in hot water, too."

"That must be why you rushed to my aid, then," she said. "Too busy covering your own ass?"

"What do you want me to do? I'm pissed, you're pissed. Everybody's pissed! You want me to throw gas on the fire? Start arguing about whose fault it is and isn't? That's not gonna help anything, because it doesn't matter. It's too late."

"You got that right," Darger said, ripping the door from his grip and slamming it shut. She wrenched the gearshift, throwing it into drive and accelerating onto the street, leaving Detective Luck standing alone in an empty parking lot.

CHAPTER 48

It's Sunday. He shouldn't be here. Got called in.

The booth feels as isolated as ever. But he doesn't mind for once. Not even solitary confinement in the wire threaded glass cage can get him down today.

The Sunday edition of The Plain Dealer sits on the counter before him. The headline beaming big bold letters:

'Doll Parts Murderer' stalks Athens County

It's crazy to him. Makes droves of moths flutter in his gut.

Seeing the story in print isn't as visceral as seeing the story depicted on TV. The shaky camera images of the bloody garbage bags on concrete.

But being the headline is a big deal. Especially on Sunday. He's going national.

The Plain Dealer is the biggest paper in Ohio with a circulation of nearly a quarter of a million. He figures similar stories populate papers and websites across the country.

Is this progress? Maybe. Now that The Daily Gawk posted the video and pictures, the story is blowing up. The brand name completes the shift from "The Trash Bag Murders" to "The Doll Parts Murders" overnight, the latter name based on a quote from a lady who peeked into one of the bags. Up until now, the papers and TV stations seemed split on the matter. But The Daily Gawk ran with Doll Parts in the headlines of their stories, and that cemented it.

The Doll Parts Killer.

He doesn't like the name. Doesn't hate it, either. It could be worse. He knows that for a fact. It has more of a ring to it than some of the media nicknames for serial killers he's read about. The Florida Gay Bar Murderer. The Alligatorman. The Sex Beast. The Weepy-Voiced Killer.

All real nicknames. All of them ridiculous.

He could live with his.

"I'm front page news," he mutters, eyes flicking to the duffel bag at his feet. "Above the fold and everything."

Nice. I bet your mom will be so proud.

He chuckles. Weird clucks of laughter climbing his throat and exiting through the segmented pink circle of his lips.

It feels wrong to have her here in the booth. To have the bag unzipped — opened — even if he can't see her for the moment. Just those two nylon canvas flaps on the floor under the counter.

She is still frozen, mostly. The process had distorted her features some. Made her nose and brow look swollen yet flattened — fatter and flatter at the same time. Almost like a sandwich someone sat on in a weird way.

But the makeup offsets these flaws. Her eyes have a kind of beauty restored to them. A femininity brought back that seemed to have drained from her little by little as the skin went slack. The places where the frost crystals glitter? They look intentional. Some makeup artist's magic touch providing a sparkle.

A crack has formed on the tip of her nose. A cleaved spot damaged by the cold. It looks a little like a cleft lip.

This, too, he covers with makeup. For now.

He knows she won't last forever. Knows that she can't. But he's thankful for the extra time the freezing affords him.

The wall unit furnace clicks. He holds a hand toward its grill. Feels the warmth saturate his fingers. The meat and then the bone almost stinging from the heat. This is the simplest feeling a mammal can feel he thinks. A warming of the blood. A thwarting of the cold.

But she can't feel that anymore. Holding the head up to the furnace would only melt that which preserves her. Would only speed the rot along.

It's too bad it works that way. That she must be cold to belong to him.

It's too bad that possession of another is all he can ever know. Not a real relationship. Not a real connection.

He can't help but think it: Maybe the newspapers are right. He doesn't have a girl. He has a doll. A toy to help him make believe.

Dead End Girl

Movement across the aisle catches his eye. Blobs shifting behind the glass in the office. It's Candice. He somehow knows before he can fully see her there behind the window.

And the old feelings come over him. That painful throb of hope and self-hatred doing battle in his chest.

Even after all that has happened, part of him thinks maybe he gave up on himself too soon. That he could have found a girl. A real one. If he really tried.

He closes his eyes. Tries to picture himself going to the movies with Candice.

And it's there. It's all right there.

The plush theater seat. The gigantic drink nestling in the cup holder at his wrist. He tilts the bucket of popcorn, and Candice's dainty hand grabs a handful. The whole world smells like butter.

She smiles at him. Such a gorgeous being. Like an angel.

And still part of him wonders what it would feel like to have her head in the duffel bag.

To dominate her. To possess her.

He opens his eyes. Sees the layers of glass that separate them. Sees the grid of chicken wire caging him away from humanity.

This is how the real world works. He sits in a little glass compartment. Uncomfortable. Apart. Locked away from all the rest.

Worthless. Powerless. Alone.

The Other.

Better to forget it. Better to live in the fantasy world for as long as he can. The place where he is God.

He fishes a hand into the bag. Feels for her. His human popsicle girl. He puts his hand over the face. Fingers touching those eyelids. The thinnest, softest part of her. He knows he's mussing her makeup, but it will be worth it.

With his free hand, he gropes for his belt.

CHAPTER 49

Violet wanted nothing more than to skulk into her motel room and hide for a few days. Maybe forever. Instead, she forced herself to march over to Loshak's door and knock. She would face her executioner with dignity.

The door whisked open so fast, it created a draft that rustled Violet's hair around her face.

"Christ, Darger," he said, rubbing his hands over his face. The rage she'd seen back at the Sheriff's office had waned, it seemed.

"I mean… Christ."

She followed him into the room, closing the door behind her.

"I didn't know she was going to turn around and sell the photos. I didn't even give them to her. I only showed them to her because she begged me. You should have seen her, Loshak. She was so much like Sierra in the way she manipulated me, it was crazy. She asked me for a glass of water and then—"

"Enough!"

Darger was so shocked at how quickly the anger returned to his voice that she actually jumped a little.

He sighed and ran his fingers through his hair, trying to control his emotions.

"Look, I know you probably think this'll be a great notch on your belt as you climb the Bureau ladder, but for fuck's sake. Girls are dying. This isn't one of those mystery-of-the-week TV shows where the good guys always get the bad guy at the end of the episode."

"I know that," she said, clenching her teeth. "I'm not—"

He held up a hand, eyes closed, as if he couldn't even stand to look at her.

"Let me finish, OK? That stakeout detail, that was the best — that was the *only* thing we had going for us on this case. And now it's gone, OK? We are back to square one, and you know what? He's going to kill again. And when he does—"

"It'll be my fault," Violet said, her voice a haunted whisper.

The words came out almost involuntarily and sounded more like she was talking to herself than to anyone else. She had a strange detached feeling suddenly. Like she was watching the scene unfold from outside.

"What? No, that's not what I meant. It's just going to be a hell-ride from here on out, as if it weren't already," he said, lifting his head and shaking it. "We're going to have to double-down and get real smart. Smarter than we've been."

"But it will be," she said, eyes swiveling over to meet his now. "My fault."

They were stretched so wide she could feel the cold of the air touching the places usually covered by the thin skin of her eyelids. Tears blurred Loshak into a muddy silhouette.

"Ah shit, Darger. Don't do that."

She turned away in an attempt to conceal that one of the tears had finally dislodged itself and was running down her cheek.

"I should go," she said, heading for the door.

Before she closed the door behind herself, she added, "I'm sorry, Loshak. Really sorry."

Those words were still echoing in her head when she reached her room. *I should go.*

And she should, shouldn't she? Look what a goddamned mess she'd made already.

She wasn't wanted here. Certainly wasn't needed. Even Cal, when he'd given her this assignment, hadn't sent her because he respected her talent. He wanted her to babysit Loshak. Just another round of political games the suits play while the people on the street get carved up by a psychopath.

Her hurt turned to anger, and she funneled the anger into motivation to get work done. She spent the rest of the day typing up two reports — one for Quantico and one for Loshak and the others. The only sound from her room for many hours was the click-clack of her fingers on her keyboard.

The report for Loshak included all of the witness statements she'd taken, along with her updated profile. All assembled into a neatly organized package, exactly how Loshak would want it.

Probably a waste of time, she thought, as she went down to the motel's front office to print off a hard copy. She didn't know if he'd use it. He didn't have much reason to, given how she'd fucked everything up.

But the last thing she wanted to do was to duck out without tying up her loose ends.

CHAPTER 50

Again he paces in the tomb. Walks the L-shaped path from his bed to the kitchenette and back. The shade falls over everything here. The darkness.

The fridge hums in the background. A faintly wet sound like a burbling fish tank.

"I'm lonely in a way I don't think anyone else can ever know. Not really. It's too big to explain."

Not anymore. You have me.

He chuckles. Looks at the head propped on the wooden chair out of the corner of his eye. Her mouth is opened wider than ever. Chin resting on the seat. Lips sagging at each corner in a way that makes her look a little like a fish.

"Nah, you know what I mean."

There's a pause before she answers.

I suppose so.

She surprises him sometimes. The things she says. He doesn't know how that works. He is scripting her lines. Talking to himself. He understands this. And yet the words sometimes just appear in his head as if from nowhere.

Water pools on her skin. Even in the shade, he can see it. And he knows what it means. A sign that she's thawing a little too much. She'll have to go back in soon. For her own good. He doesn't like it. Can't stand the times when she is sealed away from him in that frigid compartment.

But not yet. Not yet. He'll get to it in a little while.

He walks. The shoulder-high piles of books and magazines blurring past on each side.

He walks and walks. But he can't get away from it. Can't stop thinking about it. The wet. The condensation on her face like the sweat on a can of Pepsi.

The inevitable waits to take her. And it will. She will be gone. Maybe even soon.

He thinks back on their conversations. The talks they've

279

had. More like simplistic chats, maybe.

One could call him insane for talking like that. Talking to a severed head. But it's not like that. He knows it's a fantasy.

If anything he's done is insane, it's continuing to believe. Continuing to hope that he can find satisfaction on this plane. Continuing to pursue any kind of happiness despite the void. Despite the distance between him and everything. That's what he thinks. He's not delusional or anything of that nature. He knows what's real and what's not.

Are their talks anything like conversations a real couple would have? He doesn't know. He thinks maybe not. Maybe a real couple would exchange more complex thoughts. More nuanced points of view. He has a hard time imagining it.

He looks at her. Really looks. The open mouth. The saggy eyelids.

The face still displays a personality to some degree. He knows that. Even if her expression is clearly a dead one. But his imagination can't conjure the intricacies of the thoughts and feelings she might have.

Maybe he is just as dead as her in a way. She just happens to be physically dead while his death is on the inside. His dead imagination can't conceive of human thoughts or feelings outside of himself. Not really. His mind renders a childish version. A crayon scrawl of a girl that he talks to.

He knows all of this. But what can he do about it?

Maybe controlling her body is the only connection he can really hope for. Possessing her. Without that, the rest of it would fall apart. Without the head, the face, the crudely depicted personality in his fantasies would lose all meaning.

He lets the thought die away as he walks on. A few more laps back and forth. He gazes upon her.

"I don't know what I'm gonna do without you. You know that?"

She doesn't answer. Instead, there's a little sound. Almost like a wax paper wrapper being peeled away from a piece of candy.

He stops walking. Watches. Listens.

The tip of her nose drops to the wooden chair. A chunk of

cartilage and skin that almost looks like a strange tooth lying before her gaping maw. He stares at the little nub. Motionless. Silent.

"Aw, Christ."

He rushes to her. Kneels. Pinches the thing between thumb and finger and pushes the puzzle piece back into place. It plugs right into the hole in her nose. He holds it. Adjusts his hand so the tip of his index finger keeps it lodged.

This is how it will end. He understands that. But he holds the fallen piece in place for a long time before he removes his finger.

He doesn't bother with the freezer. Not tonight. He brings her to bed. Nestles her on the pillow next to him.

He can't really see her in the dark. Just the faintest sense of shapes in the shadows. A rounded object in the darkness.

For hours he tries to sleep. Closes his eyes. Empties his mind. Drifts a little.

But then he shakes himself awake. Nervous. Frightened. Afraid he'll somehow lose her if he goes under.

Over and over he does this.

He can't help but check. Fingers reaching out into the dark to find her. To feel her. There. That skin still cool but warming in slow motion. Clammy and strange. Her weeping dampness presses into his palm. And fluid of some kind drains from her neck flaps into the pillow.

Despite the wetness, he can feel how she has gone dry from the freezer. Rough and mummified and leathery.

It's not enough to preserve her, though. Not even close.

She is meat. Decomposing.

He doesn't speak to her anymore. He knows she won't answer.

The night stretches on and on. The melting picks up speed, and the rot follows right along with its pace. Kicked into some kind of bacterial overdrive.

Electricity sizzles in his skull. His mind flickering from thought to thought with great force. Great violence.

He realizes that sleep is impossible now. That he must

wallow in this nightmare. Feel every second of it without relief.

The smell of death surrounds him. Envelops him. Decay. Putrescence. But he doesn't mind it anymore. It is her smell. And she is his.

For a little longer, anyway.

CHAPTER 51

It was almost 10 PM when Darger finished with the work. On her laptop, she glanced at a list of flights leaving Columbus the next morning. The first plane to DC was booked, but she figured she might be able to get on standby.

She slept fitfully, visions of Sierra haunting her dreams. Sometimes alive and sometimes dead.

When the first faint glow of the sun was visible on the east horizon, Darger got up. She showered, dressed, and packed.

At Loshak's door, she lifted her fist intending to knock and stopped.

She couldn't do it. Couldn't face him. Leaning the packet up against his door so she'd have a flat surface to write on, Darger scrawled Loshak's name across the front with her pen. Just as she stooped to slide the manila folder under the door, it opened. She found herself staring at Loshak's feet, clad in black socks.

"What're you doing?"

"Oh, I—" Darger's mouth felt dry. She swallowed.

Goddamn it. Why was he all bright-eyed and bushy-tailed this morning of all mornings? All she wanted to do was to slip away without further drama. She held out the folder.

"I was leaving this for you."

"Leaving it? You headed somewhere?"

"What?" she said, wondering how he could have figured that out so quickly. "Well, yes. I was going home. Back to Quantico."

He exhaled loudly, a mannerism that reminded Darger of a disappointed gym teacher.

"That's it? You run into a little adversity, and you're just going to take your ball and go home?"

"I don't want to argue with you, Agent Loshak. I know I fucked up…"

He flapped a hand in the air.

"Come in here."

When he'd shut the door behind her, he went and sat on the

bed. He gestured to the chair against the wall.

"Sit."

Darger glanced at her watch.

"I have to drive all the way back to Columbus for my flight—"

"Hear me out, and then you can do whatever you want. Stay, go, whatever."

Darger set the folder down and lowered herself into the chair.

"Who's Zara?"

Violet reacted as if she'd been physically struck. She stared at him, unblinking, her heart already pounding in her chest.

"How do you know that name?" she asked.

"Something didn't sit right with me last night, after our chat. So I did a little poking around into your history with the Bureau."

Violet's chest rose and fell with each breath.

"And?"

"And a name came up. One of your last cases in Victim Assistance. Girl named Zara. Died during an investigation. File said you were there when it happened."

Violet had a hand on the hedgehog brooch again, squeezing it. She felt the spines digging into her flesh, but she didn't care. A tear dropped from her eyelashes, splattering onto her pant leg.

Damn Loshak. Damn him.

"Violet," Loshak said softly. "Tell me what happened to Zara."

And so she told him about the girl, the sixteen-year-old orphan and victim of human trafficking she'd been assigned to handle. About how cold and distant her eyes had been the first time they met. About how, as Violet counseled the girl over a series of weeks, a spark seemed to have ignited something inside her, burning brighter and brighter all the time. She started to laugh and smile and tell jokes. She came back to life inside.

She told him about preparing the girl to testify against the man who had corrupted her. About the arguments with the lead agent and the federal prosecutor over getting the girl in witness protection.

"I should have argued harder. Been louder. I thought about going over their heads. But I already had a reputation for being difficult. My boss's advice was that I should 'play the game.'"

She swallowed, looking down at her palms laid out in her lap.

"So I did. I played the FBI's game of sit down and shut up and don't question your superiors. And I lost. Zara lost."

Loshak sat motionless on the bed, barely breathing from what Violet could tell.

"We went through trial preparations. Forcing Zara to relive one abuse after the other. And one night, when we were walking to my car, we came face-to-face with a man with a gun. A hitman hired by the defendant."

Zara died in her arms, as her life flowed from the wound on her neck and out into the street. A river of blood, carrying her away, carrying that spark of life away for good.

Violet still remembered everything from that night. The feeling of her wool scarf, the one she'd wrapped around Zara's neck to try to staunch the wound, the way it got warm and sticky.

Zara's fingers clutching at Violet's arm, and how Violet wanted to hold her hand in hers and tell her it was going to be OK, but she couldn't take her grip away from Zara's neck. She had to keep applying pressure. If she just kept holding on and the ambulance got there soon…

The ambulance didn't get there soon. It was twenty-two minutes before they arrived. Zara was long gone by then, and Violet knew it, but she kept holding the girl, kept pressure on the wound, kept rocking back and forth, telling her it was OK. By then, Zara's flesh had already gone frigid, too much blood lost to keep the body warm now.

Violet remembered the choking, wet gasps. The feeling of Zara's grip growing weaker. The way Zara's blinking grew slower, more and more of the whites of her eyes showing. Her lips turning grayish under the shiny layer of lip gloss the girl always wore.

And when the paramedics finally arrived and pried the girl

from her arms and dragged Violet to her feet, she remembered seeing all the blood. She'd been sitting in a pool of it herself. Black, black, black under the street lamps. That's how it looked. Black on her pants and her hands and her face. Dark and black and drying now in a strange, sticky film.

She uttered a single word before she died. It was barely a whisper, no real intonation to it since her vocal chords had been damaged by the bullet. But Violet could read her lips.

"Mommy."

When Violet finished, she held very still. Her eyes were dry now. She felt empty of tears and everything else. Like a strange, hollow shell.

"Jesus," Loshak said, swiping a hand down his face like he might be able to squeegee away whatever feelings he was having. He hooked a finger at her hands that she held cupped in front of her.

"And that was hers, I take it?"

Violet stared down into her palms. She held the hedgehog brooch there. She must have pulled it off her jacket while she talked, in a daze.

"No. Well, yes," she said, swallowing. Her throat was dry and felt like sandpaper. "I bought it for her. It was going to be a gift. A surprise. Right before the trial started. So she'd have something to look down at. Something to hold in her hands when she was on the stand. When she had to face him."

Violet ran a finger over the green gemstone eyes.

"I found it in an antique shop. She loved hedgehogs. Wanted one for a pet, she said. When she got her own place. She talked about it all the time."

"So when I asked you why you left OVA before…" he said. "That BS about the limelight?"

She squeezed her eyelids together.

"I thought becoming an agent would mean I might actually be able to save lives instead of only doing damage control after the fact. Waiting around to pick up the tattered remains. Broken lives. But so far it looks like I'm better at screwing up investigations and getting people killed."

Loshak blew a raspberry.

"Who got killed?"

She looked up and met his coppery eyes.

"Sierra Peters."

He held up a finger.

"That wasn't your fault. She was marked long before you showed up. It never occurred to us that he would go after her again, and you know that's the truth."

"I should have figured it out."

"If anyone missed something… if someone's to blame, that person is me."

She barely heard him.

"I could have kept her safe, but I didn't. I messed up. Just like with—"

Loshak's voice was hard when he cut in.

"Quit it with the self-pity crap. We don't have time for it."

"We?" Darger asked.

"Yeah. We. You think I'm gonna let you skedaddle on outta here after you rubbed your stink all over my investigation?" He shook his head. "Oh no, Darger. You're going to finish what you started. I don't suffer quitters. And let me tell you something else. You gotta wise up. You're like a wounded dog, covering up and pretending everything's fine because you don't want the rest of the pack to know you're hurt."

"Don't profile me," she said, more angrily than she'd intended.

He ignored her.

"You think you can hide your true feelings and emotions, pushing away anything negative and refusing to deal with it because — you think — it'll only slow you down. But the real reason is that you're afraid that if you do confront your feelings, that if you face the truth straight on, maybe you won't be strong enough to survive it. So you put on a smirk like a suit of armor."

Violet held her breath.

"Burying the truth is what will break you. You stack up layer after layer of denial, and eventually, you buckle under the weight of it."

The silence stretched out before them, and then he said, more softly, "Neither of those girls dying was your fault. The world is a fucked up place, and we do what we can to stem the tide, but sometimes…"

His eyes went to the ceiling and then swung down to fix her with an unwavering gaze.

"Sometimes you get caught in a tsunami of shit, and it's all you can do to keep from drowning in it yourself."

A knock came at the door, and they both seemed to rouse from some kind of trance. With a grunt, Loshak hoisted himself to his feet. The girl from the front desk had a stack of newspapers in her arms.

"Here are those papers you wanted," she said.

"Thank you, kindly," Loshak said, removing a battered leather wallet from his back pants pocket. "What do I owe ya?"

"Three dollars and fifty cents," the girl said.

Loshak handed her a five-dollar bill.

"Keep the change."

The girl thanked him and retreated back to her post in the office downstairs.

"What are those for?" Darger asked

"Assessing the local damage," Loshak said, laying out the papers on the bed. "I wanna know what details the area newspapers used when they ran their version of the story."

"You know all that's online now, right?"

"Can't clip an online newspaper," Loshak said, thumbing through a copy of The Columbus Dispatch.

"Putting together a scrapbook of shame for me?"

"Believe it or not," Loshak paused to lick his thumb, "not everything is about you. I'm trying to think what our killer might do with his newfound fame, and I bet he's reveling in it."

The paper slapped onto the bedspread as he traded it for another. Paper rustled as he paged through, and then he stopped, eyes glued to a story buried deep in The Athens News.

"What is it?" Darger asked.

Loshak's eyes flicked back and forth over the black and white newsprint.

"I know what we're going to do."

CHAPTER 52

Darger scanned the article announcing a candlelight vigil for Fiona Worthington being organized at the local college. Her right leg bounced up and down, a nervous habit she sometimes had when she wasn't letting herself shred her nails.

"So after two accidental tabloid disasters, your idea is to engineer a third? On purpose?"

Loshak's face scrunched up like he'd just sucked on a wedge of lemon.

"Fuck the tabloids. I wouldn't throw them a life vest if they were drowning."

"I don't get it then."

"The local papers. We need this," he tapped the story about the Worthington vigil, "in every paper in Ohio, and we need it to be big. A fucking extravaganza. If I had my way, there'd be a front page story in every local rag, every day leading up to the memorial. Profiles on the victims, interviews with the family, with law enforcement."

Darger leaned back in the chair.

"You want to lure him to the vigil."

He winked.

"Now you're gettin' it."

"And what? Record the plate numbers of every dark sedan that rolls through?"

"Bingo. And don't forget the orange doohickey on the rear view."

He raised a finger in the air, wiggling it as though flicking something hanging from the invisible rearview mirror hung above him.

It could work, Darger thought. It could also be a colossal waste of time and manpower. But she didn't have any better ideas.

"You don't think he'll be too leery of showing up to something like that? After the leak about the stakeouts?"

"Not if we make it worth his while."

"How?"

Loshak opened his mouth, stretching the muscles on either side of his jaw.

"That's what we have to figure out."

"You think everyone will go along with it? The family, I mean? And the local PD?"

"Might take some convincing, especially with the task force. I guess I should handle that, 'til your little snafu has a chance to blow over."

A little bit of heat spread over her cheeks at the mere mention of her screw-up. She couldn't imagine it being forgotten anytime soon.

"Bureau's not gonna like it. If we're in the newspapers again, even if it's only local."

"We," Loshak said, raising his eyebrows for emphasis, "aren't going to be in the papers. Our part is strictly behind the scenes."

Darger watched a smile spread over Loshak's face.

"Oh yeah," he said, seeming to be talking to himself more than her. "He's perfect."

"Who?"

"The young Detective Luck, of course. Good lookin', squeaky clean guy like him? The cameras will love him."

Darger felt an involuntary tightening of her chest at Luck's name. She picked a piece of lint from her sleeve cuff, hoping her discomfort hadn't shown.

"What a bunch of dumb, superficial apes we are, eh?" he said.

"Huh?"

"Oh, nothing. It's just that we like our pretty things."

They agreed that Darger should wait outside while Loshak met with the two Sheriffs and Chief Haden that afternoon.

"Well?"

"Well, let's just say it's a good thing your scrap was mostly with Sheriff O'Day. He's still fuming over it, but he's deferring to Chief Haden being that the last two victims are his."

"But they agreed?"

Loshak nodded.

"It's on. Luck is going to talk to the Worthingtons, make sure they're OK with us horning in on their memorial a little bit. We'll meet tomorrow to start going over things. Get Luck up to speed, write up some press releases and whatnot."

"Did it take much convincing?" she asked. "I can't imagine they were wild about the idea of more press."

"They had their doubts. But when I mentioned that amping up the news coverage might actually buy us more time before another murder, they were all ears."

"You think that's true?"

Loshak's eyebrows appeared from behind his sunglasses.

"Maybe. I sure as hell hope so."

CHAPTER 53

He blinks. His eyelids swiping tears away like windshield wipers. The wet blur slides aside to reveal the road for a while. But more water wells to take the place of that which has fallen. Beads of liquid that cling to his lashes for as long as they can.

This is goodbye.

He eyes the duffel bag on the seat next to him. Zipped up tight. It will be gone soon. Falling away from him. Forever. And still, he cannot imagine it. His mind blocks him from picturing it. From feeling it all the way.

The hurt he feels now is just a sliver of what he'll feel when it's done. He knows this. And knowing it does him no good.

The night sprawls before the Prius. The headlights piercing the blackness. Reflecting from the blacktop. The engine's vibration makes the steering wheel tremble in his hands.

It's late. Some unthinkable hour. And he's the only thing stirring for miles. The only source of sound or movement. The only thing all the way alive.

He couldn't sleep now if he wanted to. Not tonight. He has to finish this first. Has to be rid of it.

He rolls through the slumbering city. Surrounded by unconsciousness. All of the windows darkened. The curtains drawn.

This is a different kind of loneliness. Somehow stimulating and strange. Not as unpleasant as the lonesome stab he gets when he's surrounded by people and somehow apart from them. This one has an innocence to it. A peacefulness.

He exhales. The fumes spilling out of him. Hot air. Heavy with booze.

How did it come to this? To killing these women. Cutting them apart. Mourning the loss of the body parts.

It is madness. Isn't it?

He doesn't know anymore. None of it makes any sense. Like life itself is an abstract painting. A crappy one at that. Lines and curves and smears that add up to nothing if you take a step back. A mess of color. Feelings and impulses are there to experience. Yes. But they are meaningless. A trail of stimulation that goes nowhere.

The water tower looms overhead. Spotlights pointing at its rounded dome. Muted blue metal the color of a cartoon dolphin. Big black letters etching the name of this place across its belly.

He is close now. Less than a mile from the end of this journey.

His mind races.

This world holds its meaning away from him. It hides it. Locks it behind glass. If it has any meaning at all.

Even when he was young, he couldn't be part of it. Not the way everyone else was. He couldn't picture himself getting the girl. Couldn't picture himself becoming the hero. These doors were never open to him.

He was an Other. A loathsome creature.

So the pictures in his head shifted. Morphed slowly but surely. And soon the girls in his fantasies were dead. Lifeless bodies. Those he could have and hold. That was something his imagination could believe.

And the violence was just the means to that end. It was how he asserted himself. How he proved he was here.

Because he was. Because he is.

He is here. A man. Not some meek thing for the world to walk upon. Not some eunuch that exists for society's convenience. Not the faceless, worthless nothing they treated him like from childhood to present.

A man.

And the world has to see that. Has to feel it like a blade jammed in their guts.

And every garbage bag proves it. Every thrust of the knife proves it. Over and over again.

He sails the seas of black nothing. Holds the infinite in his head even if it will break him. The void. The distance between himself and everyone.

But he is here. And he is a man.

Right fucking here.

He takes his foot off of the accelerator. Lets the car drift to slower and slower speeds.

An electric prickle pulses in his torso. Gaining intensity as the vehicle's momentum tapers off.

He applies the brake. Watches the ruddy light flare in the rearview mirror.

This is it.

He puts the car in park. Kills the engine. The silence makes the prickle in his chest rage to new levels. An itchy tingle crawling over his skin.

His fingers scrape the surface of the bag. Find the zipper and peel it back.

And his hand fishes into the black opening. Finds her hair. Pulls her free.

Her face looks like a Halloween mask now. A sheen to it like latex. A rotten thing. The flesh taking on a faintly green and black undertone in recent hours.

Her skin shifts with every movement like under the thin outer membrane is a layer of runny custard ready to slide away from the bone. Liquefying. Is that how it works? He doesn't know. It seems so.

She smells like roadkill. And he retches. Hears his stomach contents lurch for his esophagus. A sound like a wave slapping at rock formations along the shore. He tastes bitter acid on the back of his tongue. But he manages to keep most of it down.

He lets his eyes go blurry. Tears filling them in slow motion. All of reality fading to a soft focus.

And he doesn't see the rot anymore. Doesn't see the putrefied thing she has become. He sees who she was. The girl that he made and froze and tried his damnedest to keep. The companion he brought with him everywhere he went over the past many days.

How strange to feel nostalgia over someone who was never real. Over a decapitation victim used as a prop.

That's what she is. Right? A prop at worst. An imaginary friend at best.

But no. No. Maybe that's what she is from afar. To him, she

is more.

He brings her near. Hovering the severed head over the steering wheel. Inches from his face.

Those dead eyes seem to look into his. At least through the prism of tears. He believes what he sees. He wants to believe it.

A connection. One last connection. And it's real. The realest thing he will ever feel.

He kisses the rotting head passionately. Lovingly. His tongue probing the strangely dry gums and teeth. The white, shriveled tongue. His teeth scrape her top lip, and it stays puckered. Pinched from the pressure. It looks like a pasty worm drooping over that gaping mouth.

He weeps openly now. Putting her back in her duffel bag with care. Zipping her closed.

Water pours from his eyes. His body spasms. Silent sobs that shake him. Rattle him like he's freezing cold.

No sound comes out, though. None at all. He keeps it all inside.

He plucks the two handles dangling on each side of the bag. Weaves them around his hand. Lifts.

It's heavy now. Much heavier than before. It pulls his arm all the way down to his side as he steps out of the car. Makes the muscles knot up and shake. Tiny flexes firing as fast as possible. Cords of quivering meat.

He'd loaded the bag with rocks from a decorative display outside the apartment complex a couple doors down from his building. Kneeling among dead flowers in the dark. Piling in a bunch of limestone gravel and a handful of larger stones ranging in size from softball to cantaloupe. For the weight.

Would he have done this without the alcohol? He doesn't know. He'd been so cautious before tonight. Never doing anything onlookers could find noteworthy. Never exposing himself to any risk aside from the fleeting moments of the abductions themselves. But tonight he had knelt among shrubs with the bag open. With the head exposed. Funneling in fistfuls of rocks.

He drank beforehand to build up the gumption. To turn off the timid part of his personality for a while. Six big glugs from the Jim Beam bottle on an empty stomach. It burned all the way down. The fumes crawling up from his stomach to fill his sinus cavities. To make his eyes water.

That was enough. And within seconds, the drunkenness began to take hold.

The booze makes him fearless. Removes all of his doubts. Restores the single-minded focus he needs to carry out these acts.

He staggers a little as he makes his way onto the bridge. The wind picking up to greet him with a burst of chilly air.

He arrives at the guard rail. Hears the water burbling. Smells the Hocking River wafting up from below.

The bag rests a moment on the rail. The gravel inside grinding out a sound. All of those fibers in his arms twitching like crazy again.

He pushes the canvas rectangle over the edge. Watches it shift into something limp. It tumbles end over end on the diagonal. Handles whipping like its tiny frightened arms. Waving for help that will never come.

It cracks into the water. A slap like shattering concrete. And after wiggling a second on the surface, the water pulls it under. Swallows it whole.

He stares down there. The black water flickering in the places where the moonlight touches its surface. He almost wants it to bob to the surface. To reveal itself to be alive in some way. Sentient.

But nothing happens.

A big breath sucks into his lungs. And he turns his head away from the scene of the fall.

His arms feel so strange with the weight removed from the end of them. Useless and naked and trembling.

The wet that slicks his whole body makes him feel opened up. Like the night air can blow straight through to touch his insides.

And the emptiness is everywhere. Inside and out. Spanning to the horizon in all directions from this bridge. Engulfing all things from here into the heavens.

He walks to the car. Climbs in. The starter beeps. The engine catches. The gear shift ratchets into place.

And he's moving again. Moving on.

Emotions burst in his head like fireworks. A black rage darkening everything.

His leg twitches. Foot pressing the pedal down. The car seeming to stand up taller on the tires as it accelerates with violent abandon.

He wants to flick his wrists. To send the car careening over the shoulder and into the woods. He can feel the impact in his imagination. That kiss of wood and steel. Mashed and splintered bits. Fire engulfing the broken pieces.

He wants it so bad. Destruction. Annihilation. Of himself. Of someone else. Of anyone.

The pedal bottoms out. Feels strange jammed all the way to floor. He grinds his foot into it harder without effect.

And the car expresses his hatred with kinetic energy. It hurtles on. Penetrates the emptiness. The engine wailing like it was about to break.

Fuck off. Fuck off. Fuck off.

The car reaches top speed. Accelerating no more. Ripping over small hills with enough force to make his stomach lurch.

The notion of getting pulled over enters his head. Arriving late to the party.

Fuck it. Let them do it. He'd happily pull over right now. Happily jam the barrel of his gun down some dumbshit cop's throat and squeeze the trigger until the ammo was spent.

He laughs thinking about it. Picturing it. Seeing some cop's brain jettisoned from his skull. Escaping from a gaping slit in the back of his head.

Heat flickers in him as these violent fantasies dance in his imagination. He lusts for them to be real.

Tears drain down the sides of his face. His intestines squishing wildly in his gut. Chest and arms reverberating electrical current that feels like insects run amok inside of him and out. He knows that he's right on the edge of psychosis. Of that plunge into an insanity that can't be undone.

The car shakes now. Fenders squeaking like bedsprings. Steering wheel rattling. It sounds and feels like it wants nothing more than to come apart.

So let it. Let it. Let the pieces fall away into nothing.

He teeters on the edge just the same as the car. The edge of what? He's not entirely certain. Of madness. Of chaos. But he somehow holds it together.

Holds the void in his skull.

It should break him.

Should.

But it doesn't. Can't.

He is still here. Still walking the Earth.

Even with the vast seas of nothing flowing into him. All the way. Becoming part of him.

Even with no hope of connecting to any other. Even with loneliness and emptiness left as the only things that are real on this plane.

Even with all he has done. All the humanity he has fouled and defiled.

He is still here.

And he is what he is. What he has always been.

He gets that now. Understands it.

Owns it.

He releases the pressure on the accelerator. Letting the car slow to a normal speed. The shaking and roaring dissipating to smooth going. Falling back under control.

He catches his eyes in the rearview mirror. Stares into them. The pupils are empty black pits like a beast's.

And he knows somehow that he will be fine.

That there's work left to be done.

CHAPTER 54

Loshak milled around outside of his motel room, pacing back and forth on the concrete catwalk that ran in front of the second story units. He looked down through the wrought iron guard rail into the parking lot, but he saw no sign of movement yet. So be it. He didn't mind stretching his legs.

He shivered a little. It was cold, but it felt good to be on his feet again. He still felt like shit, but his gut wasn't aching the way it had been. Was it real progress? He didn't know.

The sound of tires rolling over wet blacktop caught his ear. He gazed down at the police cruiser wading through the mud puddles. This was it.

He jogged down the flight of steps and peered into the cruiser, a little surprised to find the passenger seat empty. He climbed into the open spot.

McAdoo smiled, and they shook hands, but the officer looked a little under the weather himself. His chubby cheeks seemed unnatural sporting stubble, and his complexion looked yellow. Waxy.

"Where's Novotny?" he said. He caught himself just shy of saying Nose-votny.

"Oh, he won't be on duty for a couple hours yet. Me neither."

"I see."

They were quiet for a second as the car pulled out of the lot, squishing through the puddles again on the way to the street.

"You heard what happened, I'm sure," McAdoo said. "About The Daily Gawk and all the fallout. The stakeout getting shut down."

"Indeed."

"Do you think… I mean, it doesn't sit right with me is all. Ending the stakeout, I mean. I don't know. Feels like we should be watching those scenes, you know? Just in case."

"I know what you mean."

"What do you think?"

"Our guy is surely following the media coverage. I suspect the articles spooked him, and I think he's smart enough to stay away. If we had all the resources in the world, we'd keep all four dump sites staked out, but we don't, so... Not much use investing so much in a low percentage play, I guess," Loshak said.

"So we do nothing? We sit back and wait for him to kill again?"

"Not exactly. We're pursuing other avenues of being proactive. Let's just say things are in motion higher up the chain at this point. I can't go into detail, you understand."

"I see."

"I know how you're feeling, though. When you've got a piece of the case, and it gets taken away, it makes you feel powerless. Empty. But trust me. We're working on it. Doing all the things we should be doing."

McAdoo chewed his lip before he answered.

"Well, I do trust you. I guess that's why I wanted to talk to you about it. I figured if I heard it from you that we were doing the right thing, I'd believe it. And maybe that'd help me let it go. Like, move on or whatever. I haven't been able to sleep, you know? Just..."

The quiet rose up between them a moment, McAdoo's teeth working at that bottom lip again.

"It's like cats and dogs, you know?" Loshak said.

McAdoo tried to make sense of this. Couldn't. His brow crumpled.

"What?"

"Sorry. I was thinking about my pets. Two cats and a dog. Haven't seen them for weeks now. This whole thing reminds me of them, I guess. My cats are all over me when I'm the only human around. Jumping up on the couch to get pet. Screeching at me to get fed. So on. But if anyone else comes over — a stranger, I mean — they run and hide under the bed for hours.

"The dog is just the opposite. He charges to the door to confront any would-be intruder on his turf. He smells the guest, looks them straight in the eye, sizes up the situation face to face and only then will he calm down.

"It's two different ways of looking at the world, you know? A cat sees individuals above all else. Almost like an artist's point of view, I think. She sees everything through the lens of individuals and relationships. If something disrupts that intricate web of connections — such as a stranger's presence — she'll disengage and keep to herself a while.

"A dog sees territory to control. He's cognizant of individuals, but his primary concern is controlling his environment in a direct, assertive way. He wants to feel in control. If you cross that threshold into his territory, you will be dealt with. Even if that only means you'll be barked at a few times."

They fell quiet again. The cruiser rolled through downtown Athens, a strip of shops and restaurants with pedestrians out. It looked more urban than anything else in the county, and after about two blocks, it was past, the atmosphere veering back to a rural feel.

"So you're saying I'm like a dog?" McAdoo said.

Loshak laughed.

"I guess in a way. Sorry, I've had a fever. Maybe I'm not making much sense. Dogs are considered man's best friend, right? And cats are a feminine symbol. Maybe there's something to that."

McAdoo nodded, but he didn't think he understood it at all. He wondered if Loshak was going loopy, sicker than anyone realized. He'd seen the man grimace often whenever they were together. Poor bastard.

CHAPTER 55

The Athens City Police Department was located across the street from a row of frat houses. Darger smirked when she considered how much that probably put a damper on parties.

The street was old, narrow, and paved with bricks. The tires rumbled over the irregular surface. It was a pleasant sound to Violet, reminding her of childhood somehow.

Loshak parked the car in a visitor spot, and they headed up a flight of concrete stairs and through a set of glass doors.

"Gotta make a pit stop," Loshak said as they passed the sign for the men's room. "You go on ahead. We're meeting in Interview Room 1."

The door to the john swung open and Darger got a whiff of public bathroom odor: cheap toilet paper, industrial cleaners, and stale urine.

She found the appointed room, entered. The door automatically closed behind her. It was a sparse little chamber — they usually were — with three chairs, a table, and a phone. With her foot, she scooted one of the chairs closer to the table and took a seat.

A few minutes later, the door handle clicked, the steel door swinging wide. Detective Luck sauntered in.

He looked startled to see that it was only her in the room. "Where's Agent Loshak?"

"Restroom," she said simply.

The disquiet between them was palpable. Neither of them uttered a word until Loshak bustled in a moment later.

"Good morning, Casey."

Loshak sat down.

"You talk to Fiona Worthington's parents about the vigil?"

"Yes, sir," Luck said. "They are more than willing to do anything we ask if it might help catch the guy."

"Excellent."

"And the Chief told me to pass on that he scheduled a press

conference for this afternoon."

"Just in time for the evening news. Perfect."

Loshak straightened a pile of papers he'd brought along with him on the table top.

"Let's see if we can't get you prepped for your date with the camera in the next few hours, eh?"

He winced and brought a fist to his mouth, and Darger wondered if he was feeling alright. He cleared his throat and continued before she could give it much further thought.

"I know it seems silly, to coach you like this," Loshak said, "but you really are playing a part. And the fewer people in on it, the better. I've tried this before where we let the reporter in on the game, and they always blow it. Try to get cute and clever when they're writing up the story. Make a mess of things."

"I get it," Luck said.

"It'll be tempting to say 'We' and 'The Athens Police Department' and 'The Investigation.' It's what you tend to hear in most police statements, but it really would be best if you could use 'I' as often as possible. We want him to identify with you specifically."

Luck nodded and scrawled something on his notepad.

"Though giving some attention to the fact that we've assembled a multi-agency task force would be flattering to him as well. The bigger and more official we can make it sound, the better. Something with a long name and maybe an acronym. Southern Ohio Serial Killer? Or Athens Area Serial Killer. Something like that. Of course, the media will end up using Doll Parts Killer or Doll Parts Murders, but that's fine. We just want our task force to impress him."

"What about Hocking River Killer," Luck suggested.

"Sounds like an homage to the Green River Killer," Darger said, her face buried in her own notes.

"Good point," Loshak said. "He'll like that. Also, be sure to stress that you're consulting with the FBI."

"Two FBI agents. From Quantico," Darger offered.

Loshak snapped his fingers.

"Yes. Good. He's so goddamn important, they sent in a team of us."

"You said no names, though, right?" Luck asked.

"God, no. Bureau would probably shit bricks if either one of us ends up in another newspaper."

"I'd hardly call The Daily Gawk a newspaper," Darger said, half-heartedly defending herself.

"Yeah, yeah. Let's focus on the task at hand."

She shrugged.

"What if, in the middle of all the chatter that's supposed to play on the killer's ego, he drops in a line encouraging people to call the tip line?"

She couldn't even bring herself to address Luck by name.

Wrinkles formed across Loshak's forehead.

"Many killers have called tip lines for their own crimes. This guy might be too smart for that, but it couldn't hurt to plant the idea."

"Exactly."

"I like it," Loshak said.

"You really think he'd take the bait that easy?" the detective asked.

Loshak leaned back in the chair, and it gave out a creak of protest.

"That's the million dollar question. Are we just spinning around in circles like dogs chasing our tails? Or are we clever pussycats, setting a trap and then stalking our prey? Only time will tell."

Agent Loshak pondered the brick wall for a moment and leveled his gaze at Luck.

"I guarantee you one thing, though. He's watching, and he's loving it."

"What if a reporter asks a question I'm not prepared for?"

"No questions," Loshak said. "We'll do interviews on an individual basis, but opening up for questions puts you at risk of getting off-topic. The press conference is a conversation between you and the killer. No one else."

Darger and Loshak stood toward the back of the room, waiting for the press conference to start. They were tucked off to one side, out of the way of the cameras and reporters.

The podium outfitted with the logo of the Athens Police Department stood empty at the front for now, but the rest of the room was filled with a bustling excitement. Cameramen angled lights and adjusted headphones and tweaked settings on their rigs.

Detective Luck appeared in the doorway, flanked by the Chief of Police and Sheriff O'Day. She thought both the other men looked a little peeved. Like maybe they were annoyed it wasn't them headed for the spotlight. A hush fell over the mass. Luck strode to the platform at the front and took up his position.

Agent Loshak inclined his head toward Darger and muttered, "Commence Operation Angler Fish."

She smirked, not taking her eyes from the podium. Loshak had jokingly referred to the plan as Operation Angler Fish earlier in the day. Despite the fact that he'd said it in jest, the name had stuck. The idea being that they, like the angler fish, were hoping to lure their prey in close enough to catch him in their jaws.

Through the stuttering strobe of the camera flashes that had begun as soon as the detective took his place, she had to admit that Loshak had been right. Luck looked every bit the handsome, clean-cut gumshoe in front of the lights.

He read from the prepared statement they'd put together, making sure to look directly into the cameras often, what Loshak had called "eye contact with the killer." His voice was clear and sincere, with just the right amount of gravitas. Darger glanced at Loshak. He was riveted, his eyes taking on a slightly manic look.

At the end of the statement, Luck lifted his chin and stared more intently into the lenses of the cameras surrounding him.

"I'd like to take a moment, on behalf of the family of Fiona Worthington, to bring attention to a candlelight vigil and memorial service being held at the university. Fiona's family would like to invite anyone in the community who has been moved by these tragic events to join them in a night of remembrance and hope. Thank you."

Detective Luck abandoned the podium to a murmur of

unanswered queries from the reporters, despite the fact that he'd specified at the beginning of the conference that he would not be taking questions at this time.

It was a while before Darger and Loshak could make their way out of the room. The throng of news crews and equipment blocked the path, all jamming up the doorway by trying to leave at once.

They hung back until the crowd cleared, and then returned to Interview Room 1. Luck was sitting on the table inside, sipping water from a paper cup.

"Hot under all those lights," he said, lowering the cup. His forehead glistened with a thin sheen of sweat.

"You handled it well, Detective. Good work," Loshak said and held out his hand.

There was a celebratory shaking of hands between the two men. Darger hung back, arms crossed.

"I say we call it a night for the moment. Tomorrow we can start on the one-on-one interviews, and then we'll begin prepping the Worthingtons for their part."

Darger thought she would have felt some sense of relief now that the day was over. They'd done it. Their task for the day was complete. Things had gone well, or as well as they'd hoped. But she still had an uneasy tension running through her.

"You hungry?" Loshak asked, buckling his seatbelt and starting the car.

"Starving," she said.

It was a pleasant night as they rolled through Athens proper. Darger put her window down to enjoy the night air.

"You ever seen an angler fish?"

Darger shook her head.

"I don't know. What do they look like?"

"Ugly as hell. Giant upturned mouth with a big over-sized jaw and long spiny teeth. And then a little dangly thing comin' off the forehead that they use as the lure."

"Sounds adorable."

"Heh. Yeah. Also, some species of angler fish are known for sexual parasitism. Meaning when they find a mate, the male actually bites onto her, and his saliva dissolves her flesh and the two fuse together. He gets all his nutrients through her, and she gets sperm to fertilize her eggs."

"Jesus," Darger said. "What are you, a part-time marine biologist now?"

Loshak chuckled. He seemed in better spirits and better health than he had been maybe the entire time she'd been there.

"Nah, I just collect interesting factoids like that. Curiosities of the universe, if you will."

Night had fallen, and over the line of trees to the east, Darger could see a crescent moon rising.

"I guess it's extra appropriate then," she said, half to herself.

"What's that?"

"The name. Operation Angler Fish? Parasitic males and all."

"Huh," Loshak said, guiding the car into the drive-thru lane at Wendy's. "True."

CHAPTER 56

Detective Luck's red van was already parked in the Worthingtons' driveway when Darger and Loshak arrived at the house. The Luckmobile. She rolled her eyes as they passed it on their way up the front walk.

Darger rang the bell, and Fiona's mother answered, welcoming them inside.

"Good to see you again, Agent Darger," she said. "Agent Loshak."

Violet couldn't help but eye the carafe of fake lemonade in the foyer while Lois stowed their coats in a closet in the hallway.

Thankfully, Mrs. Worthington didn't mention it.

When they reached the living room, Luck was seated on the couch with a young blond girl. Darger figured she was about 20 years old, and by the resemblance, knew this must be Fiona's younger sister.

By the way they were both tapping furiously at their phones, Darger thought they were playing some kind of game.

And indeed, the girl said suddenly, "Oh man. I almost had you right there."

"Emily," Lois said, "this is Special Agent Darger and Special Agent Loshak from the FBI."

Emily Worthington was a smaller, less striking version of her sister. It wasn't that she was unattractive. But the long limbs and regal posture of Fiona had been shrunken down on Emily. She was the petite version of her sister, with a heart-shaped face and slightly upturned nose. Those features, coupled with her wide-spaced green eyes, gave her an elven appearance.

The girl seemed hesitant to tear her focus away from Detective Luck. He sat straight forward, feet facing a carved mahogany coffee table in front of the sofa, his phone clutched in his palms. But the girl was positioned fully sideways, her feet up on the cushions and folded to one side. She was leaned in, chin down, eyelashes batting away whenever she looked up at the detective.

Smitten, was the word that popped into Violet's head.

"Pause," the girl said, reaching an arm out to swipe at the screen in Luck's hand. "No cheating."

Something else thrust itself into her consciousness then, as well. Something Loshak had said a few days ago. *We like our pretty things.* Darger wasn't sure if she was thinking of Casey, Emily, or Fiona when she thought it.

"Feet off the sofa, please," Lois was saying to her daughter. Her tone made it clear that this was only the ten-thousandth-or-so time she'd had to utter those words.

Emily swung around with an insolent scoff only achievable by the young.

Lois turned to them and explained, "Emily's a senior at Ohio State."

"Mom," Emily said, her bottom jaw jutting in playful annoyance. "It's *The* Ohio State University."

Lois rolled her eyes and whispered conspiratorially.

"I went to the University of Michigan. We didn't obsess over definite articles there."

"I heard that," Emily said.

"Could I get you something to drink?" Lois asked then. Addressing Darger specifically, she added, "I made a batch of lemonade special."

Violet heard Luck chuckle from across the room, and instantly her face felt warm. Lois was smiling at her. There was no trace of mockery in her face. She was teasing Darger, yes. But it wasn't meant maliciously.

Still, Violet wished they would have forgotten about it. And now she was stuck as well. If she accepted the lemonade, the gag would never die. If she declined, she felt like she'd be putting Mrs. Worthington out somehow.

"Sure," Violet said, forcing her lips into a polite smile.

"I don't get it," Emily said. "Why is that funny?"

"Oh, just a little joke between me and Special Agent Darger."

"Whatever," Emily said. She flipped her hair back and swiped at her phone. "You guys are weird."

"Special Agent Loshak? Lemonade? Water?"

"I'm fine, but thank you," he said.

When Mrs. Worthington departed for the kitchen, Violet could feel him watching her.

"What was that all about?"

"Nothing," she said. "Forget it."

He sniffed and crossed his arms over his chest.

"So you guys are in the FBI?" Emily asked, watching them with new interest. Darger had an idea what was coming next. She thought Loshak did, too.

"That's right," Loshak answered.

"So," Emily continued, "if there were aliens, you'd know about them, right?"

Darger bit her lip to keep from grinning. She was curious how Loshak would handle it. It was a surprisingly common question, even when she'd been in Victim Assistance. As soon as she said *FBI*, apparently some people immediately thought *X-Files*.

Loshak's shoulders rose as he took a deep breath. He rubbed above his top lip with a finger, a classic nervous tic, and shot Darger a guarded look.

"We're not really supposed to talk about that."

Emily stared at them for a few seconds, mouth slightly agape. Trying to decide if Loshak was being serious.

Finally, she laughed.

"Shut up! You're messing with me."

Loshak grinned and shrugged.

"It probably goes without saying that the less you speak of our involvement, the better," Loshak said, squatting on the edge of an ottoman upholstered in patterned velvet.

"We don't want him to know you're pulling the strings, in other words," Lois said. "The killer, I mean."

"Exactly. And for the most part, we won't be. We want it to come off as natural as possible. Whatever you already have planned shouldn't need to change much. This is still, first and foremost, a memorial service for your daughter. The last thing we want to do is to get in the way of that."

"Of course," Lois said. "But as I told Casey, anything we can do to assist, we're happy to help."

Loshak's mouth formed into a gracious smile.

"And we thank you for that. Why don't you start by taking us through what you have planned?"

The memorial service would begin in the auditorium at the university, where the pastor from the Worthingtons' church would lead a group prayer. Fiona's mother, father, and sister would all speak, as well as a few close friends and relatives. Preliminary plans for the Fiona Worthington Memorial Garden would be announced, which was to be housed somewhere on the university campus.

Candles would be passed out to the crowd as people left the auditorium, and then a candlelight procession would make its way to Fiona's grave site.

"Our congregation is preparing hundreds of luminaries to set up along the sidewalks to light the way," Lois said.

"That'll be pretty," Violet said.

Fiona's mother beamed.

"Do you have a route already planned? For the procession from the college to the cemetery?" Loshak asked.

"I do," Lois said, reaching for an iPad resting out of sight. She brought up a map and showed it to them.

"That's good. Perfect," Loshak said. "Could you possibly email that to me? That way, we'll know where to have our people set up."

"Absolutely," Fiona's mother said and the two spent the next several minutes bumbling through the exchange of email addresses and trying to remember how to attach a file to an email.

There was a lot of "I think if you…" and "Here try this…" before Emily had finally had enough. She rolled her eyes and wrenched the tablet from her mother's hand. In under thirty seconds, she was handing the device back to her mother, the job complete.

"I was hoping I might ask your opinion about something," Lois said, clasping her hands together. "Emily keeps telling me I'm being neurotic."

"Because you are," Emily said, not lifting her eyes from her phone.

Lois huffed playfully before continuing.

"I know that people like to bring mementos to leave at the grave," Lois went on. "And well… I just keep picturing all those things — pictures, letters, stuffed animals — out there in the rain and the snow. Getting all dirty and mildewed, and well, eventually turning into litter. I mean, does someone clean that up? At the cemetery?"

It seemed to be a mostly rhetorical question, so neither Darger nor Loshak answered.

"Anyway, it all seems a bit wasteful to me. So I've been thinking of encouraging people to bring flowers if they want to leave something. Or donating to a worthy cause in Fiona's name instead."

Darger deferred to Loshak, who was stroking his chin while he thought.

"You know, I think that's a great idea. On a multitude of levels. And you've just given me a thought, so I'm going to excuse myself for a moment."

Darger followed Loshak through the winding path back to the foyer. He slid open the closet door and reached for the hanger holding his coat.

"How long before the reporter's supposed to show up?" Loshak asked, heading for the door.

Darger looked at her watch.

"Three hours. Why?"

"If she beats me here, try to stall."

"What? Where are you going?"

"I have an errand to run." He turned back to her, scratching his eyebrow. "That a problem?"

"No," she said. "I guess not."

"Call me if she gets here before I do."

"OK," Darger said, barely attempting to hide her exasperation. Of course he couldn't tell her what he was up to. She thought of how Cal had described Loshak as not being a team player, but she had started to suspect that his reticence was just as much about creating a spectacle. Keeping those around

312

him in a permanent state of suspense. Cloaking himself with an air of mystery and intrigue. Loshak liked a dramatic reveal.

The door swung shut behind him, and Darger felt a familiar discomfort settle over her. Loshak must have been a buffer of sorts before. She could forget about the way the Worthingtons' home made her feel and focus on the task at hand. Now that he was gone though, that protection was fading.

On her way back to the living room, she passed a stairwell. She heard voices coming from above. Emily and her mother, from the sounds of it.

"I don't understand. Why can't I have it if no one else is using it?"

Lois' voice was tense.

"You know what, Emily? I'm tired of having this discussion."

What sounded like a cabinet door to Darger slammed loudly.

Darger froze, stuck between unintentionally eavesdropping and making her presence known and risking an even more uncomfortable moment.

"You want your sister's car? Take it. I'm done."

Footsteps moved off.

"Mom, don't act like that—"

The voices retreated, and Darger let out a breath. Still, the encounter jarred something unpleasant in her memory.

She had two step-siblings, Colin and Jenna. They were older, already moved out of the house and attending college when her mother married their father. They had always been polite to Violet. And yet still they'd never felt like family.

Witnessing the argument between Emily and Lois, Violet recounted a Thanksgiving visit from the siblings. The three of them were in the den watching TV when they started squabbling over the things in the house.

"When dad dies, I get the Chinese desk in his study," Jenna said.

It had come seemingly out of nowhere, at least for Violet. Maybe this was something they often discussed among themselves. She wouldn't have known.

Completely unperturbed, Colin countered.

"Fine, but then I have dibs on the Porsche."

"What? That's not a fair deal at all. The Porsche is like ten times as valuable as the desk."

Colin shrugged.

Maybe that was the heart of it all, Violet thought. Why she'd never been at home there and felt so ill at ease here in the Worthingtons' house. The worship of the material was so apparent. So abundant. She felt like she was suffocating in the gluttony of Things.

It wasn't fair, she knew, to be judging the Worthingtons that way. Emily was young. To her, it was just a car. She might as well use it. And on the whole, they seemed to be kind people.

"What are you up to?"

The voice came from behind her, and she jerked around to see Casey watching her from down the hall.

"Nothing," she stuttered.

"Where's Loshak?" he asked, glancing around like he might appear from a hidden chamber behind a bookcase or something.

"He said he had to run an errand. Said he'd try to be back before the reporter showed up."

Detective Luck nodded, and the conversation died. Why had Loshak left her here alone?

It was an hour and a half later when her phone rang. By then, Fiona's father had returned from work and joined them. Violet had been trying to explain that no one from the family should address the killer directly in any of their interviews.

"But I'd like to ask him why," Bill Worthington was saying, handing his wife a tissue. "Why her? Why did he have to take our Fiona?"

"I understand that, Mr. Worthington. I do. But it's important right now that Detective Luck be the only person talking to him, so to speak. We want a singular focus."

"Think of me like a lightning rod," Luck offered, and Darger thought she saw Emily smirk to herself. "After we catch him, I promise you'll get a chance to ask him whatever you want."

314

Darger excused herself from the discussion when she saw it was Loshak calling.

"Reporter's not there yet, right?"

"No, not for at least another hour," Darger said.

"Meet me at the front door."

Back through the labyrinth of rooms Darger went. When she reached the front of the house, she opened the door and found Loshak outside, clutching a large shopping bag under one arm.

"What's that?"

"I'll explain, and then I gotta take off."

"Again?"

"This new idea means more moving parts. More things the task force needs to be watching out for. So take this," he said, shoving the bag into her hands, "and listen."

When she returned to the living room a few minutes later, Luck's eyes were the first to fall on the newest member of their group. It was a giant stuffed elephant, probably as tall as Darger stretched from trunk to tail.

"Whatcha got there, Agent Darger?" Luck asked, hardly concealing his amusement. "Did you just duck out for a quick trip to the carnival or what?"

"No. This is Fiona's favorite stuffed animal," Violet said.

Mr. Worthington frowned.

"I beg your pardon?"

"She slept with it every night since she was four," Violet said, wiggling one of the fur-covered ears. "The way I understand it, anyway."

Emily sat forward, the first to catch on.

"Yeah. I remember. His name is Mister Toots."

Violet snapped her fingers and pointed.

"A name. That's good."

"I'm sorry, but could someone please explain to the senile old lady in the room what in good heavens is going on?" Lois asked, starting to look a little frazzled.

"It's bait," Luck said. "If we make it sound like this really important thing that Fiona loved and cherished, he'll want it."

"You're saying the killer will try to take it?" Fiona's father asked.

"Hopefully," Darger said. "They like tokens. Trinkets. It's like a symbol of her. A reminder. If we feature Mister Toots here in the newspaper articles, the stories on TV, he might not be able to resist."

Darger sat down, lowering the elephant to the floor beside her.

"That is, if you're comfortable with it. I know it probably sounds strange to be asking you to do this. To lie about a stuffed animal."

She plucked at the trunk, which flopped back to the ground when she released it.

"We have other things in motion. You can say no."

Lois moistened her lips with her tongue, blinking at the elephant on the floor for a long while. She and her husband exchanged a look. No words passed between them, but Darger knew an entire conversation was being had nonetheless. Couples who had been happily married as long as the Worthingtons often seemed to have that kind of almost psychic connection.

Finally, Fiona's mother folded her hands in her lap and fixed Darger with a matter-of-fact stare.

"Let's do it."

CHAPTER 57

He looks to the passenger seat often. Half of him expecting to find the duffel bag there. Its lips parted.

But no. She's gone. Gone for good. And he's never going to be alright.

The distance pulls him away from the hurt. Away from the world.

He leaves the car. Steps into the night. The air cool around him. There's still work to be done.

He walks now in his mother's home. His childhood home. The wretched decor surrounding him. That smell of potpourri and the faintest hint of mildew.

His mother nags him about his appearance. About his problems and how she's disappointed.

But her words don't quite filter through. They cannot breach the gulf between him and her. Not anymore.

What does she want? What did she ever hope to accomplish? To shame him? For what? He's not sure. That's the great mystery of life, eh? What are these control freaks hoping to accomplish when they run everyone down?

She must want to feel powerful. Degrading him must do that for her.

Maybe this apple didn't fall so far from the tree.

With the diarrhea of nag fully tuned out, he moves to get what he came here for. Newspapers.

The press conference on the news merely whet his appetite for that kind of content. The media pitching in to make him feel the way he wants to feel. And that Detective — Luck — was pretty good. Maybe the two of them understood each other. Opposite sides of the coin and all.

The newspapers wouldn't be as good as that. But they were something.

He leafs through the papers stacked up under the sink awaiting their exit via the recycling bin. So many stories about

317

him. Big bold headlines that make his heart flutter.

Doll Parts Killer terrorizes Athens County

FBI assisting in Doll Parts case

Family remembers Athens victim

This last one catches his eye. Even if it's not about him directly.

The article details the large-scale memorial for Fiona Worthington that Luck mentioned. Funny. She was a stuck-up, la-de-da bitch in school. School. Yes. Would the police be able to make that connection? He doesn't know. It seems possible.

But he's a clever boy. He always was. He'd made it complicated for them.

The picture next to the article makes his eyes go wide for a second. The face looks just like hers did in high school, but it's not. It's her sister. Emily. The girl holds a stuffed elephant. Mister Toots, according to the caption. Fiona's favorite. It will be among the mementos present at the memorial service.

He licks his lips. Can't resist. He creases the page. Tears carefully along the fold. Shoves the picture deep into his pocket.

CHAPTER 58

Darger, Loshak, and Luck spent Friday morning fine-tuning the plan for the memorial that would take place the following week.

"I'll see if the Athens office can spare some of our people to do the first round of watching the grave site," Loshak said. "I don't know if O'Day and Haden will be too wild about the idea of approving another round of stakeouts. Besides, they're already doing the bulk of the surveillance during the vigil."

"Have you asked the Bureau about giving us a tracking device for the elephant?" Darger asked.

"I talked the resident office here in Athens into lending us one."

Loshak fluffed the hair on top of his head with a pencil.

"Doubt we'll really need it since the damn thing's so big," he mused. "That's why I picked that one in particular. No one's going to be sneaking off with that in their pocket."

"Better safe than sorry," Luck said.

By afternoon, they'd outlined another press release for Detective Luck's next news conference. They were expecting twice as many crews as the first one, as affiliates from farther outside the Athens area had contacted them, wanting to be notified of any future endeavors.

They had called it a day and were tidying up the interview room when Luck paused. He had been flipping through his notepad.

"Agent Loshak, I've been meaning to ask," Luck started, then hesitated. He fiddled with the button on his suit jacket.

"What is it?"

"I just wondered if you thought the body position at the time of death had any significance or not."

"What about it?" Loshak asked, and Darger immediately realized she'd made a mistake.

She vaguely recalled Casey mentioning that Fiona, unlike the others, had signs suggesting she'd been face down after death. Luck thought it might mean something, and Violet had said she'd mention it to Loshak. Only the thing was, in all the confusion since then, she had completely overlooked it.

"Fiona Worthington being different than the other three, I mean," Luck said.

His eyes flicked over to Darger, and she knew he'd figured it out now. His jaw muscles tensed. He seemed to wrestle with some decision. Whether to call her out or not, most likely. He turned his body away from her, squaring himself toward Loshak. Cutting her out.

"It was only a theory, or not even. Just something I noticed, really. But the lividity marks on Fiona Worthington indicated her being face down after death, while the other three were face up, and it got me thinking… maybe he didn't want her looking when he did his work."

Loshak's mouth was working as if he were sucking on a piece of candy.

"Show me," he finally said.

"I have the file in my van."

Violet walked behind them as they made their way out of the building and down the cement steps to the parking lot. She continued to hang back while they pored over the autopsy photos of the four girls.

"Well damn," Loshak said. "I didn't even notice it. Good eye, Luck."

"You think it means something?"

"It could. And if it does — if it means that Fiona was significant to him somehow — then even more reason for everything we have planned. We might have a real chance at getting him to walk right into the trap."

They parted ways then, Loshak and Darger heading back to the motel.

"That Detective Luck is smarter than the average Athens county bear," Loshak said as they drove.

Darger kept her mouth shut. It wasn't that she thought Luck was wrong. She'd just started to get this sense that maybe people were a little too eager to give all the attention to Fiona Worthington when the fact was, there were three other victims.

They hadn't been as rich or educated or pretty as Fiona, but that didn't make them any less worthwhile as human beings.

Saturday dawned with a red-tinged sky the same color as the turning leaves on the sugar maple outside Darger's window.

After putting together another field report for submission on the following Monday, per Cal's request, Darger had little to do.

That wasn't so true, she realized, when her eyes roved over her nearly empty suitcase. Almost everything she'd packed had been worn already, most of it at least twice.

Violet hated housework and any other menial task that had to be repeated over and over, ad nauseam, for the rest of her life. But that was the price you had to pay for clean underwear. She found the address for a laundromat in town, packed up her dirty clothes, and struck out on a quest for a fresh wardrobe.

While her clothes were agitated, rinsed, spun, and dried, she thumbed through the various outdated magazines on a rack near the row of wire chairs in the seating area. But the chairs were uncomfortable, and she was restless and antsy aside from that.

It had been a week since her argument with Luck at the Sheriff's office. They hadn't spoken of it or talked much at all during the meetings for Operation Angler Fish. And extracurricular discussion was nil.

Then there was the fact that she'd neglected to bring his hypothesis to Loshak. It hadn't been on purpose, but she felt bad about it anyway.

Watching her clothes tumble in the vortex of the dryer, she dialed Casey's number. It rang twice, then went to voicemail. Was he screening her calls? Avoiding talking to her? She thought not. For all he knew, she was calling about the case. He wouldn't ignore that.

When she'd finished with her laundry, and everything was smelling Mountain Fresh again, she tried his phone a second time. Same deal: two rings, then the pre-recorded voicemail message.

Screw it. His house was only a few minutes from here. She

might as well drop by and see if he was home. She opened her trunk, tossed in the plastic bag full of freshly laundered clothes, and slammed it shut.

Her plan, however, seemed less and less wise the closer she got to Luck's house. What if he wasn't home? But she could see that wasn't the case from two blocks away. The Luckmobile was parked in the driveway.

As she brought the car to a halt across the street from his place, her mind came up with ten more excuses to abandon the idea. What if he was busy, and she was intruding? What if he had guests?

What if he had a *lady* guest?

She glanced at her reflection in the rear view mirror and rolled her eyes at her paranoia. You are such a wuss. All this because you don't want to apologize *that bad*?

Her footsteps skimmed over the asphalt on the way up the front walk to his door. She had one final bout of neurosis before she lifted her finger to ring the bell.

What if he opens the door, sees it's you, and slams it in your face?

Ding dong!

She heard the bell's sing-song chime reverberate through the house. She fidgeted on the step while she waited, pacing back and forth across the tiny concrete platform.

After a good half a minute of standing on the stoop, she turned back and headed for her car. He had to be home right? The van was parked outside. Maybe he really didn't want to see her. She was crossing the yellow line painted down the center of the street when she heard a *yip* from the backyard. Morty.

Violet crept to the side of the house, and over the gate of the wooden privacy fence, she saw him. Casey Luck was bent over, one hand reaching for something in the grass. In his other hand, he clutched a bottle of beer. Blue Moon, she knew without even needing to see the label. Cops were creatures of habit.

He wore a pair of faded jeans and a long-sleeved gray henley tee. It was the first time she'd seen him without a scrap of police garb on. No suit. No gun. No belt.

When he stood straight, she saw that it was a tennis ball he'd been plucking from the ground. He lobbed it across the yard for Morty, who took off instantly to retrieve it. Right. So he was outside with the dog and maybe hadn't heard the doorbell.

Or maybe he had heard it, maybe even peeked through the sliding glass door at the back, had seen it was Violet, and decided not to answer. Violet was struggling with whether she should call out to him or scuttle back to her car like a coward when he pivoted and caught sight of her. His brow furrowed, though he didn't necessarily look angry or disappointed to see her. If anything, she thought he looked confused.

"Hey," he said. Morty immediately noted that his master's attention had shifted to something outside the perimeter of the yard and took off to investigate.

Her cover blown, Darger realized she'd have to go ahead with it now. She let herself through the gate, just in time to meet Morty, who wagged and sniffed and spun around in excitement at the prospect of a visitor.

Luck had followed the dog to the edge of the yard, and now he stood, one hand on his hip, the other occupied by the beer.

"Sorry to show up unannounced like this," she said. "I called but…"

"Ah, crap," Casey said, reaching into his pocket. "I probably forgot to turn my phone back on."

Glancing at the screen and then pressing a button, he muttered, "Stupid thing."

Alarm passed over his face suddenly.

"Did something happen with the case? Is something wrong?"

"No," Darger said. "I mean, not with the case anyway."

She tucked a strand of hair behind her ear and sucked in her cheeks. Why was she stalling? What was so hard about apologizing?

She squatted down to pet Morty, who accepted her attention gratefully.

"I've been thinking that I… well, I think I maybe reacted in not-the-best way after the whole tabloid thing. Blaming you for not backing me up or whatever."

Morty licked her hand, which she took as encouragement to

go on.

"And I wanted to explain things."

Luck was silent for a while, and she wondered if this had all been a mistake.

"What things?"

She stood up with a sigh.

"I know it probably *seemed* like I was way out of line," she said, and his eyebrows reached for the heavens. "OK, I was definitely out of line. But there was a reason."

He took a sip of beer, appearing doubtful.

"I'm messing this up," she said with a groan of frustration. "I'm trying to apologize!"

"Then go for it." He tipped his beer to one side, the brown bottle appearing to shrug on Casey's behalf.

She looked him in the eye and swallowed.

"I'm sorry."

His chest rose as he inhaled, watching her.

"Apology accepted, Agent," he said, but she sensed that all was not right between them still. She felt a strange pain in her chest.

Casey scooped the ball from where it lay a few feet away and threw it again for the dog. Darger thought of what Loshak had said. About the weight of denial, and about her fear that she wouldn't be able to bear the burden of her true feelings.

"There's something else," she said, and Casey must have heard something in her voice, because he paused mid-throw and twisted to face her.

"I lied to you before. When you asked how I came to be an agent. That stuff about my dad being a cop? It's not true. That's just something I tell people so I don't have to tell them the real reason."

He tossed the ball away with an absent flick of the wrist, listening intently. A good trait for a detective, she thought. To know when to speak and when not to.

"I never really even knew my dad," she said, squeezing her eyes shut. "But that's not the point. The point is… before I was an agent, I was in Victim Assistance. Kind of a therapist-slash-social-worker. I counseled victims of sex crimes and human

324

trafficking mostly. We had this girl, Zara…"

By the time Darger finished telling Zara's story, the sun was setting, and a few stray crickets had begun to sing.

"We found out later that he had paid this guy $1500 to kill Zara. $1500 dollars. That's all her life was worth.

"But they were able to get the guy, the hitman, to testify. They got their conviction after all. US Attorney's happy. Bureau's happy. The agent who wouldn't approve protection for Zara got a promotion. He's now Special Agent in Charge in Maryland. The guy who actually pulled the trigger got a deal for his testimony, of course. He'll be eligible for parole in four years."

She filled her lungs with the cool autumn air.

"And they all lived happily ever after. The end."

Violet stared at the black outline of the trees against the darkening sky so she wouldn't have to look at Luck.

"Everyone but the girl. Zara," he said finally. "And you."

"Yeah, well… I'd say I got off a little easier than she did."

Casey studied her for a while, then turned back to the house. A welcoming glow radiated out from the windows.

"Why don't you come inside? It's starting to get cold out here."

She followed him in the house, and he handed her a beer without asking. She accepted gladly, twisting off the cap and taking a drink. They sat side by side on stools in front of the kitchen island for some time without speaking.

When he finally broke the silence, he said, "I guess I should take this opportunity to admit that I maybe lied a little, too."

"Really?"

She raised an eyebrow.

He flicked her bottle cap over the counter top, the metal skittering over the smooth surface.

"It wasn't my dad who was the cop. It was an uncle. My dad died when I was eight. Hit and run. And then my mom got ovarian cancer and died when I was twelve."

"Wow. I'm sorry."

He scratched at the back of his neck.

"We — my sister and I — came here to live with my aunt

and uncle then. He was the highway patrolman."

"I see," Darger said, running her thumb over a rough edge on the label pasted to her beer bottle. "And are you sure there isn't anything else you want to fess up to? Something else you might have left out?"

He turned toward her, a look of utter bewilderment written on his face.

"Tell the truth now, you totally dressed up in his uniform when you were a kid."

His cheeks slowly pulled up into a smile, the corners of his eyes crinkling.

"Maybe. *Once.*"

"I knew it."

They seemed to pick right up where they'd left off after that. Or at least, one thing led to another, and Violet found herself perched on Casey's kitchen counter, half-undressed, with her legs folded around his waist.

His teeth grazed her earlobe, her neck, her collarbone, and she ran her fingers through his hair.

"I missed you," he said, his hands tracing their way up her waist, over her ribcage, and then cupping her breasts.

"You missed this," she said, wrapping her thighs tighter around him so his bare chest pressed against hers.

"That, too."

He scooped under her hips, lifting her from where she rested, and carried her to the bedroom.

CHAPTER 59

They lay in bed for a while afterward, still tangled in each other's limbs. Eventually Casey leaned across the pillow and kissed Violet on the forehead.

"I'm gonna jump in the shower," he said. "You can join me if you like."

He walked two fingers over her belly as if they were miniature legs.

"I would," Violet said, grinning, "but I'm starving."

She sat up and felt around for her clothes in the darkened room.

"There's food in the fridge. Fruit. Yogurt. Cold pizza in the box on the counter. Help yourself to whatever," he said, flipping on a lamp next to the bed.

Violet found her underwear and slid those on first.

"No jokes about caviar and truffles? You're losing your edge, Detective."

She stood up to button her pants and suddenly felt Casey's lips at the nape of her neck.

"Well, we *are* all out of foie gras, Special Agent. My apologies."

He kissed her once more before retreating into the bathroom.

When she'd finished dressing, Violet padded out to the kitchen. She ignored the refrigerator and headed straight for the cardboard box next to the stove. She ate two slices, licked her fingers clean, and then fell into one of the black leather couches in the living room.

For the first time, she noticed all the crayon drawings stuck to the fridge with magnets. He had mentioned a sister. Perhaps he had nieces and nephews.

Casey's phone went off then, rattling over the glass surface of the coffee table in front of her. She had an itch to look, to see who it was, but refrained. She hated being nosy.

The ringing cut off, and she pulled out her own phone and checked her email. Nothing but a new notification that her current bank statement was ready and a coupon for 10% off at Kohl's. She didn't remember signing up for the Kohl's mailing list.

Casey's phone rang again. This time Darger peeked, not out of intrusiveness, but because she feared the worst: that another body had been found. Or something else, maybe. In either case, when she peered over the table at the screen, it said simply, "Grandma."

"Oh," she muttered and went back to her own screen.

The phone rang a third time, and she gave it little thought, other than that Casey had better call his grandmother.

A few minutes later, Violet heard the front door open. She was sitting on the couch, her back to the entrance. She craned her neck around to see a little girl, maybe 4 or 5 years old, slipping inside.

"Morrrrrty! Puppy!"

The child screeched and disappeared down the hallway that led toward the bedrooms. Morty jumped down from where he'd been nestled against Violet's thigh and followed the girl to the back of the house.

"There you are!" she heard the girl say with a giggle.

Violet set her phone down on the couch. What the devil was this, now? Her first thought was that the girl must be a neighbor, someone Casey let come over and play with the dog.

She wondered if it was routine for the girl to just let herself in. Did Casey know about that?

When she'd been in high school, not long after her mother married Gary and they'd moved into his house in a swanky gated community in West Bloomfield, she'd been home alone, as usual, after school. She heard the screen door creak open, and then footsteps on the stairs, and she knew instantly it wasn't her mother or her stepfather by the strange cadence of the footsteps. It almost sounded like an animal trotting up the steps. A four-legged creature. Violet, still not totally at ease in the new house (actually, she was never totally at ease in that house, even now), picked up a poker from next to the fireplace and crept quietly down the hall. From the kitchen, she heard the clink of glass jars and other containers rattling together. Tiptoeing over the tiled floor, Violet sidled around the large marble-topped island with the fire poker held out in front of her. The fridge door was still open and blocked her view of the intruder.

"Who's there?"

A small head popped into view. The gleaming black hair of the neighbor boy from across the street was what she saw first, and then his terrified green eyes. He screamed. Violet screamed. The little boy ran from the room, a dill pickle still clutched in his fist. She heard the *rat-tat-tat* of his feet on the stairs and the door opening and slamming shut. He'd been about the same age as the little girl, she thought. Four or five. What she remembered most was the pickle, of course, and the fact that he hadn't been wearing any pants.

She didn't even remember his name now — Billy? Bobby? Roddy? Something like that. She smiled to herself. She'd never spoken of it to anyone. Not to her mother or her stepfather, not even to little Bobby Whatshisname. And it never happened again, at least not while she was at home, but she'd always wondered if it had happened before. For all she knew this pantsless kid was marauding all over the neighborhood on a regular basis.

Darger stood, planning to make her presence known to the little girl (sans fire poker). Before she got a word out, an older woman bustled through the door. She was tall and statuesque with a coif of chestnut hair on top of her head.

"Jillybean, you didn't even kiss Grandma goodbye," the woman said, pausing to make sure the door was shut. When she turned back from the knob, her eyes immediately fell on Violet.

"Oh!" she said, looking startled.

Violet realized then that this must be Casey's grandmother. The one who'd been calling just before. She was younger than Violet would have expected.

She started to introduce herself, but at that moment, Casey materialized from the bathroom. His hair was still wet, and he clutched at a towel around his waist.

"Claudia," he said, wearing a look of confusion, and then a

trace of worry passed over his face. "Is everything OK?"

"Casey! There you are," the woman said, clasping her hands in the air in front of her. "I am so sorry to show up unannounced like this! I tried to call but—"

"Yeah, sorry. I must have been in the shower," Casey said, his eyes darting over to Violet, who was still standing motionless next to the sofa like she'd been zapped by some supervillain's Freeze-ray.

"One of my clients just went into hospice, and I really need to be there, and I just—" now the woman was the one glancing at Violet, and she was starting to get a very uneasy feeling. Something about the dynamic was wrong.

"No, Claudia. It's fine," he said.

Claudia. That was what was bothering her. Who called their grandmother by her first name?

"It's just obvious that you're busy," the woman said.

Casey started to say something, but the little girl finally resurfaced from the other end of the house then. She was awkwardly carrying Morty in her arms. She could manage about the top half of the dog, and the rest hung limp like a ragdoll. Morty wore a blue knit winter hat with a large pompom on top. To the dog's credit, he didn't seem to mind being manhandled by the child one bit. His tail wagged furiously, and his tongue lolled out for a taste of the girl's cheek.

"Daddy, look. Morty is wearing my hat."

"I see that, little bean," Casey said, squeezing her head as she passed by.

It was a beat before it all sunk in for Violet.

Grandma.

Claudia.

Daddy.

This was not Casey's grandmother. It was his *daughter's* grandmother.

Casey had a daughter.

God, why had she not thought about it before? That explained why he swore like a nun. He was used to trying to keep his language clean in front of his kid. And the drawings on the fridge? Duh, Darger.

And then a second realization. Casey had just told her his parents were dead. That meant the woman standing before them was the girl's maternal grandmother.

Violet was certain her swallow made an audible *gulp* noise.

Casey's ex-mother-in-law. She hoped ex, anyway, or he'd have a lot more explaining to do than he already did.

"I feel terrible," Claudia said, then gestured with a hand toward Violet. "I really hate to interrupt when you're entertaining."

"Oh, God," Casey said, and Violet could hear the strain of awkwardness in his voice. "I'm being rude, not even introducing you."

Darger stepped forward to shake the woman's hand before he could say more. She probably should have let him handle things, because what came out was, "Darger. Special Agent Darger, I mean. Err… Violet."

"Oh, so you're…" Claudia paused to search for the right words, "a friend from work?"

"That's right," Darger said. She resisted the urge to shoot Casey a furtive glance. It would have been totally transparent, and things were uncomfortable enough as it was. "I'm consulting on one of Detective Luck's cases."

Claudia brought her hand to her mouth and looked pained, but Darger swore she saw a flicker of relief cross the woman's face.

"Oh my goodness. This is about those girls isn't it?" She closed her eyes and waved her hands between them. "Never mind! I know you can't talk about it. But, oh. How awful."

She turned back to Casey.

"Anyway! I really have to get going. And again, honey. I'm so sorry to drop it on you like this."

"Really, Claudia. It's fine," Casey said.

He started to approach, then remembered he was only clad in a towel. He gestured to his half-nakedness.

"I'd give you a hug, but…"

Claudia laughed, then raised a hand to Violet.

"It was a pleasure to meet you, Agent Darger."

"All mine," Violet said, finally getting up the nerve to look at

Casey.

When Claudia turned to call out to her granddaughter, he mouthed, "I'm sorry."

Darger could only shake her head.

"Jillybilly, I'm going now," the woman called.

"Bye, grandma!" the little girl shrieked as she ran into the room and threw herself at the woman's legs.

Claudia kissed the girl on the forehead.

"You be good for daddy, yes?"

The little girl nodded.

"And if I don't see you tomorrow, then I'll see you Monday after preschool, OK?"

"OK, grandma," the girl said before careening back into the living room to find the dog.

After Claudia left, Casey went to get dressed. Violet didn't know what to do with herself, so she stayed in the kitchen where she was, absently running her finger over the polished surface of the counter.

She felt a strange lump in her throat, as if she might cry. She didn't know why.

She could hear the girl in the living room, cooing at the dog over cartoons in the background. Should she go talk to her? Introduce herself?

No, Darger thought bitterly. There was a reason Casey never mentioned having a daughter.

Ah, so *that* was why she felt so emotional. She felt slighted. Like maybe things weren't as serious as she thought. And really that was stupid. Why would they be serious? At some point, Darger would have to go back home. And Luck obviously had a life rooting him here.

What a fool you are, Violet, she thought to herself. Falling for a guy who lived a couple of states away? Who's the rube now?

She wondered if she would have felt this way had she not told him about Zara. Something about opening up to him had made it all seem more… real.

Casey glided around the corner, his head tilted so he could peer into the living room and check on his offspring. Satisfied that she was properly enthralled with the TV and the dog, he went to Violet, putting a hand on each shoulder.

"Good," he said. "You're still here."

"What, did you think I was going to go running away, screaming?" she said like the thought hadn't occurred to her.

His eyes searched her face, trying to read her, she knew. She made an effort to appear impassive.

"I'm sorry, you know. That wasn't exactly how I'd intended for you to find out I have a daughter."

He slid his hands down to her waist.

"I *was* going to tell you."

"It's fine," she said.

"Fine? Like on a scale from 1 to 10, you're only at like a Level 7 Freak Out?"

"Fine, like fine. Really. It's not a big deal."

She crossed her arms.

He moved one hand to her elbow, prying it away from where she held it near to her body. His fingers moved down and encircled hers.

"Well then, why don't you come meet her?"

He pulled at her, and she resisted, removing her hand from his grasp.

"Actually, I think I better get going."

She said it lightly, not allowing any trace of resentment into her voice.

"Violet."

He frowned, and the disappointment on his face was clear. "Don't."

"It's not like that," she said. "We have a lot to prepare for this week, right? I really should go."

He gazed down at his bare feet, nodding.

"OK. I guess you're right."

When he went to kiss her goodbye, Violet turned so his mouth missed hers. Instead, his lips barely brushed her cheek.

"Goodnight," she said and disappeared into the darkness beyond the front door before any more could be said.

CHAPTER 60

He waits outside her building. Watches the light shine in her window. There are no other signs of life or movement. Just that rectangle of glow in the dark.

He looks out over the parking lot. The hulking cars all around his. Concealing him among the pack.

The streetlights reflect off of the wet blacktop. Clumps of soggy leaves huddling along the perimeter. It rained earlier. The wet still clings to everything.

His eyes swivel back to the window. Watching. Watching. Waiting.

Maybe she will show. Maybe not. Probably not. And that's OK. All he can do is wait. Watch. Let the time go by.

Observe her routine.

That's what it really comes down to. Her routine. Her companions or lack thereof. Those things will determine her fate.

He cracks the window. Smells the rain. It's a nice change after so long sealed up in the car.

The Prius lacks his smell. His scent. It smells clean. Sanitized. That new car reek that he loathes so much.

He misses his car. This is when that fact always hits him. In these idle moments. The sitting. The waiting.

The car. The Buick. Dark blue. He'd been right to dump it. The witness had seen it. Reported it. The Daily Gawk article mentioned that specifically. Knowing these things didn't make it hurt any less to be without it.

It occurs to him that the Buick is his only friend. His only companion over the past many years. The only one who knows who he really is. What he's done. Especially now that the head is gone.

How can he fuse bonds with objects like a car or a severed head so easily and seem to struggle with it in terms of humans? He doesn't know. None of it makes much sense to him.

Relationships and what not.

He stares at the window again. Checks the time. It's 9:43 PM. Typically her light goes out within a few minutes after 10:30 PM. No visitors. No late night trips. She is very faithful to her routine from what he's observed. And that's good. That's just what he wants.

Still. He has to watch it play out. Has to trust but verify that her habits remain consistent. Steadfast.

But the wait leaves time to kill. Idle time. Empty time. Sitting in the Prius doing nothing.

And then he remembers.

The muscles in his face go taut. Almost stinging from the excitement. It reminds him of being a kid. Opening a present. A new toy.

He draws the newspaper clipping from his pocket. Gazes at the picture of Emily Worthington holding the stuffed animal. It's hard to tell through the distortion of the newsprint pixels. But he thinks she looks very much like her sister. A similar proud smile. An uncanny resemblance in the chin and brow.

The images of the FBI agents snap into his head. One after the other. Loshak and what's her name. Darger. Could they be using the media and the families to try to draw him out? Using the sister as bait? Setting up a memorial and making sure he knew all about it. That would make sense. He'd read Loshak's book. That's exactly what he said about these serial killer types, right? They return to the scene of the crime. They contact the police or the families under the guise of trying to help with the investigation. Things like this are really common.

The excited empty feeling in his chest wanes. It's another trap. Like those little boxes along the curb where the rats get caught.

It would be a thrill, though. He can't deny that. To walk among the friends and the families and all manner of law enforcement. To linger there in front of them all. Rub shoulders with them and get away with it. Maybe even to take the prized stuffed animal once all the others had moved on. A trophy to keep. Something to help him remember.

The reward would be sweet. God. So sweet he could almost

taste it. But it didn't quite match the risk. Did it?

Something flits in the window above. He catches the movement out of the corner of his eye. Looks up too late to see what it was.

Shit. Well. The light is still on. That's something.

His gut feels empty. Strange. He's worried there's a guest. A male guest. The worst of all possibilities.

Shit. Shit. Shit.

He watches. Licks his lips.

Movement again. A figure in the window. The silhouette appearing there. Entering the frame slowly. Is it her?

No.

Broad shoulders. Thick arms. A little scruff lining the jaw.

It's a man. The routine is beyond shattered. It's ruined.

He slams the heels of his hands into the steering wheel. The pain so sharp in them that he can only picture the skin all split open. Flaps of white around red slits.

He hesitates a moment. Turns them over.

No wounds. He's fine.

A little laugh exits his nostrils. His eyes checking the window one last time. This one won't work, but it's OK.

She is not his only project.

CHAPTER 61

The cruiser sloshed through the layer of rainwater collecting on the asphalt, tires flinging liquid against the wheel well to make a hollow sound.

"Loshak said he doesn't think the guy will come back, but… " McAdoo said. "I don't know. I can't stop thinking about it, I guess."

"You can't stop talking about it. I'll give you that."

"Well, what the hell, Novo? We just go back to patrolling? Setting up the radar gun to catch the speeding college kids as they leave campus? It doesn't feel right."

Stifled laughter grated out of Novotny's throat and sinuses, exiting his nostrils. It almost sounded painful, McAdoo thought, as though his partner had tried his best to hold the laugh in and couldn't.

"What's so funny?"

"Nothing. Just… This is the first time I've ever heard you express interest in any kind of police work beyond doing the bare minimum."

"Oh. Right. Hilarious, I guess."

Novotny chuckled again.

"Well, no. I had never really thought about it before is all. The idea that you're just going through the motions with this job, and it seemed funny somehow, you know? Nothing really wrong with it. You do good work, and most of what we do is handing out tickets, right? But the only things you've ever really sounded enthused about before now are your kid and the damn boat you're going to buy someday, which you also never shut up about, by the way."

McAdoo stared at the floor, his eyes peeling open and closed in a series of slow blinks.

"Well, I guess I'm just trying to fully impress upon you how rad my boat is going to be. That's all."

More laughter escaped Novotny, this time popping free

from his lips. Muscles all over his body broke into an involuntary tremor, shoulders bobbing, abdominals squeezing. He had a hell of a time getting the chuckles to cease all the way.

Once he did, he pulled the can of Skoal from his breast pocket and nestled a brown wad in his lip.

"Seriously, man. What can we do about it? Go sit outside Burger King in our free time? Would that make you happy?"

McAdoo thought about it, more slow blinking interrupting his vision.

"Well... No."

"I thought not. So you're only venting, right? I get that. But there's nothing to be done beyond doing our job, you know? That's all there is to it, and you've got to let that be good enough. For now."

McAdoo grit his teeth for a second. Then he took a deep breath and let it out.

"I guess you're right, but you know something?"

"What's that?"

"You'll always be twice the cop that I am. Of course, most of that surplus is nose, but still..."

More stifled laughter scraped its way out from deep in Novotny's throat.

CHAPTER 62

He doesn't belong. Not here. Not anywhere.

His hands grip the wheel once more. The upholstery warm under his lower back. Almost sticky through his shirt.

It smells like him in the Prius now. Maybe last night's desperation did the trick. His musk overpowering the new car smell. Acrid. Leathery. Earthy. A distinct bodily odor. It reminds him of violence in some way he can't pin down.

No work today, so he drives around all day. Watches the people. Peeking into their cars as they pass. Peering through panes of glass that may as well be doorways to other galaxies. Spaces and realities so far from his own in so many ways.

Some of the drivers sing along with their stereos. Some of them worm their hands into greasy paper bags for fries. Shoving empty calories into their faces. Some wear thoughtful expressions. Some look blank as hell.

None of it means anything. None of it.

Just creatures passing out here on the highway. Mostly mindless. No different than animals walking the beaten trail to the watering trough. Docile cattle. Too dumb to sense the predator in their midst. The wolf.

He knows that it was there all along. Whatever it is that squirms and writhes inside of people like him. Before his mom or anyone hurt him. Before all of it. It was always there. That's what he thinks.

He can't remember where the idea for his projects truly came from. One day it was just there. A fully formed picture in his head. Like maybe it was always there, and he finally noticed. Not in him. Around him. Around everyone. Everywhere.

Like there's a wave in the air if he listens for it. A broadcast. A voice that will guide him if he gets opened up to it. No. Not a voice. A stream of pictures and feelings. Visceral. Moving. A kind of thought process that predates language. Beamed into his skull from the unknown. From the outside.

Whatever it is, it knows him. And it knows you. It knows the forbidden things you think and dream and want. It opens pictures of them. Folds them into your dreams. Sleeping first. Then waking. It consumes your imagination. Your fantasies. The morbid fascinations. Evolution couldn't erase them. All those prehistoric years of animal violence and hatred that haven't quite been bred out of you yet. They wake up all at once.

And they're hungry.

And if you feel what's in the air, really feel it, it will let you throw away your modern self. Throw away the docile self that can only be used to produce and consume. Can only be used to do a job you don't care about so you can have money to buy things you don't care about. Can only be used to chat about the weather.

His modern self is worthless. To him. To everyone. To society at large. This message is reinforced everywhere. Both personally and in the broadest possible sense.

From the people flinging change at him in the booth and driving off to the dirty looks he gets from his female coworkers. All the kids who made fun of him in school. The girls who laughed at him. Curled their lips in his presence like he was some hideous deformed freak.

But bigger than that. Bigger. Everywhere.

From the children starving to death in Africa to the sweatshop workers in China working 120 hours a week for pennies to the homeless people and prostitutes in every goddamn town. "No human involved." That's what the police called homicides involving prostitutes.

No human involved.

All around the globe the human body is a commodity. In every country. In every city. That's all it is. A thing to be used up for an owner's gain. Sold. Consumed.

Chewed up.

The way he sees it, we're already being funneled into the kill chute at the slaughterhouse. We're already garbage. Already meat served on someone's plate.

So throw that self away. Throw it all away. Forget it.

None of it means anything. None of the work he's ever done

340

at his string of menial jobs. None of the things he's ever owned.

It is meaningless. Nothingness. The negation of.

He scratches his nose. Watches a Hyundai pass him in the left lane. The girl behind the wheel with a somber look on her face.

Was all life hollowed out like that?

Produce. Consume. Repeat until death.

No more. Block it out.

He tells himself these words over and over: Just listen to that wave in the air. Feel it. Let the old appetites swell in your gut.

And obey the pictures beamed into your head. Forget all else.

So he keeps going. Keeps driving. Keeps pressing forward.

There is no comfort here for creatures like him. No rest to be had.

So seal him in this car and turn him loose on the city. This box on wheels. This coffin he drives around in. Watch his obsessions blossom into something worth remembering.

He drives on and on. The light swelling in the sky.

He pictures the Prius racing down a hill into a line of cars waiting at a stoplight. Jamming the accelerator. Hitting top speed. The bang of the impact. His body jolting. The metal splintering. Glass shattering. The last thing he'd see is his car turned into a missile. Delivering death to as many people as possible. Crushing their bodies in their seats. Grinding blood and meat into the upholstery. And then the steel coffin closing in on him. Folding him up. Compressing his flesh and then piercing it. Cracking his bones. Pinching everything into something dark and tight and small.

The spectacle of it all makes him smile. Two puffs of laughter hissing between his teeth.

So how did this happen? How did he become this way?

It was always there. It was always everywhere. Around everyone. That's what he thinks.

Written in the sand. And spread across the stars. Etched into the spirals of our DNA.

Always. Forever.

CHAPTER 63

Gasping for breath, Darger jolted awake. She felt at her neck, sure she'd find the flesh torn open and sticky with blood. But no. She was fine. It was only another nightmare.

She dreamed often of the night Zara was killed. Sometimes Darger had a gun of her own, which she pulled from her bag. But when she pulled the trigger, there was an innocuous click where the bullet should have been. That was if she was able to pull the trigger, of course. In some of the dreams, she couldn't even do that right. Once, the gunman had been her stepfather, which made no sense considering he'd always been more than kind to Violet, and she had no reason to fear him. Another time, the masked man stabbed Zara instead of shooting her.

This morning's twist was that Violet tried to rush the man when he pointed the gun at Zara and demanded her purse. She couldn't get her arms and legs to move right. It felt like she was trying to jog underwater, her limbs slow and heavy. The man suffered no such decreased speed. He turned the gun and shot Violet instead.

Knowing Loshak's preference for hard copies, Darger showered, dressed, and headed out to the local supermarket to buy a copy of the local newspaper that would be running the latest story about the Worthingtons and the memorial. Also donuts. If she was going to be up this early, then there damn well better be donuts.

It was the front page story in the local paper, The Athens News. Nearly every other area paper had or would run their version as well. The Worthingtons had been generous with their time, agreeing to do over half a dozen interviews before the vigil.

Darger grabbed a box of assorted donuts on her way to the checkout. While she waited in line, she perused the story. The headline read: **Slain girl's mother: 'She was so much more than a victim.'**

Dead End Girl

Darger skimmed the article for Lois Worthingtons' quotes:

"It's painful to see her boiled down to something so ugly. I cringe every time I read her name and then 'third victim of the Doll Parts Killer.' She was so much more than that."

"It's just hard because she had so much more to do and to give. People won't ever know her as the brilliant woman she was. Her name will always be a footnote as part of these horrible crimes."

"She was funny and smart and kind. She had so much enthusiasm for everything she did. She never did anything halfway. It was all or nothing."

Details regarding the vigil followed, and Darger didn't have to read those. She knew the schedule forward and backward.

Next to the article was a large photograph. In it, Lois Worthington gazed out her living room window. Next to her, seated on the arm of the couch, was Emily, hugging the stuffed elephant to her chest.

The caption read: *Lois Worthington ponders the loss of her eldest daughter. Beside her, Emily Worthington clutches her older sister's favorite stuffed animal, which the family plans to leave at Fiona's grave site after the candlelight vigil on Tuesday.*

Loshak beamed when he saw the story. Maybe it was the nightmare from that morning, or maybe what had happened with Casey, but Darger had a knot in her stomach she couldn't seem to shake.

"You did a damn fine job coaching the Worthingtons. Almost got me with that BS about the elephant," he said and pretended to wipe a tear from his eye. "And I knew it was bogus."

"Donut?" Darger asked, extending the box toward him.

He peeked into the depths of the folded cardboard and wiggled the fingers on his left hand.

"Don't mind if I do."

The only sounds for some time were the chewing and swallowing of fried and glazed dough. Darger licked a smear of sugary goo from her finger.

"What's with you?" Loshak asked.

"Huh?"

"You have a puss on. Like something's eatin' at you."

Springs squeaked as he sat on the corner of one of the beds.

"I didn't sleep well, I guess."

"Butterflies in anticipation of our big day tomorrow?"

Loshak almost pulsed with a manic energy. It was by far the most animated Darger had seen him.

"No, but I can see you're excited."

Loshak rubbed his hands together.

"This could be it. I mean, I don't want to get ahead of myself, but… I just have a good feeling about this."

Darger said nothing, but she couldn't help but feel quite the opposite.

CHAPTER 64

When aimless driving loses its charm, he gets back to his projects. He doesn't stop to sleep or eat. He finds her. And he follows.

He weaves through traffic. Staying well back from her SUV but keeping her in view at all times. A red Rav4. Less than a year old.

He knows with a high level of certainty that she is going to the gym on the edge of town. She does so four days a week around this time. This is her routine.

He floors it to make it through a yellow light and keep her within his view. The car jerks. Lurches at his touch. But it remains soundless.

The Prius is so quiet. Dead silent most of the time. It largely runs on the battery. The gas engine only kicking on to recharge it every few minutes. It's more like a large computer than a car, he thinks. Still. It has that going for it at least. The quiet.

At the next intersection, he pulls up alongside her. Braves a glance.

This one is older than most of his projects. She is tall. Scrawny to the point of being bony. Teeth bleached. Hair dyed an unnatural shade of blond. Almost yellow.

This combination excites him somehow. This grooming pushed past normalcy. Pushed to the extreme. He doesn't know why. There is something fake about it that he finds stimulating. Something that makes her beyond clean. A different kind of pure.

Will this be it? Will it be her? He doesn't know.

Maybe. Maybe not.

He never knows when it will happen. It just does. He follows and follows and follows. And he never plans it. Never tells himself that today will be the day.

The opportunity just appears. And he takes it. Sometimes it's the first time he follows a particular girl. Others he has followed for months and never made a move on.

And that's fine. Fate plays a role. He accepts that. So far it hasn't steered him wrong, has it?

The green light flicks on. The whole world moves again. Cars spilling down the streets.

They reach the gym three blocks later. He circles in the lot a while after she parks. Not settling into a spot of his own until she gets out.

She rises from the vehicle. Drops her keys into her purse. Walks toward the building on light feet like a cat.

She is so tan. Skin glowing orange like Fanta. There are moments when he thinks she's not right. That she doesn't quite fit what he wants. But when she is out in the sun — when he can see the strange color of her — he knows she will be his.

The sliding doors part, and she disappears into the doorway. There's always something exhilarating about that moment when she steps out of his field of vision. The idea that he might lose her washing over him. Making him sweat. Making his desire more intense.

And now he waits. He squirms a little in his seat. Leans his back this way and that. But stretching is impossible in the Prius.

His lower back is sore. Stiff. His spine all compressed and tight from being stuck at the same angle for so long. He tries adjusting the seat. It doesn't help.

How long has he been in this car? He doesn't know. More than a day. He's pretty sure of that. He's eaten just once. A bag of crap from the Taco Bell drive through. Some hours later he pissed into the paper cup that had previously held his Pepsi. Emptied his full bladder. A surprising amount. Chucked it out the window on Nichols Road.

His back spasms. The muscles twitching and clenching up. Sharp pains jolt through his flesh in lines perpendicular to his spinal column.

Jesus. Should he get out? Stretch out? It'd feel incredible to fully extend his legs. To stand upright. To reach his arms up over his head and let all that pressure on the lower lumbar region go. He could feel the pleasure in his imagination. Each vertebrae pulling free of the one below it with a slow rise like a suction cup detaching.

But it's such a risk. An upmarket gym like this? They'd almost surely have security cameras in the parking lot. Probably fairly high-res ones at that. Something that could tie him to the victim later. Actual facial recognition.

No. Not happening.

He waits.

He stares up at the sign above the gym door. Three figures: one running, one lifting a barbell, one swimming. It's not lit up right now, but the silhouettes still seem to glow.

He found her here. His current project. Picked her out of the crowd. He'd sat in the parking lot several times without luck. And then she appeared. Gliding out of that doorway some months ago. Her skin was a different shade of fake tan at the time. A ruddy undertone. Almost the color of an overcooked hot dog.

He waits and waits and waits. Watches the people file in and out of that sliding glass doorway.

Will she be the one? Will today be the day? He doesn't know. Doesn't know.

Maybe it's the same with the memorial. Will he go there Tuesday night? Drive by? Hide himself among the mob of police and family members?

Maybe. Maybe not.

CHAPTER 65

The day before the memorial, Darger, Loshak, and Luck met with all the personnel that would be assisting with their sweep of the vigil.

"We're particularly interested in the larger, dark-colored sedans. Buicks, Crown Vics, you know the type," Luck said. "Navy blue, black, maybe dark green or gray."

"But get the mid-size and compacts too, if you can," Loshak said. "And be on the lookout especially for something orange attached to the rearview mirror."

Sheriff O'Day and Chief Haden were present, so Darger made an effort to keep her comments to a minimum.

"You can use your bodycams to get most of the plates," she said. "But if you think you have one that seems promising, it doesn't hurt to write it down as well. We're going to have a lot of plate numbers to sort through by the end of this."

Loshak raised his palm in the air.

"The most important thing to remember is that this is a recon mission only. The last thing we wanna do is spook the guy before we know we have enough evidence to nail him."

"That's right," Luck agreed. "We don't need any John Wayne's here."

He pointed at Detective Porto, who sat toward the back.

"Aside from our own John Wayne Porto, of course."

There were cheers and applause and laughter at that, the loudest of all coming from Porto himself.

With the meeting adjourned and the group dispersed, Luck handed Darger and Loshak each two pieces of paper.

"What's this?" Loshak asked.

"A list of guys who Fiona went to school with. Four graduating classes worth from her high school, and anyone registered for any of the same classes in both undergrad and grad school. The second page is the same list, but narrowed down to those with a criminal history."

348

"Not bad, Detective," Loshak said. "We can crosscheck these guys with any plates we get from the memorial. See if anything matches up."

"Thank you, Agent Loshak."

Darger scanned the names on the second list. Ryan Abbott, Anthony Barber, James Clegg, Tony Federer. It went on and on. She hoped that Loshak was right about his gut feeling that the memorial would be fruitful.

"Agent Darger?" Luck said. "I was hoping I could have a word."

"Sure," she said. Having some notion of what Casey wanted to talk about, Darger told Loshak to head back to the hotel without her.

"Don't stay out too late, kiddies," Loshak joked. "We have a lot of work to do tomorrow."

Violet followed Casey to his van and climbed into the passenger seat. He put the key into the ignition but didn't start it right away.

"What do you say we get a drink first? Somewhere quiet, so we can talk."

"I guess that means The Elbow Room is out, then?" she said with a smirk.

"Yeah, if I know Porto, he's downing tequila shots and insisting they fire up the karaoke machine so he can get pumped up for tomorrow."

"Good God," Darger said. "I can't believe we're going to miss that."

Casey winked at her.

"Another time, Agent."

They landed in a brewery near the university. It was all exposed brick and weathered wood, and instead of a crowd of cops, it seemed mostly inhabited by college students. They each ordered a pint from the bar plus a basket of truffle fries to share and found a small table in the back where it was a bit quieter than up front. Darger took a swallow of the Dark Farmhouse Ale and eyed the other patrons. They looked so young, she could hardly believe they weren't in high school. Had she looked that young when she was 21?

Their glasses were half empty when Casey exhaled loudly and started to fidget with his shirt cuffs.

"So about the other night…" he started.

Darger cut him off.

"You don't have to explain yourself to me, Casey."

"But I do. I want to. Just listen," he said. "You probably already guessed that I haven't dated much since my divorce, and the truth is more like I haven't dated at all since then. I haven't worked out yet how and when I'm supposed to mention these things, but I know it's not supposed to happen like it did. I'm sorry."

"It's OK. Really."

"Her name is Jill, by the way. My little girl."

"How old is she?" Violet asked, knowing it was the polite thing to do.

"She turned four in August," Casey said, smiling.

The amusement faded as he swirled the beer left in his glass, gazing into the turbulent golden liquid.

"Her mother… my ex… she was a nurse. Worked at one of the nursing homes in town. She hurt her back lifting a patient and wound up hooked on painkillers. Once she got started on those, she branched out. She'd take whatever she could get her hands on. Xanax, Klonopin. She admitted she'd tried meth a few times, even."

Violet felt a crushing guilt come over her as she remembered how angry Casey had been when she was dismissive of arresting Sierra Peter's dealer, Jimmy Congdon. No wonder he'd gotten so upset.

"It's easy to blame her addiction for ending the marriage. But the truth is, I didn't notice anything was going on because I was too busy. Or maybe the real truth is that I didn't *want* to notice anything going on. There were signs, of course. And I'm a cop, for Christ's sake. I know better.

"Anyway, it went on for a while before I picked up on it. And even then, it took her wrapping her car around a tree for me to wake up.

"We convinced her to go to rehab. We started going to Nar-Anon meetings — me, her parents, even my sister came to a few

350

meetings. Things were good for a couple of years. She got pregnant. We had a healthy baby girl. I thought we'd finally gotten things back on track, and then her dad had a heart attack. Him dying was like hitting a reset button. I came home from work one night and found her stoned out of her mind on Klonopin. Hadn't changed Jill's diaper the whole time I'd been gone. And I realized then, she couldn't be around our daughter like that. I couldn't *trust* her to be around our daughter. I gave her an ultimatum. Get clean or get out. But this time, she didn't even stick it out for the full treatment. She bounced after ten days.

"I tried to give her some time to get her shit straightened out, but eventually I filed for full custody of our daughter. At first, I thought her mom was really going to fight me on it, but we ended up coming to terms with the fact that it was the best thing to do. She's been a godsend, too. Jesus, if I didn't have Claudia, I don't know what I'd do."

He took a long drink then.

"So that's it. The mess behind the flawless and unblemished facade of Detective Casey Luck," he said, gesturing to his person with a wry smile.

"Flawless and unblemished, huh?"

He adjusted the knot in his tie.

"I think I pull it off OK."

"I give you an A minus," she teased.

"Better than any grade I ever got in school. I'll take it."

Cold rain poured down from a leaden sky when they left the pub. Thankfully, the Luckmobile was parked right out front. They skipped across the sidewalk and dove inside as quickly as possible, hopping over the puddles at the side of the road. Violet wiped raindrops from her forehead and cheeks.

"Why don't you stay over tonight? I'll make you breakfast in the morning. You can meet Jill."

He said it last, but Darger suspected that's what he really wanted more than anything else. And she knew it was the worst possible thing she could do.

She shook her head.

"You heard Loshak. Big day tomorrow. No late night

shenanigans."

"Damn. I had my heart set on that exact type of shenanigans."

When he dropped her off in front of the motel, he leaned over to kiss her. She met him halfway.

"See you tomorrow?"

"Roger that," she said, before dashing out into the rain.

Darger grabbed a towel from the bathroom and tousled her rain-damp hair. She frowned at her moist reflection in the mirror.

Something was wrong with this picture. She should be excited about the vigil tomorrow night. Loshak was. Luck was. But she wasn't. At all. She felt uneasy.

She tossed the towel over the shower curtain rod and went back to her room. As she took a seat on the edge of the bed, her eyes went immediately to her copies of the newspapers from the previous day. Fiona's blue-green eyes and perfect smile beamed up at her from the front page of The Columbus Dispatch.

She considered the quotes from Fiona's mother. *Her name will be a footnote...*

As far as Darger was concerned, it wasn't Fiona who was the footnote. It was the other three victims. Even after Sierra's 15 minutes of posthumous tabloid fame, the papers had all gone back to running the big full-color photos of Fiona when they wanted to reference a victim of the Doll Parts Killer.

She reached out and flipped the paper over, tiring of Fiona's unwavering gaze.

Her mind wandered to earlier tonight with Casey. She'd been miffed when she found out about his daughter, that was true. So shouldn't his explanation have made her feel better?

It hadn't. In fact, she felt worse. Why?

Because, you fool, she thought to herself. He wouldn't be telling you these things if he was thinking clearly about where this was headed. He sure as hell wouldn't be suggesting you meet his daughter.

She had done the math, but Casey clearly had not. At some point, Darger would leave Athens. She'd go back to Quantico, get her next assignment, and move on. There was no future for the two of them.

Violet rolled off the bed and began pacing from one end of the small room to the other. Her sock got wet when she stepped on the part of the carpet where her boots had dripped rain, but she didn't slow.

The off feeling she'd gotten at the mirror returned. Something wasn't right. Was it just nerves in anticipation of tomorrow? Her revelation with Casey? Or was something else bothering her?

She didn't know. So she returned again to the files. To the photographs. To the interviews.

She listened to the Sierra interviews in reverse order, starting with the one they'd had here in this very hotel room. It wasn't until she reached the original interview that she stopped, clicked back in the file, replayed.

DET. JANSSEN: And what about this woman you saw?
SIERRA: Woman? What woman? There was no woman.
DET. JANSSEN: Says here you said you saw a woman jogging by. A witness, I guess.
SIERRA: No. There wasn't a woman. It was just the one guy.

It was tucked at the end, after Sierra mentions chloroform for the first time, which always distracted Darger because she almost hadn't believed the detail herself the first time she'd watched the interview.

Why was Janssen asking about a woman? Sierra hadn't mentioned it in any of the other interviews, but he'd gotten it from somewhere. Where?

Who had Sierra talked to before Janssen?

That's when it hit her.

She grabbed her jacket, still dripping from the rain earlier, and headed back out into the night.

CHAPTER 66

The curtains twitch. Light spilling out from the window. From the room beyond.

He sits forward in the seat. Arms draped over the steering wheel. A weird yip emits from deep within his throat.

It's the first movement in a long while. Shakes him out of a daze right away.

This is a new project. One that excites him greatly. One that seems irrational. Dangerous. Maybe impossible. And yet he is here.

He doesn't have to pursue it. Not yet. But a time may come when it makes more sense. When his options go away.

The police will close on him. Sooner or later. And when they do, he will move on her.

She will be his last victim.

The fabric at the window shakes again. Shifting closed. The dark returning to extinguish the light.

Damn. He watches the window covering wag back and forth for a long time before inertia wins out and it keeps still.

Darkness surrounds him on the other side of the parking lot. It seems oppressive after that brief burst of light in the window.

He makes the mistake of taking a deep breath. Gags a little.

He smells like ammonia now. A caustic odor that overrides his earthy smell. Overpowers everything. It stings his eyes if he sniffs it straight on.

He blinks. His eyelids scraping over his dried out eyeballs like fine grit sandpaper.

He's not sure how long he's been at this. Time lost meaning somewhere in there. He should maybe sleep soon. But it's hard to stop. He can't wait to see what will happen next. Can't wait to see what she will do next. What he will do next. Where all of this will go.

He sniffs out a laugh. He's sitting on the edge of his seat. Literally. All scooted up. Legs quivering. It seems funny to him

354

in this moment.

He's never watched at a motel like this before. With two floors of occupied rooms right on top of him. All of those doors facing out at him. It's intense. Immediate. He feels safe at the moment, but he can't say what might happen. Just thinking about it gets the adrenaline pumping in his bloodstream again.

The suspense of it all is intoxicating. Drool pools in his mouth. Some Pavlovian response when he gets excited.

He smiles as he rests his head on the steering wheel for a moment. He knows the latest jolt of excitement will keep him awake. Takes the opportunity to close his eyes for a bit. To relax the muscles in his neck. It feels incredible. Those long strands of red fiber finally releasing the strain.

He drifts for a while. Letting his mind go blank. Letting the silence be the only thing. A warmth settles over him. Starting in his torso and spreading into his limbs.

The chasm of slumber swallows him in stages. Taking him under little by little. He bobs deeper and deeper. His being gone utterly still.

Then the saliva finds a slack spot near the corner of his mouth. A dribble leaking out to wet the stubble along his chin. He shakes himself alert. Dabs at the drool with a finger. Smearing it around.

Damn. His mind is foggy. Fuzzy. Blurred. He doesn't let this happen. Even sleeping. He stays alert. Keeps his mind clear.

It takes a concentrated effort to lift his head. To flutter his eyelids and get them to stay open. It's just as well, though. Adrenaline or not, sleep came close to taking him. Too close. How long would he have stayed down? A long while he thinks. Maybe six or eight hours without waking. What a disaster that would be.

And then something scrapes from the direction of her room. His head snaps to attention. All of the sleepy feelings erased from his mind and eyes. The fog vanquished. Replaced with intense focus. With electricity.

The door wiggles. Opens. Something like a surprised bark coming out of his mouth.

Brilliant light shines out of the place where that wedge of

wood swings wide. It stings to look at after so long in the shadows of night. Stabbing pain assaults both of his eyes. Water draining out of the corners of each. But he can't look away. Can't even blink.

He watches through the tears as she steps into the opening. Lit up from behind so he only sees her in silhouette. But even with her features shrouded in black, she is striking. The most feminine thing he's ever seen. Her movements effortlessly graceful like a cat's.

She stands in the doorway. Fiddling with something in her fingers. Keys maybe. The light behind her shining so bright.

And then she closes the door. The light cutting out.

And he feels like he's falling. Like he's lost. His throat constricts. Pinching itself closed like a strange valve at the back of his mouth. A sour taste forming on his tongue. A surge of warm fluid erupting from his throat with an almost rotten odor to it. Bile maybe.

He struggles to find her. Scanning along the catwalk for a dark shape in the blackness. Squinting. His eyes still smudged with tears. Still stinging like mad from the lack of sleep.

A black flutter catches his eye. It's her. Standing next to a sedan. A Honda Civic or Toyota Camry, he thinks. Hard to tell in the dark.

The dome light clicks on within the car. And for a moment he sees her face. That entrancing collection of features he's only really seen well in pictures on the internet. The creamy skin speckled faintly with freckles. The intelligence and complexity in her eyes and brow. A perpetual feline cleverness to the set of her lip. She is otherworldly in a way he can't pin down. Primal and celestial at the same time.

And then the moment passes. She climbs into the driver's seat. Her back to him now. Her hair and the corner of one shoulder all he can really see.

The brake lights cast a red glow over the parking lot. A flash of light that seems to bring out malevolent contours and clefts in the shadows swathing the surrounding cars. Strange phantoms that he knows can't be real. The engine grinds to life a moment later.

Dead End Girl

She does not hesitate. She pulls away and is gone. The taillights trailing away from him. Dimming into nothing. After so long watching the world in slow motion, her retreat seems to happen in fast speed.

Her absence is palpable. Something torn out of his environment. Some sense of precious things falling away from him.

The quiet stretches out, and then he remembers to breathe. The air scrapes into him. Wheezing as it enters his throat. Enters his lungs. Puffs up his chest.

He smiles. Not all is lost with her gone. Not at all.

He can go through her room.

CHAPTER 67

Janssen's house sat on a corner lot. An American flag fluttered over a small wooden porch on one side. The clock on the dash said 9:20 PM. Late for an unannounced call. But she could see lights on inside, so she at least knew she wasn't waking him.

Darger rang the bell, waited. Nothing happened. She banged her fist against the door.

"Detective Janssen?" she called loudly.

Finally, she heard the click of a deadbolt. The door handle turned and the grizzled visage of Leroy Janssen appeared on the other side of the door. A can of PBR was clutched in his fist.

"Darger. The hell do you want?"

His tone was apathetic but not nearly as frosty as she'd anticipated.

"I'm sorry to bother you at home, but I had a question."

"And God forbid you wait until morning."

He lifted the beer to his mouth and took a long gulp. He didn't ask her to go on. He just stood there, waiting.

"The first time you interviewed Sierra Peters, you asked her about a woman. But she didn't seem to know what you were talking about, and I was wondering if you remembered why you'd asked that."

Janssen blinked at her slowly.

"Christ, Darger. I don't know. I asked her about a lot of things. I can't remember the rhyme and reason to every damn question."

Darger pulled the file from the bag slung over her shoulder. Janssen made no attempt to hide the rolling of his eyes. She read the last few lines of the interview to him. When she looked up, his mouth was pressed into a hard line that obscured his lips. In the shadows, he looked like some kind of strange slit-mouthed creature.

"Right. I do remember. It was in her 911 call."

It was what she'd suspected when she'd rushed out of her

room in the first place. Now she just needed to get her hands on the recording. Violet stared back down at the paper as if a transcript of the call might appear.

"I need a copy of that call. Do you know which 911 dispatch center it went through?"

"Entire county goes through a call center in Logan," he said.

The metal of the can crinkled in his fist as he polished off the beer.

Darger was already searching the address on her phone.

"But if you think you're gonna get the recording tonight, you can forget it. They only have dispatchers at this hour. Mary Wilcox handles the filing of old calls, and she's only there during business hours."

"Shit," Darger said. "I *need* that call."

Janssen sighed. His regulation mustache wiggled to and fro as he seemed to weigh something in his mind.

"You're like one of those cats, aren't you? The ones that sink their claws in and don't let go."

"I'll take that as a compliment," she said.

He chuckled, then said, "I might have a copy of it."

"The 911 call? Really?"

"On my laptop. Might as well come inside," he said, abandoning his post at the door. He tossed his empty into the kitchen sink as he passed.

Like Casey's house, Detective Janssen's home reeked of bachelorhood, but in an entirely different way. Where Luck was all modernity and cleanliness, Janssen was out-of-date and messy. Dirty dishes and cookware littered the counters, along with several pizza boxes and more empty cans. In the hurried glance she got of the living room, she'd seen a step ladder, a TV tray, a large empty cardboard box with a mass of bubble wrap half pulled out, books, magazines, DVDs, and a folded up camping chair.

At the end of a narrow hallway, Janssen ducked into a doorway off to the left. Darger heard a click and light spilled across the threshold. The bedroom Janssen had converted into an office was as cluttered with junk as the rest of the place. Stacks of papers and files littered every possible surface. She counted three mugs filled with dubious contents. Old coffee or dip spit, she didn't really want to know.

An orange and white cat coiled around Darger's ankles as they waited for Detective Janssen's computer to boot. She wouldn't have figured Janssen to be the cat-type. Then again, she also wouldn't have figured him to help her out like this.

"I know we got off on the wrong foot before," Darger started to say, but Janssen cut her off.

"Spare me the kumbaya shit, or I might change my mind. Sometimes two people don't get along, and that's all there is to it. Nothing personal. Just the way things are."

She opened her mouth to argue but settled on, "Fair enough."

He leaned back over the computer and used the touchpad to open one of probably 40 folders on the desktop. His virtual office was as cluttered as the real one.

"Here we go," he said, double-clicking a file. The audio clip opened in a new window, and Janssen bent to turn up the external speakers hooked up to the computer.

Darger heard a crackle of static, and then the 911 operator's voice. "911, what is the address of your emergency?"

Darger held her breath and listened.

CHAPTER 68

His heart knocks in his chest. Banging so hard it makes his breathing hitch. A little hiccup interrupting each inhale.

He doesn't let his state of frenzy effect his movements, though. He walks normally. His head down. His arms slack at his sides. Dangling. Everything fluid. Everything loose. He approaches the motel door like it's his own.

The key slides into the hole. He twists. Hears the tiniest click. And it's done. Just like that.

Funny. He'd almost forgotten he had the key. Left it lying in a pile of similar mementos in his chamber with that weird milky ring. If the image hadn't struck him, hadn't popped into his head out of nowhere, this project never would have spawned.

But here he is. Violating her space.

He steps into the room. The light still on overhead. The brightness narrows his eyes to slits as he closes the door behind him.

Why leave the light on? Will she be back soon? He'd need to be quick.

The decor is of the usual trashy motel variety. All the fabrics look tired. The worn carpet. The frayed blankets. The odor, however, is glorious.

Her smell overruns the stench of decay that must normally occupy this room. It positively reeks of her.

She smells like fresh baked bread and pine and coconut. A hint of lavender. Some bodily note that ties it all together. Like brie cheese, maybe.

His scalp tingles when he inhales her. Sucks her into his nostrils. Funnels her into his sinus cavity. He is almost drunk with it.

He moves to the luggage at the foot of the bed. Unzips the wheeled duffel and flings the lid wide.

Tops and slacks and socks reveal themselves.

He digs a hand in the pocket and finds what he's looking for.

Underwear. Panties. Nothing too garish. Just normal cotton with a little rim of lacy elastic along the top.

He closes his eyes and brings them to his face. Sniffs. Her same scent intensified. A new note in the odor that he can't place. Like that faintest hint of char in a piece of salted caramel.

He shoves the underwear in his back pocket. Closes the suitcase. Zips it.

Yes. This is good. He can leave here undetected. Can come back another time perhaps. For more practical purposes.

His chest throbs with electricity as he moves to the door. His hand finds the knob. The metal cold against his feverish skin.

He knows he should go. Now. But he finds himself lingering.

He looks back over the room. At a glance, it's almost underwhelming. Only a dingy motel room. Verging on rotting. But it's more than that. To him, it's much more.

This is it. The motel room of Special Agent Violet Darger.

It's funny. No matter what else happens, they have one thing in common now.

They are hunting each other.

CHAPTER 69

When Sierra spoke on the recording, it was like she was right there in the room with Darger once more. Alive. Resurrected. It made the hair on Darger's arms stand up straight. A chill coursed all through her, cold enough to constrict her breath.

Sierra's voice was slurred, whether from her own drugs or those of the killer, Darger couldn't be sure. Her panic, however, was still discernible.

Dispatcher: 911, what is the address of your emergency?
Sierra: He's tryna kill me!
Dispatcher: Ma'am, can you please tell me where you're at?
Sierra: He's— I'm at... at the... next to the, the... Dairy Mart on Broadway.
Dispatcher: What's that?
Sierra: Across the street from the Dairy Mart.
Dispatcher: What's the problem?
Sierra: He's gonna kill me! He's got a knife and a gun and he's gonna kill me! Please hurry!
Dispatcher: Ma'am, are you injured?
Sierra: No. Yes. A little. Hit my head, I think.
Dispatcher: He hit you in the head?
Sierra: I don't know. I can't remember.
Dispatcher: Where is he now?
Sierra: I don't know, but if he finds me, he's gonna kill me. You have to hurry. Please! I'm scared.
Dispatcher: You can't see him?
Sierra: No. No, I ran. I ran from the room.
Dispatcher: He had you in a room?
Sierra: And I was tied up.
Dispatcher: Are you tied up still?
Sierra: I kinda freed myself. He put me in the room and then he left. And I ran.
Dispatcher: How far did you run?

Sierra: I don't know. A mile. A couple miles. I was in the woods. I don't know.

Dispatcher: Do you remember seeing anything else when you were running?

Sierra: When he first put me in the room. There was a woman.

Dispatcher: There was a woman with the man?

Sierra: No, not *with* him. She was outside. Outside of the room. Across the street. She was running. A whaddyacallit…

Dispatcher: A jogger?

Sierra: Yeah. Wait, no. How much longer?

Dispatcher: What?

Sierra: How much longer? I'm scared.

Dispatcher: Just a few more minutes.

[Pause]

Sierra: I see lights. I see the lights. I hear them.

Dispatcher: You hear the police lights?

Sierra: Yes. Oh, thank god. Oh, thank you. I thought I was going to die.

Dispatcher: Just hang on with me a little longer, until the officers get there, OK?

Sierra: OK. Oh God. He was going to kill me.

Dispatcher: Can you see the cars now?

Sierra: Yes. Yes, I see them.

Dispatcher: OK, just stay with me until the officers get there.

"That's it," Janssen said when the file finished playing.

"A woman outside of the room, she said. Across the street. Running. It seemed like she was going to say something else after that, but she was rattled. She lost track."

"Yeah, she was pretty messed up that night."

"What do you think it means?"

"Who the hell knows? Mighta hallucinated it for all we know."

Darger didn't think so. Sierra had been confused that night, her memory foggy, but she hadn't been delusional.

"Can I copy that onto my phone?"

"The call?" Janssen asked, then glanced at the computer with mild distrust. "I'm not really very technical."

Darger was already pulling the USB cable from her bag.

"I know how," she said.

She took a step closer to the laptop and paused.

"If you don't mind."

He raised his hands in defeat, not looking thrilled about it, but probably figuring the sooner she got what she wanted, the sooner she'd be out of his hair. Darger connected her phone to the computer and dragged the file over. It was done in under a minute.

"There. Finished."

Just to be sure everything had worked correctly, Violet opened the audio of the 911 call on her phone. It was all there.

"Great. Now, do you mind?" Janssen said, flipping off the light to the office.

He led her back to the front door. The cat followed in their wake, and before Darger exited the house, she bent to pet the top of its head.

She paused on the stoop and readjusted the strap of her bag.

"Janssen. Thank you."

"Yeah," he said and unceremoniously closed the door on her.

Well, she thought as she strode to her car, you can't win 'em all.

CHAPTER 70

Sandy Metcalf couldn't believe how cold it was. The chill hit her in the foyer as soon as the automatic doors of the gym parted, and it only got worse when she left the building and walked across the parking lot, the frigid wind battering her in the face all the while. Her hair was still a little wet from hopping in the shower after her workout. It was only a quick rinse, but her face and scalp were paying the price for it now. The harsh air seemed to not just strike her but scrape across the exposed flesh, abrading it in bursts like aggressive swipes of steel wool.

Walking between two SUVs provided her some cover, the pocket of stillness enveloping her. An empty warmth seemed to well in her there. Almost a sense of weightlessness. Her nerves all confused after the violence of the wind. She took a deep breath, her chest fluttering.

"Windy enough for you?" a man's voice said right next to her.

She jumped a little, the voice startling her, but she recovered quickly. The voice had come from a mustached man sitting in the driver's seat of the Explorer parked next to her RAV4. His window was part of the way down.

"It's brutal," she said. "If this is what we're getting in October, who knows what winter will be like?"

The man chuckled.

"Oh, it'll be nightmarish. I promise you that."

She climbed into her car, her torso still tingling with cold tendrils of adrenaline from that moment of fright. There was nothing quite like feeling alone and finding out you weren't in visceral fashion like that, she thought. It got her whole body stirring. Again, she took a deep breath into a quivering chest. The wind whipped across the hood and roof, whistling a little in that hollow just beyond the bottom of the windshield.

She started the car and applied some lip balm to her lips. That was one of her nervous ticks, even if her lips were genuinely dry at the moment. She applied it whenever she was spooked. Something about the ritual of it comforted her. The little snap of the lid popping off. The feel of it on her lips. This kind was coconut. A little greasier than she preferred, but it smelled nice. She closed her eyes as the flat surface brushed the perimeter of her lips. Then she clicked the lid back on, and the ritual was complete.

She pulled out of the parking spot, not looking back at the mustached man in the Explorer. She got another chill as the SUV eased out of the lot, goose bumps rippling over her arms. Funny how she couldn't quite shake the fright of that man violating her private moment. No matter how sure she was that everything was OK, that creeping sensation wouldn't quite leave her alone.

CHAPTER 71

He waits a time before he follows her out of the lot. Drums on the steering wheel with the heels of his hands.

Something had changed in him as he watched her this time. The shift. Some switch flipping in his head in that moment of fright he saw on her face right before she got into her car. The mustached man had spooked her somehow. And she glowed.

It always works this way. The voltage cranks up in his head. The current lighting up his brain. Making his jaw clench.

The shift is upon him.

He moves now. His Prius trailing well behind her RAV4. The SUV falling out of view now and again. Snaking around corners and bends. But he feels no fear of losing her now. No fear at all.

The clouds roil above. A relentless gray wall separating the earth from the heavens.

He no longer perceives himself as in control. No longer chooses what will happen next. No longer even wants to. It feels like a dream. An intense dream with his awareness turned all the way up. He watches the events unfold. Watches his body go through with it. Watches himself close in on the inevitable.

The current just surges and surges in his head. Such a powerful impulse. Something beyond desire. Beyond compulsion. It beats in his chest and pulses in his limbs. It presses him forward to the next act. To the next deed. It's not merely a throb in his skull to be obeyed. It is everything. Everything. The only thing that's real.

The shift.

He feels it in the tightening of his jaw. In all those cords and muscles in his neck drawn taut enough to snap. He feels it in the cold sweat slicking his skin. The surface of his body prickling with a tiny version of that electrical charge burning out in his head.

He crests a small hill and she comes back into view. The red

RAV4 waiting at a blinking red light. He already knows where she will go. Knows her every move three steps in advance.

But what will he do? That he doesn't know. Not yet.

But he will. Soon.

He can almost smell it. That electric current in his skull. It's like the ozone odor of a computer's power supply. Sharp and clean.

CHAPTER 72

Sandy's hand moved to the stereo in the center of the dash, but her fingers stopped shy of the touchscreen. She'd gone to turn on the radio reflexively and thought better of it. The noise would be too stimulating just yet — either music or talk. She needed a little peace and quiet. Something to clear her mind of that anxiety. She took another deep breath, trying to fight that tremble of the muscles in her chest and failing.

The RAV4 moved out of a wooded area and into the open, and that change in atmosphere seemed to calm her some. The wind howled through the open space, however, its restlessness not so easily quelled.

The image of the grocery store flashed in her head. She needed half and half and she'd planned to break her post-workout tradition by swinging by Seaman's to grab a quart. But now... Her skin crawled again. It didn't feel right.

The incident in the parking lot had rattled her in a way she couldn't shake, and she didn't want to do anything out of the ordinary. Didn't want to break her routine.

God, this was so weird. She hadn't felt this vulnerable in a long, long time. She was a woman in her late 30's who'd lived alone since the divorce. Five years on her own. She didn't spook easily. Not anymore. But this had her wound up. And something about that only frightened her more.

She'd been with Dan for over ten years before they split. The divorce was his call, but she wasn't shocked or even particularly upset. They'd never been very close and never had children. They just went through the motions in both their relationship and their lives. Maybe they'd both been too focused on their careers at the time. She appraised homes, something she liked doing as it involved travel and photography. He worked in auto insurance. She had never quite been clear what his job actually entailed. Paperwork. That's all she knew.

Still, she had always felt safe at night with him there next to her. The first months by herself were rough. Those long, black nights. Wide awake. Listening to every creak and groan of the house settling. The patter of her cat's feet on the carpet in the hall. The wind swishing through the trees and bushes outside.

It took over four months before she could sleep the night through undisturbed. But she'd gotten there. And she'd really blossomed after that. The doldrums of a lackluster marriage lifted, and her life felt renewed. Re-energized. She started taking care of herself, both physically and mentally, in new ways. She upped her exercise regimen, switched to a vegetarian diet, and started treating herself to the kind of leisure activities that left her feeling fulfilled. Gardening, both vegetables and flowers. Vacations to Europe and South America. She dated some, too — enough to keep things interesting — but that seemed secondary to her other endeavors. For the first time, her life was all about her.

The grocery store approached in the plaza on the right. She wouldn't be stopping. No, she would trust her gut. She'd follow her normal ritual of hitting Starbucks after her workout and leave it at that. A tall mocha. Sugar-free. Just like always.

The clock on the dash glowed green. Maybe she'd stop by Pam's for a quick visit, bring her a coffee. Sandy and her sister texted back and forth nearly every day, but she hadn't seen Pam in person in almost two weeks. She tried to remember Pam's favorite drink at Starbucks. Caramel something something… or was it cinnamon?

Her eyes flicked to the rearview mirror as she stopped at a blinking red light. The road behind her was empty. No one following. Nothing suspicious going on. Everything was perfectly normal. She knew this, but some part of her still wouldn't believe it.

CHAPTER 73

The stark silhouettes of trees that had already dropped all of their leaves rolled by as they drove into town for the memorial service. The branches reminded her of skeletal arms, reaching for the darkening sky. Crooked claws of bone.

Darger had forced Loshak to listen to Sierra's 911 call three times that morning. He'd seemed distracted, his mind probably wandering to the vigil which was only a few hours away from commencing.

"If there was a witness to Sierra's first abduction, and we could find her—"

"Now hold on, Darger. It could mean anything. For starters, it's one of the things she recanted in her first interview. Janssen specifically asks her about the woman, and Sierra says she doesn't know what the frig he's talking about."

"Yeah, but she was terrified and all screwed up from the drugs and getting hit in the head. It would make sense that she'd have the details mixed up, even an hour later."

Loshak's head tilted to one side and then the other as if he were weighing it.

"Maybe we should have Luck mention it in the next press conference. Anyone who might have seen something that night. Any women that may have been out for a walk or a run," Violet continued.

At a stop sign, she watched a gust of wind pick up a pile of papery golden leaves and swirl them around like a miniature tornado.

Loshak said, "One thing at a time. Let's get through the memorial tonight, alright? Can't we just focus on that for now? For all we know, by the time it's over, we won't need this mysterious jogging woman, because we'll already have a suspect in custody."

"You're gonna jinx it, talking like that."

Loshak scoffed with amusement.

372

"Don't get superstitious on me, Darger."

The tires bumped up and onto a bridge spanning the Hocking River. Loshak turned to gaze upon the silvery water running beneath them.

"We're about to catch a break. I can feel it."

As they pulled into the lot near the auditorium, Darger spotted three officers already making their rounds through the rows of vehicles. They were in plainclothes, but as usual were easy to identify as police if you knew where to look.

The Worthingtons were stationed at the main entrance of the auditorium, greeting each visitor as they came through the threshold. It was a handsome historic building with red brick, arched windows, and large transoms over the doors. Mission-style sconces between the doorways emitted a welcoming glow.

Lois smiled broadly when she saw them.

"Agent Darger, Agent Loshak," she said, holding out a hand for each of them. "Thank you so much for coming. And for everything else you're doing."

"Our pleasure, ma'am," Loshak said.

After exchanging pleasantries with the rest of the family, they made their way into the auditorium. It was a huge space with two mezzanines. So far, it appeared they were limiting seating to the lower level, but judging by the large crowd, Violet wouldn't be surprised if they opened one of the upper levels as well. The acoustics of the room magnified the sounds of the mob; a clamor of voices so constant it was like the babble of a stream. Offstage, Darger could hear people doing vocal warm-ups. The program she'd been handed at the door listed two performances by the choir from the Worthingtons' church.

"What does your spidey-sense say now?" Darger asked Loshak.

"Huh?"

"You think he's here?"

Loshak's eyes scanned the room and ran a hand through his hair.

"If he is, then it's a damn good thing we have a solid plan in motion. If we'd been trying to sift through this crowd, we'd be screwed."

Tucked into the shadows under the balcony of the first mezzanine was a line of cameramen testing their equipment. Loshak squinted over Darger's shoulder and then wrapped his fingers around her bicep.

"We've been spotted. Let's skedaddle," he said, pulling her further into the mass of people clustering among the seats.

Behind them, Darger could hear a woman's voice calling after them.

"Agent Darger!"

They ducked around a group of younger people and up a row of seats.

"Why, hello, Detective," Loshak said.

Casey Luck was sitting at the end of the row, cloaked somewhat by the fact that this corner of the seating area was darker than the rest.

"Oh hey. I was trying to hide from reporters," he said.

"Same here," Loshak said.

Darger settled into the seat between them.

"Everything set at the grave site?" Luck asked.

Loshak nodded.

"Yeah. Already got one car on it. I'll join him for the first round of surveillance after the vigil."

Darger wasn't listening. She had the program clutched in her hand. It was coiled into a tube, her thumb and forefinger wrapped around it. She stared into the hole in the center, going over Sierra's 911 call again in her head.

One of them said her name, but it barely registered. Not until she felt a tap on her shoulder.

"Did you hear what I said?" Luck asked.

She shook herself from the daze.

"No, I didn't. Sorry."

"We're still on for the second shift, right?"

"That's right."

Before more could be said, the lights dimmed, and the crowd noise hushed along with it. The memorial was about to begin.

CHAPTER 74

Again, the wind assailed Sandy as she made her way from Starbucks to her car. It scraped her skin with its claws, flicked strands of hair into her eyes. The hot coffee was the only thing she had to fight the cold off, but it wasn't much of a weapon. A trickle of steam coiled out of the mouth holes of the white cups in her hands.

Looking beyond the RAV4 into an adjacent lot, she saw a man struggling with a baby carrier, a diaper bag, and a few plastic bags of groceries. He wobbled and grunted, dropping a bag as he fumbled for the door. Then he dropped his keys as well.

He looked up at her through a pair of thick glasses, embarrassed, his eyes wide and innocent like a child's.

"Need a hand?" she said, setting the drinks down on the roof of the RAV4.

"Oh, no, I've got it," he said, his gaze falling to the ground. "Just, uh…"

As if on cue, he lost another bag, and the baby carrier swayed with great force. She was sure he was going to lose it, but he managed to regain control. A pair of lemons rolled away from the dumped bags, somehow heightening the sheer pathetic force of the scene.

The hair on the back of her neck prickled as she took the first step away from her vehicle. Was it fright or just the wind? She didn't know. In any case, she ignored it and jogged over.

"Thanks," he said. "I'm sorry to trouble you like this."

She stooped and gathered the spilled groceries, half watching the man and the baby out of the corner of her eye. He had such a meek presence, unable to even look at her. She felt embarrassed on his behalf. Almost disturbed. The baby's face was mostly covered with a blanket, a sliver of the forehead peeking out. Maybe he or she was sleeping.

She stood, the bags of groceries now heavy in her hands.

"It's unlocked," he said. "If you could lean in and put the groceries in the backseat, it'd be great."

She hesitated. It was a two-door. She'd practically have to get into the car to unload the groceries. But then she saw the frame buckled into the passenger seat where the baby carrier would snap into place. That made the backseat drop-off make sense. She always thought baby seats were supposed to go in the back, but what did she know?

She popped the door open and crawled into the Prius, resting her knees on the passenger seat. As she leaned into the back, it occurred to her that aside from the lemons and a few candy bars, the bags were mostly full of magazines. Old, beat up magazines. And then she remembered the moment when he dropped the keys. She had a Toyota, and knew you didn't need to be holding the keys to unlock the—

The clatter of the plastic baby carrier striking the asphalt made her jump, her shoulders hunching and freezing in that position, all of the flesh on her back tingling ice cold right away. That crawling skin spread over her shoulders, down onto the backs of her arms.

And then he was on her.

One of his arms looped around her shoulders, pulling her back into his chest. His body pressed into hers. The opposite hand shoved a rag over her nose and mouth. The chemical stench was suffocating and strange. It stung her eyes, and her head felt heavy right away.

She screamed a moment too late, the cloth muffling her sound. And she squirmed, but he was too strong. His body corded up tight. Stiff. Almost like he was made of wood.

He said nothing, and peering over her shoulder, she could read no expression on his face. Just a blank stare. Cold and distant.

And then things went wavy. A shimmer blurring everything like heat distortion. Like she could see the fume she'd inhaled hovering all around her.

The black opened up and swallowed her whole.

CHAPTER 75

"My Song in the Night" was the title of the song that opened the service, according to the program. It was an a cappella number, which Loshak felt suited the space. Something about the voices echoing in the large chamber sounded right.

Watching the members of the choir singing, Loshak couldn't help but think of Shelly, his daughter. She'd always been a self-proclaimed "choir geek." In fact, one of the last things she'd done outside of the hospital was a recital with their local community chorale.

Thinking of her, his next breath caught in his chest, and he felt the moistness of tears clinging to his eyelashes. He couldn't let his emotions get in the way tonight, though. It was too important.

He looked over his shoulder, scanning all of those faces in the crowd, checking the exits for any sign of movement.

Was the scumbag here now, cowering in the crowd? He thought it possible.

A man took the stage and introduced himself as Reverend Curtis Smith.

"On behalf of the Worthington family, I would like to thank all of you for joining us here tonight to celebrate the life of Fiona. To see how many of you have come to honor Fiona fills my heart and the heart of her family, I know. Grief is a horrible thing to bear alone. For the family to know that they are supported by the entire community is going to be crucial for them in the coming months."

He folded his hands before him on the podium.

"I'd like to begin with a moment of silence for Fiona, but also for the other three girls that will forever be tied to her: Cristal Monroe, Katie Seidel, and Sierra Peters."

The reverend bowed his head and closed his eyes, and Loshak followed suit. The quiet was peppered with the small noises of a group: stifled coughs, throat clearing, the murmur of a small child.

After a minute or so, Reverend Smith gazed upon them once more.

"A number of Fiona's friends and family members have been asked to speak before you tonight. To share a little of who Fiona was. I hope their stories will give all of us a chance to appreciate the unique individual her family will never forget: kind, generous, driven. A daughter, a sister, and a friend. A caretaker and a lover of animals."

A screen was lowered from behind a black curtain. Images lit up the white rectangle: Fiona as an infant, sitting on a bathmat wrapped in a towel. Fiona, perhaps five years old, holding a hula hoop at her waist. Fiona wearing a cap and gown at her high school graduation.

While the slide show continued to play, several of Fiona's friends and relatives went up to tell stories about the girl who had only ever been a series of photographs to Victor Loshak.

The last person to speak about Fiona's life was her mother. Lois Worthington stepped to the microphone dressed in a long-sleeved black dress with sheer sleeves and pearls embroidered at the neck and cuffs. Two huge heart-shaped wreaths of pink and white flowers flanked her on either side.

"Wow, I'm just… overwhelmed," Mrs. Worthington said, her voice breaking with emotion. "Fiona would be so touched to know that we are all here tonight sharing memories and stories of her life."

She took a deep breath.

"As you've heard from some of the others, Fiona was never one to suffer from much indecision. She always seemed to know what she wanted, and once she had her heart set on it, that was it. There was no convincing her otherwise. For her fifth birthday, she asked for cherries on top of her cake. Now, Fiona's birthday is in March, and I couldn't find fresh cherries anywhere. So I bought a can of cherries. And when she marched into the kitchen and saw me putting those black wrinkled things on top of her perfect white cake, I knew I was in trouble."

Scattered chuckles reverberated around the room.

"She said, 'Momma, why are you putting olives on my cake?'

And I explained to her, 'Honey, they didn't have fresh cherries at the store. I had to get the kind that comes in a can.' And she put her hands on her hips, and she looked up at me, and she said, 'No, momma. Those aren't going on my cake.' And that was that."

The crowd laughed, and Lois paused before she continued.

"Another time, when she was a bit older, we were riding in the car. I had the radio on. And 'Another One Bites the Dust' by Queen came on. And she started to laugh. She said, 'This sounds like that song 'Another One Rides the Bus.' And I said, 'Well this is the original song. 'Another One Rides the Bus' is a parody that came out later.' And she gave me that look. All you other moms out there know the look I'm talking about. And she said, 'Mom, I'm pretty sure 'Another One Rides the Bus' came first.' Even when she was wrong, she was right."

This time, Lois Worthington joined in the laughter, but hers ended in a choked sob. She struggled for a moment to compose herself.

Loshak's heart ached. He knew firsthand how the line between joyful reminiscence and painful recollection became a blur. How quickly the laughter could turn to tears.

With a sniff and a dab of tissue at the corners of her eyes, Lois reigned in her sorrow.

"I just have one more story to tell. When Fiona was about three years old, she was absolutely fascinated by the moon. She wanted to know everything about it. What was it made of? How far away was it? Why did it disappear sometimes? One night, we were driving home from I-don't-know-where. It was a clear night, with a big full moon. And from her car seat in the back, I heard Fiona say, 'Look, mom. The moon has a car, and he's driving with us!'"

This time the group's response was more reserved, and Fiona's mother didn't have to wait long to finish.

"I don't know if anyone else noticed, but tonight is a full moon. And I can't help but think that's a sign from Fiona and from God. I feel her with us tonight. Her warmth. Her love."

CHAPTER 76

The Prius moves without sound. An almost eerie quiet. Like the car is holding its breath.

He looks down on the crumpled figure in the passenger seat. She looks different this close up. Her skin dark and leathery. Not wholly unpleasant. But weathered.

He waits at a red light. Watches the eyes for a long moment. Looking for any motion. Any flutter of the lashes. Any sign of consciousness. There is none.

This is how it works when the fantasy is made real. He cannot lose this game. When the dream comes to life, they cannot fight back. It becomes impossible. Like a magical force rules over them. Renders them powerless. Bends them to his will.

The Peters girl escaped. But that was different. He'd done something wrong, maybe. Messed up the dream. Anyhow, he got her in the end.

The hybrid's engine kicks on with a rumble as he pulls away from the intersection. And he remembers to breathe just then. Not realizing he'd been imitating the car's held respiration until then.

Maybe if she'd parked on the other side of the Starbucks parking lot, none of this would have happened. He can't stop thinking about it. Tumbling that bit of fortune over and over in his head. The idea that both of their lives had turned on that decision. Even if it had probably seemed mundane to her when she made it.

The drive-thru window would have stopped him from acting. He wouldn't have the privacy he had. He wouldn't have been able to draw her into the emptiness of the adjacent lot. Wouldn't have been able to block things correctly so the blacktop stage they functioned on was screened from the view of any windows. Wouldn't have been able to pull her that 200 feet or more from any living soul.

Maybe he would have moved on. This project discarded for another. This day of following forgotten like so many others.

Maybe he would have gone to that memorial tonight. Reveled in knowing that the police might suspect he was there and have no means of proving it. Or maybe he would have skipped that as well. Waited. Gone to the scene of the event late at night to steal the stuffed elephant. Undetected.

He gazes upon her again. This motionless creature he's captured. This is the way the world works. None of it means anything. Life and death teeter on the fulcrum of random chance. Her parking spot sealing her fate.

But he also knows that it had to be this way. That it couldn't have happened any other way.

CHAPTER 77

McAdoo huddled in the gas station bathroom stall. Again.

Damn burritos. Again.

The hand dryer hummed in the main chamber of the room, the sound echoing off of the tiles and mercifully drowning the heinous noises out. He thanked God for that with absolute sincerity, firing off silent prayer after silent prayer, offering up his gratitude to any deity who might be listening.

He sighed. He must really hate himself to keep doing this. It was self-abuse, wasn't it? To submit his body to this kind of torture twice a month? He knew exactly what would happen, and he did it anyway. And the worst part was that the burritos weren't even good. He could get something better at Taco Bell, for God's sake. A couple of mexi-melts and a chalupa supreme. Hell yeah. At least then the insane diarrhea might be worth it.

The whir of the hand dryer cut out with a loud click, and the ensuing silence seemed strange. Intense.

He moved his feet just to hear the scuff of his shoes on the ceramic flooring. The heavy bulk of his gun shifted with the movement, holster and all leaning its weight against his ankle.

He never felt more vulnerable than when he sat here vacating his gut like this. Especially in public and when it was so damn spicy. Is that why he did it? To keep that fear sharp? To stoke the flames of those jitters that kept him focused, kept him vigilant?

Maybe. He could be over-thinking it, though. Maybe he was just a glutton — for both punishment and, apparently, microwave burritos smothered in the hottest salsa available.

Novotny sat in the cruiser, his thumbnail picking at a blistered spot in the rubbery enamel on the steering wheel. He traced his nail around the oval-shaped bubble and then peeled at the edges of the cracks running through it.

He didn't need to wonder what was taking McAdoo so long.

He knew full well what his partner was doing. He wished he'd hurry up.

The sun fled the sky, blushing along the horizon for the moment. The memorial service was tonight — going on this very moment, in fact — and he wanted to drive by the cemetery and see how things were shaping up. Maybe the killer would show. Maybe not. But it made him tense either way. Made his stomach muscles clench up just thinking about it. Juicy sounds sloshing about in his abdomen.

He watched the traffic trickle by. He had the radar gun out, but he wasn't watching it closely. It was quiet, even for a Tuesday night. Everyone had taken to shutting themselves in as much as possible with this killer on the loose. The rumor was that gun sales had quadrupled countywide. But that made him think even more people would come out for the memorial, somehow. Some symbolic display of community; of toughness and a reclaiming of dignity in the face of this adversity.

He shook his leg, calf muscle twitching his knee up and down, pistoning the ball of his foot. It was an anxious habit. An old one. Something he didn't think he'd done much at all since high school, those jacked up moments in the locker room before the football team sprinted onto the field.

Jesus. McAdoo spent more time in the bathroom than anyone he knew. The stereotype was that women took forever putting on makeup and what not? Novotny's wife was like an Olympic gold medal bathroom sprinter compared to McAdoo. If he didn't have a job, the guy would probably just shit for days at a time.

A Prius scooted toward him. It stuck out for some reason, maybe because it looked like it was moving pretty good. He checked the radar display. Yep. Eight over the limit.

He turned his gaze toward the gas station, peering through the window. The clerk read a magazine behind the counter. No sign of his partner inside. Still crapping, of course. Damned fool.

He watched the Prius jerk to a stop at the stop sign, and suddenly the story about Joel Rifkin popped into his head. The routine traffic stop that led to the arrest of a brutal serial killer, the dead body rotting in the bed of the truck. What had Loshak said during that conversation? That sometimes something as simple as a police officer trusting his gut saved lives in these cases. Something like that.

His chest tingled, the flesh atop his sternum throbbing and itching. It was, he realized, a very particular sensation. One he'd never experienced before this moment.

It felt like someone or something was trying to tell him something.

He started the car and wheeled out onto the road, gunning it, the tires thudding over the curb and jostling him around in his seat. Fuck it. He couldn't wait for McAdoo. He had to obey this whim. Had to. He figured there was a 95% chance that it was nothing at all, only a weird feeling arising from an overactive imagination, but what if this really was the guy? He'd never forgive himself.

He flipped on the lights and gave the siren switch a couple of quick on and off flips as he tore after the Prius. He'd swing back and get McAdoo in a few minutes. It was probably nothing, of course.

Probably nothing at all.

McAdoo was grappling with the painful combination of the silence and the spicy sting when the siren interrupted. He flinched a little at that WHOOP WHOOP call. It sounded like it was right on top of him.

Goddamn. It was their siren. That close? It had to be. Novotny must need him for something. Hell, it must be an emergency, even. In all their years together, he'd never done anything like that before.

Christ. He'd have to pinch it off.

He struggled to his feet, that incredible vulnerability a roiling chasm in his gut. He held an emptiness inside of him somehow. He didn't know any other way to describe it. A vacancy in his intestines that somehow made him feel exposed and powerless.

He fumbled to get his pants up and buttoned, the weight of the gun fighting him all the while. And the wrongness he felt at leaving this job half-finished was almost on a religious level. He was violating the laws of man, the laws of nature, some sacred code maintaining all that was good in the universe.

He flushed, washed up, and waddled out of the bathroom. He didn't stop and chat with the clerk like usual. He rushed straight past, flinging the glass door out of his way and stepping into the open.

But Novotny and the cruiser were already gone.

CHAPTER 78

Dark falls quickly as he moves through town. The gray day giving way to purple. The days are so short now. He can never get used to it.

It occurs to him that the memorial service will be underway already. Will likely be wrapping up very soon. The candlelight vigil the last thing left.

Funny. Right? Funny how these things work out.

He hovers a hand over the crumpled woman in the passenger's seat. He doesn't touch her. Doesn't want to risk waking her. But he feels the body heat radiating from her core. Waves of warmth touching his palm.

She seems so small. Curled in a semi-fetal position. Her chest rises and falls. Breaths slow and even. Apart from that motion, he might believe her to already be gone.

He watches the road. Looks at the graveyard sloping up the hill to his right. All those stones with names etched into them. All those people dead and gone.

The final few blocks of this trip form the peak of his vulnerability. He drives in a heavily populated area. A strip of gas stations and fast food joints. It's a stretch that's often thick with police. And there'd be no talking his way out of this one. The evidence is a living human sitting next to him.

But it's almost over. He'll be in the clear in a few blocks. Out of the city limits. Knowing that it's right there troubles him.

A clamminess seems to spread from his armpits. Sliming his chest and arms. Turning all of him strangely cool and wet like some fleshy mollusk plucked from the sea.

And then he hears it. The little whoop. The shrill cry that is unmistakable. And then another of the same. It almost sounds like the chirp of a strange bird. But no. He knows the noise.

It's a siren. Flicked on and off quickly.

Lights twirl in the rearview mirror. Red and blue. His eyes swivel to the twinkling rectangle of glass. Stare into the reflection. Already knowing what they'll find. Police lights.

He's being pulled over.

Funny. Right?

He checks the bulk beneath his knee. It's ready. And he thinks on it a second. Just a second. But there's nothing to think about. Nothing. It's already decided.

He slows. Eases the Prius over the strip of dirt where the asphalt ends. Juts onto the grassy shoulder. He's so close to the edge of town. So close to where he needs to go. But it wasn't meant to be.

He puts the car in park. Kills the engine.

Looks at the unconscious woman in the passenger seat. The crumpled doll with the skin like well-tanned leather.

"Better let me do the talking," he says, unable to suppress a smirk from curling his lip.

He chuckles a little. The idea that this could turn into a full on fit of giggling crosses his mind. He almost thinks it will.

But it doesn't.

Novotny sighed as he eased the cruiser onto the shoulder and stopped.

The vehicle pulling over right away made him smirk. What a fool he had been to believe that strange feeling. The killer would try to get away, wouldn't he? And what kind of a serial killer drove a Prius, anyway? This was probably some yuppie coming home from Starbucks.

He sighed again. Wiped his hand over his eyes. His hand fumbled for the radio microphone, but it hesitated upon grabbing it, not quite lifting. Any other day, he would call the plate in and have dispatch check for outstanding warrants before he approached the vehicle. He wasn't one of the antsy cops who feared death in every encounter, but it was just smart to know who you were dealing with.

He released the mic, spindly fingers peeling away from it like spider legs. Not today. He wouldn't bother calling it in. He'd let the guy off with a warning and be done with the whole embarrassing situation as quickly as possible.

He popped the door and stepped out of the vehicle.

McAdoo took a few steps into the parking lot in disbelief. His partner had left him. He'd actually left him in the bathroom stall at the damn Shell Station. What the hell?

He felt like a little kid who couldn't find his parents in the grocery store. Alone. Paranoid. Right on the edge of panic.

His feet scuffed against the cement, and then the sound changed when he moved onto the asphalt. He walked toward the empty parking spot. He blinked a few times, part of him hoping the car would magically reappear there just past the pumps. It didn't.

His fingers pressed into the flesh of his forehead. What the hell was he supposed to do? He had his radio on him, but if he called it in or even tried to reach Novotny with it, someone would surely hear. He'd be a laughingstock. Officer McPoopypants or something dumb like that. McAdoo-doo. What a nightmare.

As he stepped into the empty parking spot, a twinkle caught his eye in the distance. Police lights. It was the cruiser. He squinted, gazing down at the scene, not able to make out much aside from the car itself.

It was hard to judge the distance in the fading light, but he figured it must be about a quarter of a mile. He looked both directions. Time for a hike, he supposed. He could use the exercise.

Goddamn Novotny. What was he thinking leaving him behind like this?

Then again, at least he didn't feel like a lost puppy anymore. No, he was going to be fine. Everything would be back to normal in five minutes.

CHAPTER 79

The pastor from the Worthingtons' church returned to the stage and read another psalm, one that began, "Like a deer that longs for running streams, my soul longs for you, my God."

Several hundred "Amens" reflected off the walls and ceilings in a tremulous echoing pattern when he finished.

"And now, to complete this portion of the service, the First United Methodist Church Choir will perform 'The Water is Wide.' At the conclusion of the piece, the family is inviting everyone to join them in a candlelight procession to the State Street Cemetery. Candles will be distributed at the doors as you exit."

He started to walk away from the microphone, but a woman in the front row approached the stage and said something Violet couldn't hear from this distance.

Reverend Smith bent toward the woman, listened intently, and then hurried back to the mike. The choir members had already started to fan out across the stage.

"My apologies," Reverend Smith said. "I've been reminded that we have some folks with physical limitations who might struggle with the walk to the vigil. If you'd prefer to drive there, you are more than welcome. There is ample parking available on and around the cemetery grounds."

He clapped his hands together and vacated the stage. In the silence before the choir began, Luck leaned in.

"I was just thinking how strange it is," he whispered, "that both of our careers are likely to be made on this investigation."

She turned to look at him, thinking it an odd thing to say under the circumstances.

When she didn't respond, he shrugged.

"I don't know. Just something that occurred to me when I was avoiding the reporters earlier. It's like… now I'm a little bit famous or something. Everywhere I go, people know me from the press conferences. It's kinda surreal."

"I guess I never thought about it that way," Violet said.

She shifted in her seat. The room suddenly felt a little stifling. Like the crowd was sucking up all the fresh air in the place.

He wasn't wrong. Even so, she didn't like it. She supposed one might make the case that it was "looking at the bright side." But she didn't care to try to look at the bright side in the case of four murdered young women.

It reminded her a little too much of the placating words after Zara's death. Something that sleazeball of a prosecutor had said.

"A real tragedy," he'd said, smoothing his $2,000 suit and flashing a mouthful of overbleached teeth. Too quickly, he added, "But hey, we're gonna nail the guy to the wall with this."

The trill of the piano signaled the end of the choral performance. Applause filled the room. Violet squeezed her eyelids shut against a wave of claustrophobia. Or was it agoraphobia, since she was in the midst of a crowd? She didn't know. All she did know was that she wanted out of this place. Luck touched her shoulder. When she opened her eyes, she saw that people were already leaving their seats, choking the aisles as they waited their turn to leave.

"You OK?" he asked.

She nodded.

It was time to go. And not a moment too soon.

CHAPTER 80

He watches the cop exit his cruiser in the side mirror. The hatted head the most discernible part of the silhouette gliding toward him.

That smirk pulls on his lip again. He pushes it flat.

He's thought about this possibility so many times. Worried about it. And yet he finds himself utterly calm now that it's here. Almost amused.

The policeman knocks on the window. The clean-shaven face just there on the other side of the glass. He'd look like a Ken doll in a cop costume except his nose is too big. One of those big, bony Eastern European snouts.

He hesitates a moment and presses the button. The glass barrier between them sliding away.

"Good evening, officer. What seems to be the problem?"

His voice sounds so confident. So calm and assertive. It is nothing like the meek character he played with the baby carrier a short while ago.

"Can I get your driver's license, registration, and proof of insurance? I pulled you over because you were going a little fast back there. The speed limit is only 25 until you get past Spring Street. You were hitting it a couple of blocks early."

He digs in his wallet. Gets one of the licenses out. Hands it over.

"I'll have to dig a second for the other stuff."

"Not a problem."

The cop held the license in front of him. Hands fumbling at his belt for the flashlight to get a better look. Something passes over the officer's face. A quirk of the brow. Like maybe he's noticed the girl in the passenger seat.

But it's too late.

Because this is it. The moment he's daydreamed over and over.

He plucks the Ruger from under his leg. Aims and fires. The

muzzle flashing and popping. Jerking his arm a little.

The first shot bursts a small red cloud from the officer's chest. Knocks him back a step.

He fires again.

The second bullet mangles that huge nose. Opens a red hole in the middle of his face. He doesn't dwell on the wounds. He watches the eyes. Watches the light drain from them.

It's so fast. From the first shot to death transpires before the cop can even click on his flashlight.

The Maglite slips from his fingers. Clatters to the ground a beat before the officer does. It busts open. The D batteries spilling out and rolling away.

The cop bends at the knees. Buckles. And then he tips forward. Splatting face first. His face slaps the asphalt. The sound somehow soft. Like a chicken breast flopping on a cutting board.

He steps out. Looks down to make sure the officer is dead. Holding his breath to listen for any sound.

Nothing.

No rise and fall of the chest. No strange suction sounds of the breath rasping in and out of that fresh hole in his face.

It's done. Good.

The .22 isn't powerful enough to push out a fist-sized wad of brain from a gaping exit wound. But it was easy to conceal. And at close range like this, it did the job.

He stoops to the ground. Scanning. Grabs the fake ID.

Police chatter chirps from the walkie-talkie in the cop's belt. Startles him. Makes him jump.

Then he crouches and takes that as well. He wouldn't have thought of it if the thing didn't speak to him. Now he could listen in.

And then he's back in the car. Shifting gears. Speeding off. Up the hill. Around the bend. The twirling lights disappear from that rectangle of glass hanging above him where they've shimmered for so long. And it's all gone. All back behind him like everything else he's done.

Back in the mists.

His hands shake. It takes him a second to realize that it's not

from the vibration of the steering wheel. It's adrenaline.
Stimulation.

CHAPTER 81

McAdoo was about halfway to the cruiser when the shots rang out. He watched the bursts of light from the rounds, his legs doing a little stutter-step beneath him, his lungs pulsing in his chest with a dry gasp.

And then he took off running.

Heat flushed his face as he moved. His fleshy cheeks bouncing wads of warmth.

Shots fired. What the fuck?

He unsheathed his gun as he got near the car. No fumbling. No stumbling. Not this time.

And then he saw the figure sprawled on the ground. It was Novotny. He lay along that white line at the edge of the road, his feet dangling across the lip where the asphalt gave way to dirt. Blood pooled around his neck and torso. Too much blood.

Was he…

Could he be…

McAdoo approached in what felt like slow motion, the gun at the end of the outstretched arms wobbling before him, though he sensed no immediate danger. The perpetrator was long gone by now. The threat removed from this situation entirely.

He couldn't quite make out the details of his fallen ally. Not yet. And in some way that made it feel like anything was possible. Until he knew for sure, anything was possible.

The face sharpened into focus at last. Most of Novotny's nose had been blown off. A strange hole occupied his face, segmented down the middle by an intact shard of septum. The flat face somehow reminded McAdoo of a serpent.

He lowered the gun, watching that motionless figure on the ground. The whole world was still now, the sky blackening all around.

The sprawled figure coughed, and McAdoo's shoulders jerked.

Jesus Christ. He was still alive.

He rushed to his partner's side. Holstered his weapon. Knelt. "I'm here, Novo."

"He has a girl. Another one."

Novotny looked at nothing as he spoke. Eyes staring off into space like some glass-eyed doll. He spoke with a lisp, his mouth sounding mushy, his tone lifeless.

McAdoo realized that his partner had never seemed so weak before. So fragile. Before this, the idea of Novotny dying had never crossed his mind as an actual possibility. He was this strong, decisive man. Novotny wasn't the one who was supposed to die. The bumbling fat idiot was.

"Gotta get you to the hospital, buddy," McAdoo said. "Let me call it in real quick."

McAdoo brought his radio to his lips.

"No time now. Just listen. The orange parking pass. It's for the airport. Little plane on it and shit."

"Hey, don't say that. There's still time, man. I'm not gonna let you… You're gonna make it."

"Little silver plane. Like chrome. Plane."

Random syllables now gargled out of that mushy mouth. McAdoo watched his friend fade some, eyelids going droopy. Novotny veered toward unconsciousness. Toward the end. And all at once, time snapped back from slow motion to the fast speed the hectic scene called for.

McAdoo jabbered into the radio. His head going hot and dizzy. Hot and dizzy. Everything blurring together into scenes his short term memory couldn't sequence correctly. He was going into shock. And it felt like he was skipping in time. Arriving in the middle of situations, unable to remember how he'd gotten to them.

He screamed at the lifeless body. Sometimes asking if he'd call the plates in, asking what kind of car it was. Sometimes bellowing things that maybe didn't make sense at all. He didn't know for sure. He couldn't focus long enough to put the fractured bits together.

The dizziness swelled into wooziness. The world spiraling around him a bit. Almost like he was hitting that last stage of drunkenness where just sitting upright and not drooling became quite the chore.

And he couldn't remember what he'd said when he called it in. Had he even called it in for real? It seemed like something that had happened, but he couldn't call the concrete memory to mind at all. When he reached for things in his thoughts, he found nothing but the heat and that nauseating swirl of the world beginning to spiral again.

Novotny's gibberish had cut out, and now he would no longer speak when addressed. McAdoo knew that much for sure. He must be passed out. That's all it was. He had passed out, but they'd fix him up soon. The doctors would patch him right up. All the king's horses and all the king's men.

He pressed a hand to his partner's forehead. And the flesh had gone chilly. Cold and damp. Already. Just a few minutes at most laid out here in the road. It was like touching that dead frog they dissected in high school biology. A slimy, cold thing. He recalled the feel of pressing the scalpel into its pale belly. Its skin tore as much as it sliced. Fibrous. Almost papery.

And then the heat took hold in his skull. All the way.

When the ambulance and backup arrived, they had to pry the corpse from McAdoo's arms. The surviving officer's face was smeared with the dead man's blood, and he was bawling like a wounded child.

CHAPTER 82

Night had fallen by the time they reached the doors. Darger could see the inky purple of the night sky through the windows as they waited in line. At the doorway, a pair of high school aged girls held out pre-lit candles for those who hadn't brought their own.

"Thank you," Darger said as she took a candle from the girl closest. The top was fitted with a small white cup that acted as a drip catcher and a baffle against the wind.

Behind her, Loshak and Luck followed suit, each taking a candle in hand.

There was another girl behind the first two, who had apparently been tasked with candle-lighting duty.

"Hurry up, Millie!" one of the girl's said.

The one named Millie fumbled frantically with the lighter in her hand.

"I'm trying. My thumb is sore from pressing this stupid thing over and over," she complained. Finally she got the lighter to flame again. She lit the two candles the girls held out to her, and then released the button on the lighter.

"Here," Darger said, handing Millie the already lit candle in her hand.

"But I—"

Darger stooped, grabbed two fresh tapers from the box next to Millie's feet, and lit them from the dancing flame in the girl's hand.

"Ohhh," Millie said.

"We are so dumb," one of the other girls said, and they all giggled.

Violet helped herself to a new candle from the box and lit it herself. The line started to move much faster now that the girls were able to each light two candles at once.

"Thanks." Millie smiled with a mouth full of braces.

Darger winked back at her.

397

"No problem."

She moved down the stairs from the entrance to where the throng was gathering. A paper bag filled with sand and a candle had been placed on each step. More luminarias led off to the right, the golden lights dotting the darkness, lining the path that led to Fiona Worthington's final resting place. Above the sidewalk, more glimmering lights seemed to float in mid-air in the distance. She knew it was the beginning of the procession, led by Fiona's family, and that their hands held the lights aloft. But from here, the blackness blotted out the people. Only the gleam of their candles could be seen, as if carried by spirits.

It was beautiful, and yet there was that ghostly quality to it. Violet felt a shiver run down her spine.

She found Luck and Loshak huddled together under a crabapple tree across from the auditorium. Neither one of them could stop their heads from swiveling around in constant assessment of the crowd.

"It's a good thing you're not supposed to be undercover," she said.

"What's that?" Loshak asked.

"You guys are so obvious. You might as well have COP and FBI tattooed on your foreheads."

Loshak opened his mouth, poised to argue, when a black and white squad car parked a few yards away suddenly roared to life: flashers on, siren screaming. It accelerated out of the parking lot and Darger didn't have to peek behind her to know that the entire horde had turned to look.

"What the hell?" Loshak said.

Before any speculation could even be uttered, they heard more sirens and saw the telltale strobe of red and blue speeding by.

The three of them exchanged glances, and then Casey took off in a jog toward the parking lot. Darger and Loshak followed.

By the time they reached him, he was already firing up his van, his radio still in hand.

"What is it?" Darger asked.

"Officer involved shooting."

Loshak hesitated for not a moment.

Dead End Girl

"Let's go," he said, heading for his car.

CHAPTER 83

The Prius judders over the gravel. Rips through the lot aggressively. Flinging sharpened stones with every turn.

He needs to be quick. Needs to finish this and be gone. Can't dally a while like he usually does.

He pads over the rocks to the rear end of the car. Kneels. Finger and thumb working at the loosened screws on the license plate. It takes him less than a minute to switch out the stolen plate for the real thing. He hates it. Hates the idea of driving around with the real license plate on the car. Something that would trace back to his mom. But he has no choice for now.

Maybe the cop ran his plate. Maybe not. But the possibility changes everything.

The police radio makes no mention of the Prius or the plate. A panicked voice reports the officer down. And the chatter that ensues is hard to follow. He can't be sure.

He slides open the aluminum garage door. Tosses the plate into the unit.

Now to finish his project.

She never stirs. When he wraps her in blankets. Plucks her from the car. Slides her into the chamber. Lowers her to the cement floor.

Not a twitch. Not a tremble. Just the flimsiness of slack limbs. Of dead weight. These are the moments he fantasizes about. When they are at his mercy entirely. When they submit to his domination. When they just lie down and die for him.

That is how it's supposed to be.

He rolls her onto the plastic sheeting. Face down. Lifts her head. Feels for the right spot with his blade. Guiding its edge with his index finger.

He hesitates for a moment in that position. Feeling one last rise and fall of her chest. He flicks his wrist and forearm. Makes one quick incision underneath her chin. A slit.

And she leaks. He holds her head up. To keep the wound

400

open. Bursts of spray emit from her throat. Steam rising from where the red warmth drains and slaps the plastic.

Gallons. That's what it seems like. He can never prepare himself for the sheer quantity of fluid.

And just when it seems poised to go on forever, it begins to slow. Her heartbeat grows weaker. The pace fades. Fades. Stops.

The whole thing is over quickly.

He lowers her face to the plastic and releases her. Then he turns her over so he can see. Takes a step back. Eyes locked on that tiny figure. And everything is terribly, terribly quiet.

The stillness is overwhelming. Almost unbearable. It feels so final. So momentous. So complete. He has to check and make sure his own heart still beats. Frozen fingers jabbing at his neck. Adjusting their placement. Frantic to find some sign of life.

Yes. It is there. The vein still throbs. The blood still rushing through him. He's still alive. Still well.

He watches her for a long time. Waiting, he thinks. For what, he doesn't know.

Her flesh glistens. The thin layer of sweat still wet on her skin.

He hates to leave. It doesn't feel right.

The idea of bringing her along occurs to him. As crazy as it might seem at first blush, it makes sense as he ponders it. He has switched the plates. That could greatly lessen his chances of getting pulled over again. If he does get stopped by police once more tonight, he's probably sunk either way. Even cops as dumb as the ones around here would have to figure it out at that point. Wouldn't they?

He's not quite willing to leave the gun here, either. The murder weapon. The gunshot residue on his hands. No. They'd have him.

He can't do the usual thing, though. Can't spend time with her.

He has to leave town. Now.

CHAPTER 84

The scene was only a few minutes from the university district. When they arrived, the entire street was lined with police cars and ambulances. The radiating pulses of colored lights were almost dizzying as they approached the area that had already been cordoned off with yellow tape.

Luck ducked under the line and held it for Loshak and Darger to follow. Chief Haden approached and Darger knew from his face it wasn't good.

"It's him," the Chief said.

"Who? What the hell happened?" Luck said.

His eyes were wide, taking in the cruiser on the shoulder with the door open and the pool of blood on the ground, and the yellow numbered markers already being placed by crime scene techs when they discovered something of importance.

"The goddamn Doll Parts Killer, who else?" Haden said, biting off each word.

For a moment, she allowed herself to hope that the blood belonged to the killer and not to whomever had been driving the black and white. It didn't last long. Like Luck, Darger saw a mix of panic and horror on Haden's face.

Loshak intervened.

"Hold on. Start at the beginning."

Chief Haden took a breath and went into report mode, which seemed to center him some. He explained the sequence of events in an even voice. Officer Novotny pulled over an unknown subject and was shot twice at point-blank range by a small caliber firearm. Officer McAdoo arrived at the scene moments later, called it in, and awaited paramedics.

Throughout Haden's retelling of events, each dramatic moment was punctuated by a "Jesus!" from Luck.

"Novotny?" Loshak asked.

"He didn't make it. He was gone by the time the EMTs arrived."

They were all quiet for a moment while it sank in. Once again, it was Loshak who spoke up and broke the silence.

"And why do we think it's our guy?"

Haden fixed him with a haunted stare.

"Because when McAdoo found him lying in the puddle of his own blood, the first thing Novotny told him was that the guy had a girl in the car."

Loshak deflated like a punctured balloon.

"Shit."

"There's one more thing," Haden said.

He gestured for them to follow, and they approached one of the waiting ambulances.

Officer McAdoo sat in the back while a paramedic took his blood pressure. She recognized him from the first task force meeting. He wore a shell-shocked expression, eyes glassy and far off. His fingernails were caked with dried blood, and there were red-brown smears on his cheeks where more had been wiped away. Darger's eyes went to the wet spot on the concrete only a few yards away, and suddenly all of it was a little too familiar. She felt something bitter rise in the back of her throat.

"Hey, Mac," Haden said.

McAdoo turned when his name was called, though his focus didn't quite fix on them.

"Chief," he said flatly.

"Can you tell them what Novotny told you? About the plane?"

McAdoo blinked and some of the fog seemed to clear.

"A silver plane," he glanced back and forth at each of them, as if he wanted to be sure they all understood.

"Plane?" Loshak said.

"On the parking pass," McAdoo said. "Orange with a silver plane. It's an airport parking pass of some kind. That's what he said. He always notices little things like that. Always—"

He broke down into sobs before he could get the rest of the words out. Loshak stepped up onto the back of the ambulance so he could lean in and put a hand on McAdoo's arm.

"Hey, it's... You did good."

They took a few paces away from the ambulance then,

forming a small circle.

"A plane," Luck repeated. "Like he's a pilot or something?"

Darger smeared a hand over her forehead.

"Could be that," she said. "Could mean any number of things. Pilot, baggage handler, flight attendant. Fuck, he could work at the Cinnabon for all we know. Or maybe he's a frequent flier."

She inhaled as something else struck her.

"Jesus, what if he's someone that flies all over the place on business. What if he does this other places?"

"We need to figure out what airports in the area use an orange parking permit with a silver plane," Loshak said. "Now."

"I'm on it," Luck said, getting out his phone and moving off from the group to make a call.

The Chief's phone rang, and he answered before the first ring was through.

"Haden."

His already stony face grew harder, the craggy lines in his cheeks seeming to deepen.

"Where at?"

There was a pause.

"And it's been how long?"

He turned to observe the techs buzzing around the crime scene with evidence bags and cameras.

"Alright, here's what I need. Nobody gets into the car for now. Nobody. If it is a crime scene, we don't want family disturbing things. I'll send a team over, and in the meantime, no one touches anything inside that car, got it?"

He hung up the phone and stared down at the ground for a moment, composing himself.

Finally he looked up and said, "We might have an ID on the girl."

"That fast?" Darger asked.

"Worried family member. Says her sister was supposed to stop by, even called to ask her what she wanted from Starbucks, but then never showed. It's been two hours. She watches the news, has seen the stories. But she was hoping for the best. She and a neighbor drove through town, just to see. Anyway, they

404

found her SUV, abandoned in the Starbucks, latte or cappuccino or whatever the hell still sitting on the roof."

He crossed his arms over his chest.

"Normally we wouldn't even think of taking a report this early, but as soon as I heard what Novotny said about a girl in the car, I told the desk sergeant to prioritize any calls about missing girls."

"You got a name?" Loshak asked.

Chief Haden's face softened for a moment.

"Sandy Metcalf," he said.

Loshak and Darger exchanged a look, and she knew they were thinking the same thing.

If Sandy Metcalf wasn't already dead, she would be before the end of the night.

CHAPTER 85

He knows he should go home to his tomb. Knows that he should lie low for a while. Get some sleep. But he can't do it. He's too keyed up. Edgy. Gritting his teeth.

He grips the wheel like he's trying to choke the life out of it. Hands twisting now and then. Fingertips pressing so hard that the nails turn a pale yellow. The color of maggots.

He rides around Columbus again. Flipping around on the radio to try to check the news stories tonight for any mention of the Prius. Finding mostly commercials.

It's strange to be back in the city. The endless sprawl of concrete. Of that strange gray liquid poured onto the ground and hardened into a stone-like mass so that nothing can grow here. And somehow he feels that in his chest. Like all of that industrial material hovers over him. Threatens to crush him under its weight.

His fingers dab at the touchscreen without thought. Flicking through the endless commercials and terrible music playing on every radio station. Finally something catches his ear.

"In breaking news, a police officer has been slain in Athens County," the compressed voice says from the speakers.

His fingers twitch against the touchscreen. Catching themselves short of pressing the scan button again.

"A member of the APD was shot dead during a routine traffic stop this evening. Authorities are not releasing the officer's name, and no further details are known at this hour."

The remaining news stories blare on. Nothing important. He turns the radio down a moment so he can think.

So that was it for now. Not much information. Is that good? He doesn't know. Not yet. It might not mean anything. Still, it could be worse. No mention of the Prius. No mention of the possible connection to the Doll Parts case. It could be a hell of a lot worse.

He drives through suburban areas now. A narrow street.

406

Lined with trees. All of the houses nearly identical. Little boxes. Cramped as hell. The streetlight illuminates the harsh reality.

This isn't as bad as the worst parts of town. There the awnings nearly touch in some places. Tiny slits of alleyways running between the buildings. Barely wide enough to accommodate an adult.

Here there are little yards between the houses. Grass and boxwoods to decorate the boxes.

And this is it. The great dream. The masses of humanity huddling right on top of each other. Squatting together on their little islands of grass amid the endless concrete. This is what we're supposed to want. Apparently. It's what we're supposed to slave after. A house. A car. A wife. Some kids. Just like the folks in the box next door. All the next doors stretching out to infinity.

A tremor rips at his shoulders. He thinks he's going to be sick. Waits for the vomit to spray out of him. For the projectile spew gushing over the dashboard. But it never comes. He feels empty on the inside. That negative space spiraling where his innards should be.

Empty. Empty. Empty.

He wants to go home. To lie down on his bed. He knows he won't sleep. Not tonight. But maybe lying down would help in some way. Maybe some peace or calm could be possible if he kept still for a little while.

But no. He drives. On and on he presses forward. Some part of him can't stop. Can't go home.

The traffic thins as he drives. The people go home little by little until the streets are mostly vacant. Until the city is mostly dead.

But he is here. And he is awake. Alive. The wires in his head still frying. The knobs and dials still cranked all the way up.

And the night doesn't end. Doesn't fade. This darkness is infinite. It just goes on and on and on.

CHAPTER 86

By the time they got back to the motel, it was past 3 AM. Darger didn't even try to sleep. She was so wound up on adrenaline, she knew it would be pointless.

From the scene, they had moved to the station, taking over a conference room to make calls to the local airports. They spent the next several hours making dozens of calls, trying to find someone at one of the airports who would tell them anything about the parking permits in use. Unfortunately, because it was late, they struggled to even get a live human on the phone. When they did reach an actual person instead of some kind of automated system, they were inevitably transferred to the line of "someone that might be able to help" who only worked normal business hours. More answering machines.

They had no choice but to wait until morning. It was a fact that sat well with no one. Least of all, Detective Luck. She knew — despite orders from Chief Haden to the contrary — that he was probably pacing back and forth across his living room at that very moment, making calls. He still thought there was a chance to save the girl. It didn't matter that even if they'd found the right airport, they'd still have to sift through God-only-knew how many names.

This time the knock came on her door. When she opened it, Loshak stood on the other side.

"Can't sleep?" he asked.

"Hell no."

"Well, I come bearing gifts," he said, raising the bottle of Hennessy in his hand.

She unwrapped the disposable cups and held them out while Loshak poured. Before they drank, Loshak lifted his cup.

"To Novotny."

They drank. The warmth of the liquor spread over her tongue and down her throat. A pleasant burn that tingled in her chest and stomach.

"I guess you were right after all," Loshak said after a long bout of silence. "I jinxed it."

She laughed a short bitter laugh, but something in Loshak's face told her he wasn't really joking. He felt responsible.

"No one could have seen this coming."

"No? All the news stories, the press conferences? It's a double-edged sword, and I knew it. Like kicking a bee's nest and then being surprised when you get stung."

Loshak tipped back his head and finished off his drink. Darger watched him for a while, and then she leaned forward.

"Do you remember what you said to me when I wanted to quit?"

He glanced up at her.

"Knock it off with the self-pity shit," she said. "There's no time for it."

She swirled the cognac in her cup, spinning it into a golden tornado.

"At least I think that was it."

"I believe I said 'crap.' My mother taught me manners."

Darger snorted and then got serious.

"We're going to get him. His clock is ticking down. Minute by minute," she said.

Loshak sighed and rubbed a hand over his face. He was looking drained again. Tired, sickly, and pale. She hoped whatever he'd had before wasn't making a comeback. She thought about asking how he'd been feeling the past few days. The words were on the tip of the tongue. But then he spoke, and the thought left her.

"You know, I'm glad you didn't quit. You're good at this."

Darger's hands fidgeted in her lap.

"Thanks."

"I mean it. I've met guys — and gals — who've read every criminal psychology book ever written. They're profiling encyclopedias. You wanna know what Richard Ramirez ate for breakfast every morning growing up? They probably know. But when it comes to actually getting in the head of one of these guys in the wild, who for all we know is some new breed of monster we've never seen before? Forget it. They're in the weeds."

He'd refilled his drink again, and she thought he was starting to sound a touch drunk.

"I always say, it's 10% by the book 90% by the gut. You can't teach the gut part. But you've got it."

Propping her elbows on her thighs and leaning forward to rest her chin in her hands, she asked, "How can you say that before it's over? I could be wrong about everything."

"Were you not listening to what I just said?" Loshak said, then gestured to his gut.

"You sure that's not just the lingering effects of your bout with food poisoning?"

He chuckled a little at that.

"Come on, now. You were the one that insisted on talking to Sierra Peters again when everyone else wanted to write her off," he said, pausing to sip at his cup.

"Remember it, Darger. Trust your instincts. I know it's not very scientific, but that doesn't make it not true."

A leaden quiet fell over them for a while. The only sound was the steady drip of the leaky bathroom faucet.

It was Loshak who broke the silence.

"So tell me. Why'd you join the FBI in the first place? What led you down the violent and disturbing road of criminal psychology?"

Darger frowned down at her drink.

"Do you remember the Leonard Stump murders?"

He scoffed.

"Of course. I was there. One of my first cases with BAU."

"I know," she said.

"I worked my ass off to get Stump, and then he escaped from the county jail a month later. Not something I can easily forget."

He was watching her intently now, his curiosity piqued.

"Why do you bring him up?"

"Well, one of the suspected victims — Penelope Frasier?"

He lifted a finger in recognition.

"Right, right. She was one of the girls who went missing around that time and was never found. I remember."

Violet nodded.

"I was in her mother's English class when it happened. Seventh grade. The whole thing captured my imagination. I guess I was a fairly morbid twelve-year-old. Anyway, I knew someday I wanted to pursue it."

"No shit?" he said.

One corner of her mouth quirked into a smile.

"I thought your mother taught you manners."

"Eh," he said, shrugging. "She tried."

CHAPTER 87

When he finally sleeps, he is all the way out. All the way under. Tangled in that strange web of unconsciousness.

It is intense sleep. His brain fighting for what it needed. Greedily suckling at the teat of REM sleep while it has the chance.

He's plunged straight into a nonsense dream. His eyes flick about in their sockets. Trying to keep up with the fast-motion deluge of images his cerebral cortex conjures. Forgotten as fast as they appear. Eyelids twitching like mad.

His jaw clenches and unclenches all the while. Teeth scraping forward and back. Grinding at each other. He hears it sometimes. The sound of the molars clicking and gritting and gouging each other. It filters into his dream.

It's dark when he wakes. Shadows filling his tomb. The furnace hissing from the vents.

His apartment is full of that earthy smell he gives off. The air thick with the odor of damp leaves and leather with some sharper animal stench that is somehow reminiscent of Doritos. Cool Ranch.

Shards of memory come back to him as he lies there half awake. The violent images flicking in his head out of sequence. The crack of the gunfire. The cop's face flaking apart.

And then he remembers her. The feel of the knife pressed into the soft flesh of her neck.

She never fought him. Not even a little. Total submission.

That's the memory he wants to dwell on. The face blank. A little scared. Giving herself over to him.

That's his desire. His fantasy. The way she gives in. The way they all give in to him in the end.

They suffer unto what he wants.

And in those fleeting moments the world makes sense. The universe makes sense. He feels complete. Feels powerful. Like nothing can hurt him.

He sits halfway up. Propping his weight on his elbows. His mind is clearer now. And a calm settles over him. The kind of calm he hasn't felt in a long while. A sense of actual relief.

There is a strange contentment to realizing that the game has mostly played out. The choices were already made. The pieces moved into place. And all that is left is the ending. The grand finale.

He takes a deep breath and lets it out slowly. He knows in his heart that it is almost over now.

CHAPTER 88

Darger had already worn her funeral outfit three times during this trip. Maybe it's bad luck, she thought, eying the rumple of black crepe. She'd tossed it on the floor next to her suitcase after Fiona's vigil. She hadn't thought about how she'd need it again for Novotny's service. Did propriety insist that she make a trip to the laundromat? Or could she just revive it with a bit of water from the sink and a blast from her hair dryer?

She picked it up, noting the distinct note of booze smell. Right. Loshak had insisted on filling her cup again, and she'd spilled some of the cognac in her lap. That's when they'd finally decided to call it a night.

Well crap. That decided it, then.

She headed out into the early morning in search of a new dress. The sky was a pale, colorless gray. A sky for mourning if there ever was one.

At the local Goodwill, she found a navy blue number with a straight skirt and a square neckline. It looked as if it had never been worn, fit her near perfect, and was priced at $4.44. On her way back to the hotel, she stopped and bought two lattes — one for her and one for Loshak. By the time she was finished changing into the "new" dress, it was time for the viewing.

She met Loshak on the landing outside of their rooms and passed him a lidded cup.

"Much obliged," he said, lowering his sunglasses over his eyes despite the fact that it wasn't very bright out.

He looked pale again, and she hoped it was only the remnants of a hangover and not his so-called food poisoning returning with a vengeance. Again she avoided asking if he felt alright. He didn't like being fussed over, he'd made that clear enough.

"Have you ever taken a peek at the Leonard Stump file?" he asked on the drive.

"No, but I've been meaning to. I didn't have clearance

414

before, when I was in OVA," she said.

"I can send it over, whenever we get back to Quantico. You know he kept a journal when he was in jail?"

"I didn't."

Loshak eased the car into an empty parking space and undid his seatbelt.

"We kept that pretty hushed. Didn't want the media trying to get their dirty mitts on it."

Luck was loitering just inside the front door of the funeral home, out of the sprinkling mist that had begun to hang in the air. By the way he hopped to attention when he caught sight of her and Loshak, he'd been waiting for them.

"Don't you look like a dog with a bone," Loshak said.

"Whaddya got, Detective?"

"Some good news and some bad."

"Good first," Loshak said.

"It's an employee pass for Union Parking," Luck said, the excitement in his voice coming through despite his hushed tone.

"What airport?" Loshak asked.

"Well, that's the bad news. Union handles parking for Cincinnati, Columbus, Dayton, Akron, Pittsburgh... I mean they're all over the country, but those are just what's in the area."

"Jesus," Darger said. "I guess at least it narrows the list down to just airport employees. But that's still gotta be a fuckton of people."

"You don't get it." Luck couldn't keep the grin off his face now. "It's a pass *only* for employees of the parking company, not the entire airport."

"I'll be damned. That is good news," Loshak said, rubbing his hands together.

His eyes sparkled with the knowledge that they were closing in on their prey. He glanced around the room, almost as if he thought the killer might be there with them. His gaze fell on Novotny's family, who were stationed at the chapel door to greet people as they came in. Loshak straightened suddenly, the hungry gleam fading from his eye.

"Let's put a pin in this for now. We're here to pay our

415

respects to Novotny. We can talk shop after," he said.

The three of them joined the line of people entering the viewing area. While they waited, Darger considered their next move. They were still on the hunt. They needed to be smart. And careful. Her initial instinct had been to start calling around to the various airport parking facilities and asking about any of their employees that drove big, dark sedans. But that was too sloppy. Too easy for their lead to be blown by office gossip. The safest thing would be to send out a team to each airport. Take them by surprise. But what were the odds that local law enforcement would authorize that? She thought slim.

The French doors leading to the chapel loomed ahead. Darger snapped out of it, and each one of them took turns shaking the hands of the family members and murmuring words of condolence. Novotny's widow had dark circles beneath her eyes and the dazed look of someone still coming to grips with the awful truth. Darger knew he had a daughter as well, but she didn't see any children around. Maybe that was for the best.

Darger felt her heart seize in her chest. How many funerals in how many days now? It wasn't right, so much death being visited upon this place all at once. And the knowledge that there was probably another death waiting to be revealed — that of Sandy Metcalf — made it that much harder to swallow.

When they reached the front of the room, where the casket lay among a jungle of floral arrangements in every imaginable size and color, Darger kept her eyes averted.

"Go ahead," Darger said, indicating that Loshak should step to the casket first. She wanted to give him a moment on his own. She trained her eyes on the flowers and on the carpet as he moved forward.

"You alright?" Luck asked from beside her.

She blinked, startled.

"I'm fine. Why?"

"You just look a little pale is all."

She inclined her head toward him and lowered her voice to a whisper.

"I hate open caskets," she admitted.

416

Casey's brow furrowed.

"With all the screwed up stuff you look at on a day-to-day basis," he said, then gave a slight nod to the gleaming coffin in front of them, "and *that* bothers you?"

She knew it must give comfort to some, to actually see the person they'd known and loved when they said their final goodbyes. For her, she could only ever think how wrong it looked. The powdery makeup and the dull hair. The way the mouth wanted to pull away from the teeth. The wax plugs in the orifices to keep fluids from seeping out.

From what she'd heard, Novotny's facial injuries had been extensive. The mortician had to do some sculpting to reconstruct the nose. Glancing at him laid out now, she couldn't tell where the flesh ended and the sculpture began.

Casey rested a hand on her shoulder and squeezed. She turned to smile at him, but then saw that he wasn't looking at her. He was staring straight ahead, a grave expression on his face. She swung her head up. Loshak was still standing at the casket, but he'd bent forward, hands on his knees.

"Loshak," she said, and he straightened.

She'd taken a step forward but stopped then, thinking he'd managed to compose himself.

And then Loshak took one odd, shaky step toward the casket, almost falling into it before he caught himself on the edge. That got her moving again, but before she could reach him, his knees wobbled and buckled under his own weight. He teetered to the right, taking out a tripod holding a large framed photograph of Charles Anthony Novotny. Glass shattered as it struck the ground. Darger barely noticed the crunch of the shards under her feet as she rushed to Loshak's side.

"Loshak!" Darger shouted, and he crumpled to the floor.

CHAPTER 89

Automatic doors whooshed. The wheels on gurneys and wheelchairs click-clacked and squealed. Feet pattered. A drinking fountain down the hallway hummed. After a while, the sounds all smudged together into one low murmur that she barely took notice of.

She didn't know how long she'd been staring at the wall when she felt a hand on her arm. It was Luck.

"Your phone, Violet."

She looked down at her lap, reached into her pocket for the buzzing device. It barely registered that the screen said "Cal Ryskamp" before she pressed the button to answer the call.

"Hello?" she said.

"What the hell is happening out there, Darger? First an officer-involved shooting, and now Loshak's down?"

She didn't know what to say.

"Well, what is it? A heart attack?"

"Um no. They don't know yet. Or won't tell me. I don't know. I'm not family."

"For fuck's sake."

"He wasn't right. I knew he wasn't. He's been sick since I got here," she said, feeling a sharp stab of guilt. She should have been more firm. Should have tried to make him see a doctor. She'd known something was wrong. But she'd been so focused on the case.

"Christ." Cal sighed into the phone. "Well, this is what happens when you don't take care of yourself."

Darger bit back an angry retort. His tone was not-at-all sympathetic, and it pissed her off. But it wouldn't do anyone any good to get in a spat with Cal right now. Least of all Loshak.

Cal was still talking. She struggled to focus on what he was saying.

"Look, no one blames you for this, alright? Like I said before, Loshak's one of these guys who thinks the rules of the

418

universe don't apply to him."

Blame her? Blame her for what? But she only listened while Cal went on.

"There's a meeting scheduled for tomorrow afternoon, so we'll need you on the first flight back. I'll have—"

That got her attention.

"Meeting," she interrupted. "A meeting for what?"

"Violet, this has been one big mess from start to finish, and Assistant Director Linville wants a full report."

She sat forward, trying to make sense of what he was saying.

"What about the task force? We just leave all these guys here sitting around with their dicks in their hands?"

People passing by in the hallway beyond slowed at her shouting, peering into the small waiting area with mixed concern and interest before moving on.

"We're dispatching another team to take up where you left off."

"Where we left off? That's insane, Cal. They'll just be playing catch up. They don't know this case—"

"Violet, these are experienced agents from BAU. They'll handle it fine."

Now it was all falling into place. *No one blamed her. One big mess. Experienced agents.*

Bullshit. They were going to lay this all on the shoulders of a so-called inexperienced agent in over her head. And Loshak would take his share as well, she knew. That enraged her even more than being taken off the assignment. He wasn't even there to defend himself.

Cal was still yammering on, regurgitating excuses and platitudes.

"They'll actually be in on the briefing, so you can get them up to speed along with the rest of us. Oh, and that reminds me…"

She considered arguing with him, but she knew it would do no good. He wouldn't listen.

She pulled the phone away from her face and stared at the screen. She could still hear a small, tinny version of Cal's voice coming from the speaker.

Her thumb punched the red button, ending the call. The voice clicked out.

He'd call back of course. Her finger found the power button and turned the phone off.

For a long while, she just stared at the black screen in her hand.

"Everything OK?" Casey asked from beside her.

She'd forgotten he was even there.

"Sure," she said.

"Did I hear something about you going back to Quantico?"

Darger gave the phone one last look before tucking it into her pocket.

"I'm not going anywhere."

CHAPTER 90

The heart monitor chirped. Slow and steady. Special Agent Victor Loshak sprawled on the hospital bed, arms lying awkwardly at his sides, the angle of his neck strangely slack. The tall man looked even longer laid out like that, at least that's what Deputy Donaldson thought.

The deputy sat beside the bed, a folded up newspaper clutched in his fist before him. He cleared his throat. Swallowed. Cleared his throat again. He couldn't quite bring himself to speak to the inert man. Not yet. He could only continue to observe him.

Loshak looked stretched out. Bony. And his face looked gaunt and dour. Those clever lines around his eyes and mouth, the ones that made it look like he found the world perpetually amusing, had smoothed out into something somber. Melancholy. His complexion had gone ashy, too. He didn't look the same man anymore to a degree Donaldson found deeply unsettling. He couldn't help but think of a body laid out in a coffin. The way they never look quite right.

He cleared his throat one more time, and at last, he spoke.

"I wanted to come by. Let you know what happened in the game — well, some of the games, you know — I heard that, uh, it's good to read to someone in a comatose state and whatnot, so…"

Donaldson wasn't certain about that last part. He might have heard that it was good to read to a baby in the womb. He couldn't remember for sure. Anyway, he figured it wouldn't hurt.

"Well, the Bengals got smoked. Shocker, right? The final was 37-17. So the over hit, at least."

Sweeney brought the paper closer to his face, focused on the box score.

"They got outgained 457 yards to 296. Gave up 319 through the air. Secondary got shredded like you said they would.

421

Looking for a bright spot. Jeez. I don't know. I guess they averaged 4.8 yards per carry. Maybe something to build on there. The rookie running back looked real good."

Unbeknownst to Sweeney, Dan McAdoo stood in the doorway, looking on as the deputy read the sports page to the comatose agent. He watched the two of them for a long time, saying nothing.

Some hours later, it was Darger watching over Loshak. She stood there for a long, quiet moment. Not saying anything. Just watching the rise and fall of his chest.

The hospital room smelled like a funeral parlor. Sickly sweet. Darger knew it must be all the flowers people had sent. Bouquets and wreath-like displays set on stands dominated one side of the room. She took a couple of arrangements out and dumped them in the big trash bin near the nurse's station. She knew Loshak wouldn't mind.

Acute pancreatitis. That's what the doctor said.

She'd lied and told the nurses she was his partner. At first they thought she'd meant "life partner," until she explained. She wondered what Loshak would think of that declaration. At the very least, she thought he would have gotten a chuckle out of the life partner thing.

"Has he shown any signs before this?" the doctor asked. "At this stage, there's a tremendous amount of pain. Decreased appetite, nausea, vomiting. I can't imagine he would have been completely asymptomatic."

"Yeah," she said, nodding. "A week or two ago. He was throwing up a lot."

She frowned then, thinking back on the precise wording of the doctor.

"At this stage, you said. What does that mean? What stage is he at? How many stages are there?"

The doctor shook his head.

"It's not exactly like that. But he is very, very sick. It doesn't surprise me to hear that this has been going on for a while now. There is necrotic tissue present, which has led to bleeding and the beginnings of a systemic infection."

Violet had a hard time remembering much of what was said after that, other than they were preparing to transfer Loshak to a larger hospital in Columbus in the morning. Even now, hours later, the same cluster of words kept swirling around in her head like the leaves she'd watched dancing in the wind a few days ago.

Necrosis.

Hemorrhage.

Sepsis.

Morbidity.

Surgical intervention.

Coma.

Her phone buzzed. She didn't have to look to know that it was Cal. She'd turned it back on when Casey left, so he could call her with any updates. He'd tried to convince her to come home with him, but she'd refused.

She pressed the button on top of her phone and the buzzing stopped.

Behind her, a large window showed the street lights reflecting on the wet pavement below. It must have started raining at some point, but she hadn't noticed when. She turned so she could rest her head on the back of the chair and watch the droplets run down the glass.

By the time Officer Dan McAdoo slipped into Loshak's hospital room, it was late enough to be past visiting hours. The room was dark, and the hallway was only a little better. Both were lit only by the streetlights pouring through the windows and the half light trickling from the nurse's station a few doors down.

McAdoo managed to sneak past a cluster of said nurses, unsure if they'd say anything because of his uniform or not. He knew at least some of them would probably be strict, by-the-book types, badge or no badge.

He eased the door shut behind him, careful to be as quiet as he could, and strode into the room, butterflies dancing fluttery jigs in his belly. He scooted the chair toward the bed, cringing at the scrape of the wood on the tile.

He stopped, waited for the nurse to come busting through

the door to shut him down. No one came. Not even so much as a dark flutter passing the window into the hall.

He wondered, for a split second, what Novotny would say when he heard about all of this ridiculousness. Then, of course, he remembered that Novotny was dead. That was the hardest part of death for him to accept, he realized. That the person never got to chime in. No final thought. Just nothing. Forever.

He leaned toward Loshak.

"I don't know if you can understand this, but I feel like I should do something, ya know?" he said. "See, I saw Donaldson reading to you from the sports page, and I liked that. Liked it a lot. I figured I could do the same. I don't mind it or nothing."

He flipped through the paper to find what he was looking for.

"I, uh, don't know if you follow the NBA, but the Cavs have a hell of a team this year."

CHAPTER 91

When the ambulance transporting Loshak to Riverside Methodist Hospital in Columbus left the hospital in Athens, Darger was right behind it. But she had to make a stop before she followed.

At the motel, she showered quickly and packed a few things in her bag: a toothbrush, an extra shirt, some clean underwear. She also grabbed her laptop and files.

Downstairs, she made sure that both her and Loshak's rooms were paid up through the next several days. The last thing she wanted was for Loshak's room to get turned over, and all of his files chucked.

She sent a quick text to Detective Luck, letting him know she was heading for Columbus, and then she got in her car and headed west on US-33.

The hospital was easy to spot as she drew near. It was a large structure of concrete and mirrored glass, occupying the equivalent of several city blocks.

After she parked her car in the visitor lot, she wandered the halls for some time before she figured out where they'd taken Loshak. A receptionist seated behind a kiosk in a greeting area told her that Loshak was in the Inpatient Surgery Ward on the second floor.

The girl behind the desk at the nurse's station looked barely old enough to be out of high school, but the ID badge clipped to her chest said "Anita C. — Registered Nurse."

"I'm looking for Victor Loshak," Violet said.

"He's actually being prepped for surgery right now."

"Oh. That was quick."

"Are you his daughter?" the nurse asked.

"Yes," Violet said, figuring one more lie wouldn't hurt.

"Well, it's liable to take a few hours. I'd suggest you take some time for yourself in the meantime."

"Right," Violet said.

"I know that's easier said than done," the woman said. She slid a small card across the desk. "If you fill this card out, I can make sure you're contacted once he's out of surgery."

Darger filled in her contact information, wondering if she was violating some kind of HPPA law by doing so. Fuck it, she thought and handed the card back.

"Thank you," she said. The girl smiled.

Darger paced the hospital, meandering wherever she found an unlocked door. Eventually she ended up in a large cafeteria. She didn't think she was hungry, but when her nose got a whiff of food, her stomach disagreed. She couldn't remember the last time she'd eaten something that hadn't come out of a vending machine. Over a day, she thought.

Violet picked up a small salad in a plastic clamshell container and filled a bowl with chicken noodle soup and found a table near a window. She ate in a daze, barely tasting any of it. As she dropped her tray on a conveyor belt for dirty dishes, her purse buzzed.

She almost ignored it, assuming it was Cal, but then she remembered that the nurse had said someone would call when Loshak was out of surgery. Could it have been that fast? She didn't think she'd been gone from the surgery floor for more than an hour. A small surge of panic hit her when it occurred to her that something might have gone wrong. But when she finally wrestled her phone from her bag, the screen said, "CASEY LUCK."

"Hey," she answered.

"I'm pretty sure it's Columbus," he said, getting straight to the point. "Are you still up there? At the hospital?"

"Yeah. Loshak's in surgery right now."

"Alright. I'm heading up there as we speak. I can pick you up in about an hour."

"I'll be here," she said and hung up. Her heart was racing. She tried to imagine that they might be arresting the killer before Loshak was even out of surgery.

Shit. Loshak. Was she just going to leave him here alone? What if he came out of surgery, and he woke up surrounded by strangers? On the other hand, she tried to imagine not being there when they nailed the son of a bitch. Not seeing his face when he realized that he'd lost his little game.

She considered what Loshak would want, and she knew the answer.

CHAPTER 92

Luck picked her up near the hospital entrance. His van rolled up to the curb, and she hopped in so fast, he barely had to stop.

"How is he?"

"Still in surgery."

Her seatbelt whirred as she pulled it across her chest.

"Think positive," Luck said, reaching out a hand and squeezing her thigh.

"Yeah."

When they passed the first sign for John Glenn International Airport, Darger felt her heart skip a beat. Could this actually be it? Were they mere minutes away from finding the sick bastard?

"So how'd you narrow it down to Columbus?" Violet said. "I mean, what'd you guys say when you called?"

"I wish you could have seen it," Luck said, suddenly amused. "You met Betsy, right? The receptionist?"

Violet recalled a brief encounter with an elderly woman with a tight white perm who seemed to hold court behind the desk of the Athens Police Department. She'd witnessed the woman reading the riot act to one of the patrol officers for not cleaning up after himself in the break room. Despite the fact that the officer was probably 6'2" with a gun strapped to his hip and Betsy stood about 5'3" counting her cloud of hair, he had cowered before the tiny woman.

"Seemed like a firecracker."

Luck laughed.

"That's putting it mildly. Anyway, I wrote up a little script for her, had her call around and say that someone with a big dark sedan and a Union Parking permit scratched up her car in a parking lot. Witness left a note on her car. You should have heard her. She got really into it."

"I can imagine," Darger said with a smile.

"I didn't know if it would even work, you know? Figured most people would just hang up on her, but she knows how to get what she wants."

After a beat, he added, "You two would probably get along."

As they pulled into the parking lot, Luck said, "I called over to Columbus PD before I left. In case he's here, and we decide we need backup. They're ready for us."

"Good thinking," she said.

The man behind the counter inside the Parking Services building gave them a big smile. A little too big, for Violet's taste. He had the phony charm of a salesman, and his cleanly shaved head looked shiny up close. She wondered if he oiled it or something.

"Howdy, folks! What can I do for you?"

"We're looking for someone named Kurt who drives a large dark-colored sedan," Luck said, sliding off his sunglasses and tucking them inside his jacket.

As he did, Darger saw that the man caught a glimpse of Luck's holster, his eyes going wide.

"Oh boy. This is about that woman who called? The one who said Kurt hit her car?"

"Is he here?" Luck's eyes scanned the small building, and Darger did the same.

There was a girl manning the booth connected to the main building. She watched them in between cars rolling through the gates. Beyond that, Violet could see a second, smaller booth, set off by itself in a second lane. She could see the silhouette of someone inside, but couldn't make out any features, not even if it was a man or woman.

"Well, that's Kurt Van Ryper who drives a blue Buick, alright. Big ol' tank. Looks like a cop car. Honestly, I can't believe he'd do something like that. Scratch up a lady's car and just take off? That doesn't sound like him."

With a pressing look from Luck, the man realized he was rambling and got to the point.

"But no, he's not here today. I should say, he was scheduled for this morning, but he didn't show."

Luck and Darger couldn't help but exchange an anxious glance.

"Hey," the man said, squinting at Luck. "Aren't you the cop

who's been on TV? Down in Athens?"

His eyes went wide, realization hitting him.

"Jeez-o-pete! This isn't about that serial killer is it?"

Before Luck could answer, Darger interrupted.

"Do you have any kind of employment file we could take a look at? Something with a home address?"

"We do. I suppose technically I should ask for a warrant…"

"Look," Luck said, leaning in and lowering his voice. "I shouldn't be telling you this, but… Kurt isn't the one we want. That being said, we have reason to believe he has important information that could lead us to the perpetrator. So the sooner we track Kurt down — and the quieter — the better."

Darger was impressed. Luck was a better liar than she would have given him credit for. And it was smart to put an emphasis on tracking him down quietly. The last thing they needed was for someone the guy worked with to tip him off.

"Oh. Well," the man behind the counter seemed to mull it over. "That is a bit different. And now that you mention it, that makes a lot more sense. I mean, Rip— er, uh, Kurt's a bit of an oddball, but he's no killer."

"So," Darger smiled politely, "the file?"

"Right."

He took a few steps sideways and beckoned from a doorway leading into an office. They followed, waiting while the man dropped into a chair and wheeled over to a filing cabinet the color of pea soup. He bent over one of the drawers, fingers rifling through folders. There was a whisper of rustling paper as he plucked a file from the steel jaw of the cabinet. Not getting up from the wheelie chair, he scooted over to Luck and handed him the manila folder.

The flaps parted in Luck's hands like the wings of a bird. Violet held her breath. The file was absurdly plain. Black printed text and blue ballpoint pen on white paper. Nothing remarkable about it at all. And yet in her chest she felt a tremendous sense of awe. It was him. His hand had written those letters. His fingers had held the paper in place as he filled in the spaces.

Name: Kurt Van Ryper

Date of Birth: December 12th, 1987

Followed by his address, his phone number, his social security number.

Darger didn't need to look at Luck to know he was thinking the same thing. A kind of electric excitement was coming off him in waves.

Gotcha, motherfucker.

Struggling to keep her voice calm, she asked, "You don't have any kind of photo IDs or anything?"

"No, but there should be a copy of his driver's license."

They flipped through the sheets in the folder.

"I don't see it here."

"Huh," the man said. "Let me check the computer."

His fingers rattled over the keyboard, and he frowned.

"Nope. As I figured, we only went digital with the employee files recently. His original paperwork was just that: paper."

"The address listed is in Bishopville," she said. "He doesn't have a place he stays around here?"

The man rubbed at his shining head.

"So far as I know, what it says is where he lives. Sorry I can't help any more than that."

"That's OK. Thank you for this. We appreciate it."

Luck brought back the conspiratorial tone.

"And if you could keep this quiet for the time being…"

The man put his palms in the air.

"Absolutely! Say no more, Detectives. My lips are sealed."

As they climbed back into the van, Darger said, "Nice work with all that he's-not-the-one-we-really-want stuff."

Luck shrugged, but she could tell the compliment pleased him.

"So how long before he blabs it over the whole damn airport, you think?"

Darger looked at her watch.

"Half an hour."

They waited there in the parking lot while Luck called it in. He conferred for a while with Chief Haden and then hung up.

"So apparently the address is for his mom's house. A Ms. Rhonda Van Ryper."

"The plot thickens," Darger said, thinking about the profile, and the over-bearing mother trope that featured in so many serial killer backstories.

"Bishopville is the Sheriff's jurisdiction. They're gonna do a drive-by and see if it looks like anyone's home. Chief Haden assured me that they'd sit on the house 'til we got there."

He stopped and looked at her.

"If you're coming, that is."

"Are you kidding? Of course I am. You can drop me at my car, and I'll follow you back. It's back at the hospital."

Luck nodded.

"You gonna check on Loshak?" he said.

"No," she said. "He would want me to close the case."

She was suddenly feeling on the verge of tears. She didn't know why. Or maybe she did. It had been an emotional couple of days.

No. Strike that.

It had been an emotional couple of years for Violet Darger.

CHAPTER 93

Darger followed Luck back down US-33 to Athens county. Next to the freeway exit for Bishopville, Darger parked her rental in a Park and Ride lot and climbed into Luck's van.

Luck's radio crackled while they waited for a traffic light to turn. He picked it up.

"This is Luck."

"Luck, it's Deputy Donaldson," a familiar voice said. "We borrowed a van from Animal Services, used it to have some of our guys knock at the Van Ryper residence. Pretending to look for a loose dog."

"Anyone home?"

"It appears not," Donaldson said. "But we did find something of interest parked a few blocks away. A dark blue Buick LaCrosse. 2011 plates registered to a Kurt Van Ryper."

"Like he half wanted to dump it, and half wanted to keep it close by in case he needed it?" Luck asked.

"Exactly my thoughts, Detective," the tinny voice said.

"You're using unmarked vehicles, right?"

"Absolutely."

"Alright. Agent Darger and I will be there in about twenty minutes."

Cherry Lane was one street over from the house where Kurt Van Ryper lived with his mother. Luck pulled alongside a green Subaru Outback and rolled down the window on Darger's side. Donaldson sat behind the wheel of the Subaru, wearing a nylon windbreaker to obscure his uniform.

"Agent Darger," Donaldson said in greeting. "Detective Luck."

"Any change?"

"Not a peep so far. I have cars stationed on most of the other surrounding routes. Notified SWAT to be ready for the call. And since we know he's not driving the Buick, we ran the mother's name through the vehicle registry. She drives a white Silverado. Brand spankin' new. Made sure to circulate that and Kurt's driver's license photo to the other guys."

Through the window, he passed them an enlarged photocopy of Kurt Van Ryper's photo. Darger stared into the face, strangely unmoved. He looked plain. That was her only conclusion.

"Great," Luck said, staring down at the grainy black and white image. "I'm gonna see if we can find a place to camp out a little closer to the house."

Donaldson gave a nod.

"Give me a holler on the radio if you need anything."

Darger started to put her window up when Donaldson put up a hand. She stopped.

"I forgot to ask about Agent Loshak."

"He went in for surgery this morning. I'm still waiting on a call with an update."

"Heck of a thing," Donaldson said. "Prayin' for him."

They parted then. Luck steered them down to the next intersection and took a left. Another left and they were a mere three houses away from Van Ryper's home. Luck rolled by slowly, and they both made an effort to take in the house without staring. It was a nondescript white and brown split-level, with a sloped driveway that led down to a two-car garage nestled into the lower level.

"Weird, huh?" Luck said.

"What?"

"Just looks so normal." He smirked a little then. "No sign out front that says, 'Beware of Psycho.'"

Two houses down and across the street from the Van Ryper residence, a woman stepped out onto her front walk and strolled down to the mailbox. Luck pulled up next to her, and at first Darger saw the unmistakable glisten of fear in her eyes. It seemed to ebb when she saw Violet in the passenger seat.

"Excuse me, ma'am," Luck said. He unclipped his badge from his belt and showed it to the woman. "I'm Detective Luck, this is my partner, Detective Darger. We're investigating reports of a string of break-ins in this area, and we wondered if you'd heard or seen anything suspicious lately?"

The woman's mouth opened in a perfect "O" shape, and she fiddled with the zipper of her jacket.

"My goodness! No, I hadn't heard anything about that."

"That's OK. We're going to stick around for a while, keep an eye on things. I was wondering... I couldn't help but notice that you have two driveways."

The woman glanced behind her at a second two-track dirt path that led to a pole barn behind the house.

"Yes?"

"Would you mind if we parked in the second driveway? Less suspicious than if we park on the street."

"Oh. Of course," she said.

"You're sure it's not an inconvenience at all?"

"Absolutely not, Officer... I mean, Detective."

"Thank you, ma'am. That's quite a help."

"Don't mention it," she said, giving them a wave before heading back into the house.

As Luck backed the van into the drive, which also had the benefit of being partially hidden by an overgrown evergreen shrub, Darger shook her head.

"Telling tales left and right today. Surprised you haven't sprouted an extra long beak like Pinocchio."

Luck shrugged.

"I want my own two eyes on that house, and I don't want to screw things up by sitting right out in the open. Run the risk of spooking him."

He turned off the van, and so began their watch.

CHAPTER 94

It was tense the first hour or so. Each time a car approached the four-way stop in view, they both perked up, sitting forward in their seats to see if the car would turn down Hickory Lane. Of the four vehicles that had come to the intersection, only one had turned toward the Van Ryper residence. They held their breath as the car rolled down the pavement. It was a small silver car. A Ford Fiesta, Darger thought. It glided past them, around the slight bend in the road where they were parked, and slid into the driveway of a house up the lane. A teenage girl got out and went inside.

Luck and Darger exchanged a wordless glance and slumped against their backrests.

Darger reached for her bag, wanting suddenly to check if Kurt Van Ryper's name was on the list Luck had printed out before the vigil for Fiona. She wiggled the folder free from the mouth of her bag and set it on her lap. When she opened it, the candid photos of Sierra Peters as a child spilled onto the floor. With everything that had happened — least of all The Daily Gawk story facilitated by Sierra's mother — Darger hadn't returned them like she'd promised. Knowing what she knew now, she figured Patricia Peters hadn't planned on getting those photographs back.

Luck leaned across the console to help collect the scattered pictures. He stared at one of them for a beat before he handed it up to her.

"We went to high school together, you know."

Darger's head snapped up, the movement something like a spinal reflex, as if she were pulling her hand away from a hot stove top.

"You never told me that," she said.

"Well, I didn't really know her. She would have been a freshman the year I was graduating, so we didn't really cross paths much that I can remember. But my little sister had a class

436

or two with her."

Darger looked down at the photograph of Sierra, a melting blue popsicle in her hand.

"Do you remember her?"

Luck bent his head to one side, gazing out his side window.

"Not personally. But I remember she had a reputation."

"And?" Darger pressed.

"It wasn't great."

She tapped the photographs into a pile with her fingers.

"Care to elaborate?"

"You can probably guess," he said. "She liked to party. Got in her fair share of trouble."

Luck rubbed his hands together like he was trying to warm his fingers.

"People called her a slut. You know the type."

Darger shook her head, feeling angrier than she probably had a reason to.

"The type?"

Through her gritted teeth, the words came out strained.

"Hey, *I'm* not the one saying it. It's just the kind of talk I heard," Luck said.

After a silence, Darger said, "When a Fiona Worthington dies, we're practically tripping over ourselves to solve it. The media can't go a night without plastering her face on the news. But when a Cristal Monroe or a Sierra Peters or even a Katie Seidel gets murdered? Forget it. They're trash. I'm not like *them*, we think, so their deaths don't matter."

"I don't think that's true," Casey said.

"No? You think it was an accident that it was Fiona's memorial we used? Where was the candlelight vigil for the other three?"

Her voice had risen over the course of the tirade, and she was on the verge of shouting now. Casey only stared at her.

"Jesus, Violet. Forget I brought it up. I didn't know you'd get so upset."

"I'm sorry," she said, turning her face away and taking a deep breath. "You're right. Let's just drop it."

After a few minutes of awkward quiet, Casey said, "I think

there might be a deck of cards in here somewhere."

He flipped up his armrest and hunched over so he could scoot into the rear of the van without hitting his head. He thrust a hand into the pocket attached to the back of his seat.

"Ha!" he said, holding a box of Bicycle playing cards up.

They played a few rounds of Gin, laying out their sets and runs on the dash of the van. Eventually, they tired of the cards and lapsed into silence again.

Violet itched to pull out her laptop so she could watch the Sierra interviews again, this time imagining that the man she was describing was Kurt Van Ryper. But Luck had already accused her of being "obsessed" earlier in the week, and she didn't want to give him the satisfaction of thinking he was right.

"Fuck it," Casey said, after they'd gone at least thirty minutes without either of them uttering a word. It was the first time she'd heard him drop and F-bomb, and it immediately seized her attention.

"Are you pissed at me, or what?"

"Huh?"

"I spooked you, right?"

"No," she said.

Casey shook his head.

"Come on, Violet. You've been lukewarm ever since that night. With Jill."

"Believe it or not, the last few days have been a touch distracting. I don't know if you've heard, but there's a murder investigation going on."

She studied a scuff mark on the toe of her boot and avoided looking him in the face.

"Stop bullshitting me," he said, and his voice was hard. He took a breath and softened.

"I know something's up. Why don't you just tell me?"

Violet squeezed her hands into fists, fingernails digging deep into her flesh again. Time to tell the awful truth.

"You keep acting like this," she gestured between them, "is going somewhere. And it can't. You know that right?"

In the moment before his eyes flicked away from hers, she saw the hurt in them. The dread in her heart grew heavier.

"I'm just being realistic," she said, keeping her voice light and matter-of-fact. As if that would make it sting less.

"You live here. Your family lives here. I don't. When this case is over, I have to go back. And that's that."

A sparrow landed on the hood of the van and hopped over the shiny metal surface before fluttering away.

"I'm sorry if you thought it... meant something," she said, staring after the bird so she wouldn't have to see the damage she was doing.

Not that he would look at her now. There was a long pause, and then his head moved from side to side. When he spoke, his words were thick and strained.

"No, you're right. I was being stupid."

He sniffed and rubbed at the end of his nose.

The silence that followed was awkward. Darger went to say something, but a burst of static emanated from the radio, and they both sat up, staring at the small black box on the dash.

"Luck, you there?"

It was Donaldson.

He grabbed the mouthpiece in a lightning fast motion.

"This is Luck. Go ahead."

"Hey, me and the guys have been talking."

His tone was so blasé, both Luck and Darger instantly relaxed a little. If it was anything important, they would have heard it in his voice.

"We were just thinkin' that none of us knows how long this is gonna take. We weren't exactly prepared to be out here for the long haul. I thought we might take turns running up the road for some supper and any other needs one may have. There's a Subway in that filling station where 78 takes the bend south."

Luck's voice still sounded dead when he replied.

"That's not a bad idea, I guess. Good thinking."

"Don't mention it," Donaldson said. "Why don't you and Agent Darger take the first break?"

Luck reluctantly glanced in her direction. She shrugged.

His knuckles stood out white as he squeezed the button on the radio mic.

"Sure, thanks."

The wait was excruciating. Eating a crappy sub in a mini-van did little to help that.

Chewing the last bit of her sandwich, she wiped her hands with a napkin and wadded it and the paper wrapper into a ball. She stuffed that inside the bag the sub had been in, and tucked the lot of it by her feet. She drank a bit of water, just enough to moisten her throat and wash the last crumbs down. She sat back and gazed through the windshield. The sun had dipped below the houses before them while they ate. Twilight tinted everything in a dim blue light.

They saw the headlights first, the cones of light announcing the car before it made itself visible. Darger's head whipped to attention, and from the corner of her eye she saw Luck do the same. Donaldson wasn't back yet. If he had been, he may have been able to get a look at who was in the car, to give them a heads up. Instead, they had to wait as the agonizing seconds ticked by. The car slowed to a halt at the stop sign and seemed to hang there. They could see already that the blinker was on, signaling a left turn. It was coming this way.

Darger realized she was holding her breath and forced herself to inhale. It wouldn't do anyone good to pass out from sheer excitement.

After what felt like forever, the car took the turn, heading straight for them. The two square portals of light on the front of the car were blinding, but Darger stared anyway. She didn't want to blink. Didn't want to risk missing it.

The Nissan puttered up Hickory Lane, and Darger felt a strange heaviness as they waited to see where its path would end, as if gravity were rooting her to the seat. Holding her in place so she couldn't move a muscle.

The tires slowed and stopped in front of the split-level with the sloped driveway leading down to the garage.

Darger and Luck, still not making a sound or even the slightest movement, waited to see what would happen next.

CHAPTER 95

"Can you see anything?" Luck whispered, the words strangely formed, because of the way he struggled to keep his lips still like a ventriloquist.

"Too dark," she said.

The Nissan's passenger door opened then, and the dome light clicked on, illuminating the interior of the car. There were two men inside. The driver and a man riding shotgun. The passenger leaned closer to the driver for a moment, and they made some sort of exchange or perhaps a handshake, and then the door opened wider. The passenger stepped from the vehicle, but he had a hood pulled up over his head. She could see that he was a white male, and that was about it.

Luck clutched the radio mouthpiece in his hand, but he didn't dare move to use it. The man was still partially facing them.

The hooded subject paused next to the open door then ducked his head back into the vehicle, laughing at something the driver must have said. Darger had seen a glimpse of his jaw and cheek when he'd turned toward the light of the car. Based on the photo she thought it could be him. Maybe.

Luck took the momentary distraction to announce into the radio, "10-66 on the scene. Stand-by for positive ID."

The hooded man tensed like a gazelle feeling the presence of a stalking lion. He looked directly at them, squinting. He wore a look of bewilderment before he yelled something to the driver and jumped back into the vehicle. Gravel spun under the tires as the car pulled a tight U-turn and sped back the way it had come.

"Shit," Luck said, turning the key to start the engine.

He gunned it out of the driveway in pursuit. Darger groped for her seatbelt as they fishtailed onto the road.

"10-80," Luck barked into the radio. "Subject has fled the scene, 10-80."

His hand scrabbled at the dash. Darger could see blue and

red lights reflecting off her side mirror now that Luck had engaged the flashers on the van. The Nissan showed no signs of slowing.

What had been a paved road turned to dirt, the houses thinning and the forest growing thicker around them. Well, at least they weren't heading for a more populated area.

Gravel pinged against the van's undercarriage, and Darger heard the engine rev into a higher gear. Ahead, the road curved sharply, disappearing into the trees to the right. A black and yellow sign glinted at them, recommending they slow to 25 miles per hour for the upcoming curve. Luck let off the accelerator, but the Nissan maintained speed.

The car rounded the bend, and Darger watched as the back end swung around, skidding out of control. She was sure then that it would roll on its side and tumble into the ditch. The car juddered and shook and then somehow gained traction again, speeding away behind the cloak of the trees. They lost sight of it then, and for the first time, Darger thought they might lose him.

But as they came around the bend, they saw brake lights ahead. The red glow lit the overarching branches of the tree like a Halloween display.

The passenger door opened, and a figure fled into the dense woods at the side of the road. Darger was already unhooked from her seatbelt and halfway out the door before Luck had fully stopped the van.

"Stay on the car!" she shouted as she loped after the fleeing man.

A cloud of dust rose up where the car had taken off again, and she spat particles of dirt from her tongue.

She high-stepped into the foliage. It was dark, and she had no flashlight. But periodically she caught glimpses of him darting through the trees ahead of her. And she could hear him. His feet crashed through the dry leaves and deadfall littering the woods.

They were moving steadily uphill, toward what looked like a clearing ahead. Her lungs burned, and pain sent splinters through her thighs. Twice she came down on a low spot and almost fell, but somehow she kept her balance. Steam puffed out of her mouth and nostrils in pulsing clouds.

She was gaining on him now. They were close enough that she didn't lose sight of him in between the silhouettes of tree trunks. The end of the woods was looming ahead. A field of some kind. Corn or soybeans or whatever else they might grow out here, she didn't know. He seemed to hesitate on the edge of the woods, unsure of the wisdom of crossing into open ground. And that's when she saw her chance.

With a burst of speed she didn't know she had left in her, she surged forward, leaping at him with a cat-like aggression. Her shoulder rammed into his lower back, and she grappled around his waist. They went down together, hitting the tilled earth hard. He struggled to get free of her grasp, kicking, punching, scratching. Anything to loosen her grip. He rolled, his knee coming down on her head. She felt her cheekbone slam against a rock in the soil, and a bright white light flashed in her head. But still she held strong. She jabbed out with her fist, catching him in the gut, and he grunted. Another blow aimed a little lower, and he curled up like a dead spider, hands at his groin. She knelt next to him, grasping a handful of his hair with one hand. She turned his head so she could see his face. It was definitely him.

"Kurt Van Ryper?"

He only moaned in response.

She rolled him onto his belly and knelt with one knee pressing into his back.

"Give me your arms," she said. He was still cupping his crotch. She yanked one arm out, pulling it behind him. His groans were muffled by the dirt his face was pressed into.

A low rhythmic pulse could be heard now, getting louder. A helicopter.

She cuffed him, and he held still then, seeming to fall into a strange calm. The chopper's light appeared overhead, shining like the brightest star coming right at them.

Luck came crashing out of the trees, a crazy smile lighting up his face when he saw them.

They had him. They had their man.

So why was there that empty feeling in her stomach like it

was all wrong?

CHAPTER 96

Loshak drifted for a long time in a peaceful place. Neither alive nor dead.

Moving.

Floating.

Weightless and free of the pain he'd felt for these past weeks.

He was dreaming. Or something like it. Not all the way there. Not all the way real.

Unconscious.

Yes. He knew that much. Even if he couldn't make sense of it. Couldn't remember how things were supposed to be.

Mostly he didn't think about it. His existence simplified to a meandering serenity.

He could sense his respiration sometimes. That feeling of his ribcage expanding and contracting. Air rushing in and out.

And he reached out now and then. Tendrils of his mind stretching into the nothingness. Seeking some answer. Some explanation for his inanimate state.

But when he reached out, he sensed only the spiral beyond his being. A chaotic motion that twisted life into an ugliness. Contorted the universe to a cold and distant Other, forever closed off to him, unexplained and uncaring.

His questions had no answers. No positive or negative outcomes. Just indifference.

The infinite unknowable. The big nothing.

The void that swallowed up his daughter without reason. Without explanation. Without any sense of fairness or dignity or decency.

During those times when he reached, he felt trapped. Trapped in his skull. Trapped in this inert state. Nauseated. Lying motionless somewhere. Paralyzed.

Sometimes he drifted closer to the surface of the physical world, and he could hear it. The heart monitor beeping out its endless rhythm.

And the pain came back some. A dull version of it, like a butter knife stabbing him in the gut. It gripped him entirely.

But the self-awareness faded, and he roamed again in the stillness. The peace of the in-between. Not quite able to form complex thoughts any longer. Just there. And sometimes she was there with him. He could feel her there.

The beep of the heart monitor slowed, almost like it was relaxing. Tired after fighting for so long.

At 9:26 PM, Victor Loshak's heart stopped.

CHAPTER 97

After a night in lockup, Kurt was seated in Interview Room One. He hunched forward, head resting on his arms which were folded over the table.

Letting him stew a while had been Luck's idea, and a good one, Darger thought. Van Ryper probably hadn't slept much, and his anxiety would have only grown as the hours ticked by. Maybe now his ass would be puckering a bit, Luck had said. Maybe now he'd be a little more apt to talk.

Detective Luck took the seat directly across from Kurt while Darger sat off to the side.

"Do you know who I am, Kurt?"

His eyes rose slowly, fixing the detective with a sullen stare.

"Yeah. You're that cop that's been on TV."

Darger gripped the phone in her hand a little harder, and she thought she noticed an almost imperceptible stiffening of Luck's spine. They didn't dare risk glancing at each other. It could mean nothing, of course. A lot of people recognized Luck from the news these days. But still. It felt like something.

"Detective Luck," Casey said, placing a hand on his chest. "But you can call me Casey."

"Who's she?" Kurt asked then, not looking at Darger but gesturing with the twitch of his shoulder.

"This," Luck said, "is Special Agent Darger. From the FBI."

That got his attention. Kurt raised his chin and studied her with a surgeon's scrutiny.

"FBI? What's the FBI want?"

"Oh, Agent Darger here has been very interested in talking to you, Kurt," Luck said. "We all have, as a matter of fact."

"Yeah, well," Kurt said. "I don't know what you want from me."

There was a pause, and then he fixed Darger with irises that were so dark brown they were almost black.

"No first name for you, huh?"

447

"What's that?" she asked.

"He's 'Casey,'" Kurt said, placing air quotes around the name for emphasis. "But you're 'Special Agent Darger.'"

More air quotes.

Darger did her best not to look unnerved. She smiled.

"You can call me Violet if you'd prefer. Kurt."

Air rustled in his nostrils as he inhaled, sniffing with a shrug, as if it didn't matter to him either way. He angled his face toward the wall, and she felt Luck's eyes on her for a beat before he proceeded.

"Why don't we start by getting to know one another. You got a girlfriend?"

Kurt seemed thrown off by that, almost wincing before composing himself.

"A what?" he said. "Why? What do you care if I have a girlfriend or not?"

Luck spread his hands wide.

"It's only a question. Like I said, I want to get to know a little bit about you. You don't have to answer if it makes you uncomfortable for some reason."

That was good, Darger thought. Make him feel like not answering is worse than answering.

"I'm not uncomfortable. Just don't know why it matters," Kurt said, scowling at the table top. "No, I don't have a girlfriend."

"Good lookin' guy like you? Come on. There must be girls, though, right? Just no one serious."

"Psht."

Kurt glanced up at Darger and then over at Luck.

"I know what you're doing. I'm not a moron."

"Hey, I know that," Luck said, defensively. "Come on. I'm not trying to bust your balls or anything. How about we take a quick break. You want something to drink? Coke? Diet? Sprite?"

Kurt sat back, seeming to relax a bit.

"I'll take a Coke, I guess."

Luck shot her a look, and they both rose.

"I'll be right back with that, Kurt. Sit tight."

Just as Darger reached the door, Kurt called out from

behind her.

"Hey. Violet."

She froze, turning back to face him, her hand clutching the edge of the door. Ahead of her, Detective Luck had stopped also.

"Sorry about your face," Kurt said, gesturing in the vicinity of his cheek.

His lips and eyes were devoid of humor, but neither did they seem particularly pained with remorse either. She followed Luck into the hallway.

"What do you think?" Luck said, feeding a dollar bill into the machine. It squealed and whirred, sucking the money into its mouth like a piece of spaghetti.

"Hard to say so far. He's shut up pretty tight."

"Yeah. But he seems smarter than he looks, right?"

"True," she said.

"What about what he said to you, about your cheek? You think he's needling you?"

"I don't know. He seemed genuine, which might be weirder than if he'd just been taunting."

She prodded the tenderness at her cheek absently.

"Hard as hell to know whether we're over-analyzing or not."

Darger leaned her back against the wall and crossed her arms.

"Ask him about the car when we go back in."

Luck nodded, leading the way back to the interview room.

The legs of the chair skidded over the floor as Luck returned to his seat. He slid the can across the faux wood veneer of the table. Kurt popped the tab with a metallic click and a hiss.

"You drive a navy blue Buick LaCrosse, is that right?" Luck asked.

There was a pause before Kurt answered.

"No."

"No?" Luck said. "Huh. What do you drive, then?"

"A white Silverado."

"The new one? Parked in the garage at your mom's?"

Kurt's head bobbed up and down. He took off the beanie, revealing a tangle of greasy ear-length hair, the ends of which were bleached an icy platinum. He held the hat in his lap and fidgeted with the cuffed edge.

"Registration on that one had your mom's name. You don't have your own car?"

"We share it," Kurt said.

"OK. How long have you had it?"

"Bought it a few weeks ago," he said, and then his demeanor changed suddenly. His shoulders tensed. Agitated? Scared? She couldn't tell.

Before Luck could push him further on the car, Kurt Van Ryper spoke up again.

"Where is my mom? Does she know I'm here?"

Darger felt this was an odd question for a 28-year-old man to be asking.

"Don't worry," Luck said. "She's here."

"I want to talk to her."

"You can see your mom when we're done here. But we've got some more things to talk about."

The muscles in his face seemed to harden as he set his jaw. Darger watched the flesh on either side of his chin bunch into knots.

His eyes rolled up to meet Luck's. For a moment, he just stared, unblinking.

And then he said, "I want a lawyer."

CHAPTER 98

"Well, that was interesting," Luck said once they'd left the interview room behind them.

She grunted in agreement.

"You think we can use his mom to get him to talk to us some more? She's supposed to be the one wearing the pants, right? That's what your profile said."

Darger ran a finger down the bridge of her nose.

"It's not that simple. If he's our guy and if the profile is right—"

"Whoa, whoa," Luck said. "What are you talking about? Of course he's our guy."

"I'm just saying… everything we have is circumstantial at this point. We need more than the car and something orange hanging from the rearview mirror. You know that."

"I know. That's why I'm saying we should talk to Mother Dearest and see what's up with her."

Darger held her arm out toward the other interview room.

"After you, Detective."

They repeated the ritual. Entering the room, dismissing the officer assigned to watch the door, introducing themselves, and taking a seat across from their subject. The subject, in this case, was Rhonda Van Ryper. Cold, hard eyes peered out from behind a face weathered by sun and age. Her hair was permed, dyed, and cut short. She wore a little bit of makeup, but not a lot. What struck Darger most was that she didn't look afraid or even confused. It was as if she knew exactly what she was doing here.

"We were hoping we could ask you a few questions, Mrs. Van Ryper," Luck said, smoothing his tie and scooting forward in his chair.

Kurt's mother regarded him from the corner of her eye.

"Am I under arrest?"

Luck frowned.

"No ma'am."

"Then I'd like to leave. Where's Kurt?"

"Now see, that's the problem we have here, ma'am. Kurt resisted arrest and assaulted a federal officer," Luck said and gestured to Violet. "We only wanted to talk, but Kurt didn't really give us a chance to do that, and now he's in some trouble. We thought you might be able to help him out of that."

Rhonda's head swiveled to face Darger. The woman's eyelids squinted almost closed while she examined her.

"You're a Fed?" she asked, though Luck had already introduced her as such.

"FBI," Darger said.

Rhonda's lips pinched together as she mulled something over.

"If I'm not under arrest, then you can't keep me here. But I'm not leaving without Kurt."

"And as I made clear before, ma'am," Luck said. "You're not under arrest, but Kurt is. He's not going anywhere. But if you could get him to talk to us—"

Rhonda whirled on him, the whites of her eyes showing like a dog about to bite.

"He won't say boo if he knows what's good for him, and neither will I! I'm not sayin' another word. I know my rights, and I know I don't have to tell you a thing."

Exchanging a wordless glance, Luck and Darger got up from the table and exited the room.

When they were out of earshot of both rooms, Luck said, "She didn't ask why they're here."

Darger nodded.

"She didn't seem all that surprised about any of it. Could just be a good actress, but…" She trailed off.

"But it fits, though, right?"

"What?"

"I mean, wouldn't you call her overbearing?"

"Yes, but that isn't necessarily evidence of anything. A lot of people have controlling mothers and don't end up serial killers."

"Jesus! I know that," Luck snarled.

He closed his eyes and pressed his fingers against his eyelids.

"I'm sorry. I didn't mean to snap at you."

"It's OK," she said, her voice cool.

Luck's eyes flicked open, as if he just remembered something.

"What time is it?" he asked, glancing at his watch. "Shoot. I better call Claudia, see if she can pick Jill up from pre-school."

He started to stalk down the hall and stopped.

"Hey," he said, "maybe you should try to talk to her."

At first she thought he meant his daughter or mother-in-law, before finally realizing he meant Kurt Van Ryper's mother.

"I don't know. She seemed especially unenthused to find out I was FBI."

"Yeah, but you're a woman. She's a woman. Talking to someone like you... you can crack her."

"Crack her?" Darger repeated. "You watch too much TV."

"You know what I mean. Do your thing."

"What's my thing?"

He ran his fingers through his hair, messing up the part.

"Whatever you did to get Sierra Peters to talk. Cozy up to her. Make like you're friends. Get her to spill her guts. If we can get her to loosen up, we might get something we can use against him."

Darger felt her hackles rise. He made it sound like she'd manipulated Sierra. Like she'd never actually cared, only wanted to tease the story out of her. Luck was still talking.

"Plus, she's not under arrest, so she can't hide behind the attorney thing. If she won't leave here without Kurt, then she might as well talk to someone."

Darger thought about arguing, felt herself planting her feet, ready to dig in. She forced herself to relax.

"I need to think about it first. Get my head on straight," she said.

Luck seemed pleased by that.

He smiled.

"Great." Holding up his phone, he added, "I'm gonna go make this call real quick."

Darger watched him turn a corner at the end of the hall. She pivoted on her heel and went to find where she'd dumped her things when they'd first arrived at the station.

She would talk to the woman, eventually. But for now, she had her own idea of what she needed to do next.

CHAPTER 99

The key was Sierra. It always had been.

Violet dug around in her bag for her phone. She tried turning it on, but the battery was dead.

"Damn," she said, hunting for the charger and then for an outlet to plug it into.

She had to get down on her hands and knees to crawl under a table in the waiting room in order to reach it. She stayed there on the floor, huddled over the phone while Sierra's 911 call played again.

Violet took out a pen and a notepad, wrote "SIERRA" at the top, underlined it, and started jotting notes:

dairy mart — Broadway
had knife and gun
woman running outside

She tapped the pen against her lips as she listened to the 911 call again and then switched to the first interview video.

wore big glasses
cold, hard floor — cement or dirt
basement or garage or shed? What is Van Ryper's garage like?
lift or roll up door
metal roof
woods

She moved on to the second interview, followed by her own interview with Sierra.

rotten fruit smell (probably the chloroform)
pool nearby (residual smell of bleach?)

She was back on the first interview and had reached the part where she described the man. Dark hair. Wet, like he'd just showered or had mousse in it.

Dark hair.

Kurt Van Ryper had dark hair alright, but he'd bleached it blond, and not too recently. She wrote it down and circled it. Her pen tip dug so deeply into the paper it almost tore.

Because she had her earbuds in, she didn't hear when Luck came up behind her.

"You talk to her?"

Darger jumped a little, setting the phone aside.

"Not yet."

"What are you doing?"

He loomed over where she was hunched on the floor. His brow furrowed when he saw what it was. The lines deepened even further when he saw the notepad in her hand.

"Why this? Why now?"

"In the first interview, Sierra describes him as having dark hair."

"He does have dark hair."

"No. He has dark hair dyed a very unnatural shade of blond, and that wasn't done in the last week. It's been growing out for a while."

"So what?" he said, crossing his arms.

"So, Sierra would have noticed something like that. She would have mentioned it."

Luck rolled his eyes.

"Maybe he was wearing a wig. Maybe she didn't see his hair at all because he was wearing that damn hat."

"She was specific about the hair," Darger said. "I told you. She wanted to be a stylist. She paid attention to that kind of thing."

Casey covered his mouth with his hand and held it there for a moment.

"Just go talk to the mother. Please?"

His voice had taken on a pleading tone, almost desperate.

There was a long pause as Darger eyed the phone and the scribbled words on her notepad and then finally voiced what she'd been thinking for the last several hours.

"It's not just the hair," she said. "Something doesn't feel right."

"Oh come on, Violet. Don't do this. Not now."

Luck planted his hands on his hips and rolled his head around in a circle on his neck like he was trying to straighten a kink.

Now she was the one frowning.

"Don't do *what*?"

"This thing you do. We got the guy. And his mother. And you're still hung up on this."

He waved a dismissive hand at the phone and her notes.

"We have live bodies here. Stop obsessing over a dead girl and go get some new info."

"What?" Violet said, taken aback by his tone.

"You think I don't know what this is? You're being motivated by guilt. Guilt for Zara that got transferred into guilt for Sierra, and now it's propelling you down this twisted fucking path that only makes any sense to you. It's not good police work."

She pushed herself to her feet, hating how he was hanging over her. Her voice came out in a low growl.

"Fuck you."

She turned and left before he could say anything more.

The notepad protruding from her bag named her destination. Beneath Sierra's underlined name, the first line read: *dairy mart — Broadway.*

CHAPTER 100

Her hand flailed in her bag. Where was it?

Trying to keep one eye on the road, she glanced into the gaping mouth but saw only blackness. She should get a briefcase or something. Try to keep things more organized.

With a sigh, she pulled into the parking lot of an Applebee's so she could find her phone without taking out any pedestrians.

It turned out that having two eyes on the task didn't help any. She finally dumped out the entire contents of her purse into the passenger seat. Only then did she realize she'd left her phone hooked up to the charger back at the police station.

"Motherfucker!" she hissed to no one in particular. No one but herself, anyway.

Well, there was no way she was going back there. Not now. Casey could screw.

"Obsessing over a dead girl. Fuck you, Casey," she muttered.

Good luck to him and his career-making case. Cal was sending in reinforcements anyway. So-called experienced agents.

Loshak. He would have understood. He would have listened. What had he told her the night Novotny died?

It's 10% by the book 90% by the gut. You can't teach the gut part. But you've got it.

Jesus. She'd never gotten the call after Loshak's surgery. Her phone had been dead, and now she didn't have it. Who knew if he was even breathing?

She almost started to cry again. But no. No, she would not. Not one more tear, she thought, wiping at her eyelashes.

There had to be a way to get the information she needed.

Her eyes lighted on her laptop. That would do, if she could find a wireless signal. Striped awnings cast rectangular shadows across the parking lot in front of the restaurant.

She slid the computer from its case and checked the available networks. There it was, with full bars: NETGEAR_14.

And it was unsecured. She double clicked it, and then opened a browser window to get directions to the Dairy Mart on Broadway in Logan. She scribbled the directions down on the next sheet of her notepad and put the car in gear.

It was time to put her gut to the test.

The glittering waters of the Hocking River came into view periodically on her drive. Sometimes it crossed beneath her. Other times, it curved alongside the road, like a big green-black snake.

When she found the Dairy Mart, she used that as her starting point and branched out: north, south, east, west. Violet tried to take every possible combination of routes, looking for anything that might fit the description that Sierra Peters had given of the building she'd been briefly held in. Fold-up door, metal roof. There were plenty of lifting doors on the garages of the houses she passed, but none had metal roofs.

She drove past the Dairy Mart for what had to be the twentieth time, following another route. She'd taken the first right, and then two lefts. Had she done a left and then a right instead? It was getting hard to remember. The scenery was nondescript. Trees and the occasional home and more trees.

Luck's words popped into her head then.

Motivated by guilt.

Maybe he was right. Maybe she *was* obsessing because of Sierra. Because of Zara.

Or more like she *knew* he was right.

She worried at her guilt like a sore tooth, thinking she could fix it all somehow. That some combination of events might bring them back, like a necromancer's spell. But that was bullshit. Even if she solved the riddle and found the bad guy, Zara and Sierra and all the others would still be dead.

It was all an elaborate story she'd told herself to keep her from feeling the real pain. The hard, ugly, bitter truth about the world which was that sometimes good and innocent people died, and there was nothing to be done about it.

And that reminded her of another thing Loshak had said to her some time ago. It could only have been days, but it felt like months or even years. Something about buckling under the weight of her own denial.

Trees whizzed past in a green blur. What was she doing out here? No matter what happened, she would never get another chance to save those girls. She might save others by catching the killer, but Luck was right. She was out here chasing ghosts. It wasn't good police work.

The car rounded a wide curve, the road was bending back to the south, back toward town. As she tried to decide whether she should turn around or just keep following the road, which she thought might take her back to town on its own, the road straightened. Ahead, she caught sight of a sign for a gym. The logo was a blue circle, with the feminine silhouette of a woman running on a treadmill.

She sped past the driveway for the gym, her brain taking a few seconds to catch up with her eyes, and then her foot slammed on the brake pedal. It was a reflex, and she thought later how lucky she was that no one had been behind her. They would have almost certainly rear-ended her.

The road in front and behind was empty, so she reversed instead of turning around. When she got to the turn-off for the gym, she spun the wheel and rolled into the empty parking lot. As she got closer to the door, she saw a sign taped to the front door: CLOSED FOR RENOVATION — COME SEE OUR NEW AND IMPROVED FACILITY IN THE NEW YEAR!

She woke her laptop and punched frantically at the touchpad, trying to find the right spot in the tape.

"She was outside," Sierra's voice said, the phone line or maybe the recording itself crackling. "Outside of the room. Across the street. She was running. A whaddyacallit…"

A treadmill. She was trying to say treadmill.

She must have glimpsed the sign when the man had taken her out of the car.

She stepped out of the car looking for any sign of the room Sierra may have been in. Any garage doors and metal roofs. The gym had a flat roof. She spun around in the lot, and that's when she saw it, across the way.

A red sign with big white letters that read: STOR-RITE SELF

STORAGE.

And then it hit her: cement floors, roll-up door, metal roof. Sierra had been in a storage unit.

CHAPTER 101

The storage office was open. Darger parked in one of the many empty spaces in the lot and got out of the car. Her heart was hammering in her chest, and her hands felt like ice. She took a steadying breath before she opened the door and stepped inside.

A bell jangled announcing her presence. It was unnecessary. A middle-aged woman hunkered behind a counter watching Dr. Phil on a flatscreen TV on the wall.

"Good afternoon," the woman chimed. She had full cheeks, shiny and pink. A nest of brown hair streaked with gray was piled into a messy bun on top of her head.

Darger took out her ID and laid it on the counter.

"My name is Violet Darger. I'm with the FBI."

"Oh!" The woman's sparse eyebrows reached for her hairline. "I don't… well… what's this about?"

"I was hoping to have a look at a list of your customers."

The woman's head began to churn from side to side, her bun seeming to cling to her skull for dear life.

"Oh, no. I'm afraid not. Not without a warrant. The privacy of our customers is of the utmost importance to us, you understand."

Darger had been worried about this. If Luck were here, he would have had some polished spiel at the ready. Darger had no such pitch. She rubbed the back of her neck, pondering.

Then her gaze fell on the television with the fraud doctor and his tawdry show. Violet considered the possibility that the truth might be just as productive in this case.

"I really shouldn't be telling you this, but… " She leaned in, lowering her voice. "I'm assuming you watch the local news."

It took only a moment for the woman to take the hint. Again, her eyebrows leapt to attention.

"You don't mean," her voice had come out in almost a shriek, and she clapped a hand over her mouth before proceeding in a whisper. "The Doll Parts Killer?"

Darger pretended to glance over her shoulder, like an imaginary eavesdropper may be present.

"I technically can't confirm that, but let's just say that if you let me have a look at that list, you might possibly be saving a girl's life."

The woman chewed at her lip, considering for a moment.

"OK," she said, bun quivering. "I'll do it."

Almost as an afterthought, she held up a hand and said, "But this list cannot leave this office."

"I'll agree to that," Darger said.

"It'll take me a minute to get it printed out." The woman scooted toward a door leading to a back room. "I'll be back."

Violet didn't have to wait long before the woman returned, with three sheets lined with black text.

"Here they are," the woman said, sliding the papers across the counter. She slapped a hand against her chest.

"Oh! A chill just ran through me."

She rubbed at her pink forearms, trying to disperse the goose bumps that had appeared.

Darger ran a finger over the names. Half of her was only scanning through them. Half of her was searching for Van Ryper, Kurt or Rhonda. It was another name that jumped out at her, though.

Mary Jo Clegg.

Darger stopped with her pen hovering next to it. Clegg. Why did that sound familiar? She tapped the pen on the paper, thinking. And then it struck her.

She grappled with the straps of her bag, reaching for her file. She sifted through the pages, paper rustling, and then she found it. The list Luck had made of Fiona Worthington's classmates. It was right there, third from the top.

James Joseph Clegg.

Violet copied the name and address down in her notepad, scribbling in a sloppy chicken scratch that was the result of speed and nerves.

She shoved the whole lot back in her bag, sputtered a "Thank you!" to the woman behind the counter, and flew out the door.

Jumping in the car, she ground the gears shifting too quickly from reverse to drive, not waiting for the car to stop all the way.

Chauncey, Ohio, the address read. Chauncey was less than ten minutes from Athens, she figured. He'd been less than ten minutes from them the whole time.

CHAPTER 102

She knew what she should do.

What she should do was go back to the station and tell Luck what she'd found. About the gym with the running woman and the storage facility with the cement floors and the doors that rolled up, one of them under the name of Mary Jo Clegg.

Would he listen? She thought perhaps not. She thought perhaps he'd already made his decision.

Stop obsessing over a dead girl. We got the guy.

It was all on her now. Maybe it always had been. Maybe that's what Loshak had been trying to tell her when he told her to trust her instincts. Maybe he'd known all along — somehow — that it would be just her when it came down to it.

She pressed her foot on the pedal a little more firmly. It wasn't far now.

She took the turn north toward Chauncey, which seemed more a cluster of houses on the outskirts of Athens than a real town of its own. The tires bumped over the railroad tracks, tossing Darger from side to side in her seatbelt. Tombstones rolled by as she passed a cemetery. She thought about the superstitious game she played as a child, the one where you held your breath until you'd left the cemetery in the rearview.

She did it now, puffing her cheeks out just as she'd done when she was seven or eight years old. Before she reached the end of the graveyard, she saw her turn. The air rushed out of her all at once. She tried not to think of it as a bad omen, but it was too late. A shudder ran through her.

The turn signal ticked away as she waited for traffic to clear enough for her to make the left. Again she crossed the railroad tracks, shimmying this way and that. She went along slower now. She was getting close.

Two big Norway spruce trees almost completely obscured the house from view, despite the fact that it stood no farther back from the road than the rest of the houses on the street. The light was starting to fade from the day, and the extra shade cast by the trees made this end of the street feel like it was already night. The sweeping, untrimmed boughs at the base of the tree swished against the side of her car as she pulled to the curb and parked.

Her heart rate, which had calmed some during the drive, picked up speed again. She could feel the blood thrumming in her neck.

When her foot touched the ground, she was almost surprised to find that it still held solid beneath her. She had a strange otherworldly feeling, almost dream-like.

She skirted around the side of the hulking evergreens and into the front yard, concentrating on putting one foot in front of the other with all of the thoughts rushing through her head. Her throat felt dry, and she swallowed.

This time she had a plan. She'd come up with it on the drive. She would knock on the door, and when Mrs. Clegg answered, she would tell the story she'd come up with. That she was a classmate of James'. From high school. That she was in town visiting her parents and wondered if JJ still lived in the area. Would she happen to have his address? His phone number? After that, well… she'd have to figure out the rest when she came to it.

She was moving over the grass, rehearsing her lines in her head, when a shadow separated from the dark mass of the trees. She only saw it from the corner of her eye, a black blur that rushed at her from the gloom. It collided with the side of her head, right above her left cheekbone. She saw a colorful burst of stars, and then it was as if she'd been plunged face-first into a pile of snow. A whitewash… that's what they used to call it.

A freezing cold vapor filled her nose and throat and lungs. So cold it burned. And it was sweet, too. Like the sangria-flavored wine coolers she'd had the first time she ever got drunk. A horrible sweetness that made her feel instantly sick. It was suffocating.

She was gagging on it. She flailed her arms and kicked her legs, not so much trying to fight as to claw her way to fresh air. But the grip did not loosen. She felt herself being dragged backward, toward the drooping branches of the overhanging trees.

Her vision began to pulse in and out.

Black.

And then the sky, the first shading of dusk already visible overhead.

Black.

A bough overhead, just a smudge of dark green against the night.

Black.

CHAPTER 103

He watches the feline shape next to him as he drives. She is his. For now and for always.

He makes himself look back at the road. Hands quivering on the wheel. Bolts of lightning sizzling all through him.

This one feels more momentous than the others. More important. More significant. The queen of the la-de-da girls. He can set something right with her in a way he couldn't with the others.

There are no words for it. Just a feeling. A surge of power that forms in his chest and shudders all through him.

She lies slack in the passenger seat. Looks more like a pile of limbs than a person for the moment.

Her head leans his way. Dangling forward. Held up only by the seat belt that keeps her shoulders from folding into her lap. She is close. Yes. But they hit a bump and now her hair obscures the face. Ruins the moment somehow.

The chemical smell wafts from her mouth with every breath. Pungent. A little fruity. Like a mix of red wine and rotting toilet paper. The stench seems to fill the car.

He cracks the window to fight it. The cool air making his eyelids flutter.

The street blurs a little outside. The grass and houses and concrete and asphalt all smearing together. Everything grayed out from the dusk settling toward dark. The fumes must be getting to him a little.

But it's no matter. The storage unit isn't far off now. It will be done within minutes. He can seal their matrimony with a single kiss from his blade on the soft flesh of her neck. A flick of the wrist. The slightest tug of steel through skin. And she will be his like all the rest.

For now and for always.

CHAPTER 104

The world faded back in little by little.

Black.

White.

Black.

White wings.

Black.

Not white wings. Her hands. Splayed awkwardly in her lap.

Her fingers twitched involuntarily, and it occurred to her that she should pretend she was still out.

Where was she?

It was dark now. She could tell that. Her head felt thick, as if it were packed full of gauze. The way her dentist packed those little cotton wads in her gums when he had to fill a cavity.

She swayed, a lock of hair falling into her face, and a wave of nausea rolled over her. It took every ounce of willpower she could muster not to retch. When the feeling passed, she realized she was in a car. Yes. She felt the constricting pressure of the seatbelt over her chest. And then a sound to her left, a sharp, wet noise, like someone's throat clicking when they swallowed.

It was him of course. The comprehension hit her all at once, like a punch in the gut. Oh dear God, it was him.

The pieces all began to fit themselves together then. He must have been at his mother's house. He must have seen her, known who she was. If that was the case, he could have been following her.

A second later, she realized how bad it really was. Luck and everyone else were still back at the station. Still questioning Kurt Van Ryper. Still under the impression that they'd found their killer.

She was on her own.

Her breath hitched in her chest when the full understanding of it came. He had taken her like he'd taken the rest. He had knocked her out, dragged her to the car, and then… well, she knew quite well what happened after that. And it happened quickly. He liked his playthings to be dead first.

He must have sensed something had changed with her — maybe he heard the change in her breathing. Whatever it was, through the haze of her barely-parted eyelashes, she saw movement. He was grabbing for something, and that's when she noticed the smell that filled the small space. The sick, stinking reek of the chloroform.

She spun in the seat, planting her back against the door and turning on him, folding her feet up and kicking out with both legs. She'd only meant to kick with one leg, but she saw now that it was beyond her control. He'd already taped up her ankles, several loops of duct tape encircling the hem of her pants. It didn't matter, because it worked. The drooping washcloth he'd been ready to hold over her mouth and nose flew from his hand, landing somewhere in the back of the car.

He cried out, hand instantly moving to try to catch the rag. It was a stupid move, she thought. He left himself completely open to her then. She supposed it was just instinct that made him do it, but she seized the advantage. Her hands — also wrapped in tape at the wrists — balled into fists, and she swung at him, raining down blows upon his head. She was vaguely aware of the car swerving over the road as he struggled to drive and fight off her attack at the same time, but she cared not. She was some kind of feral beast now, dead set on wreaking the most havoc possible, whether she lived or died.

There was a cracking sound and then a stinging on her knuckles as her hands collided with his mouth, her bones scraping over his teeth. And then as fast as lightning, he brought his hand up. It wasn't the rag though. The rag was white and irregular, and what he held now was dark and angular.

It was a gun. *Her* gun. He pointed it at her face. She wanted to flinch but forced herself not to. She was about to tell him to do it. To shoot her. But before she could get the words out, his wrist rocked back. As quickly as a striking cobra he smashed the butt into the side of the head, and she was out.

CHAPTER 105

Blood seeps from his lip. He watches it in the rearview mirror. The rivulet of red draining down his chin. His teeth all gummy with scarlet.

What the fuck? Stupid bitch.

He holds one hand on her as he drives. Palm and fingers applying pressure to the nape of her neck. Pressing her down into the seat. Her breath going ragged from the way he constricts her. Hissing and crackling like radio static.

It makes him feel better somehow. To push her torso into the car seat. To hold her down. Hold her still. Even if she is unconscious. Even if she isn't going anywhere. It feels good.

He felt so small in that moment when she'd busted him in the mouth. Opened him up. And now he wants to lord his power over her in turn.

It wasn't fair. What she did. It wasn't fair. Those are the only words he can conjure for it. Things didn't work that way. It wasn't fair.

Anyway. It doesn't matter. Not anymore.

He jerks the wheel left. The tires slide a little as they rattle over the gravel. Rocks flinging in all directions as he tears through the parking lot.

They're here.

CHAPTER 106

Thump.

A familiar sound, that thump.

There were other sounds in the darkness. Scrapes and crunches. Less familiar. She tried to focus on the thump. Wanted to make sense of it. Felt some urgency to do so.

No, it wasn't the sound she was concerned with. Something else. Something else was more important.

Her thoughts spiraled for a moment, like sugar swirling in a glass of iced tea, and then they settled.

She remembered.

He had taken her. They had struggled in the car. He'd knocked her out with the gun.

As if the amnesia had been acting as an anesthetic, her head suddenly throbbed with pain at the memory of it. Her jaw ached, and her tongue felt swollen and strangely numb. She thought she might have bitten it at some point.

It wasn't only her head, either. The tape around her wrists was so tight the tips of her fingers pulsed with her heartbeat.

The ground beneath her was cold and hard, pressing its chill into her shoulder blades.

Careful not to stir, and to keep her breathing regular, she peeled her eyes apart. Slowly and barely a crack.

It was dark, yes. But not completely. Not as dark as she'd thought when her eyes were closed. Light bounced off the ceiling overhead, and off the roll-top door.

She was in the storage unit.

Panic struck her then, thinking of Sierra's panicked 911 call.

Oh God, why had she gone off alone? Why hadn't she stayed and just listened to Luck?

She thought of Sierra again and this time, a tiny burst of warmth filled her chest, a sensation almost like a shot of whiskey.

Sierra had gotten away. Once.

She could get away, too. If she was lucky. If she fought for it.

Another thump, and her ears practically swiveled like a cat's. A car door. Or maybe the trunk?

Carefully, she rotated her eyes around to peek out through the door. She didn't have the best angle, the way her head was slumped to one side. She had to sort of stare down her nose. It was a move that for some reason heightened the sick feeling that still roiled in her gut, making her dizzy.

It was no use anyway. The headlights shone directly into the space. It was too bright to see out. And then she heard the scrape of feet over the concrete floor.

She forced herself to relax. Played dead… or close to dead. Not close enough for him, that was for sure.

She was just barely squinting, her head lolled to one side. Peering straight out through her lashes, she saw what looked like a dismantled mannequin next to her. The arms and legs all jumbled up in a pile with the head propped up and facing her.

No, no, not a mannequin. A girl. The girl. Sandy Metcalf. Taken apart like a broken doll.

There was a tremendous, deafening rumble and then the whole world was plunged into darkness.

CHAPTER 107

This time the darkness was a blessing. As was the roar of thunder that turned out to be the metal door rolling shut. Both served to conceal Darger's dry heaving, her entire body convulsing in a lone spasm of horror.

There was the sight of it. The careless tangle of limbs. The pooling blood on the plastic sheet. And then there was the smell of it. Rot and decay so thick it felt like a warm, wet blanket on her skin. And then over top of that, the salty chemical tang of bleach.

She didn't let herself dwell on it as she lay there in the dark. This was it. She needed a weapon. Something. Anything. Her hands scrabbled over the cement, feeling around on the floor, but there was only what felt like another plastic sheet beneath her.

Shit.

What did she have? A pen? Anything. She patted around in the darkness, over her pockets, on her jacket and her shirt. Her fingers brushed over a sharp edge.

Click.

A beam of light. He held a flashlight now. Violet froze, not daring to even let herself breathe. He stooped, fumbling with something in the corner.

There was another click and a work light flooded the room with brightness. Too much light now. He could see her. She shut her eyes all the way, afraid he'd catch her peeking. It was hard not to squint even then, the halogen bulbs were so blinding.

She heard him. The soft patter of his footsteps contrasting with sharper metallic sounds. His knife, no doubt.

God, she hoped she'd get a chance. She would. She had to. He'd have to get close. Close enough to slide the blade across her neck. That would be it.

She waited for what seemed like a long time, trying not to gag on the stench of death. Trying not to think about the

474

mutilated corpse of Sandy Metcalf next to her.

Finally, he was there. The plastic crinkled as he closed in on her, but more than that, she could feel him next to her. A tingle almost like an electric charge.

He smelled like wet leaves.

He inhaled. His breathing was slow and deep. Relaxed sounding.

He bent over her. She could sense his body heat and his form blocking out the light through her closed eyelids, and then she felt the cold touch of metal on her neck. So sharp.

Her eyes snapped open, and she brought her fist up to his face, aiming for his eyes. Stabbing with the pathetic pin at the end of her brooch. It couldn't have been more than an inch-worth of weapon, but it was all she had.

She smashed him with it over and over, and at first he struggled with her, trying to catch her wrists, but she pulled away from him, striking again. This time she got him in the eye, and she heard the clatter of the knife hitting the floor. He brought both hands up to his face, howling like a wounded dog. Forgetting the pin now, she grabbed for the knife, scooting away from where he writhed like a rat with a broken back.

Her shoulder bumped into something metal that rang like a gong when she hit it — the door. Still watching him, she slit through the duct tape wrapped around her ankles and started working on her hands, but it was awkward, and she'd forgotten she had to watch, too. He slammed into her, crushing her against the door, knocking the wind from her lungs.

Somehow she managed to keep her grip on the knife, and she swung wildly with it, the blade glinting in the light. Just as it was about to sink into his thigh, he knocked it off course with a blow to her forearm. Instead of his flesh, the knife missed and lodged into a stack of old tires. Her hand slid down the shaft and along the sharp edge, but the pain barely registered. Her only thought was: *Do not let go.* She tried to wrench it free, but her hands were slick with her own blood now, and she lost her grip.

He was grappling at her, trying to get his hands at her throat. His fingers crawled over her face, down her chin. Too close to her mouth for his own good. She lashed out, getting two of them between her teeth and biting down as hard as she could, feeling the ligament and bone crunch like gristle on a steak. He screamed, pulling his hand away and holding it to his chest, and she used the moment of disorientation to bash her elbow into his groin. Another low growl came from deep in his throat, and the veins and muscles in his neck bulged.

She turned away, looking for the way to open the door. A handle, to her right. She gripped it, lifting. The door was heavy, but she got it open enough to duck under and slither through.

The chill of the night air was a shock against her face after the heat of their struggle. And the air out here was fresh, clean. She sucked big lungfuls as she ran blindly down the row of identical concrete units. She rounded a corner and flattened her back against one of the doors, listening. She held her breath, worried she wouldn't be able to hear over her ragged gasps. She heard nothing.

She sprinted for the floodlight illuminating the office at the front of the complex, keeping to the shadows as much as possible in case he followed. There was nowhere to hide here, but at least the dark concealed her a little bit.

As she scurried over the gravel lot, she tugged at her wrists, trying to loosen the bindings. She brought the mass of tape to her face, the stink of the adhesive filling her nose as she tore at the bonds with her teeth. It was no use, at least not for the moment. Trying to work her canine under the tape while she jogged wasn't going to happen.

Her feet thudded over the wooden ramp that led up to the office. She banged both fists against the glass, rattling the door in its frame. She pressed her face to the window, but all was dark and quiet inside. No one was there.

She turned, gazing down the straight drive that led to the road. Beyond on it, the gym was partially lit by a streetlight. No hope there either.

But then she saw a pale glow approaching and a truck whooshed past on the road. She took off so fast that she stumbled in the gravel, falling hard on her knee and elbow. Barely registering the pain of the sharp rocks digging into her flesh, she scrambled back to her feet and down the driveway.

Her biggest fear as she ran toward the road was that no one would come. She'd missed the only passing car on this road by thirty seconds. But when she reached the point where the gravel met the smoother surface of the road, she turned her head to the right and already could see a set of headlights approaching. She thrust her arms in the air, screaming and jumping up and down in the opposite lane as it rumbled down the road. The vehicle slowed.

CHAPTER 108

The pain is everything. Blinding. Piercing.

His fingers scrabble over his eyelids. And in his mind he sees them slicked with gore. Covered in blood. Opaque juice like seawater flowing from his punctured eyeballs. Spilling out everywhere.

But no. That doesn't make sense. Does it?

He takes a breath. Forces himself to peel his eyes open. His hands gliding away from his face in slow motion.

Barely any blood at all. Just a rust-colored smear. Whatever damage she's done is minor. Superficial. No matter how bad it hurts.

But she meant to maim him. She meant to wound him. She stabbed him for God's sake.

The words echoed in his head again.

That's not fair. They weren't supposed to do that.

And then he's on his feet. Moving. Scooping the gun from the cement floor. Running for that rectangle of light that leads outside.

His feet pound over the gravel. Propelling him into the brush headed toward the road.

Movement catches his eye. Bright light shining everywhere. Blinding him for a moment.

Headlights.

And in that moment as the flash hits and squints his eyes to slits, he sees the silhouette of her bound arms waving back and forth like crazy. He is too late. She is flagging someone down.

Breath sucks into him involuntarily. Painful and dry. The void contracts the walls of his chest. Threatening to implode his ribcage.

And all is lost. Everything.

She will slip away from him now. She will escape. It will all end here.

But the car zooms past. Oblivious. Uncaring. She waves her

arms for a long time in the red glow of the taillights.

He can breathe again. His chest no longer sucking in.

And heat flushes his face. Some kind of hate he's never felt before.

He raises the Glock, pinches one eye closed to line up the sight with her pretty face, and squeezes the trigger.

CHAPTER 109

For a moment she couldn't believe what she was seeing. The car slowed, swerved around where she stood next to the double yellow line, and the kept going.

She watched the tail lights, like two angry red eyes, disappear around a curve in the road and felt the sting of tears. After the brightness of the lights, the road seemed especially dark now. Her head throbbed, and she felt faint. She bent over her knees to catch her breath, willing herself not to pass out.

She couldn't give up. She had to think. Through the pain and the wooziness and the fear.

She considered heading into the woods for cover, but she remembered what Sierra had told her, that she thought she'd wandered beneath those dark trees for an hour or more. No, Violet would stay on the road.

There was an explosive *crack* from behind her and the sense of something whizzing past her shoulder at high speed. She turned back and saw the silhouette of a man standing in the gravel drive leading up to the storage facility. His form was perfectly outlined by the night sky above.

It was instinct that told her to throw herself to the ground then, just as another explosion and burst of light came from where he stood. He was shooting at her. With her own gun. And she was a sitting duck standing there in the middle of the road.

Darger crawled, sand and pebbles clinging to the sticky blood on her knees. She rolled into the drainage ditch and then scrambled along a few yards, thinking she might be able to stay concealed there. The pitch blackness of the woods was not inviting at all. But another gunshot changed her mind. Pushing to her feet, she staggered out of the ditch, and down into the woods.

It was steeper than she'd realized, and she found herself stumbling down the embankment more than running. Branches whipped at her face and caught in her hair. Roots and fallen

480

limbs tripped her continuously, but she got back up and continued on. She had no other choice.

Finally the land leveled out. She could hear the burble of water now. The river. The undergrowth was a little less dense here. That and the flatter ground made progress easier. She could go a little faster and not worry about falling wrong and snapping an ankle.

She paused once for half a second, behind a huge oak tree, and heard him crashing along behind her.

To the left, the land rose steeply away from the river. She didn't think she had the strength now to climb back out of it. And to her right, the churning of the water. How deep, how wide, how cold, she didn't know. Too cold for an October night like this, she thought, noticing how her toes were numb from trudging through the marshy area along the river.

She only had one option, she realized. If she stayed on the defensive, stayed in her role as the prey, she would lose. She had to reverse their roles. Become the hunter instead of the hunted. And she had to do it soon.

She had to kill him now or die trying.

CHAPTER 110

She runs away like a feral cat. Wild. Panicked. Reckless. Tearing through the woods.

He catches glimpses of her. A moving shape in the dark. A silhouette that keeps twisting just out of view.

A smile pulls his lips taut. Makes the wound there sting like he's dumping bleach on it.

Tree branches bob everywhere she goes. Their movement marking her path as clearly as possible.

It's a matter of time. He knows. It's a matter of *when* not *if*.

She has no way out. And he loves it.

The tension in his neck and back seem to ease.

He chases for what feels like a long time. But it's no concern. He feels good. Feels like he could run forever.

The rushing water of the river grows louder as they advance along this path. Rapids or something kicking up. The volume knob inching ever higher.

And then the woods clear out. Going sparse almost at once. Grass fields with a few trees now lining the sides of the river.

There are no more wagging tree branches to tell him which way to go. His indicators are gone. But he's not worried. Not yet. He knows she wasn't very far ahead of him.

He slows. Stops. Listens.

Nothing.

What the hell?

He adjusts his grip on the gun. His palm and the handle greased with sweat.

She's close. He doesn't know how he knows, but he does. He can feel it like a wave in the air. Like a bloodhound picking out the scent.

He steps forward. Head swiveling. Eyes rolling around in their sockets. He scans for any signs of movement. The gun extended before him.

He holds his breath to quiet it. But his blood still pounds in his temples. Great surges of fluid roaring through his head and pulsing in his ears.

She crashes out of the tall grass. Cutting him down at the knees.

CHAPTER 111

In her mind, she was a predator. The kind that skulks in tall grass and waits for the perfect moment to strike at her prey with a deadly quickness. A lioness. A leopard.

She leapt from her place in the thicket, colliding with his legs and knocking him off balance. Not quickly or stealthily enough, apparently, as he turned at the last beat, and there was a blinding flash and a deafening clap that sounded as if it came from inside her own head. A burning, searing pain erupted in her left arm. He'd shot her. The motherfucker had shot her.

A new burst of adrenaline was released with this knowledge. The gun reflected the moonlight as it spun in the air, and gave off a wet slap as it hit the water's edge. He scrambled for it, and she was on him. Clinging, biting, clawing at his flesh.

He reached over his shoulder, grabbing a handful of her hair and yanking. She heard the roots rip free from her scalp more than she felt it. Her whole body was on fire with an animal rage by then. She brought up her knee and drove it into the small of his back, and he grunted.

She got her arms, still taped together at the wrists, around his neck. She bent her elbow, trying to find purchase around his throat. He got his knees underneath him and rose up on all fours, throwing her off to the side.

She changed tactics, hands creeping and crawling up the side of his face, careful to steer clear of his teeth. She found what she was looking for. The soft fold of skin around the eye. She jabbed with her thumbs and fingers, feeling the way the muscles there clenched in an effort to protect. He yelped, sounding like a coyote yipping in the night. She was making sounds too, snarling and hissing with fury.

He rolled to the side then, trapping her underneath him. He lifted her easily where she'd wrapped her arms around his shoulders. Then he dropped backward, landing his full weight on her, slamming her into the ground and driving the oxygen

484

from her lungs.

He was too big. Too strong.

Her grip loosened, and he wriggled from her embrace.

She coughed and sputtered in the dirt at the edge of the water, arms and legs twitching in a fruitless attempt to right herself and crawl away. He caught her by the back of the neck and dragged her closer to the water before rolling her over onto her stomach. The river rushed up to meet her with icy fingers that clung to her chest and shoulders and neck. She arched her back, trying to keep her head free.

Crushing pain thrust into her back as he drove his knee into her ribs, kneeling on her spine. Still she struggled to keep her face out of the water.

A hand clamped down on the back of her neck, pushing closer. She turned her head, felt the river kiss her cheek, and then her head was forced under the black depths.

CHAPTER 112

Again he presses her down. Feels the power of his hands and weight forcing her under the flowing rapids. Cold water swirling around his wrists and forearms. Numbing him like ice up to the elbows.

She thrashes. Her whole body bucking against his. The muscles in her core lurch and shudder with incredible power. Incredible fury.

The small of her back thrusts into his abdomen. The bony spine encased in frantic, trembling flesh.

Her movements jolt his arms. Tug his shoulders around in their sockets. Meat and ligament grinding against bone. But his grip holds tight like steel.

He feels it in her. The shift. She is an animal now. A feral creature. All the way. They both are.

Defiance.

That's what it is. A kind of rage the others could never muster. Some real fight in her.

He wants to kill her right here and now. Hands scrabbling for her throat. Itching to find her windpipe and close it for her. But she starts to worm away from him. He reverts to gripping the places between her neck and shoulders. Securing her. Holding her under.

Good.

Let the water do the work for him. That was better anyway.

The river gurgles around them. Burbling its wet sound to drown out all but her crashing about. Bubbles explode all about her. And a few strands of her hair snake toward the surface. Undulating like seaweed.

And now that heat in his face is at odds with the chill climbing up his arms to such a degree that he feels nauseous from it. A stirring in his middle. A lightness in his head.

Black flutters at the edges of his field of vision. His eyelids flickering. The whole world wavering just a little.

The word "SWOON" screams in his head in all caps.

And in his addled mind, she is laughing at him. Smiling at his weakness. Defying him still.

But no. Fuck that.

He grits his teeth. Clamps down harder on her neck. And he drives her face into the muck at the bottom of the river. Bashing and smearing her. One hand sliding to the back of her head for better leverage. Fingers lacing into her hair. Nails digging into her scalp.

He feels the soggy ground give way to his force. The mud sucking her up. The earth itself trying to swallow her face.

He lets up and jams her down over and over in fast motion. Little suction sounds barely discernible. Spit spraying between his clenched teeth.

And the void is everywhere now. Inside of him and out. The black nothing that stretches out forever. The emptiness. The only thing that's real.

But his hands are making something now. Aren't they?

Total destruction. The only connection he can make with any other. The only touch he knows.

She moves still, but it's all panic. No real effort at escape left in her. Just flailing without meaning. The feral strength has fled her being. And he feels how powerless they both know she is. Feels it like a vibration channeled into his skin. Into the fevered blood beating through his face.

She lets up. All of her going slack little by little. That core not quite so ferocious in its struggling. Spasming now more than thrashing. Those balls of muscle along the sides of her neck growing softer and softer and softer. Two wads of pizza dough attached to her collarbone. She is giving up.

Good. Dumb bitch.

Look at what all that fighting got her. A mouth full of sludge and slime and scummy river water.

She didn't know how this worked. But he showed her. He showed her good.

This. This is the way the world works. And that's all there is to it. She is his now. Like the others.

This one won't leak out everywhere. Not yet, at least.

487

The water will snuff her out. Fill her throat and belly and lungs until it's over. Until her body is the vacant shell he needs it to be. The doll he needs it to be.

It won't be long. He knows that.

The splashing noises have cut out now that her limbs have gone limp and lifeless. The surge of the water and the heave of his breath are the only sounds.

He savors the quiet for a moment. The peaceful sound of the river's movements. The little eddies whirling around the two of them. Drawing lines on the surface of the water that twist and come apart as quickly as they form.

And then he jams her face down harder. Smears it back and forth in the muck. Feels all the cords and fiber in his arms quiver with raw power. All of his upper body pulling as taut as the strings on a cello.

A prickle writhes over his body. Every follicle of hair standing on end so he can feel everything. His whole body tingling with almost sexual ecstasy.

This is power. A physical sensation in every cell of his body.

He arches his back to rise higher over her. His shadow slicing right through her. The darkest space where the moonlight doesn't reflect from the water partially blocking her out.

His lips draw back from his teeth in a snarl from the effort. Jaw muscles twitching. Face going darker and darker red as the heat somehow keeps flushing into his skull.

He feels so huge looking down on her like this. All masculine. All muscle. Her body the tiny blur faintly visible in the swirling murk.

Yes, this is power. Power and submission. The opposites that complete each other like yin and yang. That spiral of black and white.

The water seems to change around them. Coiling about his legs. Circling the two of them.

And it almost looks like she is disappearing. Like the sheer force of his touch is erasing her. Flushing her away into some unknowable vortex.

He lets her up. Preparing to drive her down one final time

Dead End Girl

when he hears something strange bubble up from the water.

CHAPTER 113

She'd meant to take a good breath of air before she went under. Tried to. But the way he was kneeling on her back made it impossible to inhale very far.

She managed a gulp before she was thrust under, and half of that was water. She choked on it, big wracking coughs that came out as air bubbles under the water. Blubbing and gurgling and churning around her face. Her precious oxygen floating up and away.

She thrashed, flailing her legs. Her arms were pinned underneath her, deep in the muck at the bottom of the river. It hurt to squirm under him like that. Her ribs ached and cried out under the sharp points of his knees, but her lungs cried out louder. Craving air. Demanding it.

But still he held her down, hands gripping her neck and shoulders, driving her deeper into the abyss.

It was dark under the water. Her eyes were squeezed shut against the coldness, but she could still tell that it was pitch black under the surface. And she could also tell that the world was beginning to blur and lose focus. Maybe it wasn't visual, but she felt it that way. A dimming of all her senses.

Her chest burned as if someone had lit a fire inside her ribcage. An immense pressure was building, as if she were a bomb about to be set off. But she knew it was the opposite. When the timer reached zero, she would not explode. She would implode, water sucking into her and invading her innermost places.

She was losing.

She was dying.

From somewhere deep, an animal terror took hold, gave one final effort to wriggle free, but it was no use. He was stronger than she was, and he wasn't letting go.

The muck had enveloped her arms completely now. That was OK. It felt a little warmer than the water somehow. Her

490

knuckles scraped against the sharp edges of a rock. The rock moved. Could she use the rock? Her fingers flexed, she'd lost it in the mud. She stretched them out further, inching them forward. There. She had it. And it wasn't a rock.

It was better than a rock.

She'd stopped fighting him now, but still he held her down. If anything, his force had increased. She grappled with the pistol. Her wrists were still bound, though the water had loosened the adhesive on the tape some. Her fingers though… they were numb and slow from the icy water. And she was going to pass out soon, she could feel it. As it was she was having trouble thinking clearly. Her thoughts came in slow, broken snippets.

She held the gun backward, with the business end pointing at her own face. She hooked a thumb through the trigger guard. She tried her best to aim over her shoulder, but she had few options. She might blow her own head off, but she thought she'd get him too, maybe. It was better than nothing.

With her last shred of strength and consciousness, she squeezed her thumb. An enormous burst of hot air and water blasted her head. A deafening *whoompf* baffled her already ringing ears. Three times she pulled the trigger, in rapid succession.

BOOM BOOM BOOM.

His grip slackened, and like a jack-in-the-box she sprang back, knocking him off of her. Almost before her head had cleared the surface, she was hacking and barking and gulping for air. She thought the force of the coughing might do her in then, she might just tear her esophagus and choke on the blood, and she'd end up drowning anyway.

She crawled up onto the shore. Every muscle in her body trembling. Cold and dead. She couldn't even sit up. She just lay on the shore, shaking and freezing and bleeding.

In between the bouts of racking and heaving and nearly vomiting a few times, she checked to make sure he wasn't moving. He was sprawled a yard or so away, half in the water. She knew she should check to see if he had a pulse, but she couldn't bring herself to get that close. Didn't want to touch him. Besides, it was the top half that was in the water, and his face was under it.

She watched him for a long time before the cold and darkness took her. The back of his head bobbed to the surface every so often from the current.

CHAPTER 114

Blinding light surrounded Loshak. White and harsh. Too bright to look into. He fought to peel his eyelids apart, but they wouldn't obey, merely stinging and flooding with tears at his efforts.

Where the hell was he? Was this real? Was she still here with him?

He tried to move. To send out mental feelers for hands and arms and legs that may or may not exist or function. The results proved inconclusive. He thought he felt his wrist flop, but he wasn't certain.

And then it occurred to him that he was burning up, the heat coming upon him all at once, though he suspected it was always there and he was just now becoming aware of it. He had a vague sense of being damp, but whatever sweat his body might be producing was no help against this fever.

He tried to steady his thoughts and remember where he had been, what had been going on. He was working a case. A serial murder case. In Ohio. He could see his motel room in his mind, mostly his view of the ceiling from the bed. But that was all he could muster. The rest of the pieces wouldn't come into focus and partake in his puzzling.

His body heaved for breath, panicked wheezing audible somewhere in the distance that he somehow knew to be his own.

So that was alarming.

Was he being attacked? Kidnapped and trapped somewhere? Was he dying?

His jaw moved then, a disgusting mealy feeling occupying that orifice. His tongue scraped at the roof of his mouth, both surfaces as dry and rough as starfish.

A jab pricked him in the belly, the pain small at first, somehow familiar. He pondered it, could feel his forehead wrinkled up in concentration, but he couldn't remember. Then the numbness gave out. The full brunt of the pain in his gut hit like he'd been pierced with a dagger, and he blacked out.

He woke again some time later. Hours? Days? He couldn't say. Again, he found himself confused about most everything.

His eyelids fluttered open, but his eyes kept rolling back into his head. His vision juddered, the picture refusing to stay in the frame long enough to make any sense.

Even with his sight taken from him, he sensed someone in the room. He didn't know how. He just felt a presence.

"Agent Loshak," the voice spoke barely louder than a whisper. "Can you hear me?"

He knew this voice — a man's voice — but he couldn't place it. He stuttered out a response, a series of hard consonant sounds that added up to gibberish.

"Holy shit. I don't know if you're understanding this, but you have acute pancreatitis. You went into a coma and coded. They said you were probably brain dead, but... I'll, uh, get the doctor now. Oh, and the Bengals lost again."

He heard footsteps trail away, and then he was out again.

CHAPTER 115

The murmur of hushed voices. That was the first thing she remembered sensing.

They were far off. Separated from her somehow.

Closer, a rustling sound. Like someone turning the page of a book. She pictured her second-grade teacher, Mrs. Horning, who used to read out loud to them every Wednesday in her loud, sharp voice. A voice so piercing that you could hear her reading from inside a stall in the girl's bathroom at the other end of the hall. They would sit on the floor, criss-cross applesauce, and she would read to them from *Freckle Juice* and *Stone Soup* and *Amelia Bedelia Goes Camping*. Violet and her best friend Marnie would play with each other's hair when Mrs. Horning wasn't looking. They had to do it only when she wasn't looking because if Mrs. Horning caught them, she'd stop reading, crook her finger at them, and say, "That's how you get lice!"

Nearer than the papery whispers, so close it seemed to be right next to her ear almost, there was a dull, rhythmic clicking.

She inhaled deeply. A familiar smell surrounded her, but it was the sudden rush of oxygen that made her eyes flutter open.

A beat later, a voice.

"Darger — Violet?"

It was so bright in the room, she could see nothing but white.

"Can you hear me? Hold on. I'm going to get someone."

It was familiar that voice, but her thoughts were a confused jumble just now. A churning vortex of dark water.

Dark water, why did that seem important?

There were more voices now, louder. A commotion of other noises, too. Shoes squeaking on floors. Doors opened too forcefully and banging into rubber stops.

Her head lolled to the side. She would worry about the sounds and the seething black water later.

For now, she just wanted to sleep.

It was another day before she really woke for good. That's what Casey Luck told her later, anyway.

It was later, too. Instead of bright mid-day light streaming through the window next to her bed, it was the amber tint of late afternoon.

Casey was in a chair in the corner of the room, reading *The Wind-Up Bird Chronicle*. She watched him for a while before he sensed her eyes on him. He stirred and lifted his head. He glanced at her quickly and then back down at his book, as if he hadn't really expected her eyes to be open. But finding that they were, his gaze flicked back to her. He closed the book on his thumb.

"You gonna stick around for a while this time, or are you going to konk out again?"

She licked her lips. They felt like two caterpillars that had been caught out on a hot driveway under the noon sun.

"Sticking around. I think," she said. Or tried to say.

Her throat was dry, too. Thick and raw. There was pain when she swallowed, but it felt far away.

Her eyes traveled from the patch of tape over her hand, along the IV tube that ran across the bed and up the metal pole. Several bags hung there, suspended over her head. She couldn't get her focus sharp enough to read them, but she figured one of them had the good drugs in it. The clicking sound she remembered vaguely from earlier emanated from the IV pump.

By then, Casey had come closer, scooting a different chair next to the bed.

She asked about Loshak first.

"It was bad at first. I got a call from McAdoo not long after you took off from the station. Apparently, they lost him there for a minute. Had to use the defibrillator and everything. But they got him back. He woke up right before you did. Yesterday, I mean. He's still in and out, but the doctors sound hopeful."

"Clegg?"

"He's dead. Don't worry about that."

The memories were cloudy, but she remembered the image

of him floating face down.

"Van Ryper?" she asked. The real question she'd wanted to ask was, "So what the hell was up with Van Ryper?" But there was only so much her shredded vocal chords would allow at the present. Thankfully, Luck caught her meaning.

"Van Ryper and Clegg knew each other back in the day. They didn't go to school together, but they hung out. You know how it is. Clegg had done a doozy of a job stealing Van Ryper's identity. There was the job at the airport. The Buick. He had a passport, credit cards, a bank account so he could get the direct deposits from work. And it looked like he had other identities ready to go. Backups, I guess."

She opened her mouth to ask another question, but he held up a hand.

"You wanna know why Van Ryper — the real Van Ryper — and his mom were so damn shady when we brought them in?"

She nodded.

"Well, to start, we found a dime bag in the Nissan, so that explains why Kurt and his buddy ran. But the real revelation was that Kurt and mommy have been cashing her deceased brother's Social Security checks for the past six years, to the tune of over a hundred grand."

"They thought—" she croaked and Luck stopped her again.

"They thought that we were onto the fraud. That's why we were asking about the truck. That's why the Feds were involved. Yeah."

"How did you know?" she asked, trusting by now that he already knew what all of her questions would be.

"How to find you?" he smiled when she held up her thumb. "Someone called in a deranged woman standing around in the middle of the road. And gunshots."

She raised an eyebrow at the word *deranged*.

"I'm just passing on what the lady said," Luck said, then patted at the pockets of his jacket. "Oh yeah. I have something for you. Two somethings, actually."

He brought out his fist with a crinkle of plastic. His fingers opened like a flower's petals, and in the center of his palm sat the gold hedgehog brooch inside an evidence baggie.

"You don't need it for evidence?" she said, barely mustering a whisper.

"Nah. Clegg is dead."

He peeled the zip top open and shook the pin into his other hand. It looked like there was something else in the bag with the hedgehog, but he tucked it in his other hand. He thumbed the clasp on the brooch and bent toward her, moving to pin it to her hospital gown. She shrunk back from him. It took him a moment to realize why she was hesitant to take it.

"It's OK. I had 'em autoclave it for you."

Her shoulders loosened with relief.

He pinched the blue gown with his fingers, stabbing through the fabric with the pin end. When he'd finished, he gave the hedgehog a little tap on the head.

"Hell of a good luck charm, huh?"

She tucked her chin, staring into the emerald eyes, and bobbed her head once.

"But wait. There's more."

Once more he presented his fist and opened it in slow motion. This time there was a ring in his hand. A moonstone ring.

Violet gasped a little as he handed it over.

"Figured that out of everyone, you should have this too."

She turned it back and forth in her fingers, staring into the strange depths of the milky gem.

"Shouldn't this go to Mrs. Peters?"

Luck smirked.

"Technically, there's a little loophole in our chain of evidence policy called Fuck Her."

CHAPTER 116

Darger sat on the foot of Loshak's hospital bed while he spooned chocolate pudding into his mouth. He looked gaunt, his face longer and bonier than ever, but he also ate with more gusto than she'd seen at any point in their time together.

"You heard from Ryskamp or anything?" Loshak said.

"Nah, I turned my phone off days ago," Darger said. "I find it rings less that way."

Loshak chuckled and took another big bite of pudding. After a few more bites, he spoke.

"James Joseph Clegg. He was a crafty son of a bitch, I'll give him that. But he was no match for Violet Darger."

Laughter puffed out of Darger's nostrils.

Loshak's spoon froze mid-scoop.

"That's no joke. You did a hell of a job. The stolen identity could have bought him a lot more time. Everyone else was all in on the real Van Ryper from the sound of it. I probably would have been, too."

Darger swallowed and then spoke, her voice soft and small.

"Yeah. Well, thank you."

Loshak tilted his head.

"Careful now. You might faint, expressing all of this unbridled enthusiasm."

Darger smiled, but Loshak thought her expression looked more sad than amused.

"Doesn't feel quite how you thought it would, does it?" he said.

She shook her head.

He set his pudding cup down on the tray in front of him, careful to make sure the weight of the spoon didn't knock it over.

"It feels good to catch these guys, but it never brings the dead back. I think part of you always thinks maybe it will. No

499

matter how many times you go through it, part of you thinks maybe this will be the time. But you did good. You did the best you could do."

She blinked a few times, and then she nodded.

"It's a job, you know," Loshak said, picking up his pudding again. "Someone has to do it."

COME PARTY WITH US

We're loners. Rebels. But much to our surprise, the most kickass part of writing has been connecting with our readers. From time to time, we send out newsletters with giveaways, special offers, and juicy details on new releases.

Sign up for our mailing list at:
http://ltvargus.com/mailing-list

SPREAD THE WORD

Thank you for reading! We'd be very grateful if you could take a few minutes to review it on Amazon.com.

How grateful? Eternally. Even when we are old and dead and have turned into ghosts, we will be thinking fondly of you and your kind words. The most powerful way to bring our books to the attention of other people is through the honest reviews from readers like you.

ABOUT THE AUTHORS

Tim McBain writes because life is short, and he wants to make something awesome before he dies. Additionally, he likes to move it, move it.

You can connect with Tim on Twitter at @realtimmcbain or via email at tim@timmcbain.com.

L.T. Vargus grew up in Hell, Michigan, which is a lot smaller, quieter, and less fiery than one might imagine. When not click-clacking away at the keyboard, she can be found sewing, fantasizing about food, and rotting her brain in front of the TV.

If you want to wax poetic about pizza or cats, you can contact L.T. (the L is for Lex) at ltvargus9@gmail.com or on Twitter @ltvargus.

TimMcBain.com
LTVargus.com